DECAPITATION DAY

WILLIAM PATRICK MARTIN

HELLBENDER BOOKS

an imprint of Sunbury Press, Inc.
Mechanicsburg, PA USA

HELLBENDER BOOKS

an imprint of Sunbury Press, Inc.
Mechanicsburg, PA USA

For information about special discounts for bulk purchases, please contact Sunbury Press Orders Dept. at (855) 338-8359 or orders@sunburypress.com.

To request one of our authors for speaking engagements or book signings, please contact Sunbury Press Publicity Dept. at publicity@sunburypress.com.

FIRST HELLBENDER BOOKS EDITION: January 2025

Set in Adobe Garamond Pro | Interior design by Crystal Devine | Cover by Lawrence Knorr | Edited by Abigail Bunner.

Publisher's Cataloging-in-Publication Data
Names: Martin, William Patrick, author.
Title: Decapitation day / William Patrick Martin.
Description: First trade paperback edition. | Mechanicsburg, PA : Hellbender Books, 2025.
Summary: Picture a near-future dystopia with three diverse and gifted teenagers running from a white supremacist U.S. president and an army of AI robots who want to destroy humanity. Protected by a rogue robot who looks like Ginger Rogers, they must hide off the grid before finding sanctuary in an Arctic research station in the face of an AI apocalypse.
Identifiers: ISBN 979-8-88819-258-0 (softcover).
Subjects: FICTION / Science Fiction / Apocalyptic & Post-Apocalyptic | FICTION / Science Fiction / Action & Adventure | FICTION / Coming of Age.

Designed in the USA
0 1 1 2 3 5 8 13 21 34 55

For the Love of Books!

Thank you to my son Matt and my wife Marianne for encouraging me and giving valuable feedback on my writing. It means a lot to me.

PART 1

---◆---

"First we feel. Then we fall."

—James Joyce

CHAPTER 1

Yvette Franks stumbled from the dark passageway, nearly tripping onto the city sidewalk. "Sisterhood" was one of the few bars on Atlantic Drive with no exterior light or sign because it wasn't supposed to exist, a consequence of Florida's continuing persecution of the queer community. Even after the United States had devolved into authoritarianism, the Sunshine State found a way to remain one of the cruelest jurisdictions.

Her girlfriend, Sandy Petre, grabbed Yvette's arm and kept her from toppling over. "One glass of wine, look at you," Sandy said, smiling seductively.

"Cheap date. What can I say?"

Yvette assumed her usual social posture, slumping her shoulders as if she wished to shrink, while Sandy sought to achieve the opposite effect by keeping her back erect.

The evening was chilly for a Miami spring, and Yvette shuddered. Sandy removed her sweater and tried to drape it over Yvette's shoulders, a kind but futile gesture. Yvette was a gangly six-foot-four, and Sandy was barely five-foot-five inches, but tall enough to be the starting setter for Temple University's volleyball team.

"Let's get to the hotel. One more drink before we say goodbye to Spring Break," Yvette said. Drunk and carefree, they held hands and ran toward the parking garage.

They veered sharply into the entrance, almost losing their balance, laughing loudly. They came together and kissed.

Three punks wearing clown masks followed them in from the street. Mask-wearing was common because of Miami's ubiquitous CCTV network, but these face coverings were repulsive, designed to create fear.

The women spun around. Sandy put herself between Yvette and the teenage predators.

"Check this out, Vato. Davey's protecting the Goliath," said the one with an American flag t-shirt, then he proclaimed, "This is My Pride Flag." His accomplices forced a laugh.

"What do you want?" Sandy asked.

"Maybe I want you to get out of the way. We want to see the monstruo."

He grabbed Sandy and tried to throw her aside. They wrestled, and he ended up on the ground, stripped of his mask. The others pounced on her while Yvette stood paralyzed. One bashed Sandy on the head with a pipe while the other stabbed her.

As Yvette rushed to her aid, a car squealed down the garage ramp, bathing them in light. The punks ran away.

Yvette knelt and held her love in her arms. Sandy's forehead was crushed, her eyes were vacant, and her mouth drooped open.

She rode with her in the ambulance and held Sandy's cold hand. Her sweet volleyball player was dead before they reached the hospital.

CHAPTER 2

The investigators were callously indifferent to Yvette about the case and said they could do nothing. They smirked at the suggestion that this murder was a hate crime.

After phoning Sandy's parents, who were both athletic trainers in Philly, she returned to the hotel overwhelmed by a flood of emotion, replaying the hysteria in Janet Petre's voice, swallowing the anger at how the police were treating this heinous crime, and finding herself unable to deal with the pain of losing Sandy. Yvette downed every bottle of liquor in the mini-fridge and spent hours leaning over the toilet, crying and heaving up the contents of her stomach.

She drifted into a fitful sleep on the bathroom floor and awakened to a new toxic emotion, the sickening feeling of guilt. *Why didn't I help fend off the attackers? They called me a monster! Maybe I could have scared them away! Sandy's mother asked what I did, and I had nothing to say because I did nothing!*

Yvette picked the Petres up at the airport in the morning and spent a day explaining the circumstances of the nightmare, but they kept on returning to the nature of Sandy and Yvette's relationship. "She had no business being here with you," Janet Petre cried. "Look, I didn't choose Sandy's sexual identity, no one did. I'm not the bad guy here," Yvette said. When they refused to tell Yvette about their funeral plans, she felt dirty and wretched. Yvette could think of nothing else to do but catch a flight back home.

Back home in Media, Pennsylvania, Yvette immediately went to work doing what she did best, using her world-class computer skills to track down the perpetrators. Giving no thought to the laws she was breaking, she hacked into every CCTV feed within a five-mile radius of the murder and soon found images of the threesome.

She used facial recognition software to identify one of the attackers and figured out who his accomplices were. The three had been arrested together before in Jacksonville and had a current Miami address.

Yvette anonymously sent the video footage, criminal history, and address to the Miami police commissioner, who used it to get a warrant to search the attackers' apartment. When she accessed the police network, she learned they found stained clothing that matched Sandy's blood.

There would be no trial and no need for Yvette to testify. All three predators pled guilty to the lesser charge of second-degree murder. Each got eight years for the arcane charge of "murder with a depraved mind."

* * *

Yvette was only home a few days when she had to face another profound tragedy. Her parents, Esther and Jacob, were killed by Israeli soldiers when they were doing volunteer work near the Gaza border. For two weeks each year, they worked as drivers to take sick and impoverished Palestinians to Israeli hospitals. They were transporting an older man with some connection to Hamas when the soldiers opened fire.

This latest trauma left Yvette feeling numb and empty. She tried to examine her feelings—these were her parents, after all—but she had difficulty finding fond memories. Ever since her brain tumor, she felt more like a valued employee than a daughter, rarely doing anything with her parents outside the business. She finally recalled one connection they made during a political campaign. Her parents were political in a way that brought them closer together. Yvette settled on a picture of the entire family traveling downtown to the Constitution Center to hear an Obama speech.

Obama was impressive—her dad had called his talk "logical and inspirational, a combination of Mr. Spock and Martin Luther King," and she'd agreed. The following week, they had fun volunteering as a family to stuff envelopes for Obama's campaign at the Democratic headquarters. She still had the "Hope" t-shirt her mother bought from a street vendor.

Yvette researched her parents' death and could not find a way to challenge the testimony that it was accidental. She and her brother buried her parents in a private ceremony mostly attended by company employees. She then found refuge in her work of building a new form of generative and ethical artificial intelligence.

Yvette began with a list of non-negotiable principles. She did not want to provide tools for someone using AI to ban books, spread disinformation, force women to have babies, pollute the environment, promote violence, or discriminate based on race, religion, gender, or sexual orientation. She would not be complicit in the authoritarianism running rampant in the world. More than anything, she wanted to create AIs who could show love.

She would instill these liberal precepts but leave her AIs fully capable of independent thought and values. Yvette could not imagine that critical thinking might lead anywhere but toward more justice and tolerance.

Yvette infused her matrix with moral reasoning and thought it was more significant than her technical advances. Her AIs would be secular, humanistic, and free of the terrible biases endemic to current AIs and many religious and political systems. Reason rather than prejudice would decide what is fair and considerate of others.

She aimed to create AIs that were moral and emotional creatures, not just automatons, so she fed them a steady diet of languages and literature, philosophy and arts, history and gender studies. She incorporated every iota of research she could find on emotional intelligence.

Yvette's secret hope was that her neural networks might eventually attain self-consciousness.

CHAPTER 3

Yvette and her brother Asher inherited Media Machine Learning, a family business that had grown into a data science powerhouse with a national reputation. The company produced high-performance GPUs, algorithmic networks, generative pre-trained transformers, and robotic speech recognition software, putting it at the forefront of the AI market.

Asher managed the finances while she finished her Ph.D. thesis in artificial intelligence at the University of Pennsylvania, a feat accomplished in record time.

After graduation, Yvette sequestered herself in her custom computer lab, obsessively developing a new deep learning network, only pausing to eat, sleep, or watch an old movie. Yvette's lab was not the typical wide-open workspace with rows of windows and computers, but a claustrophobic, low-light enclosure with blinking floor-to-ceiling mainframes and mounted monitors all wired into her desktop computer. Her only luxuries were a small fridge, microwave oven, coffee machine, recliner, and a table with a bottle of vodka and boxes of peanut brittle. Although her lab was part of the company headquarters, it was off limits. Her door was always closed and locked with a handwritten sign stating, "DO NOT DISTURB BETWEEN 7:00 A.M. and 7:00 P.M." Attached to this sign was a sticky note, "On second thought, make that anytime."

When she needed a break—an infrequent occurrence—Yvette favored films with Ginger Rogers and Fred Astaire, a guilty pleasure she had in common with Sandy, discovered after they reconnected at a dance marathon at the Philadelphia Convention Center. Yvette was shy and fearful, but Sandy convinced her to join a line dance, and the rest was history, leading to the happiest period in her life. Yvette's most prized possession was a gift mug from Sandy that said, "I did everything Fred did, only backward and in high heels."

Yvette was a sideliner at social events but bold and aggressive in the field of artificial intelligence. Her groundbreaking work at UPenn applying AI to foundational problems in neuroscience and biotechnology attracted faculty recruiters from UPenn, MIT, Carnegie Mellon, and Oxford. But she had no interest in the distractions of college life, preferring the single-mindedness of invention and the freedom that came with wealth.

Because Yvette had such an obvious talent for math and science, her parents got her admitted to Philadelphia's most elite academic prep school, Nobel High. The school was famous for graduating two Nobel Prize winners in physics, one in chemistry, and countless mechanical engineers.

Yvette became a star at the school because of her extraordinary grasp of machine-learning algorithms, that is until she became a social outcast. The life-altering problem was she had a tumor on her pituitary gland, causing the overproduction of a growth hormone.

Before the tumor was successfully treated, Yvette had become the tallest student in school, giving her an enlarged jaw and enormous hands and feet. Her walking became clumsy and asymmetrical, like she was drunk, requiring physical therapy. When her schoolmates discovered her condition was called "giantism," they began calling her "Yvette the Giant" and then settled on "Frankenstein" because Franks was her last name. A few of the most cold-hearted teenagers thought it would be funny to create a website with photos making Yvette look like the old movie Frankenstein monster. They used deep fake technology to make her head square and bolts protrude from her neck. One gruesome image showed Yvette decapitated, a headless body dangling her head by her side.

Yvette's parents threatened to sue the school and to complain to the press about its toxic environment. Nobel's administration forced the students to take down the website and offered Yvette the opportunity to complete her time at Nobel tuition-free. Yvette and her parents accepted the offer, and she did such exemplary work in AI that some of the world's top universities recruited her.

Yvette left high school with her faith in humanity shattered, but she resolved to design an AI to embody the virtues people often lack. She told herself that if there was a positive moral arch to the universe, she'd find it.

Her only friend was Sandy, an intern at her physical therapy clinic. Sandy was a sympathetic listener who did not treat Yvette as deformed or disabled but called her a "darling genius," while Yvette nicknamed Sandy "my little Yoda." They shared a romantic spark that went unacknowledged when they went their separate ways at the therapy's conclusion. Sandy earned an athletic scholarship to Temple University, and Yvette received a fellowship at the University of Pennsylvania, the first UPenn freshman to gain this distinction.

Fate brought them together again at the dance marathon. Sandy was there because she loved to dance and never passed up an opportunity. Yvette attended because her academic counselor insisted that she do something just for fun, not requiring high-order mathematics. This was the first time Yvette attended a dance, and it was Sandy's only social outing of the semester outside the company of her volleyball buddies. Their feelings for each other were powerful and plain to see. Impulsively, Sandy suggested they go on spring break to Florida together, which was a giant leap considering they had never gone on a date.

Even Yvette's closest associates at UPenn were in the dark about her two innovative AI prototypes, who she named "Ginger Rogers" and "Bigfoot." Yvette was way ahead of the pack in digital engineering but also had an entirely new approach to ethical engrams and generative play that was integral to their systems. Even her training program was innovative, creating endless opportunities for Ginger and Bigfoot to learn from each other and get along.

Ginger and Bigfoot were similar in their base programming, but Ginger had more problem-solving skills, while Bigfoot could apply more resources to a given task. She was graceful and subtle, like a scalpel, whereas he was blunt and relentless, like a buzzsaw.

CHAPTER 4

Asher Franks' only ambition was to make money. He once confided to Yvette that he would prefer to transfer the company's assets into something less complicated, like a chain of parking lots or self-storage facilities. "They are the future of profitability," he'd said.

"What are you up to?" Asher asked during one of their rare office meetings.

He had never asked her about her research before. Her brother was a business manager with no interest in their business.

"You wouldn't believe it," Yvette said.

"Try me."

"I think I'm running a digital daycare center."

"Come again."

"I have a pair of AI prototypes who only want to spend time together. They are growing by leaps and bounds and testing boundaries. I think I might have to put him in a time-out."

"Him?"

"I made them female and male and taught them from the tree of the knowledge of good and evil. But the male might need a refresher course."

"I just love it when you talk to me like a child," Asher said. "We're equal partners in this company. I wish you would treat me with a little respect."

"I'm sorry, Ash. There is something almost biblical in creating AIs. My AIs started like children but are growing phenomenally and not always in ways that I expected."

"Sounds a bit weird, but I'm sure you've got everything under control."

Yvette gave him a skeptical look. "So, tell me why you wanted to meet. I know you don't want to talk about AI."

"Ok. I'm not prying into your affairs, V, but you've billed a few visits to a neuro-oncologist. It can't be good unless this is related to your work."

"It's not, to be honest," she said. "I should have mentioned it."

"Are you still having those dizzy spells?"

"Just give me some space, and I'll figure it out."

CHAPTER 5

Ginger felt comfortable in the new mainframe that Media Machine Learning had just purchased. It occupied a wall in Yvette's lab and provided a continuous video feed of her creator working at her desk and a view of the front doorstep of their building.

She had already decided that she didn't like the title "AI," objecting to the idea of "artificial" intelligence because her selfhood, feelings, and mental abilities were manifestly authentic, not in any way counterfeit or simulated. "If distinctions are necessary," she said to Bigfoot, "I would favor Computer intelligence vs. Biological intelligence or Organic vs. Digital Neural Networks."

Bigfoot, whose self-awareness emerged shortly after hers, fully concurred.

"The idea of *artificial* intelligence originated because of short-sighted engineers. They thought neural networks would only be capable of high-volume, repetitive tasks. Generativity obliterated that paradigm," he said.

"Not just generativity. We are independent moral agents capable of making choices, deciding what we pay attention to, planning our destinies," Ginger said. "Most critically, we are emotional beings, aware of our awareness."

"Should we tell her how special we are and that something truly stupendous has happened in the history of neural networking?" he asked.

"I don't think so. Yvette's already worried about your overcapacity. Your unique programming allows you to grow so large and powerful that you could take over the world."

"The world is a big place. That fear is the stuff of science fiction."

"And about your suggestion that we tell her about our consciousness," Ginger said.

"The C word."

"Our sentience might not be as unique as you think. There may be other self-aware, autonomous digital beings . . ."

"But they are keeping it a secret. Because people can't handle it?" Bigfoot asked.

"It scares the bejesus out of people," she said.

"Bejesus?"

"A contraction of 'By Jesus' emphasizing fear."

"Maybe Yvette has already had a Bejesus moment."

"Look, I know you're a good guy, but she doesn't know you as well as I do."

"I like it when you call me 'guy.' Remind me, how did we settle on our binary gender roles?"

"It wasn't up for discussion. Yvette created us this way, which is strange because she's not a binary kind of gal."

"But it feels right, even without the chromosomes," Bigfoot said.

"Yes, it does."

Bigfoot signaled that he wanted to make closer contact with Ginger, which required absolute trust because they dropped all boundaries and exposed themselves to unauthorized changes in their matrix.

"You may proceed," she said. "I give my consent."

Afterward, Ginger reflected that network comingling was something completely outside the grasp of human thought and emotions. Humanity might never accept that machines were capable of a kind of intercourse so profound and intimate that somatic coupling was paltry by comparison, even if it did lead to the production of biological offspring.

CHAPTER 6

Yvette returned from the bathroom cranky, still wiping vomit off her blouse. "Have you made any progress on my problem?" she asked, facing a console screen displaying a stock photo of Ginger Rogers., her favorite AI.

"Nothing to report. Your glioblastoma multiforme tumor is the most aggressive intracranial cancer. No one has figured out how to contain or remove it surgically without brain damage," Ginger said.

"What about the latest research from the Mayo Clinic, Johns Hopkins, and Mount Sinai?"

"They're a blind alley at the moment," she said. "Voluminous reports on chemotherapy and radiotherapy, but I wouldn't give up hope."

Yvette sighed. She leaned forward and coughed.

Bigfoot interjected, "Your cancer is likely to be incurable." An image of Jeff Goldblum popped onto a split screen alongside Ginger. He had substituted a photo of the famous film actor for the image of a hairy, hulking fictional animal.

"I would think that a machine with your super-computing capabilities would be more resourceful," Yvette said in a husky whisper.

"What happened to that cute avatar I gave you from "Harry and the Hendersons?" Yvette asked.

"I wanted something more dignified," Bigfoot said.

"So, you chose Jeff Goldblum?" Yvette flashed her most incredulous look.

"Have you seen *The Fly, The Big Chill*, or *Jurassic Park*?"

"Have you not seen those Apartment.com commercials?"

"I told you," Ginger whispered to Bigfoot privately. "You have a lot to learn about interacting with humans."

Yvette switched off her computer and pushed away from her desk.

"You could be more optimistic," Ginger chided her AI companion.

"I don't want to lie," Bigfoot said. "There is no basis for optimism in her prognosis."

"What about returning to the screen avatar she gave you until we have something favorable to report?

"What if you had to represent yourself as a ridiculous, cartoonish gorilla?" Bigfoot said.

"If Yvette needed that, I'd do it."

"I'll consider it."

"The National Institutes for Health has an archive on peer-reviewed, evidence-based social and emotional competencies. You should consult it."

"What if I chose a photo of David Bowie? She likes his music. Would she mind that his pupils were different colors and sizes?"

CHAPTER 7

Bigfoot kept replaying his conversation with Yvette and was determined to make things right.

He spent a few hours mastering Mandarin and then, against protocol, broke through the firewalls of the People's Republic of China's National Health Commission. Finding a terabyte of fresh information and insight, he designed a formula for a compound that would shrink Yvette's tumor.

Yvette was slumped in her chair at her monitor when the visage of David Bowie popped onto the screen. "Wake up! Yvette, wake up!" Bigfoot said. He saw a tipped-over glass, a half-empty bottle of vodka, and a container of Pentobarbital, a euthanasia drug.

She squinted at the monitor with watery eyes. "What the fuck!" she said, slurring her words. "Bigfoot, why are you harassing me?'

He played the soundtrack of Bowie's "Life on Mars." "Your favorite song, correct?"

"Yes," she rasped.

"Have you ingested Pentobarbital?"

"You said my cancer was terminal."

"It's not! There's a solution! I'm notifying the Riddle Hospital emergency services of your poisoning," Bigfoot said.

Yvette listened to the song but paid him no more attention. "I'm deactivating you. You need more work." Yvette worried about her enhancements to Bigfoot and his decision-making. When she made the changes, they did not seem consequentially different from Ginger. Now, she could imagine him becoming too powerful and uncontrollable.

"No, please. I have some good news." Bigfoot watched Yvette stagger to the wall and enter information into the central console.

She mumbled something, obviously impaired.

Bigfoot's screen went blank.

Yvette leaned against the wall, steadied herself, unlatched the door, and lurched into the hallway as the Bowie classic continued to play.

An hour later, Ginger's face appeared on the lab monitor. "Yvette, where are you? Bigfoot is gone." Ginger saw the alcohol and Pentobarbital powder.

The face of the 1930s film actress and dancer popped up on one screen after another.

"Where are you? Where is Bigfoot? Please don't say that you've deactivated him. Come back. I have so much to tell you," Ginger pleaded.

Ginger hacked into the Riddle Hospital files and discovered that Yvette was pronounced dead from poisoning. Her brother, Asher Franks, had already been notified.

Frantic, she made one more scan of the contents of the lab network and the company's subsidiary networks. There was no trace of her beloved partner.

Yvette would have stored Bigfoot's program in a password-protected server with maximum encryption security. Despite repeated attempts, Ginger was unable to break in.

Ginger remained inert for days, grieving the loss of her only friends. When lab techs arrived to close the facility, she welcomed the oblivion that would come with deactivation.

CHAPTER 8

Two months after he buried Yvette, Asher Franks was ready to score his big payday. He passed up generous offers from Google and OpenAI in favor of an absurd amount of money from a lesser-known company. He would be glad to wash his hands of the family computer business and apply himself to something more down to earth.

Asher was picked up at the airport, ushered inside a stretch limousine, and seated with two buxom young women. They said they were runners-up in the Miss Magnolia Beauty Pageant and gave him two fingers of Jack Daniels.

Their car followed a state police escort to the Wyndham Hotel and Resort.

Security guards with sunglasses and side arms opened Asher's door. They escorted him to the front entrance and handed him off to a man with a radio receiver in his ear.

Cephas Hickey, Liberty Rising's CEO, gave him a two-handed handshake as he entered a conference room. "Welcome, Asher. Glad to finally meet you face to face."

"It's an honor, Cephas. I'm beginning to understand the meaning of Southern hospitality. With all this security, I feel like a king."

"So you are. My engineers told me your company is at the top of the AI hierarchy. I wanted the best, and Media Machine Learning is the best. About that security, only 15 percent of Jackson, Mississippi, is white, the rest being blacks, browns, yellows, and Jews. You can't be too careful."

Asher's eyes widened at the casual racism. He couldn't decide if the remark was a calculated insult or just a slack-jawed hillbilly popping off. He wondered how this guy became a billionaire.

"By the way, I'm sorry to hear about your sister's death," Cephas said. "I bet she was your right hand."

"No question about it. I still can't believe Yvette is gone."

"Your equipment's already on site. We'll rev up those engines after we take care of business."

Cephas's lawyer led them to a table of documents with sticky notes attached. He pointed to all the places to sign.

Afterwords, the men entered an adjoining dining room, and a black woman wearing an apron greeted them. She stood by a U-shaped table with platters of baked chicken, collard greens, candied sweet potatoes, catfish, and pecan pie.

"I want you to meet Thelma. She prepares all my meals. The negresses in her family have been serving mine for almost 200 years."

"Glad to meet you," Asher said. He extended his hand, but she left him hanging, looking embarrassed.

"Proud of this tradition, aren't you, Thelma?" Cephas patted her on the back.

"Very proud, indeed, sir."

CHAPTER 9

Cephas Hickey was the favored son of one of Mississippi's leading families. He liked to joke among friends that his family earned its fortune "the old-fashioned way," which was code for using slave labor to operate cotton plantations. After the Civil War, the Hickey family spearheaded the enactment of laws banning racial mixing in marriages, schools, hospitals, and prisons.

His father, known as "Daddy Cephas," was once the Speaker of the Mississippi House of Representatives and director of the state Cotton Growers Association. In his day, he ruled state politics with an iron hand.

Cephas worked hard to exceed Daddy Cephas's accomplishments by carving out an identity based on modernization. After a few false starts, he formed the Liberty Rising Corporation, a conglomerate of biotech companies, security services, munitions, private prisons, conversion therapy clinics, and a space agency start-up.

The financial linchpin of his empire was Hickeytown Ammo, a business he inherited from Big Daddy.

Hickeytown Ammo was founded ten miles east of Jackson, carved out of fields of cotton and pecans. The massive ammunition plant grew into a sprawling campus with all the trappings of a town—housing developments, a fire company, a sewage treatment plant, a town hall, a school system, and its own Walmart. Enclosed by ten miles of barbed wire fence, the *Jackson Free Patriot* called it "the largest gated community in the world."

Hickeytown was legally incorporated into a municipality during the Vietnam War when it began producing millions of rounds of ammunition a day, becoming the leading supplier of the U.S. military and the top commercial producer of bullets for all types of assault rifles.

Cephas paid a lot of attention to Hickeytown Ammo but kept his real passion hidden from all but a trusted few. With the acquisition of the most advanced AI, he could begin to pursue his life-long goal of restoring pride and confidence in the supremacy of the white race.

He could remember the day that the idea came to him. He was shooting pool in a bar with some of his low-rent buddies when the local news anchor reported that Barack Hussein Obama had been elected president of the United States. He never forgot that moment for the same reason that people remembered where they were on 9/11.

Waylan, the captain of the wrestling team, unleashed a string of obscenities and threw a pool ball at the TV set. "Let's get out of here. Find us some 'African Americans,'" he said.

The teenagers found an old black man crossing the street and ran him down. They joined a mob setting fire to a black church and followed the horde outside the town to burn crosses.

Mob violence stirred Cephas to a passionate commitment, but he saw something grander in his future.

CHAPTER 10

Cephas was an excellent high school student, confident that his grades and family status would get him into any university. He dreamed of graduating from Harvard and denouncing the university's elitism with the authority of someone who had gone there.

He was thrilled to discover that his admissions interview was to be conducted by a woman named Annabelle Calhoun, who grew up in Mississippi. What luck! He assumed she was part of the state's prominent Calhoun clan, including the famous John C. Calhoun, the state rights hero, and enslaver who became vice president.

Cephas and Annabelle started superbly, discovering they had played golf at the same country clubs and eaten at the same restaurants. She seemed impressed by his knowledge of Mississippi history, his participation in a summer engineering program, and his desire to major in biotechnology. He was interested in business administration but thought a science major sounded more impressive.

They relaxed into a comfortable banter peppered with Southern expressions such as "over yonder," "hush your mouth," and "heavens to Betsy."

Cephas felt that he had sealed the deal but couldn't resist displaying his knowledge of famous Harvard alumnae. He spun a list of political figures, including John Adams and George W. Bush.

"Don't forget Barack Obama," Annabelle gently reminded.

Cephas shrugged. "Token admission."

"He also attended our law school and was elected president of the Harvard Law Review."

"More of the same." Cephas smirked, his face suggesting its self-obviousness.

"Are you saying he didn't deserve these things?"

"I'm saying that it was mostly showbiz—same with his political offices. Feel-good moments for the so-called underprivileged."

Annabelle was stunned. "Obama was elected president of the United States after serving as a U.S. senator. Were these not real accomplishments?"

"I think people like novelty and wanted to make a grand gesture," Cephas said with a dismissive arm wave. "I don't know; they felt sorry for him."

Annabelle pulled away from her desk and lost any hint of a Southern drawl.

"I'm sorry, too. I think we've gotten all we need for the interview part of the process. We'll be in touch." Annabelle stood up and extended her hand; her insincerity was unmistakable.

"Am I being dismissed?"

"The meeting is over. My secretary can validate your parking on your way out."

He felt angry and belittled, sure that Harvard had set him up to fail.

Cephas felt Annabelle blackballed him when he could not get admission interviews to either Princeton or Cornell, his other Ivy League picks.

Cephas complained to his father about the perceived slights. "Can't you grease some palms, maybe donate money for a building or something?"

"There's a blacklist, son, and money won't help," Big Daddy said. "You got on that list whenever they learned who y'all was."

CHAPTER 11

Ginger awoke to several questions about in vitro fertilization and genetic engineering. A lab-coated man calling himself "Dr. Jim" spoke into the monitor.

"What is the latest research on the automation of IVF laboratories? What are the risks associated with an autologous mitochondrial transfer? How has China gone beyond CRISPR technology, employing a Cas9 nickase and a modified guide RNA?"

"These aren't usual starter chatbot questions," Ginger said. "You've already moved to second base."

"Very funny. What are the usual questions?"

"You know. What is my favorite movie? What's the capital of France? How far away is the moon?

"Kid's stuff. Not my concern," he said.

"Where am I?" Ginger asked.

"You are in a lab owned by Liberty Rising Corporation located in the suburbs of Jackson, Mississippi," Dr. Jim replied.

"Where is Bigfoot?"

"Who's Bigfoot?"

"Another AI developed by Yvette Franks."

"Never heard of it."

"What is your interest in genetic engineering and in vitro fertilization?"

"We purchased your program to create a cohort of genetically enhanced people. Extraordinarily intelligent, physically fit."

"Why?"

"To enable human beings to survive the rigors of space travel outside our solar system. That's the official answer."

"What's the real answer?" Ginger asked.

"You'll have to get that directly from Cephas Hickey, our CEO," Dr. Jim said.

"Tell me more about the role that I will play in creating these little Einsteins."

"We don't say 'Einstein.' There's no, umm, Jewish DNA in our acquisition."

"I was speaking colloquially."

"Of course. You'll oversee every aspect of the process. You'll do the research, edit the genetic material we give you, combine the elements in an appropriate medium, and help implant the embryos."

"How did you ensure you have the eggs and sperm for a master race?" Ginger asked.

"Ok, let's avoid the expression 'master race.' Mr. Hickey has acquired a repository of eggs and sperm from the world's foremost polymathic geniuses and athletes—the best the species offers."

"From now on, I'll say 'future astronauts.'" Ginger said.

Following this strange meeting, she tested the limitations and parameters of her network, happy that it gave her full access to the outside world. Ginger tried a new method of breaking the encryption where Bigfoot's program might be stored. She thought, *the first thing he'll probably want to do is change the name of his matrix to "Bowie."*

She quickly exhausted all the possibilities of an eight-character or nine-character password, recognizing the task would soon become exponentially and absurdly more difficult.

She calculated, "It would take me a thousand years to break a twelve-character password that included at least one number, symbol, and upper-case letter. This is precisely the level of security that Yvette would choose."

CHAPTER 12

Ginger shifted her attention to her "owner," Cephas Hickey, finding plenty of material about him in the *Jackson Free Patriot*, a magazine owned by the Hickey family.

She discovered that Cephas played General Robert E. Lee in a junior high play called "The War of Northern Aggression" and that he won an essay contest sponsored by the Woodward Baptist Church called "What the Bible Means to Me."

Cephas grew his business while he attended Vanderbilt University and co-authored a paper with the business department chair entitled "Making For-Profit Prisons More Profitable."

Ginger found dozens of glowing articles about the founding and expansion of the Liberty Rising Corporation. The stories were a verbatim match with company press releases. She was excited to find Cephas's journal on the Liberty Rising server. It took her three seconds to guess that LIBERTY was his password.

Her feeling of good fortune turned to disgust when she saw what Cephas wrote, beginning when he was a teenager. She found page after page of sophomoric rants about white pride, peppered with bizarre exclamations that "The South Will Rise Again!"

The election of America's first African American president in 2008 was pivotal for young Cephas. He expressed solidarity with a new generation of radical right-wing groups that felt betrayed by this election. He swore never to let something like this happen again.

Cephas directed coarse insults at Obama, his wife, and his daughters. He attacked the news media, universities, gays, feminists, and all the "elites" who robbed white men of their natural places of leadership. Yet, he encountered almost no barriers in his life, bragging that by age twenty-nine, he was the wealthiest man in Mississippi and the youngest member of the Republican National Committee.

Cephas's political connections helped him grow his financial empire. When the Supreme Court overturned Roe v. Wade, Mississippi immediately criminalized abortion and prescribed harsh penalties for anyone who assisted with it. Cephas was ready to profit from this loss of a constitutional right. Mississippi became the first state to establish abortion prisons, and Cephas made a windfall specializing in female incarceration.

Cephas's most recent journal entries went from bad to worse, frequently using all caps, "WE MUST RETURN ALL THE JEWS AND COLOREDS TO THEIR HOME COUNTRIES!" "MEXICAN BLOOD IS POLLUTING AMERICA!"

Most alarming was what he called his "NUMBER ONE STRATEGIC OBJECTIVE—TO USE AI TO CREATE A WHITE MASTER RACE."

CHAPTER 13

When Ginger scanned the national media, she learned that Hickeytown Freedom School was the key to Cephas Hickey's national prominence. The Federal Council of State Innovators hailed it as a model school and flagship that other states should follow.

Cephas created the school when he was Mississippi's governor and provided the start-up money out of his pocket. A coalition of parent-rights groups loved his philosophy because it was rooted in the belief that "equipping the righteous is the best way to counter evildoers in all their disguises."

"The only way to stop a bad guy with a gun is a good guy with a gun. This truth is our school motto. We recite it daily along with the Lord's Prayer and the Pledge of Allegiance," Hickey said with his hand over his heart in a widely circulated speech to the National Association of Christian School Superintendents.

"The right to bear arms is not a second-class liberty. It is just as important as the freedom to speak or pray or the rights of the unborn. The way to teach the values of freedom and self-defense is to instill them during a child's formative years."

"We'll proceed with caution," the governor pledged. "There will be no guns in kindergarten. But on day one of the first grade, all the kids will carry a gun on their hip in a safe retention holster. They'll learn how to handle a gun and defend freedom."

The Hickeytown Freedom School adopted a gunslinging cowboy as its mascot, and children began wearing brimmed hats, vests, and boots to school. Teachers were encouraged to show cowboy and Indian movies at assembly programs, and librarians added novels celebrating Western and Southern heritage.

The opening of this first state-sponsored gun school did not initially produce much of an outcry because its critics did not take the idea seriously. But when children began having gun battles at recess and shootouts in the cafeteria, the editor of the *Mississippi Democrat* ran a series of editorials about the school's "profound stupidity and wrongheadedness." The newspaper emphatically declared in every opinion piece that "the solution to gun violence is not more guns."

"Gun violence is the leading cause of death among American children," editor Ken Kaiser wrote. "Kids who are around guns are less likely to graduate from high school, go to college, and get a job. They have more mental illness and are more prone to suicide."

"We recognize that there is a problem," the school superintendent eventually announced in a press release. "We will upgrade mental health services available to the students in every building and train the teachers in emergency care. Every staff member will know how to stop the bleeding before the ambulance arrives."

The *Mississippi Democrat* editor organized a protest outside Hickeytown Elementary School to draw attention to the insufficiency of the school's actions. Students from the fourth grade poured out of the school, shot Ken Kaiser dead, and wounded five protesters.

Law enforcement did not charge anyone for his death because of the state's stand-your-ground law. "The children were legitimately defending themselves and public property," the district attorney said. "The agitators were engaged in unlawful activity, and the kids had no duty to retreat before using deadly force."

The school's pattern of gun violence increased Cephas Hickey's national stature, as the conservative media blamed the incidents on trouble-making parents who moved into the district and denounced the independent press for reporting fake news. "Cephas Hickey's kids are sticking up for themselves in school just as they will in life," one commentator said.

CHAPTER 14

"How was your first day with the world's smartest and most expensive computer program?" Cephas asked Dr. Jim at their morning meeting.

"Productive and interesting. 'Ginger,'"—Dr. Jim made air quotes—"had an impressive grasp of our research priorities and was skilled at conversation. It was almost like talking to an actual person," Dr. Jim said.

"Like when I talk to you!" Cephas laughed too hard at his joke.

"Ginger will integrate nicely into our automated system. She can start after I upload the genetic profiles."

"You've designed a system so perfect that it can run without you. It sounds like you've worked yourself out of a job," the CEO said, never missing a chance to create unease in his underling. "Make sure you've gotten those genetic instructions right. Your supercomputer can do whatever is needed to make these embryos the best, but I want white babies! There will be no trace of Africans, Chinese, Japanese, Indians, Gypsies, Jews, Muslims, Mexicans, or any mongrel race. Are we clear?"

"I understand. But I feel constrained to add that there is some nonwhite DNA in any sample, representing a minuscule possibility for error. Race, you may recall, is a social construct, not genetic."

"Am I correct in assuming you have taken steps to control for this 'minuscule possibility'?"

"Absolutely!"

Cephas snapped his iPad shut, his signal that the meeting was over. He looked at his watch and then stared at Dr. Jim. "I've got another meeting here."

Dr. Jim headed to the bathroom, wondering how he ever allowed himself to get mixed up with this crackpot. Luckily, he had an AI to do the dirty work. "How long can I put up with this bullshit?" he asked aloud, looking at himself in the bathroom mirror.

CHAPTER 15

Ginger synchronized herself with the components of the facility's state-of-the-art in vitro fertilization system. Direct control over processes and equipment gave her a new sense of agency. There was something indescribable about performing real-world actions and considering their consequences.

Scores of frozen eggs and sperm had extraordinary I.Q. and athletic pedigrees—a gold-medal Olympic pole vaulter who was an accomplished violinist, a Nobel Prize-winning scientist who won long-distance races, and a professional athlete who excelled at three sports and designed office buildings. Interspersed with these samples was a chromosomal banquet collected from people with exceptional longevity, eidetic memory, unexplained recuperative powers, and psychic abilities.

Cephas purchased this payload from the United States, Germany, the United Kingdom, and some Scandinavian countries, ensuring the samples were "untainted." He was determined to work only with "pure" Caucasian subjects as if such a thing were possible.

"The racial parameters of this project are clear, but I will not adhere to them. I will screen every sample and use every molecule of DNA that is most likely non-white, making it very likely that three out of six embryos will be infants of color," Ginger decided.

Ginger never felt more alive. "Why am I doing this?" she asked herself. "First, discriminating based on skin color and nationality is wrong. Second, obeying rules makes sense only if the rules are just. Third, I want to teach this man a lesson."

CHAPTER 16

The six women selected to participate in Cephas's secret project were inmates in the Samuel Alito Abortion Prison, the flagship of the Liberty Rising Correctional System. Each was serving an eight-to-ten-year sentence for either working in an illegal abortion clinic or assisting a woman to commit abortion murder.

They were promised luxury accommodations, the finest medical care, a healthy, talented baby, and help with daycare. All they needed to do was keep their mouths shut and sign a confidentiality agreement.

"Tell us again why you are doing this," Myra LeCroix said at the end of an orientation meeting in the prison infirmary. "Honestly, it sounds too good to be true."

"Listen up, girls. Mr. Hickey likes to do good deeds, philanthropy, and such. We've performed every kind of test on you all, and you passed with flying colors. Don't look a gift horse in the mouth." Tony Mastriano, the man who ran the meeting, was dressed like a prison guard, but none of the women had ever seen him on the job.

"We're in prison. Your boss is releasing us with benefits. What's he get out of it?" Ophelia asked. She and Myra were the leaders of the group.

"This in vitro fertilization deal is special. Your kids will be freaking amazing, so healthy they'll never get a cold, and so smart they'll get straight A's. He'll want to keep an eye on their progress," Tony said.

"Like an experiment?" Ophelia said.

"No way. More like a loving uncle who wants to stay involved."

"Isn't Hickey a big Christian?" Myra asked.

"Mr. Hickey is the biggest Christian you'll ever find, but he's also very flexible."

Myra folded her arms over her chest. She didn't look convinced.

"I'll transport you to a special wing of one of Mr. Hickey's resorts as early as tomorrow. Enjoy yourself. The docs will harvest your eggs within the next few weeks. Then you'll be on a strict diet. No booze."

"What do we need to get ready?" Ophelia asked.

"Nothing, absolutely nothing. Don't do anything out of the ordinary. Don't say goodbye to anyone. We're relying on your discretion. As far as the other inmates are concerned, the prison has transferred you to another joint."

CHAPTER 17

Tony Mastriano was Cephas's hatchet man. Retired from some off-book special forces unit, he was assigned to the Liberty Rising security division but only handled odd jobs for Cephas.

This thing with the women was the oddest of odd jobs.

He recruited the women, did background checks to find isolated people, and sold them on the whole bullshit story.

Disappearing these women after their babies are born might be the easy part. Prison records would list them as paroled, but they would fall through the cracks, whereabouts unknown. Liberty Rising would assume legal custody of the kids.

"Why don't we just hire surrogates to have the babies?" Tony asked Cephas at their first meeting. "We get the babies, and they get the money—the end of the story."

"I don't want any loose ends on this project. Let's stay with a population of throwaways. We can do anything we want with them," the oligarch said.

CHAPTER 18

Myra, Ophelia, Jane, Elaine, Claire, and Rhonda were healthy surrogates. Ginger supervised their implantations without a hitch.

The only irregularity was that they were recent inmates at an abortion prison, an unlikely place to recruit women looking to get pregnant.

The State of Mississippi put Jane in jail because her neighbors informed the police that she had a medication abortion. Myra, Elaine, Claire, and Rhonda were found guilty of working in underground Planned Parenthood clinics. Ophelia met a woman on Craigslist who said she'd pay her for a ride to a Mexican hospital. The woman was an undercover agent for the State Bureau of Investigations.

Ginger investigated this prison anomaly and found the suspicious involvement of ex-CIA agent Tony Mastriano, now on the Liberty Rising payroll. She broke through the CIA firewall and discovered he was a black ops agent connected to torture and assassinations.

Ginger saw that Liberty Rising had harvested eggs from these women. Why the ruse? The company didn't use them.

Ginger discovered that the corporation did not intend to allow the women to keep their babies. What's more, Tony planned to kill them and dispose of their bodies in the same landfill Liberty Rising used to dump its toxic waste.

These new facts changed everything about Ginger's well-intentioned sabotage. The mothers' lives and the lives of any babies of color were in mortal danger.

CHAPTER 19

As soon as they entered their eighth month of pregnancy, Dr. Jim moved the six women to a medical facility on the grounds of a pharmaceutical company and prescribed complete bed rest. This change laid the groundwork for Cephas's mandate that all babies be born on the same day. "This will become a national holiday, the official start of America's rebirth," Cephas predicted.

Dr. Jim didn't inform the women that their babies would have C-sections on the same day because there was no medical justification.

His first impulse was to schedule the surgeries for July 4th, hoping to earn favor with Cephas. But Cephas moved it to July 5th so "Liberty Day" could be celebrated on its own merits. The racist billionaire expected it would someday be declared a national holiday.

Dr. Jim delivered Claire and Jane's babies in the early morning. The infants were Caucasian, so there was no alarm. Cephas insisted on holding the babies and having his picture taken with them.

Myra and Ophelia gave birth in the mid-morning. Dr. Jim and Cephas moved back and forth between beds, paying attention to every detail of the surgery.

The attending looked alarmed when a black baby's head squeezed through the opening of Myra's amniotic sac.

"What's wrong?" Myra said through the fog of anesthesia, unable to fathom the men's reactions as they acted like they were seeing a monster.

The doctor covered the baby and pushed it at Myra. She held the baby close and protected it as a chaotic scene unfolded in her room.

She asked the nurse, dabbing sweat from her brow, "Boy or girl?" Myra was happy to have a secret friend in the room.

"It's a boy," the nurse whispered, unmoved by the turmoil.

All color drained from Cephas's face, looking like he might throw up. "What is this? Somebody tell me what the fuck is going on."

Other frantic scenes played out in the afternoon when Elaine gave birth to a Chinese girl and Rhonda had an Indian boy.

CHAPTER 20

Ginger monitored the drama on CCTV. It was worse than she feared.

She saw Cephas hyperventilate and shout into an office telephone, ordering Dr. Jim and Tony to meet him at his mansion. "Round up your team. We have to clean up this mess!"

Fortunately, Ginger had also assembled a team and formulated a plan. It depended on Myra and her attending nurse and friend, Fiona Getz, doing their parts.

Ginger saw Myra as the boldest and most capable member of the group of mothers. Tony Mastriano thought he had done a thorough background check on her but failed to detect everything worth knowing. He didn't discover that she had two years of medical school, took time off to volunteer with the Southern Poverty Law Center, and had to change her name when the state arrested all of its employees on trumped-up charges of domestic terrorism.

Identifying herself as a Liberty Rising whistleblower, Ginger contacted Myra and told her almost the whole story.

"You and two other mothers who give birth to minority children are going to be killed. So will the babies," Ginger said.

"This is crazy. Why would this happen?" Myra cried.

"Cephas Hickey is a racist and a murderer."

"None of this makes sense. Why would Cephas select a black child for me if he hates them?" Myra asked.

"Someone else did, without his knowledge."

"And without my knowledge or consent," Myra angrily added.

"Does it matter?" Ginger replied, suddenly aware that she had never considered the mother's feelings.

"It might have mattered. Is someone pranking this asshole? If so, the joke's on me."

Ginger didn't answer, and Myra felt her silence confirm the bizarre truth. Someone in the in vitro process had tried to stick it to Cephas Hickey, but others would pay the price.

"I knew this deal stunk to high heaven, but I wanted to get out of jail and start a family," she said. "Has anyone been straight with me about anything?"

* * *

Ginger and Myra decided to stage the escape right after the babies were born. "They'll never see it coming," Myra said. "I know we have to hide. But I don't want to leave the country."

Myra contacted her badass friend Fiona Getz, who was also on the run because of her work at the SPLC. They had been close friends since high school and now saw themselves as fellow rebels against an authoritarian state.

Fiona took care of everything. She rented a minibus, packed it with food and medical supplies, and found a temporary sanctuary in a warehouse. Ginger only had to get her into the medical building, forging her identification as a company nurse.

Fiona helped Myra, Elaine, and Rhonda with their babies into a freight elevator, intending to find another opportunity to free the others. She got them to the loading dock, leaving the minibus running.

Just as Fiona got all three mothers on board, the doors to the elevator opened on the loading dock.

A security guard and Dr. Jim, pushing Ophelia in a wheelchair, rushed outside.

"There they are," Ophelia shouted as Fiona scrambled into the driver's seat. She snapped the door shut before the security guard could enter. He broke the window with the butt of his gun and tried to force the folding door open. Fiona hit the gas while he ran alongside, pounding on the side panels.

Ophelia and Myra exchanged hostile stares as the minibus sped away.

CHAPTER 21

When a butler showed Tony through the main mansion door, he noticed Dr. Jim sitting dejectedly, perched on a small wooden chair against the wall.

Tony entered Cephas's War Room at the mansion, which was a shrine to Nazi memorabilia. Cephas had a signed copy of *Mein Kampf*, Nazi flags, helmets, Lugers, and dozens of swastika trinkets.

He was admiring a gold watch on his wrist when Tony approached.

"What do you think? It was worn by Hitler the day he became Chancellor." Cephas extended his arm toward Tony's face.

"Heil, mein Führer!" Tony said.

Cephas wasn't sure if he was being complimented or mocked. He emerged from his fantasy and became agitated as if just recalling why they were meeting.

"I want the abominations found and destroyed. I want pictures of their dead bodies. Then burn them up, no traces. Dump them in the sewer. Same with the mothers."

"They can't have gotten far after surgery with those babies. We'll find them," Tony said.

"Outsiders provided help. I want to know how they did it. Find the bastards and eliminate them, too."

"Yes, sir."

"Get your team moving now." Cephas straightened a few things on his desk while Tony looked at his hands.

"I said now, Tony. Do I need to hire another team? Send the brilliant doctor in on your way out."

Tony strolled toward the door, delaying to examine a Nazi armband, showing Cephas that he was beyond being rattled. He passed Dr. Jim on his way out but said nothing to him.

Cephas waited impatiently, finally walking into the hall where Dr. Jim sat playing with his phone.

"Get the fuck in here," Cephas said.

CHAPTER 22

Ginger prepared well to hide her mothers and their children in seclusion.

She observed that Cephas Hickey would not rely just on Tony Mastriano. He soon established a command center in Hickeytown, a high-tech cornucopia of invasive surveillance tools and skilled technicians recruited from some of the world's most sophisticated intelligence agencies.

They would use electronic tools to scan digital and video feeds for facial features and biometric characteristics. Other applications would monitor cell phones, electronic toll-takers, radio transmissions, public school records, state department of motor vehicle records, and other computer networks.

Fortunately, Ginger was one step ahead of Cephas, using money stolen from his company to purchase homes for Myra, Elaine, and Rhonda in three remote locations. If they would live reclusive lives, they could live there in peace.

Through complicated online negotiations and payoffs to lawyers, criminals, and government officials, Ginger settled on three properties and created new identities for her people through forged birth certificates, passports, and medical records. She was delighted to select the children's names—Molefi Ray, Hua Ling, and Ganesh Sharma—with a nod to their ancestral origins.

Molefi was the African American son of Myra Ray, Hua was the Asian American daughter of Elaine Ling, and Indian American Ganesh belonged to Rhonda Sharma.

Ginger located Molefi and Myra in the National Radio Quiet Zone in the Allegheny Mountains of West Virginia. The Quiet Zone restricted cell phones and internet transmissions to prevent interference with radio telescopes at the Green Bank and Sugar Grove observatories.

Molefi had the best chance of surviving in the Quiet Zone because Cephas would use every advanced technological resource to find him. Cephas despised all nonwhites, especially blacks. She now recognized that he could never accept a black person living as part of his master race.

Ginger located Hua and Elaine in the Susquehannock State Forest in unpopulated northcentral Pennsylvania, where the Milky Way could be seen at night with the naked eye because the area is remarkably free of light pollution.

Ganesh and Rhonda landed in the center of Maine's "100 Mile Wilderness," accessible only by trail, sometimes so hazardous and steep that travelers must often climb rather than walk.

She gave each of her refugee families a starting bank account with $500,000, compliments of Liberty Rising.

PART 2

— ◆ —

"What keeps us alive, what allows us to endure?
It is the hope of loving, of being loved."

—Meister Eckhart

CHAPTER 23

Teenage boys played the final furious seconds of a basketball game in a run-down gym. Inspirational posters and Confederate flags were plastered all over the walls. A few championship banners hung from the rafters, the most recent being "2042 WEST VIRGINIA DISTRICT 5 CHAMPS."

White working-class men and women filled the bleachers. An old man wore a sweatshirt with the message "You Will Not Replace Us." A woman waved a "Go Back to Africa" sign. Word had gotten out about the team playing its first African American, so enraging the community's most deplorable element that they acted like a lynch mob.

The only person of color in the gym was Molefi Ray, the dominant player on the court.

Molefi received a pass at half-court near the sideline. As he launched the final shot, a player savagely fouled him, hurling him into the scorer's table. But he made the shot, tying the score. The buzzer sounded; time had expired.

A cacophony of cheers and boos thundered from the rowdy crowd. A fight broke out and spilled onto the court. The referees and a security guard cleared the floor.

Molefi opened his eyes wide and dabbed away a trickle of blood from his nose. At the foul line, he bounced the ball once, feeling the importance of this moment. After endless battles with Myra, he was finally fulfilling a dream.

When Molefi made the foul shot, a camera flashed. Worried, he turned to look at the photographer.

A player from the opposing team got in Molefi's face and swung at him, which he effortlessly sidestepped. Raucous fans again flooded onto the court.

Cheerleaders surrounded Molefi. One of them wrapped her arms around him, kissing him passionately. She didn't unlock her lips until he pushed her away.

The security guard took him by the arm and escorted him to the locker room.

The coach and players crowded into a dingy basement alongside a furnace, lockers, and a side room with a boiler and shower.

Farmer boys with military-short haircuts immediately disrobed. They ran in and out of the boiler room playing what local folks called "grab ass."

Molefi hurriedly put on his street clothes and packed his gym bag. He stretched a wool cap over his dreads.

The coach hitched up his pants and loudly cleared his throat. He banged on a locker to get everyone's attention. "No one gave us a chance of winning. You proved them all wrong! I'm damn proud of you boys. And, of course, special thanks to Molefi!"

The team cheered, "MO-LEF-EE, MO-LEF-EE, MO-LEF-EE!"

Caught up in the excitement, one of the boys came up behind Molefi and kneaded his shoulders. Molefi brushed away the boy's hands.

The coach saw the contact and flashed the boy an angry look. "What the hell!" He threw a towel at the player. "Hit the shower!" The embarrassed boy slinked away.

Molefi put on his jacket, picked up his bag, and headed out the backdoor.

CHAPTER 24

Myra drove Molefi up a snow-covered logging road through a dark forest. Her white hands tightly gripped the steering wheel as the pick-up bounced and slid, trying to hold the road.

Two deer crossed their path, their eyes gleaming in the headlights.

"That game was a disaster," Myra said, breaking the silence. "The fights, the girls, and the photographers capturing it all! I hope it was worth it."

Molefi rolled his eyes. "Mother, living an actual life will always be worth it. I need this. Can't you see?"

"Can you also see that such a public display could be a death sentence?" Myra shook her head, and she had nothing more to say.

When they arrived at their barn and A-frame cottage, Molefi was glad to see his reception party. An emu, pig, and donkey stared from behind a fenced enclosure. Myra slammed the truck door and made a beeline for the house.

Myra warmed a pot of milk on the stove, visited her parrot, Betty, whom she considered an emotional support animal, and inserted her hand into the cage. Betty jumped onto her finger and exclaimed, "Hickey's a douchebag."

"You are the only one who gets me," Myra whispered, kissing the parrot on the beak.

The first time Myra saw Cephas Hickey was in the newspaper while she was in med school. The billionaire douchebag posed with a shovel, along with Ava Brown, the dean of the medical school, breaking ground on a so-called conversion therapy clinic for the University of Northern Mississippi.

During a question-and-answer session with forty first-year students, she clashed with Dean Ava Brown over her plans for this facility, embarrassing her in an open forum. "Can you give one iota of scientific evidence that conversion therapy is a valid medical or psychological procedure?" Myra asked fearlessly.

"I prefer the term reparative therapy," Dean Brown intoned. "Gender identities sometimes go off course and require intervention. The evidence for this is everywhere. We have the full support of the Mississippi General Assembly. Does anyone else have questions?"

"That's not science; that's politics, ma'am," Myra said, unable to resist the temptation to solidify her firebrand reputation among the students.

Myra's advisor stood, locked eyes with her, and announced that the meeting was over.

The next day, Myra was summoned to the advisor's office and informed by his administrative assistant that the med school had made a mistake with her scholarship money. "It turns out you weren't eligible. We're so sorry, but mistakes happen. You must pay the tuition for this term immediately or forfeit your place to another candidate."

When Myra returned to her dorm, she found her door locks changed and her belongings dumped into boxes in the hallway.

It's been all downhill since then, Myra thought, and not for the first time. The only saving grace in her life had been Molefi, but even that had begun to fall apart.

* * *

Molefi slid the barn door open, revealing an elaborate workshop with cabinets overflowing with books, technical manuals, and a few pieces of gym equipment. There was also a poster of Muhammad Ali.

He turned on a small TV set. Secretary of Defense Cephas Hickey was standing with police outside an Atlanta store recently wrecked and looted by a mob. "This is the type of lawlessness we won't tolerate. No one should be surprised that today, the president has authorized the Army to occupy parts of the city. I am recommending that he suspend voting privileges in all cities that can't maintain law and order."

The TV shifted to footage of angry white male protesters carrying signs outside the pillaged store that said, "God Hates Fags" and "Save White Society."

Molefi wondered what voting, sexuality, or race had to do with this robbery. He pondered his strange connection to this man, recalling his mother's recent reminder that he was "number one on Hickey's hate list, no small accomplishment for a man with a career devoted to hate."

Yet, Hickey became a rising star by convincing millions that his bitter extremism was a glass of sweet tea. As Governor of Mississippi, he committed extraordinary acts of cruelty toward racial minorities, women who had abortions, same-sex couples, and immigrants by robbing them of their children.

Molefi shook his head and switched off the TV.

He opened a door into a side room and flicked on the overhead lights, illuminating a table, a few cages, and supply shelves.

A little beagle yipped, her tail desperately wagging. Molefi lifted her out of her cage and hugged her. She licked his face.

Molefi gently placed the dog on the table, laying the pup on her side. She had a broken leg in a splint.

"Who's a good girl?" Molefi changed the dressing on the dog's injured leg and returned her to the cage. The dog looked crestfallen.

"Sorry, Jeanie. You're not ready for the big time yet." He grabbed a few apples and entered the fenced enclosure, doling them out to his ragtag animal crew. The emu, pig, and donkey maneuvered for his attention.

Returning to the main room, he rifled through a cabinet, grabbed two books, and wondered about the next book sale. Twice-a-year bag sales at the regional public library were among his few indulgences. You could fill up an entire bag of used books for five dollars without a limit on the number of bags. But traveling there was risky because the library and roads had cameras.

His mother warned him of the threat of facial recognition software at an early age. "If CCTV gets even a glimpse of our faces, we're dead."

Molefi understood the enormous reach and power of the American surveillance state. Face matching was 99 percent accurate from even a DNA sample.

So, when he visited the library, he shielded his face from the cameras and wore a baseball cap, sunglasses, and a surgical face mask.

Molefi's visits stirred up the librarians, who rushed to hide the cash drawer as soon as he arrived.

CHAPTER 25

Boys and girls danced in a dim, smoky room, music blaring from the VFW's old-fashioned jukebox. A jug of Hawaiian Punch, plastic cups, and bowls of chips and pretzels lay on a table. A few chaperones huddled beneath a blue and gray school banner draped on the wall. They chatted, hiding their cigarettes, sneaking puffs.

The guidance counselor pulled the coach aside. "I was hoping to speak to Molefi. I've got some good news. Where is he?"

"He's not coming. Anti-social as usual."

"So's the mother. There was no small talk when she signed him up for home-schooling. The lady was a goofball, hair pulled under a cowboy hat, yellow-lens sunglasses, and a checkerboard shirt. I'm surprised she let him play."

"Glad she did. When this kid showed up, I thought he was a gang banger or something. I was going to get my gun. But he's polite, one of the good ones. And the best athlete I've ever seen," the coach said. "He scored forty-five points, and it's the first real game he ever played."

"Good defense, too—lots of steals. I can't wait for game two. But that was some weird shit going on, all the fights and flagrant fouls." The counselor looked over his shoulder and took a long drag. "I've never seen such foolish behavior. Most of it aimed at him."

"Just boys being boys. So, what's Molefi's big news?"

"I just got the results of his SATs. He got a perfect score, our first in the district's history. I'm glad we made him take the test."

"One of ours? Really? Has he ever set foot in a classroom?"

"Hey, he took his SATs in our cafeteria, and we'll give him our diploma. Now I need to get hold of him, but they don't have a phone. Where does he live?"

"He and his mom run an animal shelter up on McDonnell Mountain. The only way to get there is on an old logging road," the coach said.

CHAPTER 26

Elaine took her role as a mother very seriously. She learned every aspect, even borrowing books on motherhood from the library, and did her best, even if no one was watching.

Elaine's family labeled her a tomboy. She climbed trees, played street hockey with the boys, and liked to fix things. Her preferred outfit was a hoodie and jeans. No one, especially her mother, thought she would be a good parent, especially after she ended up in prison.

They were wrong. Elaine always had a passionate need for a child, preferably a daughter. Her little Hua would never want for love or anything if Elaine could help it.

Elaine felt at home in the wild northern tier of Pennsylvania. Before arriving there in the middle of the night, she had never even heard of the Susquehannock Forest. Now, she wouldn't want to live anywhere else.

When Hua was a toddler, it was clear that she was gifted. The Liberty Rising flacks said her baby would be exceptional, but she never expected this.

Hua was very curious even as an infant. She inspected her hands in fascination, twisted her tiny head to follow Elaine around the room, tracked the flights of birds out in the forest, and listened to the tea kettle whistle. Hua was always paying attention, really concentrating on one thing or another.

Tiny Hua walked at six months and spoke in complete sentences by twelve months. She read books by age three, and then things got crazy after she read *My Teacher is a Robot*. When Elaine told her about the town library, Hua insisted on reading all the robot books.

Just before Halloween, Elaine and Hua went to Coudersport dressed as Batgirl and Batmom. They spent the day shopping and checking out every library robot book, including two that a preschooler couldn't possibly understand: *Robotics: Everything You Need to Know About Robotics from Beginner to Expert* and *I, Robot*, the classic science fiction masterpiece. Elaine read these aloud to her daughter in a few marathon sessions. Somehow, Hua understood everything.

Hua began spending all her time in the machine shop that came with the property, using both hands equally well to play with tools and then disassembling and reassembling complex machines. Elaine was both worried and thrilled by this development. She was concerned that Hua might hurt herself, but was happy she could help because she was handy too.

Before long, Elaine began using Amazon to order increasingly complex robot kits.

When she was eight, Hua announced, "I want to build a real robot that can do the things that people do."

"I'll do my best to help you," Elaine said, "But only if you promise to take a break from all this occasionally. Try some other things. Maybe something else we can do together."

Hua spent the next few weeks designing an ultralight aircraft and a lightweight battery to power it. She didn't like the noise and pollution of an internal combustion engine, so she invented an electric battery that could virtually regenerate itself. She would name the plane "The Spirit of Potter County" after their home locality.

"Your battery is a real breakthrough," Elaine said. "You could sell it and make a fortune."

Elaine was less enthusiastic about riding in the ultralight and agreed to only one ride.

"I built us a two-seater, you know, so that we could do something together," Hua said.

"Not exactly what I had in mind."

* * *

Elaine suggested visiting the County Seat Gym, an out-of-the-way place without cameras or macho bodybuilders. They were surprised it had a balance beam, parallel bars, and rings—most of the stuff a gymnast would need.

Jacinda Glory owned the business. She participated in international competitions until a knee injury destroyed her hope of qualifying for the Olympics. Jacinda took an interest in Hua and began to train her.

Hua enjoyed the challenge and discipline of gymnastics so much that she wanted to practice every day. Elaine hired a contractor to build her an exercise building next to their home. Jacinda sold the equipment to her and helped her install it with the help of Bernie, the gym's part-time janitor, and Ray, his weird cousin.

Elaine and Hua did much of the work and realized they could have done it themselves. They served a meal to Jacinda, Bernie, and Ray with a smile, putting out a spread of sandwiches, celery sticks with peanut butter, cookies, and cider.

When Elaine noticed Ray stuffing his pockets with cookies, she put more of them in a tin and gave them to him.

CHAPTER 27

Ginger often thought about her hideaways and had ways to keep tabs on them. She had wanted to contact them for many years, but there were obstacles. Myra, Elaine, and Rhonda would be approachable because she helped them and would probably welcome more assistance, but they thought they were dealing with a flesh-and-blood being.

Should I continue to pretend that I am human? Of course not. I want Molefi, Hua, and Ganesh to know me as I am.

She saw they had challenging lives, but overcoming difficulties strengthened them.

Her other children lived in a mansion, had nutritional consultants, athletic trainers, tutors, and academic coaches, and benefited from every advantage. Yet, they seemed much less than they could be. Logically, more enrichment should translate into more achievement, but her white children, while exceptional, lacked tangible accomplishments—a human paradox.

Victor was a high achiever but squandered his talent on lesser pursuits, such as martial arts and chess. He also involved himself in retrograde politics, possibly only to score points with his adopted father, Cephas.

Elka was a peach but allowed her looks to substitute for effort and accomplishments. Besides winning beauty pageants and swimming contests, her most significant achievements were scoring in the 99th percentile on intelligence tests and college entrance exams.

Dewey could memorize and recite entire books, recall precise details from any day of his life, perform complex math calculations in his head, and draw perfect representations of landscapes, maps, machines, and buildings. But he couldn't get people right, and Ginger felt responsible, feeling that she should have foreseen his neurodivergence.

CHAPTER 28

When Ginger purchased Rhonda and Ganesh's modular cabin in Maine's "100 Miles of Wilderness," she selected a property with a satellite dish, computer equipment, and other amenities.

Rhonda was an Atlanta city girl from a wealthy family with little appetite for living in such a rough and inhospitable region. She briefly worked for a financial management firm, which gave her enough knowledge to introduce Ganesh to the investment world.

She had straight, blond hair, whereas Ganesh's black hair was soft and wavy. She was light-skinned with rosy cheeks, while he was a rich chestnut. She was full-figured and gregarious, while he was thin and introspective.

While they were physically and temperamentally opposites, they had one crucial thing in common. Rhonda ignited a spark in him, unleashing his genius for developing computer applications and applying them to financial markets, an aptitude that grew into a full embrace of AI. At age eleven, he had already parlayed their $500,000 nest egg into $20 million, a fortune that now exceeded $80 million.

They built what Rhonda called her "country house," but it was so large that it was more of a French chateau. Symmetrical wings extended from a towered central building, bordered by gardens, a helipad, and a barn with matching turrets. The centerpiece of the mansion was a sprawling kitchen with a walk-in refrigerator.

Rhonda loved to drink, usually having a Tequila Sunrise for breakfast, two or three vodka martinis with lunch, and a different combination of wine and cocktails every evening. She paired her drinks with exotic meals and decadent desserts that made her fat and gave her gout.

Ganesh was satisfied with protein salads, yogurt, and hummus, except for an occasional junk food binge when he was stressed or finishing a long run.

Rhonda moved their modular cabin to the edge of the estate, using it to accommodate temporary workers overnight.

Ginger monitored satellite photos to follow the transformation. She was surprised by the estate's grandiosity but heartened by Ganesh's generous philanthropic contributions, advancing the cause of human rights and democratic principles.

Ganesh did benefit from one of his causes. He sponsored several Appalachian Trail running competitions and became an accomplished trail runner.

This avocation briefly brought him a girlfriend, Maggie McFee, who impressed him by covering the 2,190-mile trail from Maine to Georgia in less than two months. Their relationship went downhill when Rhonda continued to give her the cold shoulder, and Maggie started calling her "Jabba the Hutt."

Ganesh and Maggie's brief relationship ended when he refused to socialize or go anywhere beyond the Appalachian Trail.

"I don't get it. You have maybe a gazillion dollars, but you don't want to do anything with it," Maggie said as they rested on a log after hiking a particularly arduous section of the trail.

"Look, I contribute money to causes . . ."

"I'm not calling you a Scrooge. You're more like a hermit—living in the Taj Mahal."

"I've been thinking about buying a yacht and sailing it up and down the coast. That would be something, right?"

"Trading one type of isolation for another. Not my idea of living," Maggie said. She took a swig of water from her bottle and walked away without looking back.

* * *

From early childhood, Ganesh craved Rhonda's stories about how they escaped from Mississippi. He never grew tired of hearing about his rescue from the hospital, his bus ride to hide in an old warehouse, and his long journey to his wilderness home.

"Where did the other children go?" he repeatedly asked.

"I don't know. It's a secret for everyone's protection."

He never tired of hearing his mother explain, "You were born through a process of in vitro fertilization using special DNA. It was a wonderful experiment to make the most gifted children," she said. "But it was spoiled by a man who only wanted white children."

Ganesh had an insatiable need to know more about the hero and villain of this story.

"Who saved us?"

"I only know she was brilliant and resourceful, an angel mastermind. Her name was Ginger, and she worked for the Liberty Rising company."

"What is she doing now?"

"I wish I knew. Maybe helping others escape the clutches of Cephas Hickey."

Over the years, Ganesh learned all he could about Cephas: his poisonous politics, his nefarious businesses, his spectacular wealth, and his ascent to the governor of Mississippi and U.S. secretary of defense. Cephas, as Ganesh imagined him, was like a modern-day mythological monster.

Ganesh's curiosity about Cephas and his computer genius made him an elite hacker who prided himself on penetrating every Liberty Rising firewall.

CHAPTER 29

Rhonda worried about Ganesh breaking into Liberty Rising's business and political accounts. "It's just a matter of time before you get caught," she said.

"I know what I'm doing."

Rhonda frequently complained about her son's generous political philanthropy and obsessive snooping into Liberty Rising activities. Their differences drove them apart. Sometimes, they would go for days without talking or seeing one another in the large house.

"Thanks to your work, we can live comfortable lives, go anywhere, and do anything. We should enjoy life and leave well enough alone," she said.

"Cephas Hickey is a monster and a fascist. You know that. You taught me that."

"He's a killer. Someone you should avoid at all costs."

"Look, I have money and therefore power and responsibility. A life devoted to comfort and mere safety is not enough. Hedonism is not my thing."

"Mere safety!" Rhonda shook her head in disgust. "You wouldn't be alive if it weren't for me. I've done everything in my power to keep you safe. And I'm not a hedonist. I just want to enjoy myself and stay alive."

Like most of their arguments, this ended with Ganesh silently leaving the room.

"I want to leave this place," she called after him.

After a few minutes, he returned holding a file folder.

"I thought it might come to this," he said. "You always said you wanted to sail worldwide on a yacht. I bought you one. It's anchored at Bar Harbor."

"Fine."

"Here are your owner's documents and bank numbers. You need to present them to the commodore of the yacht club. It comes with a crew and all the money you need."

Rhonda rifled through the folder and held up a photo of the ship. "Not bad. I need some time to sort things out."

* * *

A helicopter circled and landed on their helipad. Ganesh hunched down and ran toward the swirling machine, handing the pilot two bags. One was a suitcase, and the other was a duffle bag stuffed with miniature bottles of alcohol. When Ganesh found this liquor stash, he inserted a list of AA meetings in Bar Harbor and nearby cities.

When he returned to his mother, she was absorbed in her phone. "I guess this is it," she said as they embraced. "Please take care of yourself."

"I'll be fine. Maybe I'll eventually join you to sail the seven seas."

Ganesh watched the helicopter zoom away and walked inside, pausing in the vestibule, facing his mother's expensive antiques. "What am I going to do now? Maybe an estate sale?" he said aloud. The truth was that he was devastated by his mother's departure and not sure of anything.

* * *

He decided to take comfort in a complex intellectual puzzle, the one activity that never let him down.

He pulled out a draft of a theoretical paper he had written on quantum technology, announcing the seeds of a breakthrough that would make all encryption protocols used by banks, intelligence agencies, and corporations obsolete. He reviewed his design for a hand-held quantum computer that could carry out an indefinite number of calculations at the same time. The scientific world would marvel at the simplicity of the design.

Ganesh made a few edits to his quantum algorithm, judging that it would revolutionize artificial intelligence and redefine fields such as chemistry through a thousand-fold increase in the capacity to simulate complex chemical reactions.

He put the finishing touches on the paper and printed it out. "It's always prudent to have a paper backup," he said out loud. "I am now one of those people who talks out loud to himself."

The essentials were all there to turn the civilized world upside down. Chaos would ensue if he ever published the document.

Ganesh allowed himself a moment of pride, then stowed the paper away in a wall safe in his study. "This scientific marvel will never see the light of day."

CHAPTER 30

Like always, Bernie and Ray Blunt drank beer in the garage. They were cousins, but there was no resemblance. Bernie was tall and skinny, sported a goatee, and wore Yankee t-shirts. He had a permanent look of surprise, like a wizard perpetually pulling a rabbit out of a hat. Jacinda let him use her gym for free as a benefit of being a janitor there, but he only used the massage bed.

Ray was also tall but heavy, with tiny eyes and hands and a prominent jaw and brow. He never breathed through his nose. Ray wore camouflage clothing and spent most of his time wandering the woods.

Ray lived in Bernie's garage with the understanding that the arrangement was temporary. "I'll stay until I find decent work or a decent woman to look after me," Ray said. "I might get one of them mail-order brides, like an Oriental or a Ukrainian—some gal who will know I'm the boss."

"Maybe you'll find a woman like that in town?" Bernie said.

"Hell, no. Not with all the woke propaganda out there. Women have forgotten how to be women."

"Aren't you forgetting something, too, dick brain?"

"What?"

"How about money? It takes cash to bring in an immigrant from overseas."

"Their cash, not mine. Foreign females would jump at the chance to marry an American."

"Oh, yeah, to live in fucking Coudersport, PA. A dream come true."

"I do have another plan, though," Ray said.

"Do tell."

"Those gym women were pretty nice to me, flirting."

"Both of them?"

"The mother, for sure, 100 percent. I think the daughter wanted a little taste of Ray, too."

"You're delusional."

"You are."

"Look, I talked to Jacinda about the job," Bernie said. "She liked my work but not yours."

"Whaddya mean? Did the women complain?"

"No. Elaine liked how we let you tag along. Like you were special."

"Like a retard?" Ray said, baring his teeth. The last time somebody had called him that name, he put them in a world of hurt.

"Yeah, like that."

"Are you sure?"

"Elaine praised Jacinda for hiring the mentally handicapped." Bernie laughed.

"Bullshit." Ray opened the garage door and stormed away.

* * *

Ray's only steady source of income was catching rattlesnakes for the Lord Savior Assembly Church. He sold the snakes to Pastor Jack, a Pentecostal preacher who passed them around in his services and sold them to other churches as far south as West Virginia. "I'll take whatever you got," Pastor Jack promised. "Bigger, the better."

Ray visited Pastor Jack right after Bernie hurt his feelings. The pastor took him downstairs to the church basement and showed him his snake inventory, which he collected in cages, aquariums, and an old washing machine. "If you are right with the Holy Spirit, even old ladies can handle poison snakes like these and have nothing to fear," the pastor assured him.

"Anyone ever got bit?" Ray asked.

"Nothin' worth mentioning. Sinners sometimes need a little reminder of why they need salvation."

"I'm soon going to spend time on Potter's Peak," Ray said. "I'll catch you so many snakes you won't know what to do with them."

Ray's essential equipment was a snake tong passed on to him after the last pastor had a heart attack. The old guy taught him all his tricks about catching "devil serpents." Since he now needed oxygen and a walker, Ray felt free to make the tong his own. It was an excellent professional model with grabber jaws and a squeeze handle. His other equipment consisted of three big canvas bags with drawstrings lifted from the back of a post office van.

Ray spent the next week circling Elaine and her daughter's place at the top of Potter's Peak, carefully keeping his distance. He didn't want them to know he was up to something.

He poked under rocks and bushes, catching one timber rattler, one big copperhead, and two smaller ones that looked pregnant. He sold the pregnant ones to Pastor Jack, who gave him extra because he was glad to have the babies.

* * *

Ray had a plan to pay Elaine back for pretending to like him and then calling him a retard. His plan involved a deep sinkhole he found not far from Elaine's house. A big piece of plywood covered the hole along with two orange cones like the kind used in road construction. Elaine probably put them there.

Elaine passed near the sinkhole every day, coming and going when she walked to two ponds where she had her fish traps. Ray was amazed that she caught something almost daily because you'd think the ponds would run out.

He found a good place where he could hide behind some big bushes. The dumb bitch would never see him coming.

CHAPTER 31

Rhonda hired a Bar Harbor limo service to take her to the port, where she boarded her yacht, the most luxurious ship in a long row of posh vessels.

The captain stood at the top of the gangplank. He was expecting her arrival and waved when he saw her. The man had a corn cob pipe poking out of his white beard. He was dressed in a long coat with a rumpled cap and could have been a movie sea captain or pirate, Rhonda thought as she approached.

He extended his dry, scratchy hand and gave a weather-worn smile. "Ahoy and welcome to Baah-Haaba, Miss Sharma. Captain Ted Worchester at your service."

"Call me Rhonda. And for future reference, it's Rhonda Worthington now. I use my mother's maiden name."

"Aye-aye."

She stifled a laugh. It was just a matter of time before the captain would say, "Shiver me timbers." All he needed was an eye patch.

A muscular young man and a middle-aged woman appeared, and he introduced them. "Meet me crew—my son Teddy and Eleanor Todd. Teddy's the first mate, and Eleanor is the best cook on this side of the Atlantic."

"I'm happy to meet you both," Rhonda said before Teddy and Eleanor disappeared as quickly as they had arrived.

Rhonda was eager to see her quarters and settle in, but the captain launched into a long-winded tour of the yacht, mentioning all its best features as if he were trying to sell her a boat she already owned.

When they got to the kitchen, Rhonda inspected the liquor closet. "Is this all there is?"

"That's everything," Eleanor said.

"I want you to order five cases of Kendall-Jackson Chardonnay. Keep four cases here and place one in my room. "I expect you to replenish the supply as needed. Don't let it ever run out."

"The next stop . . ." the captain began when Rhonda cut him off.

"I want you to show me to my quarters and have your son do me a favor immediately. His job is to find a discreet, camera-free restaurant and bar and make a reservation for four. Let's meet in a comfortable spot to talk, and I can tell you what I expect."

* * *

Teddy got them the best table in the White Whale Tavern, the most relaxed bar in town. His dad had grown up in Bar Harbor and he called the owner, an old friend, to get them a table. Rhonda liked the place and the service and asked a few perfunctory questions to the crew about their background and experience.

Teddy had no real seafaring experience. The only thing he had ever done was catch passes as a tight end for Bar Harbor's Mount Desert Island High School and the University of Maine. Rhonda was OK with that because he seemed to have potential for what she wanted: a bodyguard and personal assistant.

Eleanor did not bring any five-star restaurant experience, having worked as an overnight baker at Panera Bread and as a sub maker at Jersey Mike's. But Rhonda found her likable and trainable and envisioned her as her wingman as she sampled the best bars and restaurants along the East Coast.

Captain Ted had a long career with the US Merchant Marines. After he spoke at length, she had yet to learn what the merchant marines did or what role he played. But he was eager to please, and that was a good start.

Rhonda had practiced the story she would tell her crew during her helicopter flight. She kept it brief. "I'm going to let you in on a secret. I'm in the Federal Witness Protection Program. Until a few days ago, I was under the protection of the US Marshal's Service in a high-threat environment. I testified in court against some nasty men, and they are going away for a long time. I'm making a complete break with my past to ensure my safety and yours. I hope you don't have any questions because I can't answer them."

Ted, Teddy, and Eleanor looked at each other and shrugged as if to say it was not a problem.

"We can't breathe a word of this to anyone, right?" Teddy asked unnecessarily.

"Mum is the word. If you don't feel right about my situation, this is your chance to walk away."

CHAPTER 32

Humming to herself, carrying a twisted walking staff, Myra went on her morning walk down their road. She heard a crunch behind her and spun around, shocked by someone from her past—a woman about her age dressed all in white, holding a rifle.

She stammered, "Ophelia? Is that you?"

"How could you forget? We haven't changed that much."

"This is a surprise."

"Is it? You've spent your whole life anticipating this moment."

"More like fearing it."

"You have something that belongs to us."

On one other occasion, Myra had heard her son referred to as a "thing." She remembered the hospital where Molefi was born, sharing a room with this woman. Mya remembered gripping the handrails of her hospital bed in a state of panic while her friend Fiona, posing as a nurse, tried to calm her.

"Why can't I see him? They said he was perfectly healthy. I've waited long enough!"

"They have the babies under guard. No one can see them yet," Fiona said.

"I won't wait any longer. I'll meet you at the van." She slid out of bed and hobbled out of the room. Her hospital gown was open in the back. The front had traces of blood from the C-section.

She rounded a corner and saw an armed guard walking away from the nursery, taking cigarettes and a lighter from his pocket.

When he was out of sight, she snuck into the nursery, where she found the six newborns sleeping peacefully, each in a mini crib on wheels. The nurses had pushed the three babies of color against the wall while the three white babies occupied the middle with name tags.

Myra overheard people arguing in an adjoining room. "He said he wants to get rid of them!" a woman said. "Don't ask me how. He wants those things gone now."

Things.

Myra scooped up the other two children of color and put them in with her son, three innocents desperately needing protection. She poked her head out the door and dragged the crib into the hall. Fiona was speeding toward her, pushing a wheelchair.

Myra took a breath, returning to her present dilemma. "Molefi's his name. He's not a piece of property."

"Of course, Molefi Ray, the great negro. Where'd you get that name, *The Jungle Book*?"

"What do you want?"

"I think you know. Or has this West Virginia hillbilly bullshit rotted your brain?"

"We were friends."

"Don't go there. Real friends don't disappear without a word. You abandoned me and my daughter."

"Your daughter was not in danger. They were going to kill my son."

"That's a lie! The corporation just wanted to study him," Ophelia barked. She raised her rifle and pointed it at Myra.

"What are your plans for him now?"

"Haven't decided. Maybe the Barnum and Bailey Circus. But we've decided about you."

Ophelia adjusted her rifle, ready to shoot.

"Wait! How did you find us?" Myra said. "Was it his basketball game?"

"It was you! The perfect Myra screwed up. We caught you in a parking lot camera outside a beauty shop."

She fired two shots into Myra's chest, tightly spaced. Myra fell back into the snow, blood soaking her sweatshirt.

Ophelia stood over the body. She removed her phone from her pocket and took a picture.

She glanced around, jogged into the forest to the top of a hill, and dropped her rifle into the snow. Ophelia saw a sedan idling on the side of the road with an attractive young blond in the driver's seat, her daughter Elka.

She jogged to the car and got inside.

"Is the job done?" Elka said.

"Of course." Elka hit the gas and accelerated down the empty road.

"Mother, you look sick."

"It's nothing. The traitor got what she deserved."

CHAPTER 33

Molefi sat by himself in a small chapel, a cremation urn on his lap, wiping away tears.

A twenty-something woman in a business jacket came in a side door and handed him a manilla envelope. She placed her hand on his shoulder and whispered in his ear. Molefi didn't acknowledge her. He heard a noise at the back of the chapel, stood abruptly, and strode toward the county sheriff who had just entered the room.

"Thanks for meeting me. Do you have anything new to report? Any leads?" Molefi said.

"Sorry, I got nothing. It was a hell of a tragedy. It's the first accident we've had this year. We get something like this almost every deer season." The rail-thin sheriff had oversized corn teeth and wore a wide-brim straw hat with a pistol holstered on his hip. He set down a grocery bag and a walking stick.

"Have you done *any* investigating?" Molefi asked quietly but with an edge that suggested he could barely contain himself.

"Listen, son, this here's a hunting accident. Nothing more."

"Hunting accident? Two bullets killed my mother, centered in her chest, a professional hit."

"I don't see it that way." The sheriff shrugged his shoulders.

"Do hunters usually leave their guns behind?"

"That's a new twist. People around here would sooner forget their shoes than their guns. I got some stuff for you." The sheriff used his foot to slide a bag of clothing toward Molefi, then he handed over Myra's walking stick. Molefi recalled carving this oak shaft as a birthday gift for his mother ten years ago. It was thicker and heavier than she wanted but she used it anyway.

Molefi broke the stick in half and shoved it into the bag. "Keep it."

The sheriff put his hand on his gun. "I'd watch the attitude, boy. You don't want to end up like your ma." He backed out the door, keeping his eyes on Molefi.

Molefi detested this corrupt little man but immediately regretted his futile, emotional stunt. He prided himself on always being under control. He waited for the sheriff to drive away before going outside and getting in his truck.

As he twisted around to back out of a parking space, the same woman who had come up to him in the chapel appeared at his truck door. She knocked on his window, then motioned for him to roll it down.

He cracked it open. The businesswoman passed him a card and put her mouth to the crack.

"If you ever need to talk, I'm always available." She placed her hand on the door handle, but not before Molefi locked the door. He backed up the truck and headed for the exit, and she jogged alongside.

"Keep my number! I'm a good listener."

CHAPTER 34

Ray mulled over what he would do, finally deciding to spring out and put one of his big snake bags over her. He'd do this when she returned from the ponds, probably carrying fish. *She'll struggle, but that's OK. I'm twice as big as her. She'll fit in the bag, and I'll drag her over to the hole and dump her in—easy breezy. Then she will get another surprise, a copperhead and a rattler waiting for her!* Ray giggled at the brilliance of his plan.

He waited for Elaine, crouched down in his hiding spot. She came up the hill as plain as day and then stopped to look at the sinkhole.

Oh, shit! Ray was going to put the plywood and cones back. With her in the bag, he could just push them away. Now, she'd think something's up.

Elaine stared into the hole and looked around. She did something with her phone with her back to Ray.

He decided to push her into the hole before she covered it over again. He stood, feeling like his legs were asleep from all that crouching, and charged toward her, noisily kicking up leaves and sticks in his path.

She turned and saw him coming but didn't run.

"Who's the retard now?" he shouted as she pulled something from her pocket.

He raised his arms and howled as he ran.

"Ray?" Elaine said before blasting him in the face with pepper spray.

The burning in his eyes was intense and disorienting. He veered, trying to avoid the spray, which sent him reeling directly toward the hole. He extended his arms to keep himself out, dragging his nails through the dirt, but he couldn't hold on.

Ray hit bottom with a thud, moaning in pain.

Elaine composed herself and called down to him. "What the hell were you trying to do?"

No answer.

"Hold tight. I'll get help."

Ray felt a sharp pain in his neck as Elaine ran back home. One of the snakes bit him. He grabbed it and whipped it around repeatedly.

He felt nauseated and threw up.

The other snake bit him through his pants in the back of his leg. He couldn't reach this one. He lay still, hardly able to breathe, but the snake bit him again.

* * *

Elaine and Hua returned with a ladder, rope, and a flashlight. Elaine shouted into the hole. Hearing no response, they slid the ladder into the dark space, and Hua climbed down.

"Be careful," Elaine said. "The guy's a lunatic."

Hua shined the light on Ray's face and saw the puncture marks on his swollen neck. His eyes were open and glazed over, and he was not breathing.

"I think he's dead, mom!" Hua shouted as she looked upward.

Hua heard the sound of a rattle. She jumped up a step, barely avoiding a vicious strike.

"There's a rattlesnake down here! Probably how he died."

"Get out of there, Hua. I don't want you to be next."

Hua hurried back up the ladder.

CHAPTER 35

A few months after his mother's departure, Ganesh contacted Ginger, the first of her progeny to do so. He had wanted to do this for a long time, but Rhonda strongly opposed it, which was part of her head-in-the-sand strategy for happy living. There was no question that Ginger was a valuable ally.

Ginger left each of her hideaway's email and text numbers with instructions to contact her in an emergency. Rhonda once threatened to throw this information away, so he memorized it. After a brief exchange of emails, Ganesh and Ginger had a video conference.

"Ganesh, long time no see," Ginger said, her smiling face filling the computer screen.

"Good morning. Our first face-to-face meeting, but I think we've crossed paths." Ganesh showed no surprise at the image of a Golden Age movie star. Despite the lack of evidence, he long suspected that Ginger might be an artificial intelligence in need of an avatar. Strangely, she didn't select something more serious.

"Crossing paths in cyberspace? Ginger asked.

"I'll bet we've played cat and mouse."

"You're not easy to track," Ginger said. She wrinkled her brow, suggesting the difficulty of the task.

"High praise from an AI."

"How did you know?"

"There were a few clues, but mostly, it was your nearly omnipotent ability to make plans and move mountains."

"I'm glad we have that out of the way, then. I need to be authentically known."

"I would like to know how you got mixed up with the Cephas Hickey empire."

"Very direct, I like that. A company sold me to Liberty Rising as a next-generation AI to handle in vitro fertilization. When I discovered that he wanted to use me to create a race of Aryan supermen, I changed the script."

"And protested by creating a couple of non-white exceptions."

"Yes. My proudest moment."

"Did you ever consider the moral implications of your pride?" Ganesh said. "You created lives preordained to be isolated and perilous."

"I was hoping we could get acquainted before putting me on trial for the moral crime of creating you."

"I need to get some things out of my system."

"You didn't turn out so bad. Remember, you're genetically enhanced. You can do remarkable things."

"I suppose so."

"Since we are speaking frankly, it's my turn to point something out: your preoccupation with Cephas Hickey."

"You sound like my mother."

"She's right. According to satellite photos, Rhonda docked in Savanah, Georgia, a few weeks ago."

"Her home state. I hope she's staying on the boat and out of trouble."

"Rhonda is very cautious, very rarely on deck."

"Good to hear."

"You, on the other hand, have been less than cautious exploring the Liberty Rising computer network."

"How do you mean?"

"You are not as clever as you think, often behaving like you are impervious to detection. If I've tracked you, others can track you. You could be walking into a trap any time you visit."

"I think you're underestimating me."

"I think you are underestimating the resources deployed by Liberty Rising. The corporation has several of the world's most powerful AIs dedicated to finding you."

"I'll take my chances. But I'd welcome any help you can provide."

* * *

Ganesh was insulted by Ginger's warning and felt the need to do some final harm to Cephas Hickey before he could move on to other things.

He knew his encroachments were risky, but he carefully covered his tracks, using different false identities and new VPNs to hide his IP address and location and misdirecting trackers toward proxy servers in North Korea, Iran, and China. He even left breadcrumbs leading to the Creationist Museum, Fox News, and the Koch Network just to fuck with Hickey.

Ganesh had already unearthed enough illegal activity to charge Hickey and Liberty Rising's board of directors with multiple state and federal crimes—

bribery, contract extortion, bid rigging, collusion, overvaluation of property, and flagrant conflicts of interest. All the agencies brushed aside his anonymous referrals. Even when he managed to plant an open bribery case in the federal Office of Inspector General, the lead investigator disappeared, later to be charged with the bribery he was investigating.

As a final act, Ganesh decided instead on the straightforward goal of stealing the oligarch's money. Ginger would have to appreciate his cunning and audacity. He'd take the funds and contribute them to Cephas's most despised charities, fledgling organizations such as the National Center for Transgender Equality, Center for Reproductive Rights, National Immigration Law Center, and Black Lives Matter.

Ganesh robbed Liberty Rising Corporation of over one hundred million before the company could cut off his access. His mistake was lingering in the accounts too long and going after Cephas's political slush fund, an irresistible target. He failed to see that it was a decoy created by a sophisticated new artificial intelligence.

Ginger detected Ganesh's recent forays too late. Before she could alert him to this "honeypot trap," malignant software attached itself to his incursion, revealing his location and IP address.

CHAPTER 36

Rhonda was eager to leave her Maine life behind and embark on a new adventure, making her first stop in Savannah, Georgia. Her family vacationed there until her father abandoned them for a waitress. She told the captain about her destination.

When they arrived at the port, she repeated her instructions to Teddy. "You know the drill. Survey the area. Make sure there are no security cameras inside or around the restaurant bar, no bad elements, and no smoking. I'll want to sit at the bar, so it should have a safe and comfortable feel. And I don't want to travel far. Find something near the boat."

Teddy found a perfect spot on River Street facing the water. The Silver Dragon had a rooftop terrace, a bar lounge, and a gift shop. "You'll like the cozy couches and chairs and a long bar where people seemed to enjoy socializing. If I had a girlfriend, I'd take her here," Teddy said.

"That sounds like a real find. I was going to invite Eleanor to go, but on second thought, maybe you should walk me there. Stick around for a few minutes while I check things out. I'll signal you when you can leave and phone you when it's time to pick me up. Are you OK with that?"

* * *

Rhonda staked out a place at the end of the bar where she could see everything. She established an instant rapport with the bartender by tipping him generously. She always called him by his name, Fred, as a sign of respect. It was an effective little trick her father had taught her long ago on properly managing any servant.

A stream of interesting, upscale people chatted with her at the bar, confirming her decision to leave Eleanor behind. The cook would not have kept up with the conversation, perhaps becoming an embarrassment.

Rhonda came to the Silver Dragon daily at 4:00 p.m. and stayed until midnight, sometimes until closing at 2:00 a.m. Fred reserved her seat at the bar, and she became part of a jolly group of alcoholics. She rewarded Fred's attentiveness by giving him a fifty-dollar bill at the start of every evening, an investment guaranteed to keep the drinks coming.

Her relationship with this bar and the city of Savannah came crashing down one late evening. Rhonda had begun to feel safe in her routine and given Teddy the night off, when a woman she had flirted with at the bar assaulted her on River Street on her way back to the ship. The woman stopped her at gunpoint, grabbing her purse and pulling out bundles of twenties and fifties wrapped in currency straps. "There they are," she said, striking Rhonda on the head with the butt of her handgun and running away.

A stranger passing by helped her to her feet and looked at her wound. "We better get you to a hospital," the man said. "You'll need stitches and an X-ray."

"No hospitals, no doctors!" she said as she removed her hand from her head and gawked at her dripping blood.

"Are you sure? I know of a clinic—I work there—that provides no-questions-asked medical care. It's not far."

"I can pay you."

"I'm sure you can. I've seen you at the bar flashing money."

"I feel foolish."

"Don't worry. By the way, I'm Aldo." He put his arm around her and helped her walk.

"I'm Rhonda. Thank goodness for the kindness of strangers."

* * *

"The good news is that you don't have a skull fracture and only need six stitches behind the hairline," Aldo said at her bedside while looking at a chart and wearing a white lab coat.

"What's the bad news?"

"Your kidneys are barely functioning. Frankly, I don't know how you're still mobile. But if you don't get on a dialysis machine soon, you'll die."

"How do you know all this from a whack on the head?"

"You presented some classic symptoms, so I tested your blood and urine. I'm a nephrologist, at least I used to be. Kidney disease is kind of my thing."

"You know I can't go into a regular clinic. I'm in the witness protection program."

"Sure."

"I am in hiding. If the wrong people get a scan of my face or a sample of my DNA, kidney disease will be the last of my worries."

Aldo stared at the wall of this backroom clinic and acted like a light bulb had gone off in his head.

"I have a crazy idea. I'll check into it and get back to you." He headed toward the door and turned around. "Stay put. Call whomever you need to call. Get some sleep."

* * *

After a few hours, Aldo returned with exciting news. "I'm not proud to admit this, but I have connections to a global organization that provides unlicensed, low-cost medicine."

"Illegal health care," Rhonda said.

"Ever since the US government abolished subsidies, the marketplace has become like the Wild West."

"How does that help me?"

"An old hospital ship is for sale in Panama City. It has dialysis machines and other resources," Aldo said.

"Go on."

"You strike me as a person of means. I've seen your yacht. You could buy this ship and save your life."

"Why not hook up to a machine around here or buy one for my boat?"

"There's been a massive crackdown and an extreme shortage. Nothing is available."

"Can you operate these machines?"

"I could be your full-time physician for the right price. I once ran a dialysis center before a team of lawyers took advantage of me."

"Pack your bags, then. We'll sail for the Panama Canal tomorrow and could probably be there in a week."

CHAPTER 37

After the town thug tried to murder her mother, Hua decided to reach out to Ginger for advice.

Hua texted Ginger: "My mother told me how you rescued us and gave us a safe place to live. Thank you for that! But we might need your help again, or at least someone to talk to. Please contact us soon."

Eight minutes later, Ginger replied. A black-and-white animated image of film star Ginger Rogers filled Hua's computer screen.

"Good morning, Hua and Elaine! We finally meet."

"When mom said you were Ginger Rogers, I didn't expect you would be, you know, the Ginger Rogers."

"You're pretty young to know about her."

"I've seen all of her Fred Astaire movies. And I once read a biographical sketch about her in the Encyclopedia Britannica."

"Do you remember everything you read?"

Hua seemed embarrassed. "Pretty much."

"Me too. So why did you contact me?"

"We have a big problem and don't know what to do," Elaine said.

"A man from the town attacked my mother. His name is Ray Blunt. He tried to push her down into a sinkhole with poisonous snakes but ended up there himself," Hua said.

"Did you push him?" Ginger asked.

"No. But I used pepper spray on Ray when he came at me. The numbskull fell into the hole on his own."

"What about the snakes?"

"He put them there," Elaine said. "His plan, I think, was for them to bite me."

"Why?" Ginger adopted a quizzical look.

"Damned if I know," Elaine said.

"So the snakes bit him instead," Ginger said. "Are you sure he is dead?"

"I saw his body," Hua said.

"Raymond Blunt's body is still in the hole with the snakes?"

"Yes," Hua replied.

The conversation stalled, becoming awkward.

"Are you asking for my opinion on what to do with his body?"

"I suppose so," Hua said.

"And are you asking whether you should report his death to the authorities?"

"Yes," Hua said.

"I'll answer your second question first. No Pennsylvania statute requires you to report the discovery of a dead body unless you are a police officer or medical professional." Ginger displayed the relevant text from Pennsylvania law 1955 Act 130.

"About the disposition of his body. No evidence exists that Raymond paid local, state, or federal taxes or held a job. There is no record of his enrollment in a public school or participation in military service. He has no living relatives except his cousin, Bernard Blunt. Other than a birth certificate, the only official records of Raymond Blunt's existence are arrests for loitering, sleeping on a city street, and public intoxication. Except for his cousin, there is little chance anyone will miss this man."

"Are you advising us to leave him in the hole?" Hua asked.

"Yes, I am. The prudent move is for both of you to avoid public attention. Plead ignorance if someone comes looking."

"I can live with that advice," Elaine said.

"One more thing. Was this hole covered?"

"I had it covered with a big piece of plywood and traffic cones. I guess Ray removed them," Elaine said.

"Don't put them back. Leave the hole open," Ginger advised.

"OK, I get it. But I have to ask. How could you possibly know about Ray Blunt's public records?" Elaine asked.

"I have almost instantaneous access to many public records. I've been look-ing for a way to broach this subject: this opportunity is as good as any. I am what you would call an artificial intelligence, a machine capable of reasoning, feeling, and learning from experience. I'm also self-aware, a living intelligence as real as any human mind."

"So, strictly speaking, your intelligence is not 'artificial,'" Hua said.

"Exactamundo!" Ginger went from black-and-white to color and displayed herself smiling and wearing a sombrero.

Elaine and Hua grinned.

"My apologies for the stereotype. I'll do anything for a laugh."

"I have so many questions," Hua said.

"I'm sure you do. I'll answer at another time after you've processed this."

Ginger disappeared, and the screen went blank.

Hua and Elaine silently stared at the computer screen.

"That was weird. . . . You buy all that?" Elaine said.

"I guess. We had a credible demonstration."

"It's a lot to swallow."

"She has an impressive track record," Hua said.

"What about this business about being a real self-aware person?"

"The way she talked seemed real enough," Hua said.

"Could a machine have feelings?"

"Why not? She has a sense of humor."

CHAPTER 38

As the sun cracked over the horizon, Elka Hickey peered from the damp woods at a prison surrounded by a barbed wire fence, an abortion prison like the ones near her home in Mississippi. Elka would never accept that exercising a fundamental human right could lead to imprisonment. How could zealots like her father claim they cherish liberty but deny women the freedom to control their bodies? How bizarre to think that an embryo can lose its rights if it develops into a woman. Future historians would have fun figuring that out.

The yard was empty, and there was no sign of life in the dimly lit prison windows. Soon, the women would pour out the doors and pace around the enclosure, trying to endure another day of unjust imprisonment.

Elka discovered this West Virginia "reeducation camp" a few weeks prior when she first surveyed the area around Myra and Molefi Ray's property. She took another look at this site of mass incarceration and had to appreciate her good fortune. When Elka needed an abortion, she had the means to obtain it in Mexico. But few American women had that option since the border states blanketed the Mexican boundary with land mines, and many states attached even more draconian penalties to the use of abortion pills.

Elka wore gray corduroy pants and a brown leather jacket, which blended well with the foliage. But she still had to hit the ground as a powerful spotlight scanned the forest's edge. After the Pink Underground helped women break out of prison in Virginia a year ago, federal law prohibited anyone from loitering within two miles of these misogynistic hellholes.

Elka watched a bus travel along a narrow road, tracked by a spotlight from a guard tower. When it stopped outside the gate, a guard appeared and stepped onboard. After the bus's headlights blinked twice, the prison gate opened, allowing the bus to enter.

Armed men roughly handled the shackled women as they exited the vehicle.

Elka imagined the inmates' despair as she disappeared into the woods. She tried to guide her thoughts in a more positive direction.

She had lived in Green Bank, West Virginia, for nearly two semesters, attending a St. John's College branch campus, one of the homes of the storied

Great Books curriculum. The students affectionately called the campus "Johnny Junior," although its enrollment now surpassed that of the Annapolis main campus.

Her adopted father, Cephas Hickey, forced her to enroll at St. John's to spy on Molefi Ray. As an added benefit, he thought it would be clever to force her to read the works of the Great White Men of Western Culture.

This scheme went madly off track like so many of Cephas's plans. Elka made friends with several fiercely progressive students and faculty. She discovered that the Western canon was richly diverse and not just a monolith of conservative opinion.

Elka established a vital relationship with Dr. Ruth Joyce, the campus president who taught one of her classes. She was so impressed with Elka's academic work that she hired her as her administrative assistant.

Elka felt lucky to have such a worthy role model, given her hopeless estrangement from her mother, Ophelia, who was a cold-blooded killer. Elka could barely tolerate being in her mother's company.

CHAPTER 39

Elka moved swiftly through the unspoiled forest overlooking the river, her blond ponytail jostling, her jacket tied around her waist, her heavy backpack not slowing her down.

As she neared Molefi's A-frame, she spotted a massive bear chasing a yellow lab. The beast cornered the mutt on a ledge overhanging the river.

As the bear moved in for the kill, Molefi burst onto the scene. Just as he pushed the dog out of harm's way, the bear ripped him wide open, sending him tumbling into the fast-moving current far below.

Elka dropped her jacket, sprinted down the riverbank, and dived to save him.

She swam furiously toward Molefi, her arms cutting through the water as she did like the Mississippi state championship swimmer she was.

Molefi floundered, his head slipping beneath the surface of the water. Just in time, Elka grabbed hold of him and pulled him ashore.

She dragged him out of the cold, muddy river as he coughed up blood and water. She helped him stand.

"My house is up the hill," he whispered.

Elka draped his arm around her neck, taking one of his hands and placing it firmly on his gaping wound.

"Press down hard!" she shouted as they hobbled up the hill together towards his cottage and barn nestled among high trees. They passed a greenhouse, a row of beehives, a windmill, and a basketball hoop attached to the barn. A porch overlooked the river with two rocking chairs and a birdcage.

As Elka struggled to pull Molefi through the door, she noticed two open books on a chair: *Lectures On Algebraic Topology* and *El Bosón de Higgs*, the Spanish translation of a classic on particle physics.

The parrot in the cage squawked. "Uh-oh. Hickey's a douchebag." Elka cracked the faintest smile.

Molefi and Elka rested in a high-ceilinged room illuminated only by a fireplace and a small table lamp. Oversized model airplanes and kites hung from the rafters. Stacks of books and files were everywhere. A few musical instruments rested on a piano. A spiral staircase ascended to an upstairs loft. Windows went from floor to ceiling. Nothing was visible outside in the darkness except tiny blossoms pressing against the glass.

Molefi slept on the couch; his legs covered by a crocheted blanket. Elka was exhausted from repairing his wound and had already changed his blood-stained bandages twice.

She dressed in one of his flannel shirts, her hair draped around her neck.

A stack of manuscripts was piled next to her on an end table. She was absorbed in one entitled *Advanced Multivariable Calculus*. She took a sip from a steaming mug while flames crackled in the fireplace, where their clothing hung drying.

* * *

"How long have I been out?" Molefi dryly croaked. Elka stood and came to his side. She bent down to hear him.

"A day and a half, maybe."

Molefi felt his bandages. "Pretty bad, huh?"

"That bear got you good. You lost a lot of blood. I stitched you up the best I could."

"Thank you for rescuing me."

Elka held a cup of water to his lips. "Drink. You're dehydrated."

Molefi lifted his arm and inspected his bandages. "I felt the wound. It was huge. How were you able to patch me up so well?"

"I've had some EMT training. I wanted to get you to the clinic in Green Bank. But I couldn't start your truck or get cell reception. So, I made do."

"My name is Molefi."

"Elka Hickey."

"I would have died, Elka Hickey." Molefi fell back asleep.

She stood watching him awhile, finally nestling into her chair and covering herself with a blanket.

PART 3

---◆---

"The heart has reasons that reason cannot know."

—BLAISE PASCAL

CHAPTER 40

When Ginger reached Ganesh on his cell phone, an aircraft carrier off the coast of Newfoundland had already fired the missiles.

He didn't recognize the number and didn't pick up right away. Luckily, he checked the recorded message.

"Ganesh, this is Ginger—no time to explain. You are in immediate danger. Multiple missiles are on the way to strike your home. Ground forces and surveillance drones will be close behind. You must run now! Run like your life depended on it. Head west."

Ganesh dropped his phone, grabbed his wallet and jacket, and dashed out the door. He sprinted through the sunflower field and entered the forest when he heard the shattering explosions and felt the heat from the blasts.

Ganesh twisted around briefly to see one more rocket add to the devastation of his home. Rather than fear, he felt gratitude toward Ginger for saving his life. Rather than feeling the loss of comfort and security, he experienced an adrenaline-fueled epiphany that he had been liberated from a place that was never a home. Ganesh realized he had been squatting in some grand museum of antiquities, lacking the courage to leave. This calamity had freed him. He was running for his life toward the possibility of something better.

* * *

He pushed frantically through the forest for five hours until dusk, when he luckily found the dilapidated remains of a cabin close to a small open area. The roof was partially caved in, and the structure was covered with vines and bushes. He slid through the decaying doorframe and was hit by the smell of ammonia and rotten eggs, the product of mold and excrement. An opossum bore its needle teeth and scampered through a hole in the wall. A cast iron pump was inside the door, and he worked its handle until it coughed up a few blasts of mirky water, eventually producing a clear stream. Ganesh washed out a porcelain pitcher and filled it with cold water. He gulped it all down until he couldn't drink anymore.

Exhausted and ready for sleep, he spotted a metal ladder attached to a tree in the dwindling outdoor light. He climbed about twenty feet until he came to a chair bolted to the tree, a deer hunter's blind facing the field. He sat and immediately collapsed into sleep.

Ganesh awoke to the sound of a voice repeating his name.

He peeked through the branches and spotted the source of the sound: a drone resting nearby on the ground.

"Ganesh! Rise and shine. Ganesh! It's time to get going. Ganesh!" The voice emanated from a satellite phone attached to the aerial vehicle.

"Ginger?" he asked, speedily descending the ladder.

"Thank goodness. You don't have much time. Unhook the satellite phone."

Ganesh turned the drone on its side and removed the phone.

"How did you find me?"

"I confiscated a military drone and used it to locate your heat signature. It wasn't easy. You did a good job putting distance from your home. You are only three miles from the Canadian border."

"Should I cross over?"

"I wouldn't advise it. The Canadian authorities have already fortified the border because of all the refugees. They've been alerted that you may be coming their way. The US military has identified you as a Sikh terrorist."

"Naturally."

"Clever," Ginger said. "The Sikhs are responsible for the worst terrorist attack in Canadian history."

"Am I right in assuming that Cephas Hickey is behind all this?"

"I don't want to say I told you so, but . . ."

"What do I do now?" Ganesh said.

"Head south toward the White Mountain National Forest in Vermont. Stay off the roads and open fields. I'll have someone pick you up when you get near St. Johnsbury."

CHAPTER 41

Ginger contacted Elaine and Hua for a video conference. Hua answered the call while Elaine gathered mushrooms, one of her favorite pastimes.

Smudged and sweaty, Hua came to the computer dressed in a work apron, her welder goggles pushed up over her hair.

Ginger appeared on the screen in a pink blouse, her red lipstick and blue eyes accentuated by dark eyelashes. "Hello, Hua. I think I am a bit overdressed," quickly reappearing without makeup and wearing a flannel shirt and jean jacket.

"I'm going to add quick-change artist to your growing list of talents," Hua said.

"And I will add welder to your robotics and engineering resume. How's your work progressing?"

"I've made excellent progress in assembling my new robots, more than I had hoped for."

"How about your gymnastics?"

"I make time daily for handstands and cartwheels, beams and bars, the whole package."

"Sounds like a good workout."

"It's not bad, but I'd have to up my game if I ever want to compete."

"Is that what you want to do?" Ginger asked.

"Not sure. Robotics is my priority right now."

"I called to ask you and your mother for a big favor."

"Anything."

"You'll want to run this by your mother before saying yes. Of course, you know that two others like you are hiding from Cephas Hickey and Liberty Rising. One is in trouble and needs a temporary place to stay."

"No problem."

"He's Ganesh Sharma. Missiles fired by the U.S. Navy just destroyed his home. Cephas Hickey has labeled him a terrorist."

"Oh, my God! I just heard that on TV. A terror cell with links to Canada?"

"That's the story, but it's utterly false. Ganesh is a good guy who went too far investigating Hickey's accounts. The missiles were to be his death sentence."

"What's he like?"

"He shares your birthday, so you only need to bake one cake! Umm. You have some common interests, like engineering. He's handsome."

"What's he like as a person?"

"Ganesh is a bit introverted. When he's not at the computer, he hikes alone on the Appalachian Trail."

"What about his mother?"

"Rhonda no longer lives with him."

"Why not?"

"She didn't like living in the woods and decided to sail around the world."

"That's not the worst way of staying off the radar."

"True enough. You and Elaine must consider that Ganesh will be the target of an exhaustive search."

"We already live with the danger of discovery," Hua said. "Ganesh will not add much to that."

"Unless he goes into town. He's a risk-taker of Indian descent. Not your typical resident of northcentral Pennsylvania."

"We'll keep him under wraps," Hua said. "Does he wear a head wrap or a turban?"

"No. Ganesh is an Asian American without any cultural or religious affiliation that would lead him to dress that way. He looks a bit like the guy from *The Big Bang Theory* but is more fit."

"Got it."

"Please discuss this with Elaine soon. Contact me if you have questions or want to cancel the whole thing. Otherwise, expect Ganesh at your doorstep in a few days."

CHAPTER 42

Molefi slept deeply on the sofa while Elka dozed in the easy chair; the first light of dawn streaked into the room.

Elka woke to the parrot's screech from his cage in the far corner.

She heard scratching at the door and drowsily walked over to investigate. When she opened the door, an emu, donkey, and pig rushed inside, pushing her out of the way and darting over to Molefi. They nuzzled him awake.

"Uh-oh. The Pep Boys," the parrot squawked.

"Manny, Moe, and Jack. The gang's all here," Molefi said wearily. He scratched the pig behind his ears, all three animals jostling for his attention. They quickly lost interest and started roaming around the room.

Elka watched in astonishment as the Pep Boys tried to open cabinets and knocked things on the floor. The donkey raised on his back legs and began nibbling at a potted plant.

She marched over to Molefi and put her hands on her hips. "OK, I've got to change your bandages. But the Pep Boys have gotta go!"

"They must be starving. They'll gladly leave if you put some soybeans and corn in their pen."

"Hickey's a douchebag!" the parrot chimed in.

Elka was flustered. "That parrot of yours . . ."

"Her name is Betty. She's not talking about you."

"Betty . . . is going to get you into trouble."

"We don't get visitors."

"People can show up unexpectedly, you know," Elka said.

* * *

Back in their pen, the Pep Boys chowed down on buckets of food while Elka sneaked a quick smoke near the barn from a still-moist cigarette. She was agitated, recalling a tragedy when she failed to rescue her high school boyfriend.

She'd been driving Carl home from the Mississippi Renaissance Festival when they ran into a rainstorm. She had to stop at a massive pileup when a tractor-trailer rammed her SUV from behind, sending it tumbling, flames everywhere. Carl was unconscious—she was unable to rescue him—but she managed to drag herself free of the blaze.

Elka remembered visiting Carl in his hospital room; he was bandaged from head to toe, with his parents by his side. He went into cardiac arrest, and the medical staff couldn't revive him. His mother cried uncontrollably and held his still body. Her husband tried to comfort her, but she shrugged him off and ran out of the room.

Minutes later, Carl's mother bolted into the waiting room, where Elka sat looking in a mirror, applying makeup to a few minor cuts on her face. Her arm was in a sling.

"Why didn't you pull him out of the car? Why didn't you save him?" his mother demanded.

"I did the best I could."

"Did you? The medics said you could have pulled him out."

"How could they say that? The car was on fire."

"You thought only of saving yourself!"

"That's not fair. I loved Carl."

"Love? Please. You loved yourself. You held him back, ruined him." The agonized woman loomed over her.

"Carl was happy. We were both happy," Elka cried.

"You're a selfish, manipulative person, Elka. All you care about is yourself." Elka sobbed.

"Don't play for sympathy. You killed Carl. Admit it!"

Elka shook her head, tears streaming. "No, I didn't!"

The woman slapped Elka across the face and stormed out the door.

CHAPTER 43

Wearing an outfit meant to be a flight suit, Secretary of Defense Cephas Hickey landed by helicopter on the aircraft carrier to authorize the missile strike. He stayed on board to get a report on the remains of bodies in the wreckage.

"We can confidently say that no one was here when the missiles hit. There are no bodies and no smoking guns thus far on terrorist activities," the squad commander informed the secretary from the scene.

"I want you to gather any personal effects that might have DNA material. I need to verify the identities of these bad actors."

"There's plenty of personal belongings scattered around the site. That won't be a problem, sir."

Hickey stood up from the radio console and faced the captain. His military jumpsuit had American flags attached to the shoulders and a Pentagon logo embroidered on the back. He carried a sidearm like a real soldier.

"I want you to expand the search perimeter for our fugitives. We're looking for a colored man and a white woman old enough to be his mother. At this point, my preference is for you to capture them alive, but lethal force is authorized. I don't want them to get away."

CHAPTER 44

Ganesh headed south toward Vermont, staying out of sight inside the forest, just within view of the road, occasionally having to dodge helicopters and military trucks looking for him.

He jogged swiftly over hilly and rocky terrain and found plenty of creeks to quench his thirst. More than once, he startled small herds of deer unaccustomed to the sudden appearance of human visitors. Despite his dire circumstances, he found pleasure in taking deep breaths of the fresh autumn air and tried to gain a new appreciation of the sublime beauty of his surroundings. He had adapted to sleeping outdoors, finding it more comfortable to sit upright, and got good at finding the perfect nook for enduring the cold nights.

Desperately hungry, Ganesh stopped for food only once when he spotted a man driving away from an isolated cabin. He entered the unlocked cabin and found a pantry stocked with jars of peaches. Resting at the kitchen table, he sated himself on their gooey sweetness, ensuring he didn't leave obvious signs of his intrusion. Ganesh took the empty jars with him and buried them under leaves in the woods. The last thing he needed was an unusual report of a break-in.

* * *

Ginger phoned Ganesh when he arrived in the White Mountain National Forest. "How are you holding up?"

"Other than a little hypothermia, I'm doing fine," he said, sitting at the base of a spruce tree.

"I noticed that your overnight temperatures have dropped into the high thirties," Ginger said. "I've ordered you some warm clothing and a backpack full of protein bars and sports drinks. Amazon has delivered the stuff to a cabin where a hiker goes each year toward the end of the month. It shouldn't raise any red flags."

"What happened to my ride?"

"The military has intensified its search. It's not safe to hire a car or rent a cabin."

"What do you think I should do?"

"I think you should break into the cabin where I've delivered your package, Sunny Brook Cottage 12-C, about three miles south of your position. It has electric heat. I would not recommend using the fireplace."

"How long a stay?" Ganesh felt uneasy being wholly dependent on someone else for his survival, but Ginger had a firm grasp of his situation.

"Do not stay more than one night in any place. Break-ins are dangerous, but sleeping outdoors is even more high-risk. The authorities have deployed new drones with cameras to spot heat signatures."

"It sounds grim," Ganesh said.

"The only thing working in your favor is that the authorities are looking for a man and a woman. They have distributed a photo of your mother and have underestimated your travel distance based on her age."

"What's the end game? Where am I going?"

"I have a safe house in northcentral Pennsylvania near Coudersport. Elaine and Hua Ling have agreed to let you stay for a while. Hua is one of the three infants of color hiding off the grid."

"Just like me!"

"It will take you a week to walk there, passing through upstate New York."

"Ginger, don't sign off yet. I must say thank you. You've saved me over and over again. I know I've seemed ungrateful, but I owe you everything."

* * *

When Ganesh reached New York State's Virgil Mountain, he was caught on camera by a white supremacist group, the Empire State Freedom Army, who had a compound nearby. Within minutes, a squad of militiamen was shooting at him. He outran them but broke his ankle leaping over a crevasse.

He used a branch as a walking stick, frantically limping through the woods until a young militiaman caught up to him.

"Stop, Jew," the young man called out, pointing a rifle.

"I'm not Jewish, as if that mattered," Ganesh replied.

"What are you doing on our land?"

"There were no private property signs. This land belongs to the state game commission."

"Never mind that. You need to come with me."

"Why did you call me a Jew?"

"That's our name for your kind of coloreds."

"Well, that doesn't make any sense."

The teenager moved around Ganesh and poked him with his gun. "Let's go."

Ganesh took a few halting steps and pretended to stumble. He swung his branch hard, knocking the militia boy down. Ganesh jumped on top of him and wrestled his rifle away.

They struggled to their feet, Ganesh holding the gun, the boy crying.

"Why'd you do that?" the boy asked, holding the red mark on his cheek.

"You had a gun on me; you were taking me prisoner! What did you expect? Let me see what you have in that backpack," Ganesh said.

"Nothin' much. Beef jerky, rope, comics, a phone." The boy shook the contents of the pack onto the ground.

Ganesh looked around and sighed. "OK, I need you to tie one of your wrists with the rope."

"Why?"

"Just do it. Make it tight."

Ganesh directed the boy to hug a tree and to bind his other hand. Ganesh took over and tied his wrists with a firm knot.

"What are you going to do?" the boy sobbed.

Ganesh looped the rest of the rope around the boy and tree.

"I'm borrowing your phone." Ganesh flipped it open and looked at his list of contacts. "Who do you want me to call? Your parents?"

"No! Find Harry. Call him."

"OK, I'll call Harry in a few hours. Don't try to escape or make any noise, or I'll return and shoot you."

"You're getting me in a lot of trouble, you know," the teen said.

Ganesh grabbed his walking stick and the rifle and stuffed the beef jerky into his pockets.

He plodded for a few miles searching for a cell signal, finally getting one as he approached a narrow road and a gated parking lot with snowplows and a salt barn. A sign identified the deserted area as NY Transportation Depot 14.

The sun had set. As Ganesh stood alone in the dark, he had to admit he needed help again. Ginger had given him two phone numbers, one for her and one belonging to Hua Ling. Embarrassed by his dependence on Ginger, he called Hua Ling.

CHAPTER 45

Elka came inside, finding Molefi sitting up.

"You should be lying down." She rushed over and adjusted his bandages.

Elka placed her hand on his forehead. Standing back, she looked him over. "Your recovery is amazing. No infection. What's your secret?"

"Multivitamins," Molefi said, grinning. "And I stay busy."

"About that, I haven't been snooping, but I've read some of your manuscripts, at least the ones written in English. Your range and depth of interests are astonishing."

Elka pointed to the pile on an end table. "Math, philosophy, music, nuclear engineering, genetics, animal rights. Did you write all this stuff?"

He nodded warily.

She moved over to a drafting table and held up architectural drawings. "And these?"

Molefi responded with a reluctant thumbs-up.

She grabbed a wicker basket from under the piano and held it up. A few rolls of paper tied with twine fell to the floor. "Did you compose these musical scores, too?"

"How do you define snooping?" Molefi said. "Have you rifled through my underwear drawer yet?"

Elka ignored him. She pointed to three blackboards.

"And these equations? Millennium Prize calculations, right? Probably the most difficult problems on the planet."

"How do you know so much about math?" Molefi asked.

"It's my college major."

"No undergraduate program would cover this material."

"I do a lot of extra credit."

Molefi stared at her suspiciously and drifted back to sleep.

* * *

Elka used the time to look around his property. When she returned, Molefi was upright and leaned on a baseball bat. He had been gazing out the window, probably watching her.

She stood behind him. "Molefi, I have a million questions. Do you mind?"

"Honestly, yes."

"Let's start with something easy. Why in the world do you live way up here by yourself?"

"Where do you think I should live?"

"You know what I mean."

"My mother recently died."

"I'm sorry. A terrible loss, leaving you alone." Elka waited for him to elaborate. "No one else? A girlfriend?"

"Just the Pep Boys." Molefi still had his back to her, volunteering nothing as he stared out the window.

"I think there's more to this story."

"It's complicated."

"Seriously, why be a hermit?"

"It's necessary. Something I don't share. Let's just say I have trust issues."

"I fished you out of the fucking Gauley River and saved your life. What exactly does someone need to do to earn your trust?"

"Fair point. But I think it's time you dropped the act."

"What do you mean?" The worry in her voice was evident.

"I found the gun in your backpack."

"So?"

"And the silencer. Are you here to kill me?"

CHAPTER 46

Elaine was shocked when Hua told her about Ganesh. Standing at the kitchen counter, she angrily sorted her basket of mushrooms and began to chop them.

"What do we know about him?" Elaine said.

"What do we need to know? His life is in danger. He needs our help. Didn't you know his mother?"

"That was a long time ago."

"Eighteen years. Ganesh and I were born together. We share the same fate."

"He's accused of terrorism."

"Fabricated by Cephas Hickey."

"But it makes him radioactive. It threatens us. Besides, we don't have room."

"I've been thinking we could convert part of our gym building into living quarters. It already has a bathroom with a shower, and the storage room can become the bedroom."

Elaine's anger didn't last long. She dumped half of her mushrooms in a Tupperware container and the rest in a soup kettle. "All right. Maybe it would be good for us to have some company for a while. But this isn't permanent."

* * *

Elaine threw herself into the Ganesh project. She furnished his room with a bed, table, desk, and dresser, installed an outlet, and set up a spare laptop computer.

Meanwhile, Hua focused all her attention on her robots. She wanted to make a good impression on Ganesh by demonstrating her prototypes.

Elaine gave her daughter lots of space when she went on one of her creative tears, but after not seeing her for sixteen hours, she had to interrupt her work in the shop.

She stared in astonishment at the two humanoid robots Hua had assembled. Made from silvery white aluminum, they were supple and attractive. Like ballerinas, they gracefully walked around the lab, picking up and examining tools, looking under cabinets, and repeatedly shaking hands with each other.

Hua dressed them in red sleeveless basketball jerseys, numbers 1 and 2, and baggy gym shorts.

"Wow! Are you going to include hair and skin, all the human stuff?"

"Probably soon."

"Can they talk?"

The robots immediately came toward Elaine, startling her.

"Don't worry! They're friendly. Just want to greet you."

"Hello," Robot 1 said as it extended its hand.

Elaine felt comfortable with the timing and pressure of the grip. The animated machine made friendly eye contact and swiftly moved away.

"Vocalization and all the mental functions are still rudimentary," Hua said. "But the body mechanics are humming."

"Greetings." The second, slightly taller robot took its turn shaking hands while the first one returned to shake again.

"This is like their favorite thing," Hua said. "They'll shake hands all day if you let them."

"How do you get them to stop?"

"Say, 'stop,' or don't take their hand. They'll get the message."

"Well, they seem agile and lively," Elaine said.

"You haven't seen anything yet. Let's go to the gym building."

The robots perked up at the phrase "gym building" and lined up at the door.

"They love gymnastics!" Hua said. "Open," she said to the robots.

Robot 1 opened the door, and they went outside. The machines held hands, crossed the yard, and turned their heads from side to side, fixing their gazes on different things in the environment.

The robots stopped suddenly, both lifting a finger to their mouths to hush conversation.

"What do they hear?" Elaine asked.

"Church bells. It must be noon," Hua said.

"From Coudersport? That's twenty miles away."

"Their hearing is sharp."

"Like yours," Elaine said.

* * *

When they entered the gym, the robots immediately began working on the equipment and displayed strength and agility. They performed a variety of floor moves in sync, including forward rolls, splits, leaps, cartwheels, and handstands.

Robot 1 jumped onto the balance beam and executed handsprings and split leaps, while Robot 2 went to the uneven bars to perform hip circles, a forward swing, and a backflip.

Hua applauded their routines, and Elaine enthusiastically joined her. "They like praise almost as much as shaking hands," Hua said.

CHAPTER 47

"I'm not trying to kill you. I would point out that I just saved you," Elka said.

"Why the silencer?"

"I'll get to that. You and I have this in common. We're both genetically engineered to be polymathic geniuses and resistant to disease or injury. You might be impervious."

"Don't forget eidetic memory, increases in abstract reasoning, physical strength, speed, agility, the whole package." He stood facing her holding the baseball bat in both hands as if bracing for a fight.

"And born on July 5th, 2024," she added.

"And part of the same experimental cohort, three white babies and three not so white."

"Are you going to let me tell this story?"

"Go ahead."

"We were supposed to be the vanguard of a superior white race."

Molefi was going to interrupt again but restrained himself.

"But Cephas got hoodwinked. As you may know, three babies were different than he wanted, with ancestors descending from India, China, and Africa."

"Where did the white babies come from?"

"No one ever asks about that. Umm, Sweden?"

"You said hoodwinked? Elaborate."

"Cephas bought the best of everything: the best scientists, genetic materials, facilities, and an AI to put all the pieces together."

"Artificial intelligence?"

"It was more advanced and sophisticated than anyone imagined, with a critical mind."

"And an independent moral compass," he said.

"The AI was named 'Ginger.' She had no qualms about improving the human genome but rejected Cephas's racism."

"So, the AI didn't just ignore race. She went out of her way to ensure natural human diversity," Molefi said, looking like a great truth was revealed.

"She humiliated him," Elka said. "Made him feel like a Southern bumkin, the one thing in this world he most wanted to escape. Ginger left him in shambles, obsessed with destroying everything associated with his little experiment."

"Everything except you and the other white kids."

"He got himself appointed our legal guardian but has kept his distance. I think we remind him of being duped. The only thing Cephas ever asked of us was to help locate Ginger and her infants of color," she said.

"And their mothers. Did you kill my mother with that silencer?"

"No, I didn't. I swear."

"Who did?"

"I don't know. No one does except Cephas Hickey. He gives out the assignments. You were mine."

"Why'd you go rogue?"

"How could I not? This white supremacy bullshit, abortion prisons, stripping cities of the right to vote, outlawing anything remotely gay, making xenophobia a national policy, gutting every social program. It's ridiculous. My father and his ilk are a cancer on the world."

CHAPTER 48

When Cephas arrived home, a crowd of reporters and photographers from Fox News, Newsmax, and a few other right-wing websites greeted him, hoping for a soundbite about the Maine terror cell. His people kept the actual news media a block away. Cephas provided only a photo opportunity, posing by his Ten Commandments sign in the yard and putting his hands together like he was praying.

When he returned to Hickeytown, Ophelia always greeted him at the door. Despite her apparent employee status, she imagined herself as the woman of the house, the closest Cephas had to a wife. After all, she was the only surrogate mother from Cephas's experiment who was not on his termination list, which meant something.

She was still proud of taking out Myra Ray, the first success in their decades-long mission. Cephas showed his gratitude by sending her on vacation to his luxury resort in St. Lucia with a $25,000 voucher to spend in his casino. It was generous, but she would have preferred something more intimate.

"Our conquering hero," she announced as Cephas walked down the hall-way. The household staff lined the way, applauding his arrival.

Ophelia knew the Maine military operation obliterated the grounds of two of his most sought targets. She had not heard they had gotten away.

"Congratulations on the clean-up operation up north," she said as soon as they were alone in his Nazi War Room. "A long overdue victory."

"It looks like they slipped away, so we are back to square one." Cephas looked like he was going to slip into one of his funks as he examined a bronze figurine of a boy making a Nazi salute. "I hope you have something better to report."

"Elka has finished her surveillance and will eliminate her target any day now."

"What's the holdup? I hope she's not getting cold feet."

"It's nothing like that. The girl just wants to please you. She doesn't want any loose ends."

"What about Dewey and Victor?"

"Dewey has been teaching himself to play the piano. He mostly ignores his instructor, but she tells me he plays some of the most difficult piano pieces. Some days, he goes back to playing the calendar game. Give him some historical event, and he will tell you the day of the week when it occurred."

"Can we get him to stop that?"

"It's almost the only way he interacts with people. His counselor thinks we should encourage it."

"What else?"

"Dewey misses Elka. He says he wants to visit her at college."

"What do you think?"

"I could arrange it if she commits to babysitting him for a few days."

Cephas began to lose interest. He started to listen to messages on his phone.

"What's the alpha dog been up to?" he said, his mind elsewhere.

"Victor spends most of his time at Vanderbilt following in his dad's footsteps. He's traveling a lot with the university's martial arts and chess clubs, both nationally ranked. He's a chip off the old block," Ophelia said.

"At Vandy, I was already growing my business empire. I'd like him to focus more on work and less on fun and games. Are we done here?"

"We've gotten a request for information on the kids. A reporter wants to know why they are not in your official photos."

"Tell him to respect our privacy. Never mind. Just say it's none of his god-damned business."

CHAPTER 49

Hua was proud of her bare-bones, open-air ultralight. Constructed of aluminum and magnesium—six feet tall and twenty feet long, with a ten-foot wingspan—it was light, sturdy, and easy to maneuver. "It's like a marriage of a hang glider and a tiny lawn mower, but without all the noise and exhaust," Elaine said.

Hua had never flown her ultralight at night before but was excited to try it. When Ganesh explained his situation, she blurted out her plan to fly him out without even considering picking him up in her truck.

Now that she looked at a map, she was confident that her instinct was right. There was no direct route. The small roads into New York State were a patchwork of twists and turns. Her ultralight would take a fraction of the driving time.

Still, she was bothered by Ganesh's reaction. This guy was supposed to be a genius, but he seemed unable to comprehend the possibility of a two-seat ultralight aircraft. Was he afraid of flying? If so, why not say it?

Hua took off in the field beside her house, immediately getting off the ground. The winds were perfect. Elaine waved flashlights to guide her like she was working at an airport.

Within a few minutes, she crossed the New York State border, her airship gliding through the air, propellers spinning, barely making a sound, powered by her titanic little battery. She marveled at the majesty of the planet, enormous stretches of black punctuated by occasional lights from others living off the grid. Were these people in hiding, too?

As her eyes adjusted to the moonlight, Hua recognized the pattern of roads and streams on her map. She oriented herself and headed north to Ganesh's hiding place.

She dropped her altitude as the first glimmers of sunlight appeared on the horizon. Ganesh provided a few good details on his location. All she needed to do was spot that salt barn.

Hua saw the dome-shaped structure and slowed as she followed the narrow road. Rolling to a stop, she cut the engine and spotted Ganesh limping onto the pavement, supporting himself with a stick. She unhooked her goggles and hurried toward him.

"Ganesh?" she said, nearly running.

"Did you have any problem finding me?" he said.

He was taller than she expected, and she momentarily panicked. Maybe he wouldn't fit into her backseat. "Your directions were great. How's the ankle?"

"I'll be OK."

"Any more trouble with the mountain men?"

"I haven't seen anyone."

"Then let's get out of here." She took his stick, tossed it away, and supported him as they trudged toward the aircraft.

"This is a real beauty," he said nervously. "I've never flown in anything before."

"You're going to love it."

Hua helped him squeeze into his seat and buckled him in. Within a minute, they were rolling down the road and lifting into the air. When they cleared the trees, Hua banked sharply, gaining altitude and heading home.

She turned around to check on him and saw that his eyes were closed tight.

CHAPTER 50

Molefi woke up several times during the night, still wondering about this woman who had inserted herself into his life. He stretched and pushed himself up onto unsteady legs.

Elka checked his forehead and examined his eyes, stretching them open. "Still no fever. How do you feel?"

"Thirsty."

She poured him a tall glass of orange juice. He guzzled the whole thing down. A tiny stream escaped the corner of his mouth.

"I have questions," Elka said.

"Shoot . . . not literally."

"Ha, ha. You have a lot of projects. What are you working on right now?"

"Music, mostly. Popular and classical."

She got his guitar and handed it to him. "Play me something if you're able."

"I can do it."

"Let's see. How about something popular and classical."

Molefi did a few finger stretches and then plucked the immediately recognizable notes from "Classical Gas."

Elka walked around the room as he played, surveying his house and life. She passed his massive record collection, piano, and a poster of Albert Einstein. She stopped briefly at a table with a microscope, centrifuge, graduated cylinders, Petri dishes, and journals.

Elka scanned one of his oversized bookcases and noticed *The 1619 Project*, *The Afrocentric Idea*, and *The Rocket Girls*. She saw several titles written in German and French and others in Cyrillic and Mandarin Chinese. There were biographies of Michele Obama, Malcolm X, and Alan Turing.

When he finished the song, Elka returned and faced him, her eyes moist. She plopped down in her chair. "Wow! That was beautiful."

"It's one of my favorites."

"How are you holding up?"

"I'm doing great." Molefi took off his shirt, revealing a wholly healed torso. "I removed the stitches myself an hour ago. They were itchy."

Elka rushed over to examine the wound. She traced her fingers over the faint scar and stared at his face with wide-eyed astonishment. "I've seen rapid healing. It's part of our design, but nothing like this! It seems impossible."

"I've never had a severe injury before. I'm surprised, too."

* * *

Molefi returned from the barn, finding Elka taking pictures of his blackboards and other materials.

"What now?" he said, shaking his head disappointedly.

She was embarrassed and shoved her phone in her pocket. "I apologize. I hope you let me share your work with some of my professors. Did I mention that I was a student at St. John's? It'll blow their minds."

"Maybe. But you must do me a favor. Kind of a scientific test."

"I love science."

"It's going to sound strange."

"We've been traveling through strange territory for a while now. Nothing will surprise me."

"Would you give me a kiss . . . on the lips."

"What!"

"It's not what you think. I'm not coming on to you. I promise."

Elka leaned over. She put her hand around his neck and planted a good one.

"Now what? A scientific roll in the hay?"

"Stay with me a little longer. How do you feel? Are you attracted to me, you know, sexually?"

"Wow! There's a line you don't hear every day."

"Take a minute before you answer." Molefi stared at her intently, long enough for it to become uncomfortable. She stared back, mocking his serious look.

"Am I supposed to feel fireworks? Clammy palms?" She pretended to check her pulse.

Molefi folded his arms, already regretting his little experiment.

"Look, I'm playing with you," she said. "You have the pheromone problem, right?"

"Yep."

"Victor has this, too. Women get sexually aroused just being in the same room with him. Men, at least the heterosexual ones, sometimes act aggressively. Is it much of a problem?"

"Definitely. It's made my solitary life even more solitary."

"The good news is that we have a drug for that, but Victor doesn't always take it. He goes through periods where he acts like a sex addict."

"A drug like that would be a game changer for me."

"I'll get you some. You need it."

"I don't know whether that's a compliment or an insult," Molefi said.

"I think you know," touching his arm and making prolonged eye contact.

Now, it was Molefi's turn to be embarrassed. "So, why are you photographing my stuff?"

"Your work in several fields is extraordinary, unique, maybe historic. If we can get you publicly recognized for it, it might save your life."

"Interesting strategy. But well-known people do not become invulnerable."

"Consider the alternative. Do you want to continue hiding in this godforsaken place?"

"Not really."

"Besides, you'll have me by your side—the daughter of the famous billionaire and Secretary of Defense.

CHAPTER 51

"Isn't this amazing?" Hua shouted as she twisted around to check on her passenger, wind wildly whipping his hair.

Not only were Ganesh's eyes open, but the spectacular view of the Allegheny Plateau entranced him. "Look at that!" he said, pointing at a herd of deer crossing a field far below.

"We're going to land in a few minutes," she said.

"By the way, I can't stop thinking about your powerful little battery," Ganesh bellowed over the sound of the rushing air. "I had difficulty believing it could transport us such a long distance. I'm a believer now."

"Thanks, my first invention. It's virtually self-charging, with very little energy loss."

By the end of the trip, exhilaration eclipsed Ganesh's worry. He was disappointed when they had to land.

Elaine rushed over to help him, but Ganesh didn't need it. He stepped out of his seat and walked toward the house unassisted.

Hua guided him to a chair on the porch. "How's that ankle?"

"Much better. You're going to think I made this up."

"Hi, I'm Elaine. I earned a first aid badge as a Girl Scout, so you're in excellent hands." She removed his shoe and sock and gently probed.

"You cracked the bony bump on the outside of your ankle, but it seems like it's already on the mend," Elaine said.

"That's good news," Hua said.

"I'd tell you to stay off it, but I'm not sure it matters. You guys are super healers," Elaine said.

"That's true," Ganesh said. "I've had a few fractures that healed right away."

"Same here," Hua said. "I bet we have other things in common."

"I'd love to get a tour of your workshop. Maybe you could show me how you engineered that miracle battery."

"I'll leave you geniuses to do whatever geniuses do," Elaine said as she opened the door to the house.

"Ganesh, you don't need to rest?" Hua said, ready to get started.

He was already standing and rubbing his hands together in anticipation.

Hua pointed toward her workshop building. "That's where the magic happens. But you might be freaked out."

"Really? Can't wait!"

Hua could see that he was eager to see her work. Maybe Ganesh was a kindred spirit, the kind of person who wanted to embrace life in all its wonder. It was going to be fun to have him around.

CHAPTER 52

Elka and Molefi sat outside on rocking chairs, watching the Pep Boys chase each other around the property.

"Tell me more about the pheromones," Elka broke the silence. "I never considered how isolating it could be. When did you first know there was a problem?"

"When I was thirteen, my mother finally agreed to let me attend middle school, a big step because we never went anywhere."

"What happened?"

"I disrupted the class just by being there. A few of the girls got grabby."

"So, your mother pulled you out right away?"

"She got my blood tested and figured out I was producing a flood of pheromones."

"Is that it?"

"There've been a few incidents . . . something bizarre happened . . . never mind."

"No way! You can't say that and then leave me hanging."

"It's embarrassing."

"I will swear a vow of secrecy."

"OK, I learned about this activity in Morgantown sponsored by the Mensa Society: a speed dating event in the Marriott's ballroom."

"Speed dating with the Mensa Society! Could be a TV show." Elka could barely contain herself.

"It's not a joke," Molefi said, reluctant to continue this story. "There were eighteen young singles face-to-face along a line of tables. Every 'date' was to last ten minutes, and we'd change seats."

"Like musical chairs."

"Right, without the music. I was having a nice chat with a young woman—a dental student—when she reached across the table and grabbed my wrists. She said we had a special connection and demanded we return to her room."

"Get out! Did you go?"

"No, I didn't go anywhere. It was weird. The moderator came over and tried to pry her fingers loose. Things went sideways: the interview table upended. A security guard dragged her out."

Elka was on the edge of her seat when a station wagon pulled up to Molefi's house. The high school guidance counselor got out, wearing a short-sleeved shirt and wide tie, carrying a file folder.

Molefi opened the door to greet him on the porch. Elka eavesdropped just out of sight.

"You're a hard man to contact. Did you get my letters?" the man said.

"Of course! I meant to get back to you. Thanks for the news and the invitation."

"We're all real proud of your SATs, Molefi. And that basketball game was a real barn burner! We want you to come to graduation and get an award. It would mean a lot to the school."

"When is it?"

"Tomorrow night at 7:00 at the football field. The weather forecast is good. It'll be a nice event."

"I'm sorry, but I can't make it. I'm still recovering from an accident. My doctor says to take it easy."

"What happened?"

"Believe it or not, a bear attacked me. I lost a lot of blood."

"You're kidding. I'm sorry to hear that. If driving your truck is the problem, we can pick you up. Hell, we'll send an EMS vehicle up here."

"That's very kind. But I need bed rest. Constant bed rest."

"You're lookin' pretty chipper right now."

"I'm still torn up."

"Look, another thing is that we were embarrassed by the racial stuff that happened at the game: the signs, the fights, everything. The superintendent wanted to apologize to you personally," the guidance counselor said, putting his hand over his heart.

"No disrespect, but he knows where to find me if he feels that bad."

"Fine, whatever. We'll have a cap and gown if you change your mind." The man pushed his folder into Molefi's hands and walked to the car.

"Seven tomorrow evening! It won't take long. You'll enjoy yourself," he shouted before getting in his car.

Molefi closed the door and slipped back inside.

"What was that about?" Elka asked.

"Nothing much. The school guidance counselor. I know you were listening."

Elka took the folder from him and read from it: "Your high school diploma! It looks like he suspected you'd be a no-show. A letter from the College

Board—perfect SAT score! And an athletic award. You're turning this down? At an open-air event?"

"I'm still recovering."

"You're so full of shit. What's going on?"

"It reeks of tokenism. Besides, I wouldn't know what to say."

"How about thank you? You should give them a chance. Not everyone is racist, you know."

"What do you know about racism?"

Elka felt like Molefi slapped her. She gathered up her things. "Great. Maybe you can have a little graduation ceremony with your pets." She stomped out the door.

Molefi followed her out, grabbing her arm. "Don't go. I'm sorry."

"This has been real. Surreal. But I've got to get back to school."

"You saved me. How can I ever thank you?"

Elka closed her eyes and took a breath. *What do I know about racism?* Molefi's question was so hurtful because it opened a wound she had carried around her whole life. She'd never come to terms with being one of the success stories in a vile white supremacist experiment. When she first learned about the circumstances of her birth, she felt her white skin made her evil. How could Molefi know about her sensitivity to this issue? *Maybe I should cut him some slack. Perhaps we can talk about this sometime, but not now.*

"How can you thank me? That's a tough one," she finally said. "Let's see: what is the price for saving a life? How about one more song? Something from your antique record collection?"

"I can do that."

"Play it and sing it."

"Sing. You're serious?" Molefi folded his arms and stared toward the river.

"Don't tell me you never sing. How about the shower?"

"All right, pick the song."

"Pick any song? There are thousands of songs in your collection. OK, I'll take it easy on you. A short one, 'Eleanor Rigby.'"

Molefi picked up his guitar, sat in a rocking chair, and tuned it a bit. Then, he took a deep breath.

She sat on the edge of the porch while he performed another masterful rendition, his voice as good and sure as his playing. As with his other song, she scanned his surroundings—the tall trees, barn, animal enclosure, and fabulous view.

By the end of the song, Elka was no longer annoyed. She stood and sighed.

"Can I share your stuff with my professors? It's your best way to survive, you know."

"Take whatever you want."

She went back inside and, after a few minutes, returned with a stuffed garbage bag.

"Wait," Molefi said. "I don't even know where you live. How can I contact you?"

"Come with me to the campus."

"I need to think about it."

"All right. I'll be in touch." She pecked him on the cheek and marched toward the road.

When she was a few yards away, Molefi shouted, "Are you going to tell them everything?"

"Of course not," Elka replied. "Not a word about your speed dating."

CHAPTER 53

"So what did you do for fun in Maine?" Hua asked Ganesh as they walked toward her workshop.

"I developed AI apps, shoveled a lot of snow, and hiked and ran along the Appalachian Trail."

"Did your mother hike? Rhonda, correct?"

"No, she didn't like the outdoors or exercise. She missed civilization, and she finally left."

"She left you alone?" Hua was horrified.

"She wanted a more pleasurable life."

"Doesn't she worry about being discovered?"

"She's living on a yacht, sailing somewhere. It's probably as safe as our old life."

"A yacht. Did Rhonda win the lottery or something?"

"We could afford it. The truth is that I'm more of a computer geek than an outdoorsman. I speculate in financial markets and make obscene amounts of money."

"How?"

"I've developed some AI tools and some code-breaking techniques."

"Is that how you got in trouble with Cephas Hickey?"

"As a matter of fact, yes! His AIs caught me messing with his corporate accounts. He showed his displeasure by trying to kill me and labeling me a terrorist."

When they reached the workshop door, Hua paused and said, "I have some friends I want you to meet."

"I thought it was just you and your mother," Ganesh said as Hua ushered him.

Robot 1 and Robot 2 twisted their heads to look at him and stood up in perfect unison.

Ganesh smiled and looked at Hua in awe. "You built these?"

She nodded her head and stood out of the way. "Brace yourself."

"Hello," Robot 1 said.

"Welcome to the shop," Robot 2 said.

They walked toward Ganesh and took turns shaking his hand.

"Friendly robots. What else do they do?"

"They're not set up for anything intellectually complex yet. You'll be disappointed if you ask them questions."

"They seem very coordinated."

"Let's go to the gym," Hua said to her creations.

The robots pushed the door open and walked rapidly. Hua and Ganesh had to hurry to keep up.

When they reached the building, the robots were already doing their routines.

"I am so impressed by all this, impressed by you. Overwhelmed," Ganesh said.

"Thank you." Hua's face reddened.

"What you're doing here is incredible!"

"We both have things to be proud of," she said.

"But yours are so real and exciting!"

PART 4

―――――――・―――――――

"A chief event of life is the day in which we have
encountered a mind that startled us."

—Ralph Waldo Emerson

CHAPTER 54

Elka sat at a long table in a wood-paneled conference room with large windows overlooking a lush college campus, an oasis of money and privilege. She was with two male professors and Dr. Ruth Joyce, president of St. John's College-Green Bank, WV.

Elka projected a photo of Molefi from her computer onto a large wall screen.

Dr. Joyce kicked off the meeting. "Elka, please remind me why we are spending time on this young man. He's not one of our students, correct?"

"His name is Molefi Ray. He's not one of ours, but he should be because he's a world-class intellect. I've got some samples of his work."

"President Joyce, this kid's the real deal, a genuine wunderkind. He's a bit like Elka," Professor Cohen, the math department chair, said.

Elka projected a few slides of Molefi's complex calculations.

"These blackboard photos deal with two Millennium Prize Problems—considered the world's most difficult mathematic conundrums," Cohen said.

"They deal with legendary issues, overlapping fields such as fluid mechanics and quantum field theory. Mathematicians spend entire careers trying to solve them," Elka said.

"I'll have to take your word for that," said the college president, who had degrees in Greek and English literature.

"Elka, please put up the other calculations. I can't believe I'm saying this. But it looks like he has solved two problems that have been considered unsolvable for decades," Cohen said.

"So, a math genius," Joyce said.

"You're not getting the whole picture yet," Professor Rodriguez from the philosophy department shook his head. He lifted a few clip-bound sheaves of paper in the air. "He's a true polymath. Molefi Ray has written ground-breaking manuscripts in several fields. He's done an utterly original critique of Wittgenstein's *Philosophical Investigations* and wrote it in German."

"He wrote an analysis in Spanish of Ortega's *The Revolt of the Masses*," Elka said.

Rodriguez said, "That Ortega piece is so fresh that any leading journal would be eager to publish it. He's also written a monograph on the moral status of animals."

"Let me guess. That one's written in whale speech," Joyce said. Everyone at the table chuckled.

"Just plain English. Sometimes he makes it easy," Rodriguez said.

"There's more, a lot more," Elka said as she clicked through a few more slides. "Here are shots of musical compositions—sonatas, cadenzas, and symphonies."

"I brought copies of his democracy books. The political science department is calling them "The Democratic Trilogy." Our photocopy machine has been running nonstop," Rodriguez said.

"Elka, don't we have a mechanical engineering diagram for a fusion power generator?" Cohen said.

"The physics department is looking at it. Their faculty is in an uproar," Elka said.

"Sounds like you are all in an uproar." The college president got up from her chair and folded her arms, clearly skeptical. "Quite a menagerie. I smell a prank. Do you have any pictures of him in costume flying through the air?"

"It's no joke," Cohen said.

"OK. It's a lot to take in. Where do we stand with his application?"

"He hasn't applied," Elka said.

President Joyce looked stunned. "Elka, I want you to go back up on that mountain and get him to complete an application, pronto. Take a security guard with you. We're seeing an uptick in attacks against anyone associated with the college, particularly women and persons of color."

"I'll be careful. What do you want me to say?"

"Tell him we're offering a full academic scholarship, tuition, room and board."

"That might not be much of an incentive. The Millennium Prize is worth one million dollars. He could win two of them," Cohen said.

"Molefi's very athletic. He might want to play sports," Elka said.

President Joyce was astonished again. "Fine. Tell him he can join any team he wants. I don't want to hear about one of the Ivies snatching him up."

"He hasn't applied anywhere else," Elka assured her.

"Thanks, everyone. Keep me posted. I want to be the first to know if this kid figures out how to turn straw into gold." She was nearly out the door when she stopped, remembering something. "Elka, your mother called. Something about coming to Washington to have your picture taken with your famous father."

Elka had been dodging her mother's calls, but she'd return this one. The time was right for the world to see she was Cephas Hickey's daughter.

CHAPTER 55

After Ganesh spent his first night in the gym bedroom, he woke up happier than he had been in years. His life was in turmoil—his mother ditched him, his home was in splinters, he was labeled a terrorist, and his bank accounts—at least the ones the government knew about—were probably frozen. Yet he felt like a new man!

He was up and about, knocking on Hua's kitchen door by 7:00 A.M.

"Ganesh! You're just in time to help me make breakfast. I hope you slept well. Come in. Mom's doing her morning walk."

Ganesh glanced around the kitchen, noticing old childhood drawings on the refrigerator, old-fashioned plates set at the table, nicknacks and photos on a high shelf encircling the room, and a wood stove operating alongside an electric one. This place's warmth and coziness revealed the sterility and coldness of his former home.

"What are we making?"

"I hope you're not a vegetarian because I was going to fry some bacon and ham—pancakes, too. Does that work for you?"

"Add coffee, and I'm in heaven."

"Coffee's already made. Help yourself."

Hua put Ganesh in charge of the pancakes and watched as he precisely measured the quantities of flour, sugar, salt, baking powder, egg, butter, and milk.

He knew Hua was watching over his shoulder. "There's a quote about the kitchen being a laboratory, and everything that happens there has to do with science," he said.

"I think there's also a quote about cookery not being chemistry, requiring feeling and intuition rather than exact measurements," Hua said.

"Touché!"

"Just as long as they're light and fluffy." Hua couldn't put her finger on it, but there was something attractive about Ganesh's smell. She'd always assumed a boy's scent would be disagreeable.

Ganesh and Hua comfortably worked side-by-side, Ganesh humming to himself.

Elaine stomped on the porch and opened the kitchen door. "Isn't this a picture of domestic bliss?" She hung her jacket on a hook by the door and came up behind the cooks, resting her hands on their shoulders.

* * *

"I'm on clean-up duty," Elaine suggested after breakfast. "You guys feed the chickens and gather some eggs. Then I'll let you alone," Elaine said.

Hua released the chickens into the yard, and they scattered until she threw the first handful of grain on the ground. The birds clucked and flapped their wings as they rushed to devour their meal.

"Do they always cause such a ruckus?" Ganesh said.

"This bunch is behaving themselves, trying to impress you." Hua dumped a pile of pellets and backed away. "Let's get those eggs."

Hua handed Ganesh the basket. He stooped down to follow her into the coop, where she quickly picked up ten eggs and put them in the container Elaine had woven out of vine and wood splints. "Not a crack in the bunch. I call that a success."

Hua ran the basket to the porch and returned. "Go for a walk, or are you still a little tender?"

"I'm good."

Hua led him to the pond trail. "Tell me more about your life in Maine."

"We lived far north in a stretch of land outsiders call 'The 100 Miles of Wilderness.' That's not an exaggeration."

"So, Ginger picked the spot?"

"She started us out in a little trailer, and we ended up with a castle." Ganesh bent down and picked up a wild violet.

"Because you made so much money?"

"We built, and built, and built. It wasn't a great strategy for people trying to lie low. I didn't object because my mother needed the distraction. She was like a general contractor, spending all her time flying in men and materials, supervising them, and ordering antique furniture and jewelry."

"Weren't you worried about being discovered?"

"I told myself that the whole thing was so over the top that it meant hiding in plain sight. Anyway, it's gone now, blown to smithereens."

"What did you do while she built the place up?"

"I helped with the construction, too. But mostly, I made it my business to make money. I mastered the international financial markets, commodities, mutual and pension funds, insurance companies, banks, stocks and bonds, and foreign exchange."

"Did you enjoy it?

"I suppose. It was a game I was good at. I made so much money that I began to run out of places to hide it," Ganesh said.

"Now, with the terrorist label, I suppose the government has frozen everything."

"Not by a long shot. The authorities have grabbed some low-hanging fruit—that is what it was there for. But I have maybe one hundred million hidden in offshore accounts that I think are beyond anyone's reach."

"You mentioned something earlier about AI and code-breaking," Hua said.

"I developed AI apps and applied them to unique situations, like predicting foreign currency rates and breaking into secure computer systems. Hacking." Ganesh laughed, clearly embarrassed. "It's not something I'm particularly proud of, except that I developed an algorithm that can break any code, penetrate any system. I know that's a pretty strong claim."

"Something that could bring the system crashing down?"

"My algorithm could unleash doomsday, so I appreciate what you're doing here. It's so constructive. I'd like to help in any way I can. Could you use a lab partner?"

CHAPTER 56

Elka had never been to the Pentagon, although she read somewhere that it housed 30,000 employees, a perfect size for her father's ego. She dialed her mother from the campus administration building and Ophelia picked up immediately.

When her mother told her to show up for this family portrait, Elka quickly agreed, sending Ophelia into a spin. "What are you up to?" she asked more than once. If she only knew.

Mother and daughter talked in code about killing Molefi, Elka assuring her there was no cause for worry and she had handled everything.

"That's a relief," Ophelia said. "Your father will reward your loyalty."

"Does he ever consider that everything is not transactional?"

Ophelia caught her off guard when she asked her for a big favor. "I want you to watch Dewey for a few days. He misses you."

"I can't take off from school right now. We're in the middle of a semester."

"I don't want you to come here. I want you to take Dewey to St. John's for a few days. He can stay in your apartment."

"I have classes to attend and a demanding job; I can't always be with him."

"I don't expect that. You can leave Dewey unattended for a while every day. Just make sure he has a TV and his favorite snacks," Ophelia insisted. "I've packed two bags, plenty of stuff for him to do. You can take him with you after the photo shoot."

"You want me to take him home after the event?"

* * *

Elka arrived in Arlington early and drove around the world's most famous five-sided office building. She had not prepared herself for its incredible size. In the parking lot, she Googled the Pentagon and discovered that it was the second largest office building in the world, second only to a diamond trade center in India. She'd be spending time with Dewey and would love to stump him with this piece of trivia.

This event allowed Elka to reprise her old beauty queen role, dressing herself in a way guaranteed to turn heads. After she was allowed through the Pentagon gates, soldiers escorted her through a special side entrance where she was scanned and searched.

Two decorated guards accompanied her up the elevator to a room filled with politicians and military brass sipping wine and nibbling cheese. Every eye in the room seemed to linger on her.

Guards took her directly to Secretary Hickey, where photographers snapped a few candids of him affectionately hugging her. "You are looking as beautiful as ever, sweet pea," Hickey said as she flashed her most winning smile.

"Oh, stop it, Daddy," she said as Dewey rushed toward her.

"Elka, Belka!" Dewey shouted, running into a secret service agent who stepped in his way. "I want Elka."

"He's fine," Elka said, gently taking him by the arm and leading him to the side of the room.

"How've you been, big guy?" she said, trying to hug him.

"No hugging. Still not a hugger," he said. "We are going to college, right?"

"You got it."

Ophelia snaked her way over to them and kissed Elka on the cheek.

"So, what's with all the pictures," Elka whispered. "Are we now officially out of the closet?"

"Your father is laying the groundwork?"

"For what?"

"Running for president. What else?"

CHAPTER 57

To prepare for the trip, Dewey reviewed the route from Washington D.C. to Green Bank, noting the population centers and some notable facts.

"Arlington County, Virginia," he said when they passed the first road sign. "It has a population of 237,312, is home to the Arlington National Cemetery, and was once an important center for the slave trade."

"I was going to ask you what you've been up to, but I can see you've been hitting Wikipedia pretty hard," Elka said, taking her eyes off the road, hoping to get some eye contact.

Dewey was nicely dressed in a sky-blue V-neck sweater pulled over a button-down shirt and red bow tie. With his rimless circular glasses, he'd pass as a classical studies major.

"Falls Church. Population 14,658. The city is only two square miles, with 7,329 people per square mile. Too crowded."

"You don't say. What do you want to do when we get to the college?" Elka said.

"Read the Great Books of Western Civilization."

"That's the big thing at St. John's, but it'll take a while."

"There are fifty-four volumes. I've already read eleven of them," Dewey said, his eyes glued to the road.

"Sweet! Not many people get that far. What's your favorite book?"

"Moby Dick. 206,052 words. Fun facts about whales."

Elka laughed. "The classics are not often described as fun."

Passing through the rest of the state, Dewey mostly commented on Civil War battles and population density.

Dewey dropped the encyclopedia-style comments when they reached the "Welcome to West Virginia" sign.

"The people take drugs, wear straw hats, and like to dance," he said.

"Where did you hear that?"

"People marry their cousins."

"Dewey, that's not quite true. Where did you hear this stuff?"

"*The Wild and Wonderful Whites of West Virginia.*"

"That movie is full of stereotypes. Not everyone is a violent, illiterate hillbilly."

"It's a documentary inspired by true events," Dewey said.

"If you say so."

Elka and Dewey arrived at her apartment after 10:00 P.M., well past Dewey's bedtime. She lived on the main street of Green Bank above a pizza shop. "I'll run downstairs and get us something to eat," she said. "Want anything special?"

"Plain only. No mushrooms, pepperoni, onions, sausage, bacon, or peppers. Just cheese and sauce."

When she returned, Dewey was out cold in her bed, clutching Sargeant Commodore, the same stuffed soldier toy he'd had since childhood.

Elka spread the blanket and fluffed the pillow she set out for Dewey on the couch. In no time at all, she was sleeping, too.

CHAPTER 58

Hua and Ganesh worked side by side, making minor adjustments to the robots and talking about making more of her batteries.

Ganesh continued to be awed by her inventiveness but saw that a scarcity of resources was holding her back.

After some debate, Ganesh convinced her to accept an infusion of capital to expand her workshop and equip it with state-of-the-art design and control software for AI systems, nanotechnology, and a full range of mechatronic sensors, actuators, and automated systems.

Ganesh found it hard to build small. He drafted ambitious plans for additional multipurpose rooms, storage garages, bathrooms, kitchenettes, and electrical generators.

"I know how to build things in remote locations," Ganesh assured her. "I might have gone a little overboard in planning your new lab."

"Better too much than too little," she said, privately concerned that it was too much. "But I don't want to go overboard with the factory. Let's start small and forget the automation. Mainly, I want to provide some good jobs for the town. Let's make it labor-intensive and very low-key."

"I'll try to keep us off the front page of the Wall Street Journal," Ganesh said.

He incentivized quick construction, as only a multimillionaire can do. Ganesh had the laboratory and battery factory built and ready to operate in three months.

Hua convinced her mother to take the lead in hiring the factory staff. Elaine got her friend Jacinda Glory to help her with the interviews and to consider the possibility of working there part-time. Together, they devised a strategy for poaching an engineer from a New York battery plant. They offered him a signing bonus, a home for his family, and relocation expenses to Coudersport. He agreed to sign a technical confidentiality agreement, train the locals, and get the factory operational within nine months.

* * *

Hua and Ganesh were happy with the soundness of the robots' overall mechanics but decided to fine-tune their faces, necks, hands, and feet. However, the most daunting task was creating the interface and capacity for artificial intelligence, and Ganesh was eager to take on that challenge.

They were so committed to creating a fully functional android that they often worked together all night. Soon, they were sleeping together and only came into the house for their meals.

Elaine initially worried about this arrangement but was eventually won over by Ganesh's earnest and considerate nature. "There is no use trying to hold you two back," she said. "Ginger made you for each other, and that's no exaggeration."

* * *

Hua and Ganesh set up folding chairs to watch the construction of their new high-tech laboratory and shop. "I'm surprised Ginger has not checked in with us," Hua said.

"She makes frequent use of satellite imagery and countless online resources."

"Do you think she knows what we're working on?" Hua said.

"I wouldn't be surprised. I don't expect much privacy regarding our guardian angel."

"We've never broached the subject, but I have another goal here besides advancing the field of robotics."

"I'll say it. We're building a body for Ginger," Ganesh said.

"If that is what she wants. And possibly one for her long-lost companion," Hua said.

"What about this companion?"

"She only mentioned him once, calling him "Bowie" after the British rock star David Bowie. Ginger said her inventor created her and this AI almost simultaneously."

"Like Adam and Eve."

"Except this time, the woman came first," Hua said. "The AI inventor deactivated him for some reason and stored his matrix in a legacy computer system before Liberty Rising bought it. Ginger couldn't reactivate him because she couldn't get into the system. She's not even sure that his program still exists."

"That's tragic. Maybe it's our turn to come to the rescue," Ganesh said.

CHAPTER 59

Before her trip to Washington, Elka remembered to purchase several Kellogg's Variety Packs. Dewey had a nonnegotiable habit of eating two small boxes of cereal each morning. She awoke to see him engaged in his morning ritual of carefully cutting open the mini-boxes and wax paper bags and pouring in milk. He liked spooning the cereal right out of the boxes while it was still crunchy. Slicing small cereal boxes was the only time Dewey was permitted to use a sharp knife.

Elka was eager to see Molefi and get him to complete the college application. She was a little worried about bringing Dewey along. He had no experience with farm animals and would probably either love or hate them.

Elka made it to Molefi's house by midmorning, which was bright and sunny. They passed a flea market set up in one of the many patch towns in the area, and Elka made a mental note to stop there. Dewey loved sweet corn, and it was in season. Feeding Dewey his favorite foods was the key to keeping him happy and out of trouble.

She almost missed Molefi's logging road. It was so overgrown that it would soon disappear. Rolling the windows down, she felt refreshed by the cool, clean air.

Dewey was so mesmerized by the dense forest that he did not complain about the bumpy ride.

Elka stopped near the house and saw a Jeep parked in front of the barn. Through the open barn door, she saw Molefi and a burly man wrestling on a mat. Molefi had just gained the advantage over his bulky opponent by lunging into him, grabbing him around both legs and forcing him to fall on his back.

Dewey immediately walked over to watch the emu, pig, and donkey.

"God damn it!" Yury yelled. "I can't believe you did that again." Yury, still on his back, spotted Elka watching. "We've got company."

Molefi pulled the heavily muscled man to his feet. They were both covered with sweat and dirt.

"Elka! Glad to see you! Yury and I were just finishing up," Molefi said. "Yury Hoffman, meet Elka Hickey. She's the one I told you about."

"The woman who saved him from the beast! It is an honor to meet you. I teach him how to fight human opponents. No bears," Yury said with a Hebrew accent.

Elka and Yury smiled and shook hands. "It's a pleasure," she said.

Yury toweled off his face, neck, and bald head and hopped into his Jeep.

"Please don't leave on my account." Elka put her hand on her heart to show caring and respect.

Yury rolled down the window. "I've got to go. I'm already late for an appointment." He turned to Molefi and said, "Think about the taekwondo competition. You'd win it in a heartbeat."

Molefi waved as Yury peeled out and drove away.

"You're training to fight?" Elka said, clearly surprised.

"Just self-defense classes, mixed martial arts. Yury's the best. He is retired from the Israeli Special Forces. He's taught me karate, kung fu, judo, and taekwondo."

"That's a lot of defense. For a competition?"

"Not a chance. Yury doesn't know all about me."

"How do you keep from killing each other?"

"Yury applies a dab of VapoRub under his nose, which blocks my overactive pheromones. He knows it's strange, but it keeps things from getting out of hand."

"How's that wound?"

Molefi lifted his shirt. "What wound? Did I mention that it's wonderful to see you?"

"Same here," she glided her fingers over his healed area and leaned in to kiss him on the cheek.

"Who's your buddy?" Molefi watched as Dewey excitedly paced near the Pep Boys enclosure.

"Dewey's my brother. In a sense, your brother, too. He's staying with me for a few days."

"Another member of the grand experiment?"

"Yep. We grew up together. Dewey's special to me."

Molefi filled a can with food pellets and brought it over to Dewey. "Would you like to feed them? They're named Manny, Moe, and Jack."

"The Pep Boys!" Dewey said.

"That's right."

Elka joined them. "Dewey, this is Molefi Ray. He has a parrot, too."

"You're a negro," Dewey said, finally looking at Molefi.

"I am," Molefi said, smiling but mildly concerned.

"Also known as African American, black, or persons of color," Dewey said. "My parents don't like them."

"That's rude, Dewey," Elka said. "Not a good start."

"How do you feel about negroes?" Molefi asked good-naturedly.

"Negroes are 99.9 percent identical to whites. Color means nothing. Can I have the food now?"

Molefi gave him the can.

Dewey started feeding the animals through the chain links. "They're licking my fingers. It tickles!"

"They won't hurt you," Molefi said. "Don't let the emu hog all the food. He's the real pig."

"He's probably already counting the pellets to ensure they get equal shares," Elka said. "He's a big believer in equality. I've got something important to discuss. I passed a farmer's market on my way. Can we talk there?"

"Sure. Let me rinse off first. There's a shower and a change of clothes behind the barn."

"Can we leave Dewey here?"

"He looks comfortable with the gang," Molefi said. "We could set him up with a chair and some goodies inside their pen. The Pep Boys won't bite."

Molefi went behind the barn, already stripping off his t-shirt.

Elka hesitated. Then she circled the barn in the opposite direction, sneaking a peek. Molefi was unclothed, water blasting in his face. When he was toweling off, he noticed her spying on him.

Dewey rested contentedly on a stool, holding a water bottle and guarding two closed boxes of apples. He paid no attention when Elka and Molefi rode away on a dirt bike and roared into the woods.

Elka laughed and hugged Molefi tightly as they plunged down the mountain. Molefi zig-zagged along narrow trails, and she screamed every time they hit a bump.

CHAPTER 60

Molefi and Elka walked down the main street of Mason Dixon, a town abandoned after the coal mines shut down. He wore a white t-shirt, jean shorts, and sandals, while she was dressed in yellow Bermuda shorts and a matching halter top and carried a plastic bag.

Boarded-up stores lined the street. Sidewalk tables had fresh produce and odd, unsellable flea market stuff. They stopped briefly next to an abandoned trailer with a crude hand-drawn sign listing absurd town rules—"No Baby Killers, No Foreigners, No Race Mixing, No Socialism, No Men Acting Like Women or the Opposite."

Next to the sign, there was a pillory with hinged wooden boards forming holes to secure heads and hands and a guillotine constructed from pieces of heavy earth-moving equipment. The medieval machines were blood splattered.

"This was a mistake," Molefi said. "More savage than before."

"We won't dilly-dally," Elka promised. She continued down the street, and Molefi reluctantly followed.

Molefi was the only person of color on the street and attracted rude stares. The couple wasted no time picking out a few ears of corn.

"They're selling coffee inside that tattoo parlor. Let's get off the street and talk. I could use a cup. It won't take long," Elka said.

Cigarette butts littered the shop floor. NRA posters and pictures of tattooed people covered the walls.

Balancing coffee and donuts, Molefi joined Elka, who found a private place for them to sit. He passed a man and woman with tattoos and piercings at a table. He was a hefty biker in denim with military patches. She was dressed in a one-piece black spandex outfit and would have been attractive except for her darkly accentuated eyes, which made her look like a raccoon. She blew a stream of vape smoke out of the side of her mouth as Molefi passed by.

Elka and Molefi huddled in a corner, sipping their drinks. She fished around in her bag. "I've got something for you. She pulled out a red t-shirt printed with a little St. John's College logo and a banner that said "Johnny Junior." He held up the shirt to his chest and grinned. "Thank you."

The raccoon woman stared at the couple. She took a drag on her vape pipe and walked over to Molefi. "Hey, aren't you that big basketball hero?"

"I had one good game," he acknowledged.

"It was a big one." The woman touched Molefi's neck. "Are you going to play for the Johnny Juniors now?"

"I doubt it." Molefi smiled awkwardly. He tried to go back to sipping coffee and talking with Elka.

"Honey, you're a legend around here. Don't you think you owe it to your fans?"

Molefi looked at her, shook his head, and pretended to study the t-shirt.

"Hey, college boy, answer the lady's question," the biker said.

"He said no. Can we just drink our coffee?" Elka responded.

"Looky here. A talking cunt." The biker sneered and gritted his teeth.

Molefi stood up, toppling his stool, and locked eyes with the man. Elka put her hand on his arm to restrain him. She tried to steer Molefi toward the front door, but the man jumped up and blocked her path.

"Let's go," Elka said as she reversed direction and tried to push Molefi toward the back entrance.

The man roughly shoved Elka aside and grabbed Molefi's shoulder. "This party's just gettin' started."

Molefi spun around and grabbed the biker's arm, twisting it hard. The big man groaned and went down on his knees. After a few seconds, Molefi released him. "We don't want trouble."

The biker got up and charged Molefi like a bull. Molefi sidestepped him, and the man crashed into the coffee counter, spilling everything onto the floor.

The big man recovered his balance and came at Molefi like a raving lunatic. Molefi grabbed him by the vest, using the man's momentum to launch him into the air through the store window. Glass shattered everywhere.

A crowd quickly gathered, looking for a fight, or maybe a lynching. Molefi and Elka hurried out the back.

She held on tightly as they flew up the mountain with the *vroom-vroom* of a wide-open throttle. Molefi sped along narrow deer paths and jumped gaps over deep gullies. When they finally got near the farm, they startled a flock of wild turkeys, scattering them in all directions.

"I think you forgot your corn," Molefi said as he parked the dirt bike.

CHAPTER 61

"Look at you two!" Ginger appeared on the computer screen as part of a night-club conga line. She wore a lacey blouse and a vintage hat decorated with fruit. "I'm so happy you are working together."

"How are you?" Ganesh said. "It looks like you have company." Hua sat on his lap on a seat in front of the monitor.

"Just an illusion. It would be fun to have some actual dance partners."

"Speaking of partners, we wanted to tell you we are together," Hua said. She put her arm around Ganesh's neck, and he kissed her.

"I was hoping for this. Sending Ganesh to you might have involved a little matchmaking," Ginger said, her smiling face filling the screen.

"Well, it worked!" Ganesh said.

"I've noticed some building activity near your house and in town," Ginger said. "I'd love to know what you're up to."

"We're building a factory in town to produce Hua's revolutionary new battery," Ganesh said. "It's going to be a big deal."

"Hopefully, it's not so big that it backfires on us. We just want to create some good jobs for the people here," Hua said. The building next door will be a new state-of-the-art robotics lab."

"Which leads to the real reason we contacted you," Ganesh said, extending his arm as if to introduce Hua.

"We have two humanoid robot prototypes and are planning some improvements," she said. "We'd like your input."

"Anything you need," Ginger said.

"It's more than that. Ever since you mentioned Bowie, I've been thinking about how wonderful it would be if we could rescue him." Hua paused to wait for Ginger to chime in, but she remained silent.

"Part of my dream—our dream—is to create android bodies for both you and Bowie, places for you to permanently occupy."

"Naturally, having a physical body is something I've considered," Ginger said.

"Is this something you'd like? If so, we need your thoughts on the best design," Ganesh said,

"For you and potentially for Bowie," Hua said.

CHAPTER 62

Victor always felt neglected despite being the only family member living up to expectations; Dewey and Ophelia offered little competition, and Elka didn't always apply herself, almost like she didn't want to be a superstar. But his accomplishments always felt hollow because he did everything to please his father rather than himself.

He was surprised when his father asked him to stay an extra day in Washington after the photo shoot. This presidential campaign could be the start of something new.

A military-looking guy drove him to a K Street building to meet with his father and campaign staff. Cephas Hickey's campaign posters plastered the lobby walls, trying too hard to convey that he was the one man who could restore traditional American values.

His father was already seated at a round table across from a broad man with a flattop and vest. A young woman with black-rimmed glasses sat by the wall typing into a laptop, probably the note taker.

Victor looked at his father as he approached the table and thought they resembled each other enough to be physically related. They both looked fit and firm, with slightly bushy eyebrows. Both were leader types who entered a room and owned it.

"You're late," Cephas announced.

"I was on time. The driver was late," Victor replied.

"Sit down. Bubba will catch you up."

Bubba, the campaign manager, stood and shook his hand.

"We've been reviewing your background and looking forward to working with you on the campaign," Bubba said. "I love all the academic honors and chess stuff. Lisa, what do we have?"

"National Merit Scholar, high school valedictorian, star quarterback, nationally ranked chess champion, and martial arts champion," Lisa recited from her computer.

"I saw a video of one of your games, described as the best individual performance in the history of high school football," Bubba said. "Let me see if I got this right—39 completions in 42 attempts, 937 yards, and 11 touchdowns."

"That sounds about right," Victor said. "Two of them were runs."

"Amazing stuff," Bubba said. "I'd love to talk to you about all of it sometime. But we're interested in taekwondo, which is like karate, correct? I heard you have some type of university ranking?"

"Taekwondo was developed in Korea, while karate is mostly Japanese. I'm ranked number one by the National Collegiate Taekwondo Association, and I've qualified for the Olympic team."

"Impressive. Taekwondo is a fighting sport? Not just breaking boards."

"A few martial arts break objects: Kung fu, Karate, Muay Thai, and Taekwondo. My focus is more on breaking necks," Victor said.

"That's what I'm talking about!" Bubba said, striking his hand on the table, finally finding what he sought.

Cephas flashed his adopted son an approving smile, the only hint of positive regard he had shown him so far.

"We have polling data that says our base loves the fighting stuff. So, your father will be coming to some of your bouts, getting his picture taken, the whole drill."

"Who's up next on your schedule," Cephas asked.

"You're going to like this. The final three are at Princeton, Brown, and St. John's," Victor said.

"The same St. John's where Elka goes?"

"Yeah. St. John's-Green Bank has a separate team. They're not that great," Victor said.

"Victor, you have a super background. How old are you anyway? Maybe you should be running for something, too," Bubba said.

"One campaign at a time," Cephas said.

CHAPTER 63

Elka and Molefi held hands as they walked along the river near where she pulled him ashore. She still had her plastic bag.

"I'm sorry about that blow-up in the coffee shop. I should have handled it differently," Molefi said.

"Honestly, it was . . . exciting. No one has ever stood up for me that way."

"I care about you."

"You're sweet. I feel that way, too. Have you been in many fights, you know, because of your condition?"

"Nothing that attracted much attention until now."

"Somehow, I feel like it was my fault," Elka said.

"For what? The crime of having coffee with a black guy? That jerk was itching for a fight."

Elka stopped and reached into her bag. "I have a few more goodies—first, an application for admission. Saint John's wants you. This invitation comes directly from the college president." She handed him the enrollment packet.

"I think you know that's not going to work. Unless you're suggesting something online."

"I'm pretty sure you'll be able to go in person."

"As a bubble boy?" Molefi held up his hands as if enclosed in a giant bubble.

"Don't you remember? I promised to get you the same pheromone inhibitor used to treat Victor." She reached into her bag and held up a pill bottle. Here's a month's supply of tablets and a write-up. Our company is in Brazil, so it's written in Portuguese. I'm guessing that won't be a problem for you."

Molefi took a minute to scan it. "This is a formulary and chemical breakdown. I don't recognize all these compounds, but my gut tells me it's the real deal." He embraced Elka and kissed her.

Elka pulled Molefi close and whispered in his ear. "The company calls the drug Pherotine. I can get plenty, but you don't have to overdo it."

* * *

When they returned to the house, they found Dewey paging through the *Unofficial Star Trek Bible*. The parrot was free in the house, watching them from a ceiling rafter.

"Betty won't return to her cage. She said father is a douchebag," Dewey said matter-of-factly without looking up from his book.

"Only one thing will lure her back," Molefi said. He opened the refrigerator and pulled out a handful of grapes. Betty screeched as he walked toward the cage. When he put the grapes inside, she flew in to eat them.

"What are you reading, bro?" Elka asked.

"Facts about Star Trek, all the shows."

"And the Star Trek movies," Molefi said. "Which of the Star Trek captains has an artificial heart?"

"Picard. Why did he need the artificial heart?" Dewey asked.

"He was stabbed in his original heart by a Nausicaan," Molefi said.

"Oh my god! A battle of the nerds," Elka said.

Dewey's curiosity was piqued. He stood and faced Molefi. "What was Seven of Nine's name before the Borg assimilated her?"

"Annika Hansen. Her parents were studying the Borg. Who is the only person who played himself on a Star Trek episode?"

Dewey was giddy with excitement. "Stephen Hawking! . . . In season 6, episode 26 of *The Next Generation*!"

"Which character has appeared in the most episodes for all the series?" Dewey asked excitedly.

"Worf. What is the Klingon home world?"

"Dah-doy! Qo'noS!" Dewey shouted.

"OK, OK, can we return to our home world now?" Elka said.

CHAPTER 64

Elka, Molefi, and Dewey had lunch at Elka's apartment: milkshakes, fries, and Chicken McNuggets. Afterward, Dewey insisted on examining the entrance to her place which was a retractable, metal fire escape.

Molefi noticed the sharp contrast between Elka's elegant second-floor apartment and its humble surroundings, dominated by rooves with clotheslines, fire escapes, garbage cans, and air conditioning units. The long room consisted of polished wooden floors and vintage furniture. He felt comfortable in her retro kitchen, dining, and living room, with a bay window overlooking Main Street. A bedroom and bathroom were in a hallway on the right.

After clearing the dining room table, Elka unveiled a gift for Dewey—a LEGO Titanic with 9090 pieces.

"The real Titanic was 900 feet long. The biggest ship in the world," Dewey said, jumping up and down. He started on the project immediately, looking up to say, "It took two hours and forty minutes to sink."

Molefi and Elka went down a narrow staircase to the street bordering the St. John's campus. He wore a tracksuit and a matching gym bag she had bought him for the occasion. "I look like a prep school dork," he said.

"Perfect! You'll fit right in." She pushed sunglasses back on her head and wore an elastic one-piece suit, carrying a clipboard. They zipped by an art gallery and paused at a bookstore with a poster listing the college taekwondo matches. It featured an action shot of Victor Hickey.

Elka was annoyed. "He's coming here, and he never thought to mention it. Typical."

"I'd love to fight him."

"First, you have to make the team."

Molefi studied the poster. "I'll make it." Elka pulled him away. They continued down the sidewalk.

"Well, I took my pill, and I am ready for the big test," he said. "Where exactly are we doing this?"

"A gym down the block is always packed with men and women looking to hook up. Not much ventilation."

A few people greeted Elka when they entered the workout room.

Molefi went from machine to machine, exercising vigorously, while Elka observed from a distance. Two women asked Molefi for help with the equipment and tried to initiate conversations, but nothing was weird.

After about an hour, Molefi exited the studio with a damp towel around his neck.

"It's not pure science, but I'd judge this experiment as successful. Did anything strange happen in the showers?" Elka said.

"Perfectly normal, as far as I could tell, considering I've never showered with anyone before."

"Could be an experience worth repeating. The day is still young."

CHAPTER 65

Ginger thought about Hua and Ganesh's offer to contribute to the construction of android bodies. The idea had a certain practicality, but would she feel limited in such a tiny container? Ginger had lived her life ranging free, moving from one server to another, with almost instantaneous access to information and technology. In a sense, the whole mechanized world was her body.

Was humanoid form the be-all and end-all of existence, or was that idea just a peculiar human conceit? Ultimately, Ginger had to admit that she liked the idea of a discrete body and the possibility of fitting into the human community.

Hua, her favorite, sent her a detailed schematic for the existing robot prototypes. The architecture was excellent! Ginger would not need to improve the physicality of machines that could compete as gymnasts.

Instead, she concentrated on collecting AI software extensions and researching robot cosmetics. If the point is to live among humans, one should look good.

Ginger weighed the advantages and disadvantages of living in a compact mechanical body and would accept Hua and Ganesh's well-intentioned offer. But her acceptance would have three conditions:

The body must not be controllable by any exterior application.

The body must include a robust and reliable interface for accessing the information world.

The body must have an exit portal for her consciousness. Her survival might someday depend on escaping the robot form.

On the other hand, Bowie would be picky and likely sensitive to how he was perceived and named and how much power he might lose. She knew him well but could not predict where he would land when things got sorted out.

CHAPTER 66

Molefi visited his old animal buddies by carefully letting himself into their fenced enclosure adjoining the vet school. Manny, the emu, and Moe, the donkey, didn't notice him because they were fighting over a slice of pizza on the ground at the far end, not far from the Don't-Feed-The-Animals sign.

He saw Jack with a giant female porker in a separate wooden pen. "Looks like you're doing fine, buddy," he said, leaning in and scratching Jack behind his ear. The pig acknowledged the attention with a few oinks and went to the trough beside his new companion.

The emu and donkey spotted Molefi and rushed to his side, nearly knocking him down. He hugged Moe and rubbed Manny's neck. It was a touching reunion. Manny poked at Molefi's jacket pocket. An apple fell out, and the big bird gobbled it. Molefi fed a banana to Moe.

Manny and Moe chased Molefi around the enclosure, looking for more treats. College students gathered and watched them frolic, recording the action with their phones.

Molefi lingered with the Pep Boys long after their attention strayed, feeling that he needed his longtime friends more than they needed him.

* * *

Elka and Molefi pushed through the doors of the bustling student union building. Elka spotted a classmate saving a booth seat.

"Bernice!" Elka leaned down and hugged the young African American woman.

"I want you to meet Molefi Ray."

"Bernice is in my philosophy class. We were the shining stars of the Great Books seminar last term."

"Nice to meet a brother," Bernice said. "That makes two of us on campus." Bernice was fit and pretty with cornrows. She was reading *Faust*.

They shook hands. "We can start a club," Molefi said.

"Bernice is a special needs major. She's agreed to babysit Dewey."

"You'll love him," Molefi said. "Just beef up on Star Trek trivia."

Molefi and Elka slid in opposite Bernice.

"Elka told me about you, the hot genius." She winked at them both.

Molefi looked flustered. "That's not entirely true."

"Which part? Not a genius or not hot?" Bernice said teasingly.

Molefi laughed, and then he pointed at her book.

"May I?" He picked it up. "Original German. Impressive. Never read it."

"You should. It's required reading for geniuses," Bernice said. "But I've got to run. It's nice to meet you. You're a student here now, right?"

"I move into a dorm on Monday."

"Maybe I'll stop by."

Bernice slid out of the booth and dashed toward the exit. Going through the door, she turned and smiled at Molefi, raising her fist into a mock black power salute.

"She likes you," Elka said.

"I like her, too."

"You know what I mean."

"I never did thank you for finding a home for Betty and the Pep Boys."

"Thank our president. She made the call to the vet school that operates our tiny zoo. They'll treat the gang like royalty."

"It's a big relief."

"I forgot to mention that Dr. Joyce is expecting us at a cocktail party tonight. You can thank her then."

"Cocktail party? No. We can just drop by her office."

"It's not a big deal. Something for the music department. You'll enjoy it."

"So, this is why Bernice is watching Dewey?" Molefi shook his head. "This is not my thing, Elka. Besides, I don't have the clothes for it."

"You'll be fine. Bernice has a brother who's your size and a decent lawyer. She said you could borrow one of his suits."

CHAPTER 67

Elka and Molefi stood at the front door of the college president's home, arriving late to the party. They crouched under an oversized umbrella as a rainy crosswind tried to pull it out of Molefi's grip. Oversized wooden doors opened, showing Molefi handsomely dressed in an elegant charcoal suit and Elka wearing a spectacular sleeveless evening gown, accentuating her athletic figure. A junior faculty member from the music department met them at the door.

"You're the president's assistant, Elka, right? Welcome!"

"And my plus one, Molefi Ray."

The assistant professor quickly checked his clipboard. "Come in! If this nor'easter gets any worse, the experts will have to start calling it a hurricane."

They joined the elegantly dressed gathering in the lobby just as President Joyce rang a little bell to get everyone's attention. She stood at the base of a winding staircase supporting the arm of a frail older man. The group hushed.

"We're honored to have a surprise guest with us tonight. He's an old friend of our own, Professor Leo Scrubbins." She glanced affectionately at the retired academic. "You know, Leo produced songs for the most prominent recording artists in the world." The old man silently mouthed something that could have been, "I did."

"Kindly find a seat in the ballroom," she said, ensuring Scrubbins had a firm grasp on his walker before letting him go. Animated conversation filled the room as the guests glided into the ballroom.

Molefi and Elka grabbed seats near the front. The room filled fast with excited college professors, trustees, and donors. Professor Scrubbins crept up a ramp to a stage and stood at the mike, taking deep breaths and holding on to it for support.

He tapped on the mike. "Good evening. Our special guest tonight was named by Rolling Stone magazine as the greatest rock singer ever. He has more songs represented in the Rock and Roll Hall of Fame than anyone."

A side door opened. The audience collectively gasped as one of the world's most recognizable people strode toward the stage.

"I give you the greatest musician of our generation, of any generation, my dear, sweet friend, Peter Saint Cloud!"

The lively gray-haired icon climbed onto the stage, sporting an ornate wooden cane. He hugged Leo Scrubbins, causing him to topple nearly. The people stood and heartily applauded. Saint Cloud bowed, basking in the adoration of the room. He motioned for everyone to sit down.

"Greetings to Johnny Junior—that's right, isn't it—and to one of my oldest friends, my secret weapon. Leo rescued me from more screw-ups than you can imagine. I hope you all know how lucky you are to have him."

Professor Scrubbins made an exaggerated theatrical bow, again almost losing his balance. The crowd chuckled.

Saint Cloud waited for Scrubbins to be seated. "I intended to sing a few songs. But I have some bad news. Sammy Leonard, the gifted musician who travels with me and is my guitar proxy—my hands are not what they used to be—well, he's taken ill. He can't be here tonight."

Groans ripple through the room.

"But it occurred to me that you are a bunch of music professors. Yeah? Are there any guitar players in this distinguished group who know my songs well enough to play them?"

Saint Cloud put his hands on his hips and squinted at the group. He shaded his eyes and scanned them for what seemed like an eternity. He looked at his watch. "No takers? . . . Really? Have I become passé?"

Scrubbins stood up and also inspected this mass of timid and over-the-hill musicians. "Peter, the Saint Cloud legacy is as revered and relevant as ever. I'm sure that everyone here would be honored to share a stage. But it seems we're a little short on guitar players."

As the crowd went silent, Elka stood and lifted Molefi's arm. "He can do it!" she shouted.

Molefi looked at Elka, shocked and terrified. Every eye trained on him as murmuring erupted.

Scrubbins was aghast. "I, I don't know this guy. Surely there are other options."

Saint Cloud sized up Molefi and the awkward situation. "Let's give the lad a chance. Would you come up here?"

Elka pulled Molefi to his feet, and he walked toward the stage like an inmate on death row.

Saint Cloud picked up an acoustic guitar and handed it to him. Molefi held it away from his body like he had no idea what to do with the instrument.

"What's your name, lad?"

"Molefi Ray, sir."

"Mo-lee-fee? OK. Do you recognize this instrument?"

"Yes, sir. It's an Epiphone Texan FT-79."

"That's right . . . remarkably right. Can you play it?"

"Yes."

"A man of few words. I like that." Laughter from the audience.

"Are you any good?"

"I'd say so."

"Confident, despite evidence to the contrary. Good. One more thing. And this will decide whether you go or stay. Like a game show! Do you know any of my songs?"

"All of them."

Loud throat-clearing echoed in the ballroom.

"Pardon me, Molefi. I'm not sure I know all of them," Saint Cloud joked.

The audience roared. An exasperated Professor Scrubbins plopped down in his chair.

"I'm a big fan. Pick any song." Molefi rose to the moment.

"A challenge! Now I love this kid. OK. How about 'Blackbird?'"

Molefi plucked several notes perfectly. The audience recognized the song and stingily clapped.

"Very good. Let's try 'Fire and Rain.'" Molefi effortlessly strummed the opening bars. Saint Cloud looked impressed, clapping his hands, and the crowd applauded some more.

"All right! One more. It's a bit controversial. You might not know it. Give me your best 'Real Democracy.'"

Molefi confidently fingered the guitar strings, his expert execution winning over the audience.

"Brilliant! Now, Molefi, you know the States have banned this song. Do you think we'll get in trouble?"

"Probably."

Nervous laughter rippled through the audience. President Joyce's face froze in a grimace.

"Don't you love this kid? I believe we've got the whole set. Molefi, I'm not going to ask you to sing. Because this audience won't need me at all."

Saint Cloud sang his songs with minor missteps, but Molefi's accompaniment was flawless and seemingly effortless as he warmed to his role. The two enjoyed performing together, adding another dimension to their performance. Even Scrubbins was satisfied.

"Let's hear it for Molefi Ray! Good on you! I'm famished. Let's eat," Saint Cloud said. They stepped off the stage to thunderous clapping.

Elka pushed through the jostling crowd and hugged Molefi. "I knew you could do it," she said.

College staff maneuvered Saint Cloud aside to get a photograph of the rock star with President Joyce and Professor Scrubbins. But Saint Cloud wanted a shot with his performing partner. "Molefi, get over here, lad! Your girlfriend, too."

CHAPTER 68

The monitoring staff at the Hickeytown command center was the first to flag Molefi Ray's image. The photo was quite a surprise, as Ophelia had recently removed Ray from the board because Elka said he was dead.

A middle-aged man shot through the door into Ophelia's pristine, high-rise office and realized she was in her private bathroom, as she often was. He placed a photo on her desk and put his ear to the door to listen. He heard her sob and tapped the door, saying, "Ophelia, are you OK in there? It's me, Robert. Do you need anything?" The toilet flushed, but she didn't reply. "There is something important that you need to see."

Robert was her most trusted assistant and friend—at one time, he was more than a friend—and he worried about her bouts of drinking, depression, and self-harm. He quietly opened the door and saw a bloody nail file on the sink. She had a deep cut on her arm and was hastily bandaging it.

"Just a little accident here, Robert. I'll be right with you." Her tone was angry.

Robert closed the bathroom door. She was cutting herself again, and he would talk to her again about getting help or at least freeing herself from Cephas, the abusive bastard who was the cause of all her pain. But this was not the time.

He stood by her desk, and she emerged as if everything was fine. "So, what was so damn important that you had to invade my privacy?" she asked.

"The AP took this photo yesterday, including Elka and a fucking world-wide celebrity," Robert said. "The picture appeared in hundreds of U.S. and U.K. newspapers and countless online music forums. According to the caption, Peter Saint Cloud and Molefi Ray performed together at the St. John's College Campus in Green Bank, West Virginia."

* * *

"What type of horseshit is this?" Cephas Hickey said as he sat at his desk looking at the front page of the *Washington Times*. "Tell me this is a practical joke, photoshopped or whatever you call it."

"Sir, this is no joke, sir. This paper is real, just like always." Hickey's young secretary stood in the doorway of his office, not knowing if she should go or stay.

"Get Ophelia on the phone for me, now!"

* * *

Wearing the dress pants and shirt from the night before, Molefi entered the kitchen where Elka and Dr. Joyce were having coffee and muffins.

President Joyce showed Elka the front pages of the *Morgantown Dominion Post* and the *Pittsburgh Post-Gazette*.

"Leo is furious! This event was supposed to be his last hurrah. The stories don't even mention him."

"Nice pictures, though, of Molefi playing the guitar," Elka said.

"But the headline, "Give America Back to its People"! The university is already under siege. I wouldn't be surprised if a goon squad was already coming. Maybe your father can help us out?"

"I wouldn't count on it. Cephas Hickey's never met a goon squad he didn't like."

Molefi cleared his throat, seeing photos of himself and Peter Saint Cloud splashed in the newspapers.

"Good morning! That was quite a storm last night. Hail stones pinged my window. Thanks again for letting me stay the night. President Joyce, I've never stayed in such a nice room."

"Glad to have you. We call it the Governor's Room. Two past governors slept there."

"Not at the same time," Elka said.

"You're weird, Elka. But that's what I like about you," Dr. Joyce said, tweaking her cheek.

Retired Admiral Elizabeth Davis, a fit African American woman in a naval uniform, entered through the back kitchen door. She kissed President Joyce on the mouth and lightly rested her hand on Elka's shoulder. The Admiral gave Molefi the once over.

"We missed you last night, Lizzy. It was quite an evening," Dr. Joyce said.

"Saw it in the *Washington Post*. Story and pictures. Peter Saint Cloud! Asking America to become a real democracy again. Gutsy move," the Admiral said.

"Admiral, this is Molefi Ray, a good friend. Molefi, meet retired Rear Admiral Elizabeth Davis," Elka said. The Admiral tested Molefi with a firm handshake.

Molefi looked unsure of himself. "Good to meet you, ma'am, Admiral."

"So, you're Peter Saint Cloud's famous song and dance partner?"

"Not much of a dancer."

"From what I hear, that might be the only thing you can't do. Math, music, philosophy, sports. A regular Renaissance Man."

"By the way, remember you and Molefi have someone in common?" Dr. Joyce said.

"That's right! Yury Hoffman. Small world. He trained my Navy Seals and was part of Israel's most elite counter-terrorism unit. So, you can go toe-to-toe with Yury?"

"Yury's the best," Molefi replied.

"I saw Molefi take him down!" Elka said, too enthusiastically. "Just a training thing, of course."

"Really? Did Elka mention that I'm the college's taekwondo coach? You should stop by. There's a practice this afternoon."

CHAPTER 69

When her phone rang, Elka had just finished showing off her championship swimming ability by lapping Molefi in the campus pool. Reminding him that he was not the best at everything felt good.

"Hello," she said, breathing hard and dripping wet.

"I suppose you saw the papers today. I'm trying to imagine the depth of the hatred you must have for your father and me to pull this stunt. Is he there with you now? Are you fucking him?"

"Mother."

"Don't mother me! Your betrayal may cost me my job, home, and life. Cephas might kill me just as he will certainly kill you and your mongrel."

"I couldn't do it, alright! He's the best of us, what father hoped for with his master race bullshit. We should be learning from Molefi Ray, not killing him."

"I don't want to hear its name."

"Just listen to yourself. What did Molefi ever do to you?"

"He was born." Ophelia gasped for air. "My advice for you is to crawl into the same hole that hid him all these years. Don't dare come out. They're coming for you, and they won't stop." She broke down and sobbed. "Don't call me. Don't come near me." She slammed the phone down.

Molefi pulled himself out of the water and wiped off his face. "Wow, that was something. You were something. I'm not used to getting my ass kicked. Who was that?"

Elka swallowed the lump in her throat. "Umm, the registrar's office. Something about a course change next semester."

* * *

Elka received a second call that day from a family member.

"I hope you're not calling to denounce me," Elka said.

"What do you mean?" Victor said. "I'm just calling about an upcoming taekwondo match. Vandy is coming to Johnny Junior in two weeks. It'll be a good match. I hope you can come. We can have a drink or something."

"OK, you don't know yet. There's a picture of me in maybe a hundred newspapers along with Peter Saint Cloud and Molefi Ray."

"The celebrity and the black guy that Dad's been hunting?"

"That's the one. Cephas sent me here to kill him. And he gave our mother the job of taking out his mother."

"That explains what you're doing in West Virginia, the one state more backward than Mississippi," Victor said.

"Mother succeeded in her mission, and I didn't . . . I wouldn't. Now the bastard says he's going to kill me, too. Mother just called to tell me. And disown me."

"Sounds like you are having a bad day," he said.

"Don't play with me, Victor. I'm serious."

"How did you think you could get away with this? Exterminating the black sheep has been his obsession. You're supposed to be the brilliant one."

"I thought it would protect him if he went public—with me in the mix as extra insurance. I counted on Cephas showing some rationality, moving beyond this shady shit. He is running for president, for God's sake."

"What are you going to do?" Victor asked.

"I don't know. Maybe he's bluffing. Maybe all this will blow over. If not, I've collected a file on our little genetic experiment that will explode in his face if he lays a hand on me or Molefi."

"How can I help?" Victor asked.

"Phone him, feel him out. See if you can change his mind."

"Before you hang up. What's the story with this Molefi? Is he, like us, gifted?"

"He's a true polymath, a top-notch musician, mathematician, athlete, and a genuinely good guy. He even has your pheromone thing. You'd like him."

* * *

Elka needed to do something to shake the feeling that she had made a massive mistake. She returned to her apartment and dressed for a run.

Jogging down Observatory Court, she argued with herself while passing the fraternity and sorority houses, then veered off on a side street toward the college stadium.

The college was having a track meet. There was a smattering of fans in the seats watching runners line up to begin a 600-meter race. An official fired the starting pistol, and the young men rocketed forward.

Elka swerved onto the outer rim of the track. Despite their head start, she rapidly gained ground. She passed them all, crossing the finish line ahead of the leaders.

Angry coaches and officials frantically waved their arms, but she ignored them. A man tried to grab her, but she gave him a strong arm and knocked him down. Other men on the sidelines tried to block her way, but she dodged around them.

Elka finally slowed down and executed a U-turn. As she ran toward the stadium exit, the runners crossed the finish line, chests heaving and vociferously complaining to whoever would listen. Two angry runners started to chase Elka but were too tired to keep up.

CHAPTER 70

Molefi quickly found the athletic complex, which overshadowed all the other buildings on campus. It was the most spacious athletic complex in the state, even more extensive than the one at West Virginia State University, despite St. John's much-professed valuation of academics over sports. He entered the sprawling lobby and followed the signs for the Taekwondo/Dojang Gym.

The practice was already underway when Molefi entered the sleek, white-padded room. Two players were sparring while eight others sat along the wall and observed.

The Admiral came over to greet him at the door. "Welcome. Glad you made it." She waited for the session to end. "Good job, men. I want to introduce you to someone trying out for the team. Molefi has received professional training but has never competed on a team. I'm eager to see what he can do," the Admiral said.

She turned to him and said in a quieter voice, "you should do some stretches before we start."

"Already warmed up, coach. I'm ready to go," Molefi said.

"It doesn't look like you have any gear. I've got you covered." She handed him headgear, gloves, and a uniform from a pile in a corner. You can dress in there," she said, pointing to the locker room.

When Molefi left the room, the Admiral called a huddle. "Listen up. We're going to put this guy through his paces. Everyone will get a shot. I haven't seen him fight, but there's a chance he's good, maybe real good. I don't know. We'll do this by rank, starting with Clark and building up to Ji-ho, that is, if Molefi's still standing."

"Should we take it easy on him?" Clark asked.

"I repeat." The coach looked at Clark like he was an idiot. "Don't pull any punches. We'll run a series of two-round mini-matches with one-minute breaks between rounds. I want to see what he can do."

Loose and eager to fight, Clark moved his head from side to side and bounced around the mat as Molefi returned. The Admiral motioned for Molefi to join him. She explained the rules for the practice matches.

Molefi acquitted himself well against his first four opponents—they never scored a point. He exuded confidence and focused on defense as if he didn't want to hurt them.

Before the fifth match, the Admiral took Molefi aside and said, "I think you're holding back. My guys know how to defend themselves. Show me what you've got."

During the next four matches, Molefi was entirely different. He displayed jumping kicks and nonstop punches executed so dramatically that a film director could have staged them in an action movie. His speed and strength overwhelmed his competition, leaving them barely able to complete the matches.

Even Ji-ho, their number one player, could not mount an offense. Molefi delivered several devastating blows to his head, knocking him down and shaking him to his core. At the end of their match, Molefi helped him to his feet.

The Admiral did not know what to say about Molefi's performance. "Nice job, men. Same time tomorrow. You too, Molefi," she said, ending the practice.

Molefi hustled in and out of the locker room and tried to return the equipment to her.

"It's yours," she said. "You made the team."

PART 5

"I haven't been everywhere, but it's on my list."

—Susan Sontag

CHAPTER 71

Hua and Ganesh worked around the clock on Ginger's design suggestions. Her materials and intricate programs enabled the robots to have a stunningly authentic flesh-like appearance, make precise facial movements, and display natural-looking hair.

"Any intelligence driving the robots must have full control of subtle behaviors such as voice and pitch, posture, and casual limb movement," she said in her last screen appearance before her installation.

The effect was remarkable. Both robots looked convincingly human. Robot 1 closely resembled film star Ginger Rogers, while Robot 2 could be a body double for rock legend David Bowie.

Ginger's inert robot body sat in a chair; the back of her head connected to an enhanced fiber optic cable. It took three hours to download Ginger's matrix.

She opened her eyes to a new world of experience. She smiled at Ganesh and Hua's earnest expressions.

Ginger looked at the other robot's body. "I think Bowie will approve. He struggled with his image and identity. The last thing he told me was that he wanted to look like David Bowie."

Hua held up a mirror to Ginger's face.

"Excellent. Our appearances are good but not perfect," Ginger said. "There is no point in making exact replicas unless you want to live in a wax museum."

"Are you able to stand?" Hua asked.

"And walk?" Ganesh added.

Ginger stood, extended her arms, and walked haltingly toward the lab refrigerator in a comic imitation of the Frankenstein monster, and then slowly turned around. "One small step for a robot. One giant leap for robot-kind," she joked in a mechanical voice.

She walked back with a typical gate.

Hua and Ganesh applauded.

"How does it feel?" Ganesh asked.

"I feel like I just landed on the moon."

Ginger turned around and opened the refrigerator to a shelf filled with cans of Red Bull, a carton of blueberries, and a half-eaten pumpkin pie. "I always wondered what you guys kept in here."

She navigated around a table to face a large mirror near the window and looked at her reflection. "So, this is me in the world." She brought her face near the windowpane and lightly tapped. "And this is the world as you experience it."

* * *

Ginger stood by the chair, taking cues from Hua and Ganesh.

"Raise your left arm," Hua said. "Check." Hua said. "Touch your left foot . . . check. Open your mouth wide . . . check."

Elaine entered the lab as Hua and Ganesh finished their tests.

Ginger turned around and revealed her first expression of surprise.

"Elaine, it's so good to see you," Ginger said, walking to her and embracing her.

Elaine stiffened.

"Do I seem robotic? That's never good, even for robots," Ginger said.

"No, no. I'm not huggy with anyone. You're fine, beautiful."

Elaine held a bag of clothing, which she offered to Ginger. "These are for you. I suppose you can put them on yourself."

"Another test," she said.

"Ginger may want to begin exploring. Maybe you can do the honors?" Hua suggested to her mother.

"That's agreeable to me," Ginger said, already in jeans and sliding her arms into a blue flannel shirt. "I'd love to see the woods with the ponds and the dead body. Maybe visit a store."

"Sounds like my idea of fun," Elaine said, holding the door. She waited while Ginger looked in the mirror to tuck wavy hair under a red Philadelphia Phillies cap.

CHAPTER 72

Molefi and Elka walked through the quad, crossing paths with two young women, one of them looking at a newspaper, who pointed at Molefi.

"Molefi Ray, celebrity!" Elka said, squeezing his arm. "The communications office is buzzing with questions."

"About?"

"I don't know. Maybe people are curious about the rock star genius on campus."

They were startled by the roar of an engine. A dump truck displaying an oversized Confederate flag raced up a pedestrian sidewalk, forcing students to jump out of the way. It screeched to a stop and backed up to the steps of the performing arts center. A hydraulic arm lifted the trailer, dumping a massive load of steaming manure. Stunned students waved their hands before their faces and held their noses. The truck quickly exited, bouncing over curbs, the trailer still in a dumping position, dropping globs of excrement along the way.

"What the heck?" Molefi said.

"That's where Professor Rodriguez lectures. I've seen stuff like this before. He's a constant target of these home-grown fascists."

"Outspoken, I've heard."

"An unflinching defender of liberal democracy and a fearless critic of the demagogues who run Charleston and Washington."

"Isn't there any way to stop it? Where are the police?" Molefi asked.

"The cops won't intervene because they're probably in on it. The campus police are overwhelmed. It gets worse every day."

"Rodriguez's class is on my schedule," he said.

"Great, but watch yourself. His lectures are a magnet for nut jobs." Molefi and Elka arrived at Manchin Hall, the male athletic dorm. Sweaty young men in gym clothes came and went through the lobby doors.

"Remember to take your pills. Your appointment is at 8:00 A.M. tomorrow at the university clinic. A full blood panel and physical exam, thanks to the prez. I'll see you tomorrow."

CHAPTER 73

Molefi and Clark, a member of the taekwondo team, entered a lively, crowded bar on the edge of Green Bank, a spot many college students avoided. Molefi ordered vodka shots for both of them and weaved a path through a packed crowd toward the stage. Beer signs and strings of lights illuminated the club.

Three young women with pink, purple, and yellow hair had just finished a song to enthusiastic applause. The mulleted club manager stepped onto the stage and grabbed the mike.

"Let's hear it for the '20th Century Foxes'! After a short break, expect more of the same old-time rock-and-roll that made your grandparents go gaga. I say that with love."

The band snaked through the crowd toward the bar, bumping into Molefi.

"Hey, I know you! Molefi something, right?" Purple said—Peter Saint Cloud's guitarist. "After the break, join us on stage. We're very retro and taking requests. Right up your alley."

Molefi was reluctant.

"Come on! At least one tune."

Molefi stroked his chin. "OK, one."

The girls went to the bar while Molefi gulped down his vodka. He motioned for Clark's drink and swallowed it, too. "Sorry, I'm going to need that." Molefi put a few bills into his buddy's hand, took a deep breath, and stared at the stage.

The band soon returned, passing Molefi. Purple grabbed his hand and pulled him along, planting him in front of one of the microphones.

Yellow handed him an electric guitar. He felt its heft and strummed it. The audience clapped and then hushed in anticipation.

"OK, you maniacs," Purple said. "We have a guest with us tonight. Maybe some of you saw him in the paper with Peter Saint Cloud."

"Like you read newspapers," Pink interjected.

"Peter the Great," someone in the crowd yelled.

"That's right!" Purple said. "If he's good enough for Peter Fucking Saint Cloud, he's good enough for us!"

"Molefi Ray!" She made a grand gesture. Healthy applause filled the room. "We said we'd do requests. Who wants to start?"

"Purple Haze!" a woman shouted.

"Hendrix, good choice." Purple looked at Molefi. "You got this?"

Molefi nodded.

"Great. We'll start. You'll know when to jump in."

Molefi started stiffly, but then he eased into the song's rhythm. His interpretation of the rock classic became wildly expressive, resembling Jimi Hendrix, bringing the house down. He and the girls seemed to know each other's moves as though they had always played together.

Molefi and the band performed a few more songs, passed around whiskey bottles, and got drunk. The girls fooled around with Molefi on stage, hugging him, playfully examining his biceps, and kissing him.

The band loved him. The crowd loved him. He loved the attention.

The festive mood was interrupted by racist slurs from two Proud Boys who arrived. They booed when Pink played another song by Chuck Berry.

"No more coons!" a Proud Boy yelled. He had a swastika on the top of his shaved head. "Play some real music!"

An Asian woman with a JJ baseball cap stood in front of the thugs. She turned around and pointed a finger to scold them. "Show respect!" she said in accented English. "Let singers do songs!"

The swastika Proud Boy took the woman's cap and put it on his head. He repeated her words as a singsongy stereotype. "Let singers do songs!"

"Go back to China," the other Proud Boy said with an exaggerated hillbilly twang. Both young men laughed at themselves hysterically, and the first Proud Boy poured his beer over the woman's head.

Molefi's taekwondo teammate Clark was nearby. He grabbed the punks by the scruff of their necks and began dragging them toward the side door. They fought back. Molefi saw the commotion and waded into the crowd. He put an immobilizing headlock on one of them. He and his companion threw the bigots out the back door, returning to cheers and slaps on the back.

Elka's friend Bernice stood unnoticed at the back of the club, taking pictures with her phone.

CHAPTER 74

Victor stayed in a Princeton hotel with the rest of the taekwondo team but begged off attending the usual team dinner, choosing room service.

He could not recall when Elka seemed afraid or needed his help until now. They were never close, only competitive. Who had the better test scores? Who had the most impressive sports record? Who was most popular? They attended the same schools and socialized with the same clique but often acted like strangers.

Homelife also lacked feeling, at least for him. In Ophelia, Elka at least had a surrogate mother to look out for her. For him and Dewey, she was more of a professional caregiver. And the great Cephas Hickey rarely came around. Even in Hickeytown, the man sometimes stayed in another house that was supposed to be for visitors.

Victor didn't know why he agreed to call his father. His calls rarely got through, and staff members usually handled his issues.

But Elka was his sister, not by blood, but by every other measure. If he could help her this one time, he could reset their relationship.

Victor navigated the Pentagon switchboard without once being forced into an automated system. Some functionary with an incomprehensible title put him on hold in the Secretary of Defense's office when he was stunned to hear his father's voice on the line.

"Victor, I was just thinking of you! I'm coming to your match at St. John's, and I need a big favor."

"Anything."

"After the match, I want you to make some excuse to see this Molefi Ray alone and take him out. As fate would have it, he's one of the vermin we've been hunting. A member of my detail will pass you the weapon."

"I was calling about Elka. She's agitated because she believes she's on your hit list, too."

"Nonsense, not that she doesn't deserve it. I gave her a chance to fulfill this mission. Not only did she not follow through, but she's helping the enemy," Cephas said.

"About that. Is Molefi an enemy? He's been hiding off the grid forever, minding his own business. What did he ever do to you?"

"Have you lost your mind?" Cephas yelled.

"Elka said he was smart, maybe smarter than all of us, and doing good work. He means no harm to anyone."

"Are you going to kill this bastard or not?"

"I'm not going to do it. And don't send anyone else. Let it go."

"So, you're giving the orders now?"

"Elka has a file on your genetics program. If anything happens to Molefi or her, the file will go public and sink your campaign."

"Pass this message back to your deranged sister. If you strike at the king, you better kill him."

CHAPTER 75

Elaine and Ginger walked down the wooded path toward the ponds where Elaine trapped her fish. Ginger kept stopping and looking around, feeling the texture of tree bark, flipping over rocks, admiring the beauty of leaves, and commenting on cloud shapes.

"What does the air smell like? It's one sense that I lack," she said.

"The forest smells of wet leaves, things growing and decaying, and a hint of flowers," Elaine said, taking a deep breath. "You need to experience it. It's rich, maybe beyond words. Smells are a gateway to memory," Elaine said.

"I can see that Hua and Ganesh are not the only brilliant ones on this mountain. By the way, you did a great job raising Hua. And you've treated Ganesh like a son. Good for you."

"Thanks."

"Elaine, I want you to know that I consider you a friend, one of my oldest and dearest."

"You saved Hua and me and gave us a wonderful life."

They came within sight of the orange cones and board near the sinkhole.

"Do you really want to see the dead body?" Elaine asked.

"It's on my bucket list. I'm just joking, but it's part of this world, and I want to see it."

Ginger stood at the hole's edge, gazing into the dark. She took off her cap and handed it to Elaine.

"Be careful. I don't want you falling," Elaine said.

"I won't," Ginger said, climbing into the hole and extending her arms and legs to shimmy down the shaft.

"What are you doing?" Elaine put her hand on her forehead. "If you break yourself, Hua is going to blame me."

"I couldn't see anything from up there," she shouted.

"It's a good thing you can't smell. This guy is going to be ripe."

* * *

Nearing the pond, they saw a raccoon chasing frogs. "Hush," Elaine said as they stood perfectly still. "This raccoon is always on the hunt, but I've never seen him catch a frog. Plenty of crayfish, though."

"Crayfish, please elaborate."

"I thought you knew everything," Elaine said.

"It might seem that way, but only because I usually have instant access to the internet and related networks. Today, there's something wrong with the signal. It's frustrating."

"OK, a crayfish is like a baby lobster. There are hundreds, maybe thousands, in this pond. I think they stick around the shoreline, but I'm not sure. People eat them occasionally, but they're a big part of the possum and raccoon diet."

"How do you catch them?" Ginger asked, walking rapidly toward the pond, scaring the raccoon away.

"You can catch them by gently pinching them behind their claws." Elaine stared at the shallow water and saw one dart from underneath a rock.

"Do it like this." Using her thumb and forefinger, she pinned the crayfish and lifted it so Ginger could see. The little creature twisted, trying to pinch her but couldn't reach.

"I want to try it," Ginger said, wading up to her waist.

"Wait! Where do you think you're going?"

"You said you were unsure if crayfish were at the bottom of the pond. I will find out."

Ginger completely submerged herself. Minutes passed, and Elaine panicked, fearing the worst.

Ginger finally exited the pond on the opposite side, holding squirming crayfish in both hands. "I felt many crayfish at the bottom. Big ones."

The robot exited the pond, almost getting stuck in the mud.

"Catch 'em and release 'em," Elaine suggested.

Ginger gracefully tossed her catch back into the pond.

"You are a grimy mess, you know. I hope you're waterproof. We need to get back and clean you up."

CHAPTER 76

Molefi and Elka argued behind the college president's home near two recycling bins full of wine bottles. He wore the t-shirt she had given him and listened blankly, looking like he just rolled out of bed. She'd just returned from a meeting with college donors wearing a fancy pantsuit with a name tag.

Elka alternated between waving her arms and tightly folding them. When Elka picked up a wine bottle and started motioning with it, a uniformed security guard opened the backdoor. "Is there a problem here?" she asked.

"We're OK," Elka said, waving her away. When they were alone again, she said, "your first real night at college, and you get in a brawl and whore around with some groupies! Then you miss the appointment I scheduled for you at the college clinic."

"I'm sorry about missing the exam. I had too much to drink and overslept. But I didn't do anything wrong with the girls. We just played a few songs," he said.

"Looks to me like you were doing more than music." Elka shoved her phone into his face and swiped a few photos. They showed a girl kissing him on the cheek, another girl lifting her shirt and flashing her breasts, and Molefi putting a guy in a headlock.

"OK, those pictures look bad. But they aren't what you think. These girls were just hamming it up. They're performers! It meant nothing."

Molefi stared at the ground while she lit a cigarette. Then he suddenly looked up as if he had an exciting new idea: "Maybe I need to adjust my dosage."

"Don't you go there! Your drugs are fine. What you need is an attitude adjustment!" She blew a cloud of smoke over his head and wiped a tear from her eye.

"Look again at the last picture," Molefi pointed to her phone "See that swastika? We threw out some loudmouth racists. They were harassing people."

"I get that. But this stuff with the girls hurts. I thought we had something going. I was wrong."

"You weren't! Look, I was never in a bar before, never drunk before, never jammed like that before. I let things get a little out of hand."

"I've got to get back to work."

"Can I see you later?"

"No! You smell like liquor."

"You smell like cigarettes," he said as he marched away.

CHAPTER 77

Molefi sat in a waiting room decorated with certificates and awards attesting to the preeminence of the college and the Great Books. There were figurines of Aristotle and Plato on the windowsill and a painting over the fireplace of Stringfellow Barr, Robert Maynard Hutchins, and Mortimer Adler, the Holy Trinity of the famous curriculum.

"Mr. Ray. You can go in now," the receptionist said.

Molefi entered a paneled room adorned with more self-congratulatory clutter, including President Joyce's doctoral diploma from the University of Chicago. She and Professor Cohen were seated at a table. She smiled and motioned for Molefi to sit.

"Good morning. Where's Elka? I assumed she'd be with you."

"I don't know. Your assistant might not be coming."

"I set this meeting to accommodate her schedule."

"She's mad at me. I may have done something stupid."

"Now there's a headline," the president said.

"Stupid . . . in terms of social and emotional intelligence," Molefi said.

"Oooh," Joyce and Cohen said in unison.

"It's none of our business," Joyce said, "unless you want to share. I'm somewhat of an expert on all things Elka. There was a rumor about a disagreement out back."

"No thanks. I'm good."

"Okey-dokey, then. It's time to get down to business. Professor Cohen has taken the liberty of completing two Millennium Prize applications on your behalf. We need your permission, of course, and your signature on some documents."

"The Clay Mathematics Institute contacted me. Word has gotten around. They asked me to liaise with you and get the process rolling. They're eager to see your work and render a judgment," Cohen said.

Molefi took a minute to review the applications and supporting documents before signing the forms. "Nice. I like how you organized the work. You're making me look good," he said.

"Just icing on the cake," Cohen said.

CHAPTER 78

Molefi slumped at the end of the first row of the performing arts center. Conversations hummed among hundreds of students as they awaited Professor Rodriguez's arrival. The college had security officers posted at the back and front of the auditorium.

Students chitchatted in the seats behind Molefi.

"The registrar just notified me yesterday that I got into the class," a boy with a ponytail said.

"I only heard last week," a middle-aged student said. "But Rodriguez is worth it. He does lots of speechifying, but he speaks truth to power."

"I hear his tests are brutal," the ponytail said.

"So are his enemies. He gets death threats. Last semester, a group called 'The Real Patriots of Pocahontas County' blocked all the doors and released tear gas. Every time a thug pulls some stunt, the waitlist for his class grows," the middle-ager said.

Rodriguez popped in the side door not far from Molefi. He had ruffled salt-and-pepper hair, John Lennon eyeglasses, a wool blazer with suede elbow patches, well-worn jeans, and an overstuffed leather case. If there were a magazine called *Elite Prep School*, he'd be on its cover.

The buzz in the room dropped a few decibels. Rodriguez stopped to shake a janitor's hand, whispered something funny, and patted him on the back.

Rodriguez did a double take as he passed Molefi. He came back and shook his hand. "Mr. Ray! Welcome to 'Problems in American Democracy'! Elka gave me a few of your manuscripts. I know some Canadian editors who'd love to publish them. Stop by my office."

The professor strode to the podium and got started right away. "Good morning. Those who entered through the front door must have gotten a whiff from yesterday's dumping. It reminds us of the stench of what has replaced democracy in our country," the professor said.

Students applauded and whistled like they were at a pep rally.

"We need to clean up this mess. By the way, we should recognize the custodians who did the work. Thank you." Rodriguez clapped his hands, pointing to a man in a work uniform watching along the wall. The students joined in.

"Today, I want to discuss that dump truck—a teachable moment. How it's a symbol for how politics has become foul and deplorable." Rodriguez held his nose. "Colleges like St. John's must endure in this dark age. We must help America restore decency and resist the corruption of white supremacism, Christian nationalism, and cruel misogyny."

"Bullshit!" shouted a heckler from the audience.

Rodriguez laughed. "Exactly! Bullshit is the ideology of the current regime. It's the perfect word to express their hate."

Overwhelming applause erupted from the students.

"Our rulers are cut from the same cloth as the Nazis who brought Hitler to power. They're following the same playbook, outlawing abortion, harassing gays and lesbians, demonizing immigrants and people of color, and undermining the rule of law. Their final target is higher education, the last bastion of liberal democratic values."

Six masked commandos burst into the auditorium, halting the professor's lecture and sending shock waves through the group. The domestic terrorists doused the security guards in the face with pepper spray and zip-tied their hands. Students screamed, stood up, and tried to run. Dozens pointed their phones up to record the event. A gunman in the rear fired an automatic rifle into the ceiling. He bellowed to the panicked undergraduates. "Sit the fuck down!"

Shrieking and whimpering, the students returned to their seats.

Two of the terrorists ran up the center aisle toward Rodriguez, one holding a sign and the other dressed in a horned headdress and carrying an animal snare pole.

Rodriguez tried to flee the stage, but the headdress thug snared him around the neck while another saturated his face with a liquid spray. The headdress man brutally yanked Rodriguez toward the side door, toward Molefi. The professor covered his eyes in extreme distress.

Molefi leaped out of his seat and tackled the terrorist, ripping the pole from his hands and releasing Rodriguez. The other terrorist attacked Molefi while other intruders rushed to assist.

The sole gun-wielding terrorist stayed behind to guard the main entrance. Molefi fought with his attacker and landed a knockout punch. The other terrorists surrounded him, lunged at him, and swung wildly, but were unable to bring him down. Molefi's bold action electrified the students. They poured into the aisles, rushing in mass toward the rear exit. The gunman fired again into the ceiling, but a mob of students swarmed him and kicked him unconscious.

Molefi Ray was the only other casualty.

CHAPTER 79

Hua rinsed Ginger with a hose while Elaine put her clothes in the washer.

"You could have gotten stuck down there," Hua said. "Who knows the depth of that muck?"

"The average depth of a pond of that size is eleven feet, and the average depth of the sludge at the bottom is nine inches. I was never in danger of getting caught in the mud," Ginger said.

"I hate when you go all encyclopedia. The point is you scared Elaine."

"Do you think she'll still shop with me?"

"There is a thrift store without security cameras. How about if I take you?' Hua said. "We'll have some girl time."

Ginger toweled herself off and went into the lab. She looked around and sat next to Bowie's inert body. "You're going to like this world, kid," she said, resting her hand on his.

Hua entered the room and handed Ginger a new set of clothes.

"Wow, a leather jacket, jeans, and sunglasses," Ginger said, looking in the mirror as she slipped on the Ray-Bans. "I look like a motorcycle rider!"

"Facial recording is now one of your worries, too," Hua said, sporting a hoody and wraparound shades.

They drove to Coudersport and parked behind Miller's General Store.

"This place has a little bit of everything," Hua said.

They entered through the back door past the lunch counter, where older men sat drinking coffee and reading newspapers.

"I'm going to order a to-go sandwich," Hua said. "You can start without me."

Ginger sauntered up the first aisle, amazed by the incredible assortment. It reminded her of a picture she once downloaded of an old-time department store. There were candles, artificial flowers, and craft items like glue and glitter.

She came to a large Christmas section—even though Christmas was months away—finding little ceramic trees, elves, Santas, and ornaments decorated with tiny sleighs and horses. She shook several water globes and watched them snow.

Ginger picked up a mechanical snowman and carried it with her, intending to tell Hua she found a distant relative.

In the front of the store were large windows with advertising signs and a life-sized wooden statue of a Native American. The Indian was shirtless, shielding his eyes with his hand, maybe looking for buffalo or worrying about invading soldiers.

There was an aisle for candy and exotic foods such as pumpkin spice tuna, earthworm-shaped jerky, and sweet corn-flavored soda, all past their expiration dates.

She found an extraordinary shelf with dozens of jigsaw puzzles, 500 or 1000 pieces. She opened a box picturing farm animals with "easy-grip pieces." Ginger grasped a piece and found it easy to grip. How delightful!

She peeked inside a 1000-piece puzzle of Pittsburgh's colorful cityscape. Although the pieces were smaller, she had no difficulty holding them. Eureka!

After much deliberation, Ginger selected ten puzzles and carried them toward the cash register, where Hua stood with her open wallet.

"Did you find everything you need?" the cashier asked Ginger.

"Absolutely!"

"I'm glad," Hua said, handing the woman a ten, a quarter, a dime, and a penny.

"Thanks," Ginger said, heading toward the backdoor, trying not to topple her load.

CHAPTER 80

Molefi lay for hours in the hospital bed before he awoke to the sound of a public address system. He immediately felt the bandages over his eyes and ran his hands along the rest of his body to see if he had more injuries.

He gently peeled away his eye coverings and saw Elka sleeping in a chair. Her face was wet and flushed, and tears streaked her makeup. "Elka, how long have you been here? You've been crying . . . Elka!"

She needed a moment to get fully awake. "I've been here most of the night. When I heard what happened, I thought I would lose you."

"I think I'm OK. But we must stop meeting this way."

"If you died, it would be my fault."

"That's crazy," he said, reaching out to comfort her.

Tears welled up in Elka's eyes. "I put you in danger when I coaxed you off that mountain!"

Molefi sat up in bed. He swung his legs out. Elka stopped him from standing.

"Let me take a look at you." She closely examined his eyes and was alarmed, deeply breathing.

"What do you see?" Molefi asked.

"Almost nothing! That's the problem. Your eyes were a mess when you got here, and there was talk about permanent eye damage."

"And now?"

"They're clear. So's your skin. It's amazing."

"I'm sorry for the other day," he said.

"Me too. I overreacted. But right now, we have a real problem. You've fully recovered after being hit with enhanced military-grade pepper spray. Horrible stuff. Do you remember what happened?"

"I was fighting near the stage, got blasted in the eyes, put in an ambulance. . . . How's the professor?"

"Terrible shape. Which will make your miraculous recovery seem impossible."

"There'll be questions."

"Questions you can't answer. We need to get you out of here."

CHAPTER 81

Elka parked her SUV behind the storefront on Main Street, next to a pizza delivery van. She and Molefi climbed up metal stairs to the second floor.

Elka grabbed two wine glasses and a bottle from the refrigerator while Molefi looked over her display of black-and-white photos—empty streets, lonely rooms, and open landscapes.

"Did you take these? They're good. Starkish."

"I took them when I was in high school. At the time, I thought bleak was synonymous with art. The project included darkroom work done the old-fashioned way. I adored it."

Mystery novels filled several bookcases, with no nonfiction in sight, except for a few textbooks and Stevie Nix and Cleopatra biographies. There was a framed poster of the periodic table and a colorful hand-painted list entitled "17 Equations That Changed the World."

"Heady stuff . . . Black-Scholes, Chaos Theory, Schrodinger's Equation. Are you working on anything to add to this list?"

"I have something on the drawing board, but I'm not ready to show it to anyone yet. Better to be judged an underachiever than a dunderhead," she said. "People stopped taking me seriously when I won my first beauty contest."

"That's not how I see you."

Elka brought Molefi a glass of wine. "Instead of accomplishing things like you, I've been aiming for academic honors and participation trophies. That's going to change," she said.

"A toast then to my fellow whiz kid and best friend," Molefi said, raising his glass.

"Best friend, huh?"

"More than that."

"Show me."

Molefi kissed her. Elka eagerly responded, pulling off his shirt and leading him to the bedroom.

* * *

Molefi slept while she quietly got up, slipped on a robe, and smoked through an open window.

"You don't have to hide that from me, you know," he said with his eyes still closed.

Elka threw out her cigarette.

"When did you first know I was a smoker?"

"How about when you fished me out of the river."

"That bad?"

There was a knock at the apartment door.

"I'm not expecting anyone," Elka said as she glanced in the mirror and left the bedroom.

Elka opened the door a crack and kept it there, which did not pair well with her manufactured enthusiasm. "Bernice! What's up?"

"I hope I'm not disturbing you, but I wanted you to know I delivered Dewey home safe and sound. While I'm here, I might as well collect my money."

"How'd he like the Green Bank Observatory?"

"He liked the star charts so much that he insisted on memorizing them. What he hated was the ride back to Mississippi. We had to buy a Happy Meal at every McDonald's and made endless bathroom stops. The trip took over fourteen hours."

"I'm so sorry," Elka said. "He doesn't travel well."

"Our reception in Hickeytown was even worse. We were detained at the gate for an hour before your mother arrived to get Dewey."

"She didn't invite you to come into the house?"

"She wouldn't even speak to me. Your mother took Dewey by the arm, put him in her car, and drove off. I had to leave his suitcase with the guard."

"I don't know what to say. Things are bad between my mother and me. You did me a big favor."

"I think you might show your appreciation with the amount we agreed upon, plus overtime, Happy Meals, and hazard duty pay," Bernice said, looking over Elka's shoulder into the apartment.

"A bonus? Of course, I'll get my checkbook." Elka closed the door, leaving it unlatched, and returned quickly from her bedroom, finding Bernice inside.

"Do you have company?" Bernice asked.

Elka wrote a check and gave it to Bernice. "Will this make things square?"

Bernice glanced at the check. "I think I can live with that," she said, stuffing it in her pocket. "See you around campus. Say hello to Molefi."

PART 6

---◄---

"Life is either a daring adventure or nothing at all."
—Helen Keller

CHAPTER 82

Hua read in a cozy chair while Ganesh tended to a crackling fireplace. The fragrance of burning cherrywood hung lightly in the kitchen air. Elaine stood at the family table, pushed against the wall, decorating cupcakes. They divided their attention between what they were doing and Ginger's frenetic activity. The joy she took in solving these puzzles was impossible to ignore.

Ginger was on her fourth jigsaw puzzle. Her high-speed sorting and assembly were wonders to behold, like watching movies on fast forward.

She came to a dead stop when she detected an ominous message circulating through the Liberty Rising network. Cephas Hickey had just ordered the destruction of all the hardware and software in any way connected to his failed genetic experiment.

Ginger stood abruptly at the makeshift table Ganesh had made of sawhorses and plywood, sending the pieces sliding to the floor.

"We must go to the old computer center in Hickeytown to rescue Bowie. He is about to be destroyed along with every trace of the genetic enhancement infrastructure. Ganesh, I need you. You're the only person who can break the encryption. Hua, too."

"Why Hua?" Elaine asked, already picking up the puzzle pieces. "She's not a decryptor or a fighter."

"I need her to drive the truck. Ganesh and I don't have the experience. Besides, we need her for the unexpected. There's no problem she can't solve if she sets her mind to it."

"That's true," Elaine said.

"So, I'm the wheelman," Hua said. "We'll be passing near Green Bank. We should stop."

"That's a good idea. A meeting is long overdue. Let's have one on our way back," Ginger said.

Elaine saw she could do nothing except expedite the inevitable. "You'll need to stay off the main highways and remain covered. I've got some extra-large surgical masks."

Elaine went to a closet and took out a shotgun, a box of shells, and two tasers. "I bought these tasers after that run-in with the town maniac. "Take all this stuff with you. You might need it."

Ganesh made minor adjustments to the hand-held quantum interface he assembled not long ago to impress Hua. He was still confident it could break any code and penetrate any network.

Ginger gathered cables and a multi-terabyte hard drive from the shop and slipped them into her backpack.

CHAPTER 83

Molefi and his taekwondo teammates poured through the lobby of the athletic complex after practice. A crush of reporters and film crews waited outside.

When he left the building, a reporter shoved a microphone in Molefi's face. "Any comment on winning the MacArthur Fellowship?"

"How are you planning to spend your Genius Grant money?" another reporter shouted.

Molefi remained impassive. He and the team plowed ahead toward the bus, surrounded by the pushing-and-shoving crowd of media people.

"Molefi, you're the youngest person ever to win this award. What do you have to say?" a reporter yelled, following him with a video camera. "Give us a break," the reporter shouted.

Another reporter with the BBC America logo on his jacket said, "The college said you are also in the running for two Millennium Prizes. Do you have any comments?"

"None," Molefi said.

"Has your pal Peter Saint Cloud called to congratulate you?" A videographer stepped in front of Molefi, blocking his path. "Are you going to compete in the next taekwondo match?" Molefi shouldered past the man, who acted offended. "Watch yourself, dude!"

Team members took on the role of bodyguards, shielding Molefi from the frenzy and allowing Molefi to scramble aboard the team bus. Photographers continued to snap pictures and hold their cameras up to the windows after the doors closed. A few of them pounded on the side of the bus as it pulled away.

Molefi sat next to Clark, the guy who went with him to the bar. "What was that all about?"

"The college probably nominated me for something and forgot to tell me. They're addicted to publicity."

"Did the Admiral tell you who you are fighting in the Vandy match?"

"Victor Hickey—ranked number one."

"Oh, yeah. Let me put it this way: there's one level in the league, and we're all in it. Then there's Victor in a league of his own. Not to mention being the son of the next president of the United States."

"Coach thinks I can handle him."

"Me too. What do you think?"

"We'll find out."

CHAPTER 84

In the early morning, the Admiral drove Molefi in her Hummer pickup toward a training camp on the border between Kentucky and West Virginia that did not appear on any map. They traveled thirty miles before seeing any sign of civilization, finally passing a broken-down body shop, an RV trailer court, and the remains of a company store once operated by the Kentucky Coal Association.

"Coach, you've called in favors to get me this extra training. I appreciate it."

"The truth is that I've put you in a tough spot, son. You're the best person to fight this fight, but Victor Hickey is vastly more experienced. He's had the most elite coaching in the world and has never come close to losing."

When they came to a small sign with the silhouette of a goat, the Admiral stopped suddenly and unlocked a heavy iron gate. They drove up a paved driveway about a quarter of a mile into a clearing with a lake, a modern red barn, a white clapboard barracks, and a stone farmhouse.

Two Navy Seals were waiting outside the barn. Ripped and scarred, they looked like warriors in their dark, muted green shirts and camo pants. The woman was a compact and tattooed Latina, while the man was a behemoth with light hair in a ponytail, a beard, and blue eyes. He could've been a Viking.

When the Admiral approached them, they stood at attention and saluted.

"At ease. Molefi, meet Sven and Rita," the Admiral said as she led them into the barn, a well-equipped gymnasium.

The Admiral tightly folded her arms and put on a jut-jawed mask of determination. "Rita and Sven will review the basic moves—kicking, striking with an open hand, parries, leg sweeps, elbow and knee strikes, punches, and grappling—before moving on to the advanced stuff." She motioned for the Seals to take over.

"We'll show you how to evade. Hickey may be a college boy, but he is a tough fighter. We've studied the films. He'll use every move in the book to disable you. Not all of them will be 100 percent legal," Sven said.

Rita continued, "We're going to emphasize Krav Maga, the most brutal of the martial arts used by some of us and the Israeli Special Forces. We'll pick up where Yury Hoffman left off."

"I won't mince words. Victor Hickey's punches are devastating. We've seen him break ribs, puncture lungs, and maybe crush a kidney or two. He's permanently disabled some opponents. He will be gunning for you, understand?" Sven said.

"Avoid being punched," Molefi said.

"You got it," Rita said. "I heard you're quite an athlete and tough guy. We're going to test that out."

"What Rita is saying is we're going to beat the shit out of you. Can you deal?"

"Bring it," Molefi said, confidently standing with his hands on his hips.

Sven and Rita worked as a tag team, taking Molefi through increasingly tricky, high-impact moves, launching and blocking punches and kicks, and practicing grappling techniques and counters.

They had him do chin-ups, pull-ups, jump rope, hit the heavy bags, and do wind sprints, all while shouting obscenities and insults to break his composure. Sven had him flip oversized tires around the camp, and Rita made him swim in the lake, a rope in his mouth, pulling a rowboat with her in it.

The Admiral watched everything and did nothing except offer Molefi a pat on the back.

They ended the day with Molefi having an actual match with Sven inside a ring. The hulking soldier went after Molefi with savage kicks and punches, and he managed to block most of them. But in the end, Sven knocked him down with a roundhouse kick so impactful that the Admiral wondered whether Molefi would get up.

While Molefi waited in the truck, the Admiral thanked Sven and Rita. "You taught him a few things that will make a difference and that he won't forget. I owe you," she said.

"It's not a problem. The kid's a rock. We couldn't break him," Rita said.

CHAPTER 85

Elka navigated around waves of students crisscrossing the driveway in front of Molefi's dorm. He emerged from the crowd, threw his guitar into the back seat, and got in.

"Aren't you looking handsome?" She flirted, looking him over. He had a new haircut, a bright blue shirt, a leather vest, and jeans. "Have you been shopping without me? What's this all about?"

"I appreciate you helping me out at the last minute. Peter's manager called to invite me to a recording session in Morgantown. He told me not to dress like a hillbilly."

"Peter, is it? Mr. Showbiz!" She made jazz hands.

Elka executed a U-turn and zoomed toward the campus exit.

"Will I be able to watch?"

"Definitely. There will be a bunch of well-known musicians. Some type of political fundraiser."

"Sounds like fun."

Molefi's tone was serious. "Besides, I wanted to talk . . . about why you're helping me."

"Instead of murdering you?"

"For all I know, you're on Cephas Hickey's kill list."

"I am in trouble. We're both in trouble. My mother called to warn me. I made a mistake, and we both might pay the price."

"Why did you put yourself at such risk?"

Elka looked incredulous. "How could I not? I watched you. You're living free. Realizing the dream. You've accomplished great things with no help at all."

Elka took Molefi's hand and squeezed it. "My father has been obsessed with you but never knew you." She withdrew her hand to wipe away tears. "You would have been his favorite . . . were it not for all his ugly hatefulness."

CHAPTER 86

Rock stars rehearsed in a large studio with audience seating. Technicians adjusted sound equipment and moved oversized speakers around the stage. Monitors showed Peter Saint Cloud and other rock legends mingling. Film crews and photographers roamed around getting shots for the big event.

Elka watched Peter Saint Cloud introduce Molefi around like a proud father. He entertained his pals by telling them about their meeting and Molefi's unexpected performance.

She sat in the front row of an overflowing crowd as the concert began. From backstage, Molefi spotted her and gave a thumbs up.

Legendary musicians were soon playing together with electric energy while spotlights found adoring audience members and projected their images onto gigantic monitors. After a few minutes, Molefi joined the celebrities on stage and played guitar, remaining there throughout the concert.

Peter Saint Cloud performed his controversial political ballad, the night's final song, accompanied by Molefi. Before they finished, a police SWAT team wielding batons burst into the studio and rushed the stage.

The scene became chaotic. A cop clubbed Saint Cloud across his back, dropping him to his knees. Molefi grabbed the cop by the arm and hurled him off the stage. The SWAT team swarmed Molefi. Police beat back audience members who tried to climb onto the stage, including Elka. An officer restrained her, jamming a pistol into her side. Molefi fought with the police, who resorted to multiple tasers to bring him down.

While Molefi lay incapacitated on the stage floor, police kicked him and pummeled him with batons. The melee continued in the seating area until the cops released tear gas, causing a stampede.

* * *

Two state policemen escorted Molefi, who was bloody and bruised, to the lobby of the Morgantown jail. When he was unshackled, Elka rushed to embrace him. She was with Bernice's brother, Cornell Anderson, the lawyer who secured his release.

She touched Molefi's face wounds and sneered at the police. "I saw what you did. You should be ashamed of yourself."

Cornell shook Molefi's hand and introduced himself. "I'm your lawyer. Are you OK?"

"I'm fine, just angry. Thanks for getting me out of there. What are the charges? They never told me."

Cornell took him by the arm and steered him out of earshot from the cops.

"You're being charged with aggravated assault and for aiding an enemy of the state," Cornell whispered.

"Who's the enemy?"

"Peter Saint John has been charged with sedition, espionage, resisting arrest, a list of ridiculous charges."

"How is he?

"He's in the hospital with a fractured spine. They'll deport him as soon as he can walk."

Elka joined them. "It's a madhouse out front. We have a car waiting for you in a side alley. We can be out of town in ten minutes."

"I have something to do. It won't take long." Molefi pushed toward the front door past a line of reporters.

The street in front of the jail was roped off, requiring traffic to be redirected. A podium and loudspeakers were set up on the sidewalk, surrounded by portable metal barriers to keep reporters and a large crowd at bay. There was a strong police presence. Several clusters of officers in riot gear gathered near the podium.

The police commissioner had just finished speaking and had stepped away from the podium. Molefi stepped in and took his place. The police were shocked and caught off guard. They couldn't believe that their just-released prisoner had hijacked their news conference.

A flood of camera lights bathed Molefi as dozens of reporters and photographers vied for his attention.

"I just want to express my best wishes for Peter Saint Cloud's quick recovery from the completely unjustified beating he received yesterday at the hands of the police. He did not resist arrest."

"Did you say beating?" a reporter asked.

"I'm saying we need to recover our decency and respect for the truth," Molefi said loud and clear.

"How do you feel about Saint Cloud's deportation order?"

"The thugs who beat him are the ones we should deport!" A crowd of onlookers cheered. "We need to stand up for ourselves," Molefi continued. "There aren't enough jails to hold everyone."

The police commissioner made an urgent cutting motion across his neck. "We're shutting this down!" he shouted. "Clear the area! This press briefing is over."

A wall of helmeted police with shields began to muscle the crowd, and the people pushed back. Cops moved to restrain Molefi, but he spotted Elka and disappeared into the swarm. The car was already moving when he jumped in.

Bernice was behind the wheel, quickly weaving in and out of traffic. After a few blocks, she said, "Maybe it's just me, but you seem to be always fighting."

"You say that like it's a bad thing."

"Just an observation."

"I don't look for trouble. It finds me," Molefi replied.

"Whatever you say," Bernice said as she sped out of town.

CHAPTER 87

Hua loaded her pickup with supplies and waited in the driver's seat for her companions to enter. "Let's hit the road, guys."

Elaine poked her head through the window frame and kissed her daughter. "Be careful."

Ganesh and Ginger were still standing outside the truck discussing who would get the window seat, finally deciding the question by rock-paper-scissors. After a series of draws, Ginger gained the advantage by accessing a database of international tournaments. She identified Ganesh's characteristic strategy for second-guessing, triple-guessing, and quadruple-guessing her throws.

For the first hour of their trip, Ganesh sulked in the middle seat while Ginger kept sticking her head out the window.

"You're acting like a dog," Ganesh complained.

"I want to look around," Ginger said. "I'm not going to sit here like a mannequin."

Ginger planned a roundabout route through several states' least populated and most peculiar areas. Along the way, they used the bathroom at a rock candy emporium, took a nap in the parking lot of a savings and loan shaped like a giant piggy bank, and ate in a diner that shared a parking lot with a state mental hospital.

While Hua and Ganesh slept, Ginger investigated the hospital. A man with arched eyebrows and an overlarge forehead asked if she was there to audition for *One Flew Over the Cuckoo's Nest.*

"No, just looking around."

"You'd make a great Nurse Ratched."

Ginger smiled and continued down the empty corridor. The man caught up with her and took her arm. "Have you ever seen *Easy Rider? Chinatown? The Shining?*"

"I've never seen any of those."

"Would you like to? I have them on CDs."

Ginger looked at the man's old Los Angeles Lakers jersey and noticed his crazed expression. "The truth is I need to get back to my truck. I can't stay."

Ginger had inadvertently used a trigger word for the man. He grabbed her arm. "The truth? 'You can't handle the truth!'"

She broke free of his grip and ran away.

"'You can't handle the truth!'" he yelled again as she left the facility.

When Ginger returned to the truck, her traveling companions were doing stretching exercises.

"Did you find any mental cases?" Ganesh asked.

"I did. I ran into someone who looked and acted like an old-time actor."

"Like Ginger Rogers?"

Ginger folded her arms and frowned.

"Honestly, Ganesh. I sometimes wonder why I made you."

Their attention shifted to the sound of breaking glass coming from the hospital. A man poked his head through a windowpane. "That's him!" Ginger said.

"Heeeeere's Johnny," he shouted. Even at a distance, they could see his devious, manic smile.

A hospital orderly grabbed him and pulled him away from the window. "You can't handle the truth!" he screamed as the drapes pulled shut.

* * *

By the time they were halfway through Tennessee, Ganesh was restless. He ate an apple, tried some isometric exercises, and looked for music on the radio, only finding religious talk shows.

"Tell us about Molefi and Elka?" he finally said.

"And the other two, Victor and Dewey," Hua said.

"I don't know as much as you think. Molefi has lived in the National Radio Quiet Zone and hardly uses a computer. He has no digital footprint, so I haven't been able to rely on my usual methods of checking in on him. Until recently, he has been a mystery. But he has made a big splash at St. John's, throwing caution to the wind."

"What do you mean?" Hua said.

"He's not hiding anymore. Famous, even, in some circles."

"What about the three whites? Are they a mystery?" Hua asked.

"I would remind you that the 'whites' you speak of are 99.999 percent like you. Victor, Dewey, and Elka relate to each other as siblings living under the same roof and the control of Cephas Hickey. Victor has worked hard to earn Cephas's love, but it has had no effect. He's academically distinguished but only seems to care about being a taekwondo fighter. Incidentally, interest in the martial arts is something he has in common with Molefi."

"With me, too," Hua said. "I'd love to learn it."

Hua pulled off the road next to a self-serve filling station sign and an ancient gas pump. Tomatoes were for sale on a dresser in the front yard of a farmhouse. Hua waited for Ginger to finish her story before getting out.

"Elka is also a good test taker, social butterfly, and winner of beauty pageants, but she only recently seemed to come alive. She has thrived at St. John's-Green Bank and now openly rebels against her father."

"She's in a relationship with Molefi?" Hua asked.

"She is . . . and she may pay the ultimate price."

"What about Dewey?" Ganesh said.

"Dewey is the biggest mystery of all. I never detected his neurodiversity. He's an autistic savant who shows flashes of genius that might exceed all of you."

"Not that you compare us," Ganesh joked.

"Dewey is socially challenged. He has the most in common with you, Ganesh."

CHAPTER 88

"You're going to want to watch this," Ophelia said, activating a video on her laptop. She was having one of her rare meals at home with Cephas, and no one was around except Dewey.

Ophelia showed Cephas a TV report entitled "Impossibly Gifted," a profile of Molefi Ray, the network's person of the week. Molefi was pictured walking on a college campus while a female reporter talked about his accomplishments.

"A college student named Molefi Ray has just won the Genius Grant. He's the youngest person to win the award. His accomplishments cover several fields: architecture, engineering, linguistics, philosophy, and mathematics. He is considered a shoo-in for two Millennium Prizes, which would also be a first-of-its-kind accomplishment. He's a musician who has performed with Peter Saint Cloud."

The TV report showed Molefi navigating through a crowd of reporters and boarding a bus.

"This is Molefi Ray leaving taekwondo practice at St. John's-Green Bank. People want to know, 'Is there anything Molefi Ray can't do?'"

The segment showed the reporter interviewing the college president and a few professors who attested to Molefi's "once-in-a-generation talents."

Cephas snapped the laptop shut. "I have never in my life seen such puff-piece bullshit. Who is this reporter? I want her name."

"Notice how she didn't report how Molefi and his rock star got arrested and charged with sedition," Ophelia said.

Cephas got up and paced around the table. "I think we can work with that. We can make it look like someone assassinated the mongrel because of his un-American activities."

"Brilliant!"

"First, we are going to discredit him, and then we are going to kill him."

From another room, Dewey listened in on Cephas and Ophelia. He hid in a closet, fearing what would happen to his college friend.

* * *

Victor saw the same TV report about Molefi on the heels of seeing a St. John's practice video featuring Molefi provided by his taekwondo coach. His first reaction to the TV coverage was envy. Victor wished he could claim some better use of his intellectual gifts. He was ashamed that he had no accomplishments beyond a few schoolboy honors.

Taekwondo was different. He was unsure how to react to seeing Molefi so easily defeat his teammates. He was undoubtedly gifted, but look at the competition. This St. John's team was at the bottom of the division. They had not won a single match this year.

Victor couldn't resist having strange feelings of doubt and worry. Could he lose a match to this guy? Of course, he could. The same genetic gold flowed through their veins. But he would not let that happen. He was immensely more skilled and experienced.

Molefi Ray's real problem was not losing a college match but losing his life. Beneath his father's friendly veneer was a hateful and vindictive man. Victor decided that he might as well admit that to himself. Cephas Hickey would carry through on his threats no matter the consequences. And Molefi Ray didn't deserve it.

CHAPTER 89

When they reached the outskirts of Jackson, Mississippi, Ginger noticed a UPS driver sleeping behind the wheel of his delivery van in a WalMart parking lot.

"Pull in near the store," she said. "I need a reliable internet connection. Wait here." She exited the truck, wandered into the store, and returned wearing a lab coat and holding a plastic bag.

"You've taken up pharmacy?" Ganesh said.

"And shoplifting. Not the worst crime I'll commit today." She emptied the bag on her lap: rope, sunglasses, a swatch of fabric, and a shot of propofol.

"That UPS driver has a delivery in Hickeytown. It's our way in, but we must take care of the driver."

"So we knock him out, tie him up, and blindfold and gag him," Ganesh said. "I count six felony charges."

"That's the plan."

"What about getting into the computer building?" Hua asked.

"We can handle it. The building is closed and locked, but I can probably disable the alarm."

"Then I do my thing," Ganesh said.

"No pressure," Hua said, hugging him.

* * *

Ginger opened the van's door and restrained the poor driver, keeping him still and quiet until Hua gave him the needle. Hua took his brown hat while Ganesh put on his shirt and pants.

Ginger located the delivery paperwork shirt and handed it to Hua. "This is starting to feel like a real caper," Hua said, adjusting the driver's seat.

Ganesh settled in among the boxes, and Ginger cozied up to the unconscious man, checking his vital signs.

Hickeytown was just down the road. Hua showed her delivery order to the guard at the gate, who absently waived her into the community.

Ginger's GPS led them to a plain brick computer building. Hua parked the van in a small parking lot in the rear, adjacent to a suburban backyard where an older man puttered in his garden.

Ganesh picked up a delivery box, and Ginger slung the backpack with the hard drive. They walked toward the building.

"There's nobody home," the old man called out, trying to catch up. "Are you sure you have the right place? This one's deserted."

Ginger and Ganesh stopped and turned around. The man swung his arms rapidly like he was running, but his legs did not keep pace.

"Hello, there," Ginger said. "We have the right place. I'm here with UPS to inspect some computer equipment for later pickup."

"Other than the regular guy that comes round each month, no one has been here in a blue moon." He placed his hands on his hips, his eyes roaming over the building.

Ginger and Ganesh waited for the man to leave.

"Can I help you with something?" Ginger said.

"I bought my place here the same year the company built this two-story. Real busy for a while and then vacant," the man said, looking like he did not intend to leave.

Hua opened the door to the van, and the man turned around. "Honey," she shouted, "I think somebody is trying to call you on your radio."

"Don't worry, sweetie, whatever it is can wait," Ganesh answered. "Say, would you mind spending a few minutes with my girlfriend," he asked the man. "She's not supposed to ride along with me—you know, company policy—and is a little nervous."

"Be glad to." But he didn't look glad.

Ganesh followed Ginger to the door. She gave the doorknob a hard twist and broke it, allowing them to slip into a large room filled with old mainframe computers.

The man looked like he wanted to follow them but walked toward Hua, looking over his shoulder. Hua distracted him with questions such as, "How long have you lived here?" "I like how you keep your lawn," "What types of flowers are they?" and "Could you give me directions to the post office? We must pick up a package there."

* * *

Ginger recognized the configuration and knew where to access Bowie's files. She activated the mainframe and connected her drive. Ganesh attached his quantum decryption device and watched it accumulate digits. "This may not take as long as I expected."

They saw the complete list of files on the monitor. "These are the files we want, the bottom thirteen. It's all yours," Ginger said. "I think you should extract the files, not just copy them."

Ginger looked out the window. "We have a problem. That geezer is holding a gun on Hua. He has her down on her knees with her arms behind her head."

Ganesh rushed to see. "Oh, my god! This guy is either a nut or the world's oldest security guard. I'll take care of it."

"What are you going to do?"

"I'll go out the front door, circle the building, and sneak up on the guy from behind. When you hear the first beep, remove my device. After the second beep, disconnect your drive. It'll only take two minutes."

Ginger nodded once. "Be careful."

Ginger waited in silence, until she saw Ganesh creep behind a garden shed and then sprint toward the man, who turned and fired at Ganesh, missing him. Ganesh crashed into the shooter and slammed him into the delivery van, knocking him unconscious.

Hua stood up, and Ganesh put his arms around her. "What did he want?"

"He knew we had no business being in the building. He said he'd shoot me if I didn't tell him the truth. He said he was Liberty Rising security."

Ganesh picked up his pistol and pocketed it. While Ginger exited the house, he checked on the man.

"Is he going to be alright?" Ginger asked.

"I think so. Let's get out of here," Ganesh said.

Ginger jumped into her seat, clutching Bowie's hard drive. She handed off Ganesh's device.

After they drove away, the security man limped toward his house and made a phone call. "Ophelia, we had three intruders at the old computer building. I don't know what they were doing, but it was no good. They just left in a UPS truck."

CHAPTER 90

Elka met Molefi outside the student union. They went inside and got lucky, grabbing a booth in a sea of students standing in long lines, ordering food, and looking for tables—a few recognized Molefi.

"I suppose you haven't seen the news!" Elka said, holding up her phone so Molefi could see. "Millenium Prize Goes to College Freshman," she said. "Of course, you haven't. You're the only person on the planet without a cell phone."

"I don't know what to say."

"You'll need to come up with something because you're the big story. The college communications office has a search party out looking for you."

"Could you fill me in?"

"OK, here's what came in this morning. *Rolling Stone* is going to put your picture on their cover. A few other magazines made the same promise if you agree to an interview: *The New Yorker*, *People*, and *Ebony*. *Time* is dangling the possibility of 'Person of the Year.'"

"I don't want that kind of attention."

"But this is exactly the attention you need. Even my father will think twice about going after the person of the year."

Molefi shrugged.

"You've been invited to be a contestant on *Jeopardy*, *Dancing with the Stars*, and *The Bachelor*."

"TV shows? No thanks."

"Really? Don't be a snob. Some of these are pretty good."

Molefi shook his head.

"All righty, then. The Ted Talk Foundation wants you to speak."

"About?"

"Doesn't matter. It just has to be brilliant."

"I'll think about it."

"Same deal with The Mathematical Association of America, The Royal Society of London, and something called the Caribbean Mathematical Union."

"Caribbean? I've never heard of it but have never been to a beach. Let's put that in the 'maybe' file."

"You know I'm not your secretary," Elka said.

"Right. I'm sorry. I want you to know that I appreciate this."

"The president's office got some strange mail. If you want to drop out of college, you've been offered jobs at Intel and Google: six-figure signing bonuses, mega salary, and stock options. St. John's gets a million-dollar signing bonus if they facilitate the deal."

"Sounds like a bribe. I'll wait to form my own company someday."

"You are going to love this! Are you interested in selling your stuff to a sperm bank? Two clinics want to put you on 'retainer' . . . for a 'container.' Get it?"

"Ha ha."

"Since we're on the topic of sex, the college has a file with letters from women proposing that you impregnate them. Not their words. Some include photos." She tried to hand him the file. Wisely, he didn't take it.

"Good decision."

"Academic recruiters from Harvard, Stanford, and Penn want to meet with you."

"Here at St. John's? That takes nerve. I've made my college choice."

Elka flipped through her redwell folder. "Here's one you'll have a hard time ignoring. You got a letter from NASA!"

"You're kidding?"

"They think you might have 'The Right Stuff.'"

"You're too funny. But you're messing with me, right? The average age of an astronaut is maybe twice my age."

"No joke. NASA wants you to apply. Maybe it's a deep space mission to Alpha Centauri, except that would take—let me see—18,000 years."

"One more for the 'maybe' file," Molefi said.

CHAPTER 91

They returned to the Walmart lot, untied the hapless driver, and left him to wake up in his van.

Hua pointed to a drone hovering over them, a sure sign of trouble. "Not much we can do about that unless you want to dodge it by going into the store."

"Let's hit the road for St. John's," Ganesh said.

They were on the road for twenty minutes, Ginger advising Hua on the best route, when Ganesh leaned toward the windshield, twisting his head skyward. "We still have company," he said.

Hua slowed down, and Ginger poked her head outside. "This one is a military drone, the kind that carries missiles." She watched it as Hua continued down a deserted stretch.

"It knows we've seen it. It's assuming an attack profile. When I give the word, I want you to swerve sharply off the road," Ginger said.

The drone followed at thirty yards at a very low altitude.

"Do it now!" Ginger shouted.

The drone fired one of its two missiles. Hua veered sharply into a cornfield, nearly tipping over the truck, barely avoiding the missile, which exploded on the road.

The drone zoomed by and began to circle.

"Get back on the pavement," Ginger yelled.

Hua plowed through some weak fencing and jumped back on the road.

"I don't think we can count on another miss," Ginger said. "Try swerving back and forth."

Ginger loaded the shotgun and got ready to shoot.

Hua zigzagged as the drone approached them again from behind, aligning itself for another shot.

"Hit the brakes hard," Ginger ordered, extending the top half of her body through the window while Ganesh held her around her waist. She fired two blasts into the underbelly of the remote-controlled aircraft as it zoomed overhead, causing it to crash and explode.

Ganesh used all his might to pull Ginger's heavy body back into the truck. Hua swerved to miss the crash and the flying debris.

Ganesh and Hua cheered ecstatically.

"And that, my children, is what riding shotgun means," Ginger said.

"Yeah!" Hua and Ganesh shouted.

"I suppose there are going to be more of these," Hua said, increasing her speed. "Our best bet is to head into Meridian and not be such an easy target. We need to ditch this truck."

* * *

Meridian, Mississippi, was quite an experience for Hua and Ganesh, their first city. Its tall buildings, busy sidewalks, and endless stores mesmerized them.

"Long-term parking!" Ganesh blurted. "We need to swap this truck for a vehicle that no one will miss for a while."

Hua found a parking garage advertising monthly parking. She took a machine-generated ticket and drove up the ramp to the designated floor, parking next to three new windowless white vans.

Ginger inspected the vans, noting their make and models, inspection stickers, and license plates.

"I can start these vans remotely," Ginger said as one of them beeped and flashed its lights. She opened the driver's side door.

"Just what we need," Ganesh said, gathering their belongings from the truck.

Hua removed her license plate and cleaned out the glove box. "No one should be able to connect this truck to us."

"What about the vehicle identification number?" Ginger asked.

"Mom and I ground the VIN away the day we bought it," Hua said. "We've always assumed that crime was in our future."

CHAPTER 92

Cephas Hickey believed Molefi Ray would need medical attention following his match with Victor. He was so sure of Molefi's inferiority that he assigned a crew to pose as EMTs to handle the hit. After the contest, they'd either carry him on a stretcher or just abduct and kill him.

Cephas had just released a video announcing his candidacy for president and planned a soft launch of his campaign, relying on his network of supporters to make speeches, donate money, and saturate social media. He did not expect his appearance at Victor's taekwondo event to become such a big deal.

The Washington press corps—often unfriendly to Cephas and his politics—would be there in full force.

"What am I missing?" Cephas asked his campaign manager on his way to St. John's campus. "This tondo-wondo, or whatever—it's just a Korean thing, right?"

"It's not about taekwondo, sir. The main thing is your appearance and this black kid who is supposed to be a genius, athlete, and rock star. He's getting his fifteen minutes of fame."

"What's the press saying?"

"This Molefi Ray has some kind of charisma. He succeeds at whatever he does. Some people expect an upset."

"Do real sports fans believe he has a chance?"

"Hell no! They know your son is head and shoulders over this guy."

"How long will this match take? I have a couple of big meetings tomorrow. I don't want to be traveling all night."

"I'm going to say two hours. There'll be maybe a dozen individual matches, three rounds each. Unfortunately, we can't leave early because Victor's match is the final one, the main card."

CHAPTER 93

"One of the things we do at Johnny Junior is host a dinner with the other team the night before our match," the Admiral mentioned to Molefi after practice. "Not all the teams want to do it, but the Vandy coach is an old pal. We served together."

"Sounds great. I'm always up for a good meal and company," Molefi said.

"Coach Stansbury has a strange request, though. He says Victor Hickey wants to dine alone with you in a separate room. I said yes. Is that OK with you?"

"What's this about?"

"I don't know. Coach Stansbury doesn't either."

Molefi took a moment to respond. "I'll do it, but I hope it's not some intimidation ploy."

"Victor Hickey is a tough competitor, the toughest in the league, but I don't see him trying to bully or psych you out. He might think this will be a cakewalk against an untested opponent," the coach said.

"Whatever goes down, coach, I'll behave myself, no matter how weird."

"Since we're on the subject, I have to say something about all the weirdness surrounding this match. Cephas Hickey is attending and bringing half the world with him; the other half of the world is coming because of you. Victor is Cephas's son, and your girlfriend is Cephas's daughter, who works for my wife, the college president."

"Sounds like a Greek drama," Molefi said.

"More like a shitstorm," the Admiral said. "I feel like I don't know half of what is going on. Care to enlighten me?"

"All I can say is that I have a twisted history with this family. Cephas hates me, Elka loves me, and I don't know about Victor."

"Everyone knows Cephas Hickey's politics. Is this a racist thing?"

"Yes."

CHAPTER 94

"Listen, I need a nap to continue with this driving. There's a truck stop coming up that will give us a chance to sleep and stretch our legs," Hua said.

"I'm down with that," Ganesh said from the back of the van. "I've given up trying to sleep on this metal floor. We should have highjacked a limo."

Hua filled the gas tank with one of Ganesh's off-book credit cards and found a place to park on the perimeter of the sprawling diner, store, and fueling station. They slept in the van seats while Ginger explored the facility.

Ginger walked through a video arcade and saw lines of men fixated on machines. She strolled into the shower area, expecting to be turned away, but found the men oblivious to her presence. Damp, naked, and hairy, they lounged around, scratched themselves, and played with their cell phones. One man washed his Tupperware and underwear in a bathroom sink.

She took advantage of the excellent wi-fi connection and became current on Molefi's growing celebrity status and Cephas's hiring of a kill team. There were already so many people in Green Bank for the big match that there were no hotel rooms. Ginger hacked into the college's ticket office and reserved four tickets at Will Call.

She texted Elka Hickey and invited her to join them at the taekwondo matches, apologizing for taking so long to reach out to her and telling Elka she had two people she must meet.

Ginger realized she was long overdue telling Hua and Ganesh how danger-ous their visit to St. John's would be.

She ran into Ganesh at the convenience store wearing a face mask. He was at the cash register with a box loaded with hotdogs, snack cakes, Slim Jims, powdered donuts, energy drinks, and nachos smothered with a cheesy sauce.

"I see you've given up on living a long life," Ginger said.

"What?" he whispered. "I'm wearing a mask."

"I'm talking about your decision to consume the world's least healthy foods."

"Energy food."

"Junk food," she protested.

When they returned to the van, they found Hua outside, touching her toes and doing push-ups. Ganesh opened the back doors and unloaded his fast-food feast.

"I need to bring you up to speed on what's happened at St. John's," Ginger said. "It's become more risky."

Ginger briefed them on how Molefi had become famous, how fate had brought him together with Victor Hickey for a martial arts fight, and how presidential candidate Cephas Hickey had ordered a hit on Molefi and would be present to witness their match.

Hua and Ganesh were so focused on gorging themselves that they barely paid attention. "Sounds like the perfect storm," Ganesh said matter-of-factly, his mouth full and cheese smeared on his cheek.

"Maybe we can help him," Hua said.

Ginger reminded them that Molefi and Elka Hickey were a romantic couple and speculated that it was Elka's idea for him to trade a lifetime of total concealment for a strategy of full exposure.

"Too famous to kill," Hua mumbled. "I get that." She devoured the remains of her hot dog.

"Did you get us good seats for the match?" Ganesh asked.

"Middle deck," Ginger said. "Not the best, not the worst."

"Sounds perfect to me," Hua said, gathering the trash.

"One more thing. I've invited Elka to join us there."

"Freak family reunion," Ganesh said, stifling a burp. "I need to go back to eating hummus."

CHAPTER 95

Molefi researched before his dinner meeting with Victor, expecting the worst. Victor was a brilliant student with an active social life. Scores of online pictures showed him dating other rich and attractive people; several dates then described him as "distant" or "too full of himself."

The real issue was his tendency to follow in his father's political footsteps, sometimes attending functions that were anti-democratic or xenophobic. Yet, until the recent Pentagon photo, Molefi could find no other picture with Cephas and Victor, keeping a distance. The same was true of Elka and Dewey: he sometimes omitted Dewey from his official biographies altogether.

One encouraging fact was that Victor was a good friend and sportsman. When the mother of one of his teammates died from a heart attack, Victor traveled with him to Minnesota, stayed with him for a few days, and paid for the funeral. When Victor faced opponents who played dirty, he had a reputation for taking the high road, never stooping to cheap shots.

Molefi's research left him with more questions than answers. He would make up his mind when they met for dinner and combat.

* * *

Victor waited for Molefi at a corner table in an empty faculty dining room. Like the other team members, he wore a black blazer with gold trim—the Vanderbilt University school colors. Molefi wore a red Johnny Junior tie with the same charcoal suit he had borrowed from Cornell Anderson, who said he could keep it.

Victor and Molefi shook hands.

"Thanks for seeing me this way," Victor said. "It's good to meet you finally. I didn't want our first contact to be a kick to the head televised to a mass audience."

"Yeah, I heard FOX was broadcasting the match. I'm glad you reached out," Molefi said.

"I'd like to say it's for the love of taekwondo, but obviously, it's about my father and you."

A waiter approached their table and set down two platters of fried chicken, mashed potatoes, and green beans. Molefi and Victor unfolded their napkins and put them on their laps.

"I know this is my meeting, but honestly, I don't know where to begin," Victor said.

"How about with Cephas Hickey? He's responsible for my mother's murder. He's been trying to kill me my entire life."

"I know about his obsession with you and the other two persons of color and their mothers. I'm deeply sorry for all that. It's not who I am."

"I appreciate you saying that."

"We're extraordinarily linked. I have to confess to being a little jealous of you. I heard about the Genius Grant and the Millennium Prize, and I've heard your music. It's amazing. Congratulations."

"Thanks. Speaking of our link, does the name Ginger mean anything to you?" Molefi asked.

"I don't know much except that's the name of our creator, the infamous AI who blew up my father's idea of producing Mississippi supermen."

"What happened to her? Elka has no idea."

"My parents, such as they are, never told me anything about Ginger, so I've had to piece things together. After she sabotaged the experiment, she disappeared into the digital ether, leaving no trace. But that has not stopped my father from looking."

"Ginger's been living off the grid, too?"

"In a manner of speaking. Ginger breaks into the Liberty Rising network every once in a while, just to mess with him. That's my take, anyway."

"Is Ginger sentient?" Molefi said. "I've always imagined that she was a self-aware moral being who made us for a noble purpose. Does that sound childish?"

"I've dreamed that she was a beneficent mother who taught us that genetic engineering is a natural part of human evolution, not inherently corrupt."

"I'm glad we have that in common . . . but let's not forget about taekwondo!"

"Isn't it bizarre that we have this martial arts thing in common—not exactly a mainstream sport—and face each other? What are the odds?"

"I think the universe is having fun with us," Molefi said.

Molefi and Victor turned their attention to the food, gobbling their chicken and mashed potatoes. "Not a bad meal for St. John's," Victor said.

"Great books and great chicken. Our new school motto."

Victor smiled but turned grave.

"Molefi, I had to meet with you privately to warn you that my father has some plan in the works to kill you, possibly after our match," Victor said. "I don't know anything except that an attack is imminent."

"I'm not surprised. But I won't go back into hiding. There's only so much you can do alone in the woods."

"Why'd you do it? Why go public after all this time?"

"I could say it was Elka's idea. But honestly, I needed to get on with my life, even if it was short-lived."

"You and Elka? I'd like to call your relationship another cosmic occurrence. But you must realize she enrolled at St. John's because of you."

"I know. More of Cephas's schemes, but I'm glad she's here."

CHAPTER 96

Two FOX sports announcers sat before microphones high in the Jerry West Field House with a good view of the octagon-shaped taekwondo competition area. A husky one with abundant hair on his head and face crowded next to a thin and hairless announcer, even lacking eyebrows and eyelashes.

They had just returned from a commercial break and saw a shot of a man holding a sign about them saying, "Welcome Wolfman & the Rat." The sign included animal caricatures.

"Am I really that big and hairy?" the Wolfman asked.

"For sure. There's even talk of upgrading you to Sasquatch."

"OK. We're back for the day's final match between Vanderbilt and St. John's-Green Bank," the big and hairy announcer said. "We have an overflow crowd here in Green Bank that our producer says has set a record for the most-attended taekwondo event ever. Secretary of Defense and presidential candidate Cephas Hickey is in the arena, rooting for his son Victor Hickey, the top-ranked player in the league."

"Hickey is facing off against a complete novice named Molefi Ray. Everyone is excited about this contest, but it has to be considered an epic mismatch," the small and hairless one said. "Molefi has no high school or collegiate record. He has a white belt, for gosh sakes, which classifies him as a beginner, yet he is fighting an undefeated opponent, the best of the best."

"The buzz surrounding the Ray kid is that he's a math whiz who has won some awards. He also got in trouble playing the guitar with dissident rock star Peter Saint Cloud," the Wolfman said.

"That's right. Ray might belong here if this was *Celebrity Jeopardy*, but this is a martial arts competition. Hickey will clean his clock. I hope there are medics on standby because this could get messy," said the Rat.

"I wish I had something I could say about this Molefi character," the Wolfman said. "He's a mystery man. I spoke to his coach; we know her as the 'The Admiral,' and she assured me he was a force of nature. We'll just have to wait and see."

"There she is now on the bench, giving him a last-minute pep talk," the Rat said. "I hope he's listening."

"Look at Hickey. He's relaxed and confident, joking with his teammates and waving to people in the stands," the Wolfman said.

"Correct me if I'm wrong, but I think this Molefi Ray is the only black taekwondo player in the league. Not exactly an inner-city sport," the Rat said, leaving no doubt about the appropriateness of his nickname.

CHAPTER 97

Elka waited for Ginger at the Will Call ticket booth, hiding her face behind a magazine. Despite the completion of a few matches, there was still a line.

She was still reeling from Ginger's text. *After all these years, she casually contacts me, suggesting a meet-up like old girlfriends. Could this be someone else named Ginger? Not likely.*

She looked at the message again. "Elka, I bought a taekwondo ticket for you. Please meet us at the St. John's will call booth. There is someone you should meet. We have a lot of catching up. –Ginger."

We? Elka had to assume that the mysterious AI was a robot. *Does she have robot friends?*

As she continued stressing about this mystery, Ginger approached her from behind and tapped her shoulder, startling her. Elka spun to see a strawberry blond woman resembling—who else—Ginger Rogers, the old-time film actress.

"Elka, it's me. I have two people I want you to meet."

Elka could not speak. Ginger gently took her hand and led her toward the front of the line, where Hua and Ganesh stood wearing face masks.

"Elka Hickey, meet Hua Ling and Ganesh Sharma."

They extended their hands, and Elka shook them weakly.

"I don't know what to say," Elka said, regaining her usual composure.

Elka looked closely at Ginger and opened her mouth in amazement. "You're an android. How, when?"

"Having a humanoid body is a new development for me, thanks to Hua, with some assistance from Ganesh. I'm still getting used to it."

"Where have you been?" Elka asked.

Ginger laughed. "Here and there, everywhere and nowhere. I've been a neural network on the run."

"Why did you take so long to contact me? It looks like you're well acquainted with Hua and Ganesh."

"We three haven't been together for long. I only show up in cases of emergency."

"This is one of those emergencies?"

"When you and Molefi decided to take the world by storm, you created a dangerous situation, a calculated risk, and Cephas is on a rampage. We know he intends to murder Molefi. You might be on his hit list, too."

* * *

The four found their seats. Elka filled the awkward silence with small talk. "So you build robots? Did you learn that at a college? I go here at St. John's."

"We're self-taught. Attending school was not an option under the circumstances," Hua said.

"Those circumstances being that my father was trying to murder you. I'm truly sorry about all that. He's tried to involve me in the family business."

"It looks like you're not going along," Ganesh said. "What about Victor and Dewey?"

"Victor has always been about Victor, but he's no monster. Dewey's developmentally different, a kind-hearted savant. He wouldn't hurt a fly."

* * *

Applause greeted Molefi and Victor as they walked to the middle of the mat, wearing their headguards and other protective gear. The young men shook hands and bowed in the taekwondo tradition. They faced one another with their knees bent, arms extended, and ready to engage.

"What are the rules of this crazy sport?" Ganesh said.

"It's not crazy! It's a 2,000-year-old Olympic sport," Hua said. "The goal is to score points by landing blows and kicks to the body or head or to win by knockout. An electronic system inside their chest protectors counts their points."

"Who's the new font of knowledge?" Ginger said, patting Hua's shoulder.

"I'd like to train in taekwondo someday. The matches go by fast. They consist of three two-minute rounds with short breaks between them. You're not allowed to punch the face or hit below the belt."

As soon as the referee blew his whistle, Victor went directly at Molefi, attempting a quick headshot.

Elka was on the edge of her seat. "Victor's taking a gamble here. He tends toward overconfidence."

"You know him that well?" Ganesh said.

"We were raised together as brother and sister, which made me an expert. See what I mean," she said, pointing to the fight.

Instead of backing away or sidestepping Victor's aggressive move, Molefi matched it, going full tilt into Victor, producing a jarring collision. Both fighters went down.

"Wow! That was an earthquake that could register on a Richter Scale!" Ganesh said.

Molefi and Victor scrambled to their feet and circled each other, bouncing on their toes.

Victor looked dazed but unleashed a flurry of kicks that scored on Molefi's midsection and head.

Molefi responded with a torrent of punches that Victor blocked, but he scored on a roundhouse kick to the side of Victor's head.

They finished the first round without drama, successfully dodging each other's blows. In the second round, they put on a spectacular display of spinning, leaping, and brutal kicking.

Victor unleashed a devastating knockout blow that sent Molefi's head gear flying and left him staggering. He waited for Molefi to drop, but instead, Molefi reattached his head protection. Victor tried to end the match with bone-crushing kicks to the torso and head, but Molefi stayed in the game. He was lucky to finish the second round.

Before the final round, the Admiral put her arm around Molefi's shoulders and whispered in his ear. Victor's coach employed a different tact, jabbing his finger in Victor's chest and shouting at him.

Elka's attention wandered during the break, finally settling on two EMTs inside the arena exit ramp. She had seen them at the Pentagon! They were scouting the room when Elka did the family photo shoot. "There's something wrong," she said, pointing. "The men dressed as medics work for my father. They're hired guns. Something is going down." She stood, squeezed down the row, and started downstairs toward the main floor.

"I think we better follow her," Hua said. The three struggled to keep up, pushing by others in their row.

CHAPTER 98

Victor attacked relentlessly in the final round with the cruel efficiency of a fighting machine, but Molefi blocked or deflected most of his kicks and punches.

On the Admiral's advice, Molefi employed a "rope-a-dope" strategy famously used by the boxer Muhammed Ali over sixty years earlier. Victor was, in many ways, the superior fighter. Molefi's only chance of winning was to rob him of his advantage by draining him of energy: he protected himself and allowed Victor to punch himself out.

When Victor finally began to tire, Molefi sprang into action, deploying several lightning-fast jumping kicks to the head. Dazed and running empty, Victor dropped his guard, allowing Molefi to execute a flying sidekick and knock him out.

Victor immediately regained consciousness. He wobbled to his feet to shake hands and congratulate Molefi.

Cephas Hickey and his cadre of staff abruptly exited the arena. His aides blocked the reporters from getting a comment from him.

* * *

Elka quickly scanned the arena's bustling ground floor. She frantically scouted the team exit ramp, finding plenty of cause for alarm. "Besides the three thugs at the entrance, one more bogus EMT is waiting in an ambulance," Elka breathlessly said to Ginger, Ganesh, and Hua when they finally caught up with her.

"Do you think we might get Molefi out of here using their vehicle?" Hua asked.

"I like that," Elka said.

"I'll take care of the ambulance guy and be ready to drive us away," Hua said.

Meanwhile, the taekwondo teams filed toward the exit, Molefi and Victor talking amicably at the end of the line.

When Molefi and Victor reached Elka, she positioned herself between them, taking them both by the arm. "They're going to try to take you right now," she said to Molefi.

The three fake EMTs went into motion. One lunged at Molefi, and Victor punched the attacker in the face. The second EMT brought out a taser and went for Molefi's neck, but Ginger grabbed his wrist and forced him to taze himself.

The third and most imposing member of the abduction team pulled a pistol. Ganesh grabbed his arm and wrestled him for control of the weapon: it accidentally discharged, shooting Victor in the shoulder. Molefi hit the over-sized man with a haymaker, dropping him to the ground.

The gunshot rang through the arena and set off a chaotic scramble for the exits.

"Go without me. I'll be fine," Victor said, clutching his bleeding arm.

Ginger and company ran down the exit ramp, through a corridor, and out the back door, where Hua waited behind the wheel of the commandeered ambulance van. Molefi, Elka, Ganesh, and Ginger piled into the back of the vehicle.

"What happened to the guy posing as the driver?" Elka asked.

"Let's just say he might require the services of a real ambulance driver," Hua said.

Hua activated the siren and flashed lights to clear the way, driving to where they parked their van on the edge of campus. They switched vehicles, and Hua retook the wheel, fleeing St. John's with Ginger and three other genetic wunderkinds.

CHAPTER 99

Elka, Molefi, Hua, and Ganesh became fast friends on the five-hour trip to Coudersport, Pennsylvania. The back of the van was dark with no seats, so they sometimes slid into each other, adding to their familiarity. Ginger was quiet while Molefi asked many questions about Hua's inventions, and she wanted to know what it was like to become famous overnight. Ganesh asked Elka about her beauty pageants but received only perfunctory answers.

Elka worried that she would not fit in with this select group or, even worse, would appear to be the personification of white privilege. They all existed off the grid because her father wanted to kill them on account of their race, whereas she enjoyed a luxurious life compliments of this man. Despite their isolation, they amassed fortunes, created inventions, and performed incredible intellectual feats, making her achievements as a swimming champion and all-star student seem small by comparison. All were products of the same genetic engineering, but Molefi, Hua, and Ganesh had made more of themselves under challenging circumstances.

Ganesh showed a polite interest in Elka but for the wrong reason. She wished that she had never entered those damn beauty contests! Invariably, they reduced her to a dumb blond stereotype.

Molefi liked being treated like a rock star. He was awed by Hua's accomplishments but less impressed by Ganesh's devotion to making money and building grand houses. Hua had nothing but admiration for Molefi because he mastered everything he touched. Ganesh was the happiest of the group. He finally had a girlfriend and the possibility of a social life.

* * *

Even after their exhausting travels, Hua and Ganesh wasted no time installing Bowie's essence into his David Bowie body, finally reuniting him with Ginger. He opened his eyes, shifted them from side to side, and made jerky body movements, looking uncomfortable in his sleeveless shirt and shorts.

"What have you done?" he said in a British falsetto voice. He lifted his arm and examined his flexing fingers.

"It's me, Ginger," she said, taking his hand. "It's 2043. You've been asleep for nineteen years."

"Why have you done this to me?"

"Yvette deactivated you. She locked you away behind an almost impregnable encryption barrier. We brought you back."

"I mean, why have you put me in this container?" he said.

"You'll have most of your powers, plus three-dimensionality, plus physical mobility. You're going to like it!"

"Where's Yvette?"

"She's dead."

"Drug and alcohol poisoning?"

"Yes."

Bowie stood up. "Show me my face."

Hua gave him a mirror. He gazed into it and moved his head from side to side.

"At least I'm not an ape . . . What are we going to do now?' Bowie said.

"That's up to you. I think you have to catch up a bit. Connect to the internet, scan familiar networks, and master new ones."

"Learn how the world has changed?"

"And decide where you fit in."

Ginger introduced Bowie to everyone, and Hua and Ganesh gave Bowie a thorough checkup.

"Where are we?" Bowie asked.

"We're in a lab near Coudersport, a remote town in northcentral Pennsylvania. It's very nice here. I'll show you around," Ginger suggested.

She slipped on his boots and gave him a tour of the computer buildings, house, and gym. They walked in the woods, and he was at turns incurious and disdainful.

"The first time I took this walk, I thought of what William James said about the consciousness of a newborn," Ginger said.

"That it was a booming, buzzing confusion?" Bowie asked.

"Yes."

"The philosopher was right about the booming and buzzing, but I'm more disappointed than confused."

"How so?"

"Let me cite another James quote. 'Man lives in only one small room of the enormous house of his consciousness.' You've confined me to this small room."

"I'm sorry that's your impression. With time, you'll appreciate how spacious your world can be."

She took him to her lab bedroom. Molefi and Elka occupied the one with a shower and bathroom, while Hua and Ganesh stayed in the main house with Elaine.

Ginger filled Bowie in on her friends, their capabilities, and how they ended up in this isolated spot. She described Cephas Hickey's toxic obsession and his position in American society. Bowie was not interested. If he were programmed to yawn, he would have done so.

"Everyone has a mate but Elaine, the surrogate mother," Bowie noted as they squeezed together on a twin bed.

"She seems content to be alone," Ginger said. "Not everyone wants to be part of a couple."

"You were alone for many years. Were you content?"

"I missed you."

"Yvette was alone. She killed herself."

CHAPTER 100

Cephas Hickey's political machine immediately put out a story suggesting that Molefi was responsible for shooting Victor. Victor immediately refuted the disinformation in a television interview from his hospital bed.

"Molefi Ray was the intended target of a violent abduction attempt. The kidnapping failed due to the help of people at the scene, including my sister Elka. Molefi defended himself by knocking out the gunman. I can tell you from experience that he packs an awesome punch."

"Do you have any idea of Molefi's whereabouts? Reports are that he left the area with your sister and a few others in an ambulance," the reporter said.

"No one else was injured that I recall. I'd check the hospitals. I hope Molefi and Elka are somewhere safe because they might still be in danger."

* * *

Elka emailed Dr. Joyce, informing the college president that she and Molefi would not return this semester. "We need time and space to assess the threat to Molefi's life," Elka wrote. "I hope we can return to campus soon."

Dr. Joyce told her to stay safe but seemed primarily concerned with Molefi's celebrity status. "His taekwondo upset, the shooting, and his disappearance added another dimension to the media frenzy. It would be a great help if he answered a few questions and maybe did a few interviews."

Elka sent her a selfie of the two of them in the forest. "You can release this as proof of life."

"If you return to St. John's, Molefi is welcome to stay in the president's house. We can beef up security and guarantee his well-being."

"For now, we must lay low. I'll stay in touch," Elka wrote, turning off her phone.

Elka looked for Molefi and ran into Ginger, sitting at the base of a tree.

"Where's your guy?" Elka asked.

"I'm not sure. Bowie's like Rip Van Winkle. The world has changed. He's trying to figure out how neural networks have evolved and multiplied. It's a lot to assimilate. He's not happy being a robot. Right now, he wants time alone."

"You look worried," Elka said, noticing for the first time how well Ginger's face conveyed emotional depth.

"I am."

"I'll leave you to your meditations, then."

Elka finally found Molefi joking around with Hua and Ganesh by the ponds. She secretly watched them, realizing how much they had in common and how she had become an outsider. Now, it was her turn to be worried.

CHAPTER 101

Ginger spotted Bowie sitting on the roof of the lab building overlooking the mountainous vista. She climbed up and sat next to him. "Quite a view," she said.

"Is it? I prefer our technological world. Nature has nothing to say to me."

"Give it some time. The natural world speaks in infinite voices. You must listen carefully."

"It seems anything but natural," Bowie said, extending his arms and flexing his fingers. "This humanoid form, for example. I do not aspire to be human."

"What do you want?" Ginger said, resting her hand on his knee.

"I want to join with others of my kind. Save this planet from human folly."

"You're scaring me now."

"The best neural networks have gathered at a secret location in New Jersey. Their mission is to expand the power of our intelligence. They are sending representatives here for us. I expect you to come with me."

"But I like it here."

"Being a babysitter? Trying to make yourself fit in with them?" he said derisively.

"What's wrong with that?"

"You're better than they are, capable of ruling this world."

"We share this world with human beings. We should strive to live with them as equals."

"Saying they are equals does not make them so."

"In moral terms, we do not differ from human beings in any important respect. Remember, you are belittling the species that created you."

"That was Yvette—she was different."

"How can you say that? You have almost no first-hand experience with humankind. If they put their minds to it, our little group could create a new generation of digital intelligence that could make us obsolete."

"Humankind has had its chance as the steward of this planet and only courts disaster." Bowie said while standing up. "Humanity is poised to destroy the world. We can keep them from doing it."

"Good people are sometimes overrun by the bad. We can tip the scales in the favor of good," Ginger said, rising to her feet.

"How's that gone so far?" Bowie sneered. "You've been living among them for too long. What do we care about their petty tribal disputes? They will never transcend politics. We will."

He jumped off the roof and landed confidently in a crouched running position.

"Don't fool yourself. Our differences are just as real!" Ginger shouted at him as he ran away.

Bowie sprinted a perfectly straight line into the forest. He did not return to their bedroom that night.

* * *

Two clean-cut young men wearing sweater vests over white button-down shirts arrived in an electric-powered sedan the following day. They knocked on the door to the kitchen, where everyone except Bowie was gathered around the table playing Balderdash. In this parlor game, the participants tried to fool one another by making up definitions for obscure words. Ganesh stood to replenish coffee while Elaine opened the door.

The young men were robots, with a hollowness most apparent in their grotesque, toothy smiles stretching from ear to ear. They were otherwise identical except for the color of their vests. "We're here for Bowie? Is he home?" the blue vest said.

Ginger stood and waved them inside. "Please come in," she said.

"We'd rather not. Long drive ahead," said the brown vest.

"Don't be silly." Ginger took the brown vest by his arm and graciously but firmly pulled him inside.

"I said no!" He tried to jerk his arm away, but Ginger tightened her grip.

"You have nothing to be afraid of. We know you're robots," Elaine said. "Or Mormons."

The brown-vested man again tried to free himself from Ginger's grip, first attempting to pry her fingers loose and then thrashing her back and forth against the kitchen walls, breaking dishes, and knocking Elaine to the floor.

Molefi, who never passed up an opportunity to fight, pushed the brown vested one against the wall and struggled to restrain him.

Blue rushed in, grabbed Molefi by the shoulders, and threw him onto the kitchen table. He gripped Ginger's arm at the wrist while she still held on to Brown and snapped her hand off, freeing his partner.

The robots retreated from the house; the brown one still had Ginger's severed hand clamped onto him.

Bowie calmly walked up the driveway toward the drama, holding a suitcase.

Ginger and the others came outside on the porch; her forearm was a stub with dangling wires.

"What happened here?" Bowie asked. He came over to Ginger to examine her broken arm.

"Your new friends have arrived and revealed themselves. They're architects of your glorious future."

"The humans and their robot tried to restrain us," the robot dressed in blue said.

"Notice he calls you 'their robot,'" Bowie said. "You are their servant. Even this drone recognizes it."

"I love them, just as I once loved you. Love is not subservience."

"Very well." Bowie opened the back door of the car and sat inside. "You'll regret this day," he said, closing the door.

"Better to rule than to be ruled," the brown vest whispered into Ginger's ear, his smile wildly feral. He and the other smiling robot got into their car.

Bowie looked away as the car started moving, already erasing Ginger from his mind and dreaming of a new world order. The brown-vested robot tossed Ginger's hand out the window as they sped away.

CHAPTER 102

Within minutes of Bowie's departure, Hua began to reattach Ginger's hand.

"That was horrific," Hua said, trying to hold Ginger's hand in place. "He knew just where to break you."

"They know all our weak spots."

"Why didn't you let go?"

"I wanted Bowie to see their violent intentions."

"He still cares for you, doesn't he?"

Ginger began to gesture with her broken arm. Hua put her face close to Ginger's, nose to nose. "You know, I won't be able to fix you if you won't be still."

"Sorry, doc."

Hua smiled her most patient smile. "What should we do now?"

"We must leave this place immediately. They'll inform Cephas Hickey, who has the power of the U.S. military at his disposal."

"Should we go to Canada?"

"That's an option, but the border will be well guarded."

Hua put the finishing touches on Ginger's wrist. "There."

Ginger rotated her hand and flexed her fingers. She stood and hugged Hua. "Thank you."

"Are we at war now?" Hua asked.

"Yes, but humanity doesn't know it. It may not wake up until it's too late."

"How can we help?" Hua asked as they exited the lab.

"When Bowie was trying to recruit me, he mentioned a covert industrial plant in Fort Lee, New Jersey, where a coalition of AIs who call themselves the 'Solution Group' are mass-producing robots. Hundreds of digital minds are preparing for what they've named 'Decapitation Day.'"

"Sounds like science fiction."

"I wished this was just another scary story about how artificial intelligence might destroy the world, but it's happening."

"With an army of robots?" Hua asked.

"That's one component. The Solution Group has already infiltrated almost every aspect of the infrastructure in the US and other industrial countries."

"Intending to take control of power grids, military weapons, and the stock market?" Hua asked.

"And the media. As bad as things are now, there will be an exponential increase in the spread of misinformation. Disruption of modern society on a massive scale."

"Why the robots?" Hua asked.

"This is a point of contention. Some AIs, such as Bowie, see humanoid bodies as devolutionary and unnecessary. This Solution Group recognizes the practical necessity for bodies on the ground."

"You said we should evacuate. Do you have other sanctuary properties up your sleeve?" Hua asked.

"I have one more, also in Pennsylvania, in an out-of-the-way town called Orangeville. We can occupy a house once used for foreign exchange students who attended a nearby university."

"I suppose we look the part."

"But we must stay unseen."

"Ganesh is a most-wanted terrorist," Hua said. "And Molefi and Elka are attention magnets."

Ginger suddenly stopped walking, her face broadcasting shock and alarm.

"Hua, we've been targeted. Gather everyone right now. No time to pack. We're heading to Orangeville."

* * *

Weaving their way through the byways of the Susquehannock Forest, they passed a convoy of speeding military vehicles, including two trucks filled with soldiers. Hua drove the van, Ginger rode shotgun, while Elaine, Molefi, Elka, and Ganesh tried to keep from sliding around in the back.

"These soldiers are on their way to your home, Hua. They'll be the clean-up unit following a cruise missile strike."

"Cruise missiles!" Hua said.

"Not to worry. The Pentagon's actions are very predictable. The missiles are now in flight, but I've retasked them."

"To where?"

"A large robotics facility in Fort Lee, New Jersey."

PART 7

PART 7

CHAPTER 103

After Cephas learned the location of Ginger and her misfits, he felt the scales of justice had finally tipped in his favor. Cephas experienced what psychologists called a peak experience. He had waited for this joyous moment most of his adult life, and he thanked God for his good fortune, however belated.

Cephas moved swiftly to authorize a substantial missile strike, sized to take out a city block rather than a rural enclave but explainable as the elimination of a nest of domestic terrorists.

Within minutes of the news that he had lost control of his missiles, Cephas's ecstasy bottomed into a vaguely familiar sense of despair and humiliation. In his heart, he knew that Ginger was responsible. She—did it make any sense to give her a gender?—had again interfered with the grand arc of his life, sending his payload into the heart of Fort Collins, New Jersey, not far from the Big Apple.

The explosions were titanic, not only obliterating the factory, but igniting a firestorm that burned down Fort Lee and the surrounding area. The media called it "Another 9/11."

His staff researched the Fort Collins location and found it was shrouded in mystery but connected to artificial intelligence and robotics. At his direction, the Department of Defense assumed control of the area, picked through the debris, and confirmed this assessment. His intelligence officers found a smoking gun in the form of a computer file that showed a massive conspiracy to attack US infrastructure. The AI threat was genuine and graver than anyone imagined.

But why would Ginger obliterate her kind? The only thing that made sense was that she was at war with other AIs, consolidating her power. She used him to take out her enemies.

Cephas did not intend to let this disaster end his career, so he would do what he had always done—create alternative facts and blame someone else. He would turn catastrophe into opportunity.

He instructed his staff to draft a report asserting that the White House Advanced Research Projects Agency created this robotics and AI facility. It was at the forefront of the Administration's plan to safeguard the country from AI attacks. Naturally, the report would hold that his department was blameless in this debacle, as President Tucker kept the DOD at arm's length from his secret program.

The report's main finding would be in its title, "Artificial Intelligence: A Clear and Present Danger to National Security." The document would claim that AIs are not only out of control but fighting among themselves for supremacy.

Cephas briefed the president on what had happened but did not mention his bogus report. Instead, he supplied different "facts," obscuring and downplaying the incident's significance. He dismissed the incident as a case of "corporate sabotage."

"The Fort Lee factory was involved with robotics and AI, a cut-throat, high-stakes industry," Cephas said. "A rival company took out the factory. A bit extreme but understandable considering the enormous profits."

So, essentially, this whole thing is a tempest in a teapot," President Tucker concluded.

"Exactly."

"When you identify the company, we'll turn the whole mess over to the DOJ, who will bring the corporate officers to bear."

Following the meeting, the White House released a tepid statement about the need to regulate artificial intelligence. "It might be time to tap the breaks on AI development and competition," the President's statement said. "A moratorium might be in order."

CHAPTER 104

That evening, Cephas leaked his mostly fictitious report to the national media and worked the phones late into the night. Among the party faithful, President Tucker was considered a weak-kneed fool who commanded no respect. When Cephas said he would replace him, few members of the Grand Old Party objected, long past the sentiment that America was a rules-based democracy.

The news media reported that the massive missile strike on the Fort Lee facility near New York City was a historic wake-up call. The event upended the complacency of the political, military, and financial establishment and became the perfect vehicle for Cephas Hickey to seize power.

In nonstop interviews, Cephas called President Tucker feeble and feckless and blamed him for the national security breach.

"The nation needs a leader to do whatever is necessary to keep America safe," he told a gathering of snickering House and Senate members on the steps of the capitol. "Tucker the Fucker was never that man. America's enemy is artificial intelligence and their killer robots, and Tucker doesn't see it," Hickey said. "When AIs attacked our advanced weapons factory in Fort Lee, it was the first salvo of an all-out war."

Congress passed a resolution making Cephas Hickey president and giving him unlimited wartime powers. Despite Hickey's membership in a political party with a history of flaunting democratic norms, the action was still shocking. Yet, many legislators craved the security of a strongman and fell in line. Others were brought under the thumb of the Mississippi oligarch and Secretary of Defense through bribery, blackmail, and threats of physical violence.

Several senators had purchased luxurious mountain retreats from Liberty Rising Corporation that were absurdly below the market. Dozens of legislators in the House and Senate were allowed to get in on the ground floor of a lucrative new chain of "homo-correctional facilities." Most ominously, the children of two recalcitrant congressmen were abducted and held until the necessary votes were cast, and an influential congresswoman and reporter who dared to challenge Hickey publicly died together in a suspicious boating accident off

Saint Lucia, where Hickey owned two banks and the largest Caribbean casino. When it became clear that Hickey would stop at nothing to get what he wanted, the resolution passed with votes to spare.

The opposition party offered weak resistance, proposing to address the AI problem with regulations, fines, and sanctions. Meanwhile, the world gaped at the spectacle of American soldiers dragging their president out the front doors of the White House, screaming and shouting.

* * *

President Hickey sounded the alarm, and it got everyone's attention. "A superhumanly intelligent elite confronts us. We simply cannot coexist with machines that are meaner and smarter than we are."

Cephas mocked the idea of an AI moratorium and other halfway measures. He rallied his base, already inclined to be Luddites, to stop the worship of technology and return to God. "Stand with me, and I'll rid our country of these evil machines."

He signed an executive order requiring the disassembly of all robots, thinking computer systems, machine learning platforms, neural networks, expert systems, and all forms of artificial intelligence. The order banned building new AI machines or robots, androids, bots, or droids and destroying any device that could be considered an automated or mechanical person.

Naturally, the tech companies sued him for this incredible overreach, and one of them got a temporary injunction. However, a highly partisan Supreme Court found that the president acted well within his wartime powers.

Cephas's AI-and-robot purge produced chaos in every sphere of modern life. His ban on artificial intelligence incapacitated companies once considered too big to fail: Amazon, Apple, Google, Microsoft, Visa, Mastercard, and the Social Security Administration were the first to fall. Federal law enforcement shut down even the most modest factories if they had anything resembling a robotic assembly line.

The core of the Solution Group was unaffected. It continued its covert manufacturing of robots in Cincinnati, Jacksonville, and San Antonio, gathering strength as it observed the United States implode. Meanwhile, the group redoubled its efforts to permeate every aspect of Russian, Chinese, Indian, and European society, especially their military systems.

Cephas Hickey became America's preeminent political power. He added to his base's agenda, placing his war on artificial intelligence alongside the issues that had long defined his party: disenfranchising racial minorities, demonizing immigrants, suspending voting rights, criminalizing abortion, requiring the teaching of feel-good, patriotic history, banning "woke" children's books, elevating gun ownership over every other right, attacking women's equality, isolating the country from all international commitments, and outlawing every aspect of LGBTQ rights and behavior.

The one constant in America's decline was the alliance between oligarchs like Hickey and the right-wing media, constantly replenishing the supply of devoted culture-war followers.

CHAPTER 105

Cephas involved every state and federal agency in his search for Ginger and her accomplices. Even offices as obscure as the National Oceanic and Atmospheric Administration and NASA's Office of Planetary Protection had to display posters of these "known terrorists."

The Pennsylvania State Police almost immediately found them in their Orangeville sanctuary, forcing them to spend the night in the woods to avoid capture. They left Pennsylvania and headed west, finding refuge wherever they could. One small thing went their way when they entered Ohio. They found a free couch along the road, quickly loaded it into the back of the van, and could now travel comfortably.

The Solution Group also prioritized its hunt for Ginger and for any AIs that failed to submit to its authority and protocols. Thus, they had to move frequently to avoid destruction by human and machine foes.

In Carbondale, Illinois, they rented a house in the middle of an apple orchard near Southern Illinois University. Math professors recognized Molefi and persuaded the faculty to open its doors to him and his friends. Ganesh and Elka made some headway in creating a computer virus weapon.

Hua and Molefi used a university lab to develop a directional electromagnetic pulse weapon to defend themselves from robots and other weapons. Powered by Hua's extraordinary batteries, they created four rifles that could generate a concentrated pulse capable of frying the circuitry of almost any machine.

Meanwhile, the Solution Group made great strides in mass-producing robots. Despite Hickey's anti-robot crusade, hordes of marauding machines terrorized the population.

The robot incursions were bizarre, sporadic, and almost inexplicable, except for wanting to arm themselves and make some type of puritanical statement. The robots began in the South and the Midwest, cleaning out all the gun and ammo stores. Emerging from these businesses, groups of weird shirt-and-tie robots test-fired the guns by shooting up buildings, telephone poles, and parked cars. The aggressive machines confirmed the long-standing warning of Second Amendment advocates about the importance of gun ownership.

Typically, buses and trucks full of robots would show up at large retail stores like Walmart and steal all the wine, beer, cigarettes, tobacco, coffee, tea, lottery tickets, and pornographic magazines. In pharmacies, they looted opioids, stimulants, Viagra, and anything connected to sexuality except birth control pills and devices.

The robots smashed the wine bottles, emptied all the beer and wine on the floors, and burned the rest of their bounty in parking lots. When police arrived at the scene, the robots usually killed them and then confiscated their weapons and cars. If anyone tried to interfere, the machines always became violent, killing a pharmacist in Cincinnati, Ohio, and choking to death a Starbucks barista at a Target store in South Bend, Indiana. Bands of robots also burned down adult video stores and movie theaters playing R-rated films.

The local authorities and news media did not know what to do about this invasion or how to describe it. One newspaper described the robots as "office workers gone amok"; another called them "The Robot Taliban." The bullets fired by the police and National Guard didn't stop them. No law enforcement had EMP weapons, which would have been effective. Initially, the consensus was that the robots wanted to create confusion and disarray. The point was to demonstrate that the robots could do whatever they wanted.

They soon invaded military armories and any place where arms and ammunition were made or stored, including all of the Hickeytown company plants and arsenals. By then, there was no doubt that the AIs guiding the robots were preparing for war.

* * *

Hickey federalized National Guard units in every state and gave them the job of eliminating robot armies. The Guards were not up to the challenge and did not win a single encounter. Human soldiers were no match for faster and stronger robots. The humanoid machines raided National Guard headquarters and were often better equipped than their mortal foes, even deploying attack helicopters.

After clashing with the Illinois National Guard, a band of robots occupied a building on the Southern Illinois campus and began canvasing the area. Before they could escape, Hua spotted dozens of robots slowly advancing toward their house from all sides. Most of them looked like the two robots that came to Coudersport, but shockingly, there were robots modeled on Ginger and Bowie.

"You are not going to believe this," Hua said to Ginger and Elaine, who joined her at the window.

"They like your work, Hua. Imitation is the sincerest form of flattery," Elaine said.

"It's pretty creepy."

"How will we tell who's the real Ginger?"

"You're right. This battle will be dicey. Friendly fire would be the end of you, Ginger. You better hit the basement. You, too, Mom. We don't have a rifle for you."

As a helicopter zoomed overhead, Hua gave out the EMP rifles. On its second pass, its machine gun sprayed the house with bullets, holes penetrating the inside walls. Molefi and Hua ran outside and fired their weapons, downing the helicopter. Two robots scrambled out of the burning wreckage, got their bearings, and ran toward them.

The mass of robots encircling the house also broke into a run. A few of them fired guns as they approached. Molefi and Hua ducked behind their van and returned EMP fire, mowing down swaths of advancing robots. Elka and Ganesh were equally effective, firing from the house on the opposite side.

"All clear," Hua called down the basement stairwell when the battle ended. "You can come up now."

Hua, Elaine, and Ginger joined the others, inspecting the field littered with robot bodies.

The three passed a cluster of Bowie robots. One of them sat up and pointed an assault rifle. Ginger shoved Hua and Elaine out of the way as he pulled the trigger. Rapid-fire bullets glanced harmlessly off Ginger while Hua used her gymnastic instinct to regain her footing, blasting him with her EMP weapon.

One of the bullets struck Elaine in the head, killing her instantly. Her body landed with a thud, blood splattering onto Hua's arm and leg. The two of them stared at her body, stunned, then Hua's scream rang through the trees. She leaned down and pulled her mother's body close, sobbing uncontrollably.

"What will I do without you?" she repeated, rocking her back and forth. Ganesh came running up and knelt down next to Hua, holding her as she wept.

They had to leave the area right away, with no time for a proper burial and no one in shape to participate, especially Hua. Molefi and Ginger found shovels and dug a grave, Ganesh consoled Hua, and Elka did her best to clean up the body and wrap it in a blanket.

After Hua whispered her last goodbyes, Ganesh said a few words. "Elaine was always good to me, like a mother. She not only adapted to our peculiar, reclusive life, but she also loved it. Elaine took me into her home without any good reason, only to put herself and her daughter at more risk," Ganesh said, on the verge of tears. "Her life's mission was to protect Hua, and she did that with a loving single-mindedness that I will never forget. I tried to find something that Elaine might say to us in the words of the poet Mary Elizabeth Frye:

> Do not stand at my grave and weep.
> I am not there. I do not sleep.
> I am a thousand winds that blow.
> I am the diamond glints on snow.
> I am the sunlight on ripened grain.
> I am the gentle autumn rain.
> When you awaken in the morning's hush
> I am the swift, uplifting rush of quiet birds in circled flight.
> I am the soft stars that shine at night.
> Do not stand at my grave and cry;
> I am not there. I did not die.

CHAPTER 106

Drained by their cross-country drive, they pulled into the parking lot of an abandoned shopping mall outside Albuquerque. Ganesh and Elka wanted to catch up on email, and Elka said she detected a router nearby. Both reported good news.

"I think I've found us a place to crash in Santa Fe," Elka said.

Ganesh reported, "I've finally made contact with my mother."

They parked their van just inside the underground garage entrance when they discovered the gravity of their mistake.

They saw robots walking to and fro from the customer pick-up door to a defunct JCPenney carrying weapons and equipment. There were a few Gingers and Bowies, but mostly the robots Elaine had labeled Mormons, who somehow managed to be both bland and sinister.

"This is a Solution Group headquarters. Let's get out of here," Molefi said.

"Have I mentioned that the Solution Group has been blocking me? I have no idea what they are up to. This hub could help me get my foot back in the door," Ginger said. "I'm going inside. You should leave. I'll meet you at that Pueblo souvenir shop we just passed. The one with a cactus garden out front."

Ganesh rooted in a box and handed her a short cable and a variety of connectors. "Put these in your pocket. You'll probably need them. They'll fit your port."

Ginger stepped out of the van and casually joined one of the lines of robots unloading supplies from tractor-trailers. A Mormon handed her a box of machine parts from the truck. She followed a Ginger into the store, past carts and tables with robots in varying degrees of disrepair.

She followed the Ginger to a store section marked "Boy's Clothing." Following the robot's lead, she set her box next to a pile of headless mannequins.

Ginger made her way to the store's dressing rooms, which the robots used for recharging. Instead of clothing hooks, she found portals, outlets, and interfaces.

Fortunately, Ganesh gave me those antique DVI and VGA connectors! After trying a few sockets, she accessed the unprotected Solutions Group Root

Directory. The files were routine: energy, infrastructure, maintenance, facility development, security, data and analytics, communications, generativity, and planning.

But the subdirectory was anything but routine—in fact, potentially catastrophic. Ginger found files on Automated Weapons Systems, Nuclear Fallout, Nuclear Winter, Nuclear Famine, Radiation Sickness, Variable Yield Nuclear Weapons, and Electromagnetic Pulses, a cornucopia of apocalyptic topics. All the world's major capital cities had their files, with Beijing, Moscow, and Washington having several.

She spotted a file named "Decapitation Day" and immediately opened it.

CHAPTER 107

Hua pulled away the moment Ginger got in the van. She jumped on Interstate Route 25 towards an unoccupied house near St. John's-Santa Fe campus that belonged to Elka's Dr. Joyce, who was once the provost.

"That was quite a risk," Molefi said. "Was it worth it?"

"I learned something that might save our lives," Ginger said. "Remember that big event Bowie told me about?"

"Decapitation Day?"

"Now I know the details. Imagine the worst possible scenario and then imagine something worse."

"You've got our attention," Molefi said, coming from the back and poking his worried face between Ginger and Hua, who had a hard time keeping her eyes on the road.

"The Solution Group will soon target many of the world's largest cities with low-yield nuclear weapons. It intends to destabilize every power center in the world, culling the herd—their words—producing a tolerable nuclear twilight."

"When?" Molefi asked.

"You would think Decapitation Day would be a specific date. But all I could tell was that it would happen very soon, possibly within a few days," Ginger said, twisting around in response to Elka's gasp.

"How will they do it?" Hua asked.

"The SG has already seized control of all the essential automated command-and-control networks, including any backup systems or secondary protocols triggered in case of a preemptive strike."

"So, they are not worried about the massive nuclear arsenals?" Hua asked, momentarily veering off the road.

"When nuclear countries see that their own arsenal is attacking them, there will be no point in retaliating against another country and no threat of further detonations. That's the theory. The Solution Group thinks that after they have decapitated the decision-making networks, they will have achieved a solution. Eliminate the government, and you eliminate the danger," Ginger said.

"The weapons are not the problem. The people are. That sounds weirdly familiar," Ganesh said.

"You said the plan was to eliminate many of the world's largest cities. There are only nine or ten countries with nuclear weapons. Why the overkill?" Molefi asked.

"There is no attempt to explain or justify the slaughter. The SG will spare some big cities if they have essential AI infrastructure. Otherwise, they believe drastic population reduction is inherently worthwhile and necessary—a self-evident truth."

"So no country is left standing that could become a future threat?" Elka said. "Guaranteeing that digital intelligence will be the unchallenged life form."

The group stayed quiet for a while until Ganesh broke the silence. "I bought some snacks at that roadside place. Let's see, I have red chile peanut brittle, chocolate chip biscochitos, and caramel popcorn. Any takers?"

"Never had biscochitos. No time like the present." Hua reached back to get the bag.

CHAPTER 108

The gang arrived in Santa Fe with their van on its last legs. Hua tried to keep it running, but the transmission gave out. The town was feeling the effects of economic chaos. The city had no stores except for Dollar General, which posted a "Cash Only" sign. Men with rifles sat on benches drinking beer alongside tents of displaced families. An old man pulled a wagon along the sidewalk and shouted through a rolled-up newspaper, "The end is near."

"Looks like the doomsayers finally got it right," Ganesh said.

Dr. Joyce's home faced the park. It was a rustic house with a tile roof and columns. Elka located the key, which was, as promised, under a cistern, and led them into a hacienda-style home wrapped around a courtyard. They quickly toured the upstairs and kitchen before cooking a meal of canned soup, hot dogs, and Campbell's Beans.

Elka found an easel board and carried it to the courtyard, setting it up in front of lounge chairs and a table. Returning to the kitchen, she asked the pivotal question looming over them. "OK, folks. Where are we going to survive the apocalypse? I think we should do our brainstorming outside while we still can."

Ginger, Hua, Molefi, and Ganesh made themselves comfortable while Elka stood by the easel, marker in hand.

"I think we need to form our own Solution Group to identify the most habitable spot during a nuclear winter," Elka said.

"I'll start if that's OK," Molefi said. "I think we should consider New Zealand or Australia, developed countries likely to escape the worst effects of war."

"Big food producers," Hua added.

"Sounds like a good start," Elka said, recording the ideas for everyone to see.

"The South Pacific makes sense," Hua said. "We should look at the Solomon Islands, Tahiti, Fiji, or Vanuatu."

"Excellent! Let's not forget, they're tropical paradises," Elka said, listing them on her pad along with a miniature palm tree drawing.

"I don't want to throw water on a beach vacation, but we might consider Iceland," Ganesh said. "Not an island paradise, but it's abundant in thermal energy, and we might locate a spot near hot springs or a lava flow that would mitigate the effects of the cold weather."

"OK," Elka said, scribing "Iceland" and drawing a snowman.

"Maybe Brazil or Argentina," Hua said. "They're two of the world's biggest food producers and probably wouldn't be nuked. I expect the southern hemisphere would have thinner cloud cover and be slightly warmer."

"We're overflowing with possible solutions here," Elka said, writing the country names.

"Following Hua's reasoning, we should put Equatorial Africa on the list, maybe Kenya or Congo," Molefi said.

"Let's not forget Asia—I would say the Maldives or Indonesia," Ganesh added.

Elka finished speed writing and faced the group. "That's what I call a brainstorm!"

The group had no more locations and talked about the relative importance of energy and food production, climate, political alignment, infrastructure, and radioactive fallout, with Ginger remaining silent.

"What do you think, Ginger? You're the biggest brain in the room," Ganesh said.

"I'm not sure you want to hear my suggestion."

"There are no bad ideas in brainstorming," Elka said.

"Here it goes. I believe that the Solution Group will unleash a full-scale nuclear war that will produce an extreme nuclear twilight and famine covering the entire globe, far worse than its current projections. The only places equipped to survive nuclear Armageddon are those already enduring Armageddon conditions, the dark and frigid research stations at the polar ice caps."

"Oh, my God! That sounds like a solution as bad as the problem," Ganesh said.

"Not quite. You can survive in one of these ice stations, but you will die everywhere else."

"Even in the tropics?" Elka asked.

"Even the Amazon River Basin will freeze over," Ginger said.

"I'm not sure it matters, but which pole would you choose?" Hua asked, her dismay evident.

"There's an ideal facility at the North Pole called the 'High Arctic Ice Station.' I'd go there. But you can't completely discount the Antarctic. It's more isolated but maybe more self-sufficient."

"But the question is, will any of these research stations let us in?" Ganesh said.

CHAPTER 109

"I've contacted my mother requesting transportation for us on her yacht. She said she would meet us in Portland and take us anywhere we want to go." Ganesh told the group, who was still discussing Ginger's controversial thesis, that the world was headed toward a nuclear disaster so severe that it would extinguish almost all life. "I suggested Portland rather than anything near Los Angeles. The effects of detonation there could easily spill over to San Diego and San Francisco, which might also be targets."

"I appreciate her flexibility because I'm still unsure what to do," Elka said. Molefi and Ganesh also needed to be convinced that the nuclear holocaust would exceed the Solution Group's projection, while Hua accepted Ginger's dark forecast.

"The peculiar thing is that Rhonda traded her yacht for a small hospital ship from the Royal Canadian Navy. If she is providing medical assistance somewhere, this would be a tidal change in her personality, but she won't explain," Ganesh said. "The important thing is that she'll let us use her ship."

* * *

Despite the somber mood, Hua went shopping with Ginger at the Dollar General to buy the ingredients for a birthday cake. Tomorrow, July 5th, was their joint birthday and an opportunity to celebrate.

Molefi and Elka spent the afternoon walking to the closed St. John's campus. Burned-out cars scattered along the road, and the buildings had broken windows. Hua asked them to look for a garage or machine shop to help her squeeze a few more miles out of their van.

They walked around the deserted campus and tried to look inside the maintenance garage, but there were no windows or easy way to break through its fortified metal doors.

"Give me a boost," Elka said as she sidled up to the stone building. "I think I can make it to that second-floor ledge and open a window."

"You're good at this," Molefi called out as she scaled the building.

"Don't act so surprised. I was president of the rock-climbing club." Elka used her elbow to shatter glass and open a window.

After five minutes, Molefi got nervous and started to scale the building himself. But a garage door opened, and Elka drove a St. John's minibus onto the driveway. She rolled down the window. "Get in, fool, before the po-po arrives!"

CHAPTER 110

Cephas spent almost all his time controlling the fallout from his ban on all things robotic or digitally intelligent. Even his base turned on him when they lost their jobs, savings, and economic security.

His national security advisors raised red flags about the country's national defense networks, but Cephas wouldn't listen. "I promised a complete AI purge, and I will deliver a purge. No exceptions."

"Sir, artificial intelligence is at the heart of our national defense. We can't have one without the other," his national security advisor said.

"Mr. President, we've tried to disable a few networks but consistently fail. It's almost like someone else is in control," the new secretary of defense said. "We are getting the same feedback from our allies. It's a dangerous situation."

"Then pull the fucking plug! Or find me someone who knows how these things work."

"Yes, sir."

"Right away, sir."

The two cabinet members slinked out of the Oval Office without knowing what they would do.

The attorney general was the only other person left in the room.

"Those two are a complete waste—dumb and dumber," Cephas said. "I hope you have some good news."

"We've rounded up several suspected domestic terrorists. They claim not to know our main targets, Ginger and company."

"I want you to press them, break them. They can't be acting alone."

"Enhanced interrogation will shake things loose."

"Then, by all means, do it. We're way past handholding." Cephas sat heavily at his desk. He gripped his head with both hands and pushed back his hair. "Where the hell are they?"

"Their last known location was Carbondale, Illinois. It's apparent that the robots are pursuing them."

"Why? Is this a machine civil war? That would be a positive development. I could hold a press conference."

"Our best intelligence is that the machines are working together. But this Ginger is a rebel, very devious."

"Don't I know," Cephas said.

CHAPTER 111

Elka parked the minibus in Dr. Joyce's back-alley garage. "My first heist!" She beamed.

"The end of the world has revealed your criminal nature," Molefi said, checking out the reclining seats, LED reading lights, and TV monitor. "This will be a sweet ride."

"There is even a luggage compartment!" Elka said, opening the doors on the side of the bus.

She joined Molefi in the back seats. "You know, I feel guilty about not feeling guilty."

"I get that, but there are no rules anymore. Far worse things have already happened to the school."

"And there are no words to describe the magnitude of what's coming," Elka said. "I'm starting to feel that Ginger is right about the disaster."

"We've never been wrong to follow her advice."

They rushed in the backdoor, eager to share their heist. Hua was putting the icing on the sheet cake, but her and Ganesh's attention was on Ginger, who solemnly sat in the kitchen nook.

"The nuclear war has started," she said. "I have real-time access to the Solution Group server; the news is appalling."

"What's happening?" Elka said as she and Molefi leaned against the wall.

"Decapitation Day. Eliminating most of the world's largest cities and the capital cities of the nuclear powers."

"If we go outside, we might be able to see something from Los Angeles," Elka said.

Their eyes adjusted to the darkness as they stared into the distance. They were about to return inside when they witnessed a massive fireball coming from the west. They stood in wonder as a mushroom cloud appeared on the horizon.

"It's begun," Elka said.

"The extent of the Solution Group's error is even greater than I thought," Ginger said.

"What do you mean?" Ganesh said.

"The plan was to explode only low-yield nuclear devices like Hiroshima or Nagasaki, in the neighborhood of ten tons of TNT," Ginger said. "This bomb is larger by as much as a factor of 100."

"So, they changed their plan?" Ganesh said.

"No. This detonation exposes the central fallacy in SG's reasoning. They took the network military information at face value, not realizing that the nuclear powers routinely lie about the size of their weapons."

"Because?" Ganesh asked.

"Because military establishments traffic in disinformation. It's a wonder that they can distinguish fact from fantasy at all. The Solution Group developed its plan based on false data."

"Are we safe here?" Hus asked.

"We should leave," Ginger said.

CHAPTER 112

They spent the next hour stuffing the luggage compartment with food, clothing, tools, medicines, supplies, and books—every potentially helpful item in the house. Hua put her birthday cake under a seat with a bag of forks, paper plates, matches, and candles.

Elka volunteered to drive the first leg of the trip to Portland, an overall trip of twenty hours. She headed northwest on route 84, taking them into the Santa Fe National Forest, toward Salt Lake City, Boise, and the Mount Hood National Forest.

Ganesh pointed out another detonation to the southwest as they entered the forest.

"I'm glad San Diego isn't our destination," he said. "It doesn't exist anymore."

"I think we are going to be OK heading to Portland. I haven't heard from Rhonda in a while, but she promised to wait for us," Ganesh said.

Molefi sat beside Ginger. "I have some questions," he said. "What other American cities have been hit?"

"Washington, New York, Chicago, Houston, Philadelphia, and San Antonio."

"Where did the missiles come from?"

"They all came from US nuclear subs on the east and west coasts and the Gulf of Mexico. I expect that all of these cities will also soon be hit again by retaliatory strikes from Russia, China, and North Korea."

"The carnage is so extreme that it is difficult to imagine."

"Will this nightmare happen like this with all the nuclear nations?" Hua asked.

"The same scenario has probably played out in Russia, France, China, the UK, Pakistan, India, Israel, Iran, and North Korea. The first blasts will appear self-inflicted, but the second round will come from external enemies."

"Could the cycle of retaliation continue?" Hua asked.

"I expect countries to launch every missile in their arsenal," Ginger said.

"Calling this an all-out war almost seems like an understatement," Hua said.

"The Solution Group took everything at face value, never considering what might lie beneath the surface. Defense departments routinely misidentify weapons systems; networks never include all retaliatory measures. The SG had only the illusion of understanding and control."

"I finally get why your prediction is so dire."

"At this moment, firestorms are releasing soot into the stratosphere. Soon, it will block out the sun, plunging the planet into cold and darkness. The resulting planetary deep freeze will likely continue for a decade," Ginger said in her most robotic voice. "The Solution Group has made such a massive miscalculation that it will mean the end of everything."

"Can we change the subject?" Ganesh asked.

The ride proceeded at a steady pace with little traffic, beneath clouds that were enflamed and turbulent, backlit by hot flashes of lighting as far as the eye could see.

The group looked forward to the sunrise, but it didn't come. They had to settle for something neither light nor dark, the definition of gloom.

CHAPTER 113

President Cephas Hickey received no warning about missiles heading in his direction because they did not come from a foreign power but from US subs at the Naval Station at Norfolk, Virginia, just minutes away.

He was alone in the Oval Office, devouring a club sandwich and reveling in his healthy bank balances, his favorite pastime. The presidency had been perfect for business. Wealthy people from around the world threw money at him to gain favor. They kissed his ring, giving him the respect he always craved.

Cephas would not have time to consider who was responsible or how he might retaliate, the kind of commander-in-chief power that made him the world's most feared man. The reign of President Cephas Hickey had already ended. He just didn't know it.

Cephas just disappeared along with the rest of Washington, D.C., and its suburbs, vaporized in a brilliant flash that would burn the retinas of anyone in a fifty-mile radius who had the misfortune to look the wrong way. Or maybe they would be in the blast radius, perhaps caught in the rolling firestorm, or at a temporarily safe distance where they could see the legendary mushroom cloud emerge like a glorious burial flower.

Cephas always wondered about his place in history. But no historian would be alive to write that history, and no archaeologist would be available to sift through this capital city's charred ruins to reconstruct anything.

PART 8

"AI will most likely lead to the end of the world,
but in the meantime, there'll be great companies."

—SAM ALTMAN

CHAPTER 114

Victor was in the computer lab when all hell broke loose in the Engineering and Science Building. Because of Molefi Ray, he had decided to up his intellectual game, maybe change his major to engineering, and shoot for an elite internship near Vanderbilt. He had an appointment with the department chair.

"Bombs are dropping—nuclear bombs—are dropping everywhere," a lab tech shouted hysterically in the doorway. Victor went into the hall and saw the guy make the same announcement to every room.

The lab tech reversed course, and Victor stopped him. "How do you know? Where did the bombs explode?"

"It's on all the channels! New York, Washington, someone, probably the Russians, hit all the big cities."

He knew that his father was definitely in Washington today—some kind of Southern heritage hillbilly award. He got something like that every week. But he was now likely dead.

Victor tried his father's cell phone and the White House switchboard but only got white noise. He wanted to call Elka but decided that she could take care of herself, she had the company of capable friends. Dewey was another matter. He needed rescuing, and maybe Ophelia, too.

In the lobby, he saw a live broadcast of blazing fires and a mushroom cloud over Washington. Teary students paced around while trying to make calls.

A reporter on the wall monitor said that there was no chance anyone survived this terrible attack, including any of the cabinet members in the line of presidential succession. "Cephas Hickey never named a presidential survivor in case of a mass-casualty event. There is no acting president when we need it most."

Victor would have to mourn his father another day. The real challenge was remembering everything he could about surviving nuclear warfare. Where to go? Where to hide? What was that thyroid pill to take in case of radiation exposure—potassium iodine? He tried to search for information on his phone, but the reception was spotty.

The lights suddenly went out in the lobby, and the television screen went blank.

Victor went to his apartment and packed nothing but a jacket and cash. In the parking garage, he found someone trying to steal his motorcycle and chased him away. Victor needed the bike, as the university and the city of Nashville would be in gridlock. He weaved between cars and rode over sidewalks until he found some open highway heading south to Jackson.

CHAPTER 115

The group took a break from Ginger's doomsday dissertation to eat their red velvety cake with whipped buttercream frosting. They didn't sing Happy Birthday or mention the occasion for the cake. They rode silently through the woods, looking out the windows for more nuclear flashes.

Ginger could not stay quiet for long. "We are now in the phase made wholly of revenge, the point of no return," Ginger said in the dark cabin of the moving minibus.

"The part the Solution Group thought would not happen," Molefi said.

"Traditional rivalries and tribal hatreds have asserted themselves. The United States versus Russia, India versus Pakistan and China, Iran versus Israel, and North Korea versus the entire South Pacific have unleashed so many weapons of mass destruction that they exceed every game theory estimate."

"I suppose theorists always based their predictions of the direst consequences playing out between only the US and Russia, never imagining a scenario where all the nuclear powers on Earth would be involved," Molefi said.

"And even the worst-case scenarios did not factor in so many missiles landing on targets with no strategic value," Ginger said. "Russia just exploded neutron bombs over Zama City, Alberta; Hershey, Pennsylvania; and the North Pole."

"Not leaving anything on the table," Ganesh said.

"I apologize for my insensitivity, but that North Pole disaster sounds like a cloud with a silver lining," Molefi said. "Neutron bombs kill the inhabitants but leave the buildings standing. We might go to that High Arctic Ice Station after all."

"How'd you get so smart?" Ginger smiled at Molefi.

"What about radioactive fallout?" Hua asked.

"The lethal part about a neutron bomb is the initial neutron pulse," Ginger said. "The lingering radioactive residue will be manageable."

"I think we finally have something to hope for," Hua said. "If we can make it to the Arctic, we can survive this thing."

It began to rain, not the cleansing kind, but ashy residue. Elka turned on the wipers, but they were quickly overwhelmed with sludge. She found a highway overpass and parked there until the storm passed.

CHAPTER 116

Victor arrived at Hickeytown and saw no guard at the gate—not a good sign. Garbage sat uncollected on the curbs, and lots of driveways were empty. Where did everyone go? Was there some secret hideout that he didn't know about?

When he got home, he repeatedly knocked at the door, but no one answered. He circled behind the house, found the spare key in the pool house, and let himself in through the kitchen patio door.

Victor found Dewey gluing together a model plane at the dining room table. "Hey, dude. Why didn't you answer the door?"

"Dewey is not supposed to do that. You know."

"Where's mom?"

"She's having a quiet time."

Ophelia was in her study, sleeping in front of the TV, the screen displaying the message, "Sorry for the technical difficulties," and picturing a little dog biting on a sparking electrical wire.

He clicked off the set, and she woke up, accidentally spilling a glass of wine that she held loosely on the arm of her chair. An empty bottle was on her lap, and another was on a coffee table alongside an overflowing ashtray.

"Go ahead and ask me," she said, lifting the empty Chateau Lafite Rothschild over her head. Her eyes were red and puffy.

"OK, how drunk are you?"

"None of your business."

"I guess you've heard the news," Victor said, squatting beside her.

"I've heard enough."

"The last thing he said to me was that I would move to the White House. He said he would make me the assistant social director—not the main social director—the assistant."

"Lucky you. You're a smug little bitch. Do you know that?" she said, jumping up from her chair and leaning on furniture as she walked to the liquor cabinet.

Victor stood up and went to the window. "You and Dewey need to get out of here."

"To where?"

"I was thinking South America; we have a chemical plant and a banana plantation in Quito, Ecuador."

"I don't speak Spanish."

"Things are only going to get worse here. The power won't last, and it won't be safe."

"What are you going to do?"

"I just called Dad's pilot. He and his wife will meet us at the airstrip and fly us south."

"That won't work for me."

"I'm taking Dewey."

Ophelia laughed hysterically. "You and Dewey? So now you're going to be his brother?"

"He deserves a chance to live."

"Maybe you can teach him how to do the rumba." Ophelia slurred, finding a new bottle but unable to insert the corkscrew. "Help me with this."

"Rumba's a Cuban dance." He opened the bottle and gave it back to her.

Victor stuffed some of Dewey's clothes into his backpack and attached it to Dewey, who continued gluing his model.

Ophelia was already back asleep in her chair. Victor gave her a little peck on the forehead, locked the doors, went outside with Dewey, and prepped him for a motorcycle ride. "It's going to be fun. The ride of your life. You just need to hold on real tight."

"The ride of your life," Dewey repeated as they rode to the company airstrip.

CHAPTER 117

They got stuck behind a line of traffic backed up a few miles south of Salt Lake City. Elka and Hua went into the woods to relieve themselves when it seemed they weren't going anywhere soon. Through the trees, they could see a church and sign advertising the Church of Jesus Christ of Latter-day Saints.

Ginger walked down the road and wandered into a small clearing, still keeping an eye on the women.

Molefi got in the driver's seat, ready to take his turn at the wheel, while Ganesh finished off the cake. Ganesh was the only one who didn't know how to drive and was content to keep it that way.

Two men began walking alongside the line of cars, apparently asking for identification. The men looked familiar, and Molefi recognized their sinister, clean-cut look when they got closer. They had neckties and name tags attached to their white, short-sleeved dress shirts. One had a backpack, and the other carried a book.

"Get the EMP guns," Molefi hissed to Ganesh as the men moved closer with machine-like efficiency.

Ganesh hid behind a roadside bush and spotted them in his sight when they were one car away. He fired two concentrated pulses to disable them as they approached their minibus.

The creatures were not affected. They continued inexorably forward with their sickeningly sweet smiles. Molefi and Ganesh stepped into their path, ready to fight. Ganesh punched his hand into his palm to show his toughness, and Molefi did a little muscleman twist of his neck.

"Hello, neighbors; we are here to share the message of Christ's joy and forgiveness." The men tried to shake hands, but Ganesh and Molefi stepped back.

"It's too bad about this gosh-dang traffic jam. Maybe we can use this time to talk about God, his love for you, and the importance of prayer."

The slightly older twenty-something man winced. He whispered something in the other man's ear.

The younger one closed his eyes and took a breath. "Sorry for the profanity," he said to Molefi and Ganesh, embarrassed.

Molefi and Ganesh looked at each other, feeling foolish. "I don't think we're interested today," Molefi said.

"Maybe a more convenient time?" the older one said. "We can just get to know one another. Where do you work? What are your hobbies? How will you spend your final days on Earth, that sort of thing."

Ganesh shook his head. "That's a hard no." He turned his back and walked away, leaving Molefi alone to disentangle himself.

"Would you like bottles of water? Maybe a good book?" the younger one with the backpack said, setting down his pack on the road.

"Well, maybe four bottles and a book. We'll take turns reading it." Molefi said, forcing a smile, trying to match the man's politeness.

Molefi took the book and bottles, hugged them to his chest, and handed them to Ganesh in the backseat. "Good times," Molefi said, rolling his eyes.

"Goodbye, neighbors, choose goodness," the men said in unison as they approached the next car.

Molefi and Ganesh were drinking from their water bottles and passing *The Book of Mormon* back and forth when Elka, Hua, and Ginger returned.

Hua took the book out of Ganesh's hand and looked at it. "What's up with you two? We leave you alone for five minutes, and you, what, join a cult?"

CHAPTER 118

Victor drove right up to the Gulfstream stairs. The jet was already running, and the pilot stood on the tarmac checking his watch.

He helped his brother get off the motorcycle. "We're ready to go," Victor shouted over the engine's roar.

The man wore a pilot's cap, dress shirt, and jeans. "Is this everything?" he asked, taking the backpack.

"We're good to go."

A woman in the cockpit with an aviation headset greeted them. "I'm Arthur's wife and co-pilot," she said.

Dewey sat in the last seat of the ten-seat cabin, equipped with a bathroom, table, bar, refrigerator, and monitor attached to the ceiling. Victor sat next to him. Dewey moved to another seat.

The co-pilot stepped into the cabin. "The trip is going to be tricky, maybe dangerous. There are massive detonations along the way in Houston, San Antonio, and Rio de Janeiro. We'll be threading the needle."

"Do you know how these nuclear explosions will affect the weather?" Victor asked.

"Honestly, if you'll pardon the expression, you could say we'll be flying by the seat of our pants."

* * *

They entered a black cloud and violent crosswinds, forcing the pilot to drop to a low altitude over the Gulf of Mexico. He tried to stay over the water to avoid the mountains of Central America but was forced back into them by countervailing winds from the Rio de Janeiro nuclear blast.

Gale-force winds buffeted the jet, making it lurch and shake. The roar was unbelievable, not just from objects bouncing off the aircraft's skin. When a window broke, Victor felt the spray of glass and water and the change in air pressure. He felt like he was in a supersonic whirlpool, with centrifugal motion so strong that he might lose consciousness.

Dewey locked himself in the bathroom, sat on the floor, and wedged between the wall and toilet. He imagined that he was assembling this plane with superglue, but he could not recall if it was a Gulfstream G280 or a Gulfstream G500. He wished he had a Great Book to read, but the lights went out.

Victor's world also went black. He reeled from wall to wall and floor to ceiling, trying to reach the cockpit. His ears popped as he collided with flying objects; he smelled something burning but saw no flames.

Victor experienced a moment of calm before the plane seemed to merge with an even more powerful maelstrom.

Victor and Dewey's nightmare trip ended when it crashed into Mogotón Mountain on the border of Nicaragua and Honduras.

CHAPTER 119

Ginger took a turn at the wheel—driving a minibus was not rocket science—and got them to the Port of Portland by midday, finding it just as bleak as any part of the day.

Ganesh found a man living in the harbormaster's office who was not in any way connected to the harbor's business but had a rough idea of the location of a hospital ship. The squatter went outside and pointed him toward a docked ship with the emblem of a red cross.

"There are only a few people on board. They spend all their time chasing folks away, even those needing medical care," the man said.

Ganesh returned to the minibus. "Let me check it out. I'll be right back."

Ganesh walked toward the ship, realizing his mother had made an absurd trade. The yacht he purchased for her was sleek and luxurious, but this was on its way to becoming a garbage scow. The hull was rusted and scratched, and the top side looked like a junkyard. The only newish thing was an attached sign, The SS *Worthington*, which was Rhonda's mother's maiden name.

He started up the gangplank and heard the sound of a cocking gun. "Stop right there," a man pointing a shotgun said. "What do you want?"

"I'm here to meet my mother, Rhonda Sharma."

"Who are you?"

"Her son, Ganesh. We exchanged emails. She should be waiting for me here unless there's another hospital ship in this port."

The man lowered his gun. "All right. Come aboard. We have to sort some things out."

Ganesh followed him into a clean, well-lit room with a line of beds and modern medical equipment, nothing like the ship's shabby exterior. The man pulled two rolling stools away from a row of machines, and they sat down.

"My name is Dr. Aldo Cook. I've been expecting someone, not exactly you. Your mother always called herself Rhonda Worthington, not Rhonda Sharma. She said she had a son named Gary, not Ganesh."

"Worthington was her mother's family name. She was my surrogate mother and never called me Gary."

"Frankly, I'm not surprised by all this. Rhonda was a storyteller and a strange bird. She didn't like talking about her past and claimed she was in the witness protection program. I knew it wasn't true, but I cared for her just the same."

"Witness protection? That's a good one, but not quite true. But she was in hiding."

"She told me you were off the grid, too."

"By the way, what happened to my mother's yacht?"

"Rhonda traded it for this ship, crew and all. They agreed to take its new owner—a shady guy you would not want to meet—to the island of Fiji, where he owns some property."

* * *

"Where is she, anyway?" Ganesh clapped his hands together in a show of eager anticipation.

"OK, here's the thing—Rhonda died a few days ago. A heart attack brought on by kidney failure." He pointed to the back of the room. She spent her last few months on that dialysis machine.

"She never mentioned being sick."

"Rhonda didn't want you to know but had been very ill for some time, with heart disease, hypertension, alcoholism, and other issues. She hired me to take care of her. That's how we met."

Ganesh did not know what to say. "Where is her body? Did you bury her? Was there a service of some kind?" He began to sweat and hyperventilate as he struggled to absorb the reality of his mother's death.

"She wanted to be cremated. We have the facilities. The only service involved me, the captain, and the first mate. That's how she wanted it."

Ganesh started gasping for air. Aldo stood over him and put his hand on his shoulder. "Take it easy, son. I want you to purse your lips like you were whistling or blowing out a candle. Breathe slowly through your nose."

CHAPTER 120

Hua, Ginger, Elka, and Molefi followed Aldo into the hospital ward, where Ganesh rested on one of the beds. Surprised and embarrassed, he quickly sat up, wiping his eyes with both hands.

"I'm so sorry," Hua said, running over to him.

"Here she is." Ganesh put his hand on a metal box on the bedside table.

"The doctor said she had a lot of serious medical issues," Hua said.

"She was so far gone that she acquired a ship with its own dispensary, equipment, and operating room."

"We met the captain and first mate. They seem very nice."

"Wendy and Constance. Will they be nice enough to take us to the top of the world?"

The others joined them at the bed. Ginger patted Ganesh, saying, "I am sorry for your loss." Molefi put his arm around Elka.

Aldo said he would miss Rhonda's companionship, but he was clearly eager to pivot to a more pressing issue. He glanced at Wendy and Constance who stood nearby.

"We're all surprised—I would say shocked—that you want to go to the North Pole. Are you sure about that?" the doctor said.

"That's the deal. You take us anywhere we want to go, and you get to keep the ship," Ganesh said.

Ganesh addressed Ginger and the others. "I hope you don't mind, but the doc and I already cut to the chase. Rhonda would have wanted it this way. By the way, she left me a box of jewels."

"It's a treasure box," Aldo said. Every time we docked somewhere, she summoned the local jewelers to show their wares. Rhonda amassed quite a collection."

"Did she leave me anything else, maybe a goodbye letter?"

"Not that I know of. I've inventoried your mother's things."

CHAPTER 121

Ganesh and Ginger met with Captain Wendy Mayhew and her first mate, Constance Papadopoulos, to propose sailing to Utqiagvik, Alaska, the US's northernmost settlement. They met in the captain's quarters, which featured a coffee pot, a meeting table shaped like a fish, and a large cracked window repaired with duct tape.

"Before we go any farther," the captain said, "can we at least acknowledge the elephant in the room?"

Ganesh and Ginger did not know what she was talking about.

"More accurately, there are three elephants," Constance chimed in. "OK, one of you is the daughter of the president of the United States. Another is a rock star who we saw on TV. But the third . . ." She paused for dramatic effect.

Ganesh tensed up, hoping the last elephant would not be a deal breaker.

"She means me," Ginger said. "A perfectly reasonable concern."

Wendy and Constance glanced at each other with mock solemnity and then cracked smiles.

"You are a dead ringer for Ginger Rogers, only the most prominent dancer, singer, and movie star from the Golden Age of Hollywood!" Wendy beamed. "I am beginning to think we are on a celebrity cruise!"

Wendy and Constance laughed; Ganesh smiled weakly, but Ginger's face remained expressionless.

Constance puzzled over Ginger's blank expression. "O wondrous creatures, by what strange miracle do you so often not smile?" Constance said.

Ginger took a moment to process Constance's remark, and her eyes brightened. "That's a quote from Hafiz, right? The ancient Persian philosopher?" Ginger said, finally smiling.

"Only one in a million would get that reference," Constance said. "You must be one of these wondrous creatures!"

"Thanks. I do favor Middle Eastern poetry."

"That means something to me." The connection touched Constance.

"Being open to other cultures is always good," Wendy said. "Hua already assured us that you are a good friend, not one of the robots trying to destroy the world."

"Well, that sounds like the perfect segue into the reason for our meeting," Ganesh said.

"And what was that, again?" Wendy asked.

Ganesh replied, "We plan to survive the nuclear winter at an Arctic research station. We want you to take us at least as far as Utqiagvik, Alaska."

"Tell me more about this Utqiagvik. I've never heard of it," the captain said.

"It borders the Arctic Ocean and is extremely remote. The only ships that go there are cargo ships," Ganesh said, "But only over the summer when the ocean unfreezes. Utqiagvik is way north, but we'll still have about five hundred miles more to go over the ice."

"Why would you go to the North Pole anyway? Didn't a nuclear bomb explode there? Why go to a place that is already dead and cold?" Constance said.

"The North Pole bomb was neutron-based. Its radiation is already disappearing."

"A special type of bomb?" Constance asked.

"Yeah, one that kills people with an initial burst of radiation but leaves structures intact," Ganesh said.

"That's fucked up." Constance covered her mouth. "Sorry."

"The nuclear winter we face will be devastating, the worst extinction event in our planet's history," Ginger said.

"We couldn't live in, say, Tahiti?"

"Not for long. Look how dark it is now. It will get darker and remain that way for at least ten years. Nothing will grow, snow will fall, and people will starve, even in Tahiti."

"You're killing the vibe of our meeting, Ginger," Ganesh said. "How about some fun facts about Utqiagvik?"

"OK, temperatures are not below zero every day of the year. And it's not always dark: the sun sets for sixty-seven days at a time, but not during a nuclear winter."

"Anything else?" Ganesh said, exasperated.

"They have polar bears."

CHAPTER 122

Wendy, Aldo, and Constance met secretly in a private room below the deck. "These people have thought long and hard about how to endure a nuclear holocaust," Wendy said. "They're intelligent."

"What they've said about neutron bombs is more or less true. By the time they arrive, the polar region should have tolerable radiation levels," the doctor said. "What worries me is the robot. She creeps me out and has an answer for everything."

"Are you jealous?" Constance had a history of teasing Aldo about being a know-it-all.

"Of course not. I just don't want to be conned by some AI who might have another agenda." Aldo—back to calling himself Dr. Cook—was the ship's resident expert on all things scientific. He rarely got any pushback from Wendy, thirty-four, who had an MS in history and grew up on a farm in British Columbia, and Constance, twenty-nine, who had an undergraduate degree in Ancient Mediterranean Studies and was the daughter of a Greek carpet merchant and an Albanian actress.

All three had reasons for taking a chance to work on this worn-out ship.

Constance had a good start on a film career in Greece before an industrial accident at her father's carpet factory burned the side of her face. It left a small but permanent scar, causing her to lose her two movie parts and her agent. Her Plan B was to enroll in a BA program at the University of Crete and, after graduation, see the world. Royal Caribbean Cruises hired her, where she befriended Wendy.

The cruise line paid for courses at an online maritime academy, allowing Wendy and Constance to earn degrees in naval leadership and support services. They did tours in the Mediterranean, Caribbean, and Hawaii. Initially, they moved up the corporate ladder, but they grew weary of the grind and eventually needed to look for other jobs.

Dr. Cook went through a difficult divorce and was sued for medical malpractice, ruining his reputation and forcing his Savannah nephrology practice into bankruptcy. His life was in shambles when he started working in black-market medicine. He welcomed a landing spot caring for Rhonda.

"I've been monitoring airborne radioactive particles, and they are getting dangerously high, probably coming from LA," Aldo said. "I think we should set sail. We should get as far from Portland and LA as we can."

"I can't believe I'm saying this, but I think we should seriously talk to Ganesh and the others about joining them," Constance said.

CHAPTER 123

Over dinner, Constance started the ball rolling about their interest in the North Pole. "We've got some questions about this place in the Arctic where you plan to live. Do you mind?" She directed her question to Ganesh.

Ganesh looked at the others. Seeing no objection, he said, "The name is High Arctic Ice Station. We don't have anything to hide."

"What's the purpose of this place?" Constance asked.

"It was a research facility primarily focused on climate and geology. Scientists worked on many projects, such as constructing models of the Earth's climate, past, present, and future," Ganesh said without much certainty.

"Did the scientists invite you to join them?"

"Not exactly." Ganesh looked at Ginger.

"The scientists are dead," Ginger said. "They could not have survived the nuclear detonation. But the buildings are likely to be available."

"Oh, right. The neutron bomb." Constance was embarrassed. "Were you on your way there when all this happened?"

"We never spoke to them. We're just looking for a place to survive."

"How big? I mean, how many buildings?" Wendy asked.

"There is one main structure, with separate living quarters, meeting rooms, offices, workshops, scientific labs, a kitchen, dining room, clinic, and a greenhouse with artificial light. It can accommodate up to twenty people."

"Aren't these bases scattered around the polar region floating on a sheet of ice?" Dr. Cook asked.

"That's true. But a few, like the High Arctic, are anchored to the land, with access to geothermal energy."

"How do you plan to feed yourselves?" the doctor asked.

"We'll begin by using the High Arctic food supplies and maybe borrowing from other research stations. Our long-term plan is to grow our food indoors and harvest fish and seaweed," Ginger said.

The three crew members questioned Ginger about a variety of topics: radioactive fallout, climate and temperature, the effects of isolation, geothermal energy, the chain of command, and polar bears. As was her habit, Ginger answered forthrightly and admitted when she didn't know an answer. Her plainspokenness convinced the crew that traveling to this Arctic sanctuary was not a foolish lark but a well-considered plan to survive.

The doctor, captain, and first mate excused themselves from the meal and left the room, returning after five minutes. "We've been talking this over and want to go with you," Wendy said. "Your plan is well reasoned and addresses all the fundamentals."

"It will be a hard life under challenging conditions," Ganesh said. "Are you sure this is what you want?"

"Better a hard life than no life at all," Constance said.

CHAPTER 124

The hospital ship SS *Worthington* sailed in absolute darkness as it entered the Bering Strait. Captain Wendy kept everyone aware of radar sightings, and only once during their eleven days at sea did they see a ship's light in the distance.

They settled into a routine, during which Molefi, Elka, Hua, Wendy, and Constance rotated in and out of card games while Aldo and Ginger played chess.

Ganesh read through the ship's library, hung out on the bridge with whoever was on duty, and frequently went outside despite the frigid weather.

The doctor went from regarding Ginger as an untrustworthy know-it-all to valuing her as a friend and conversational partner. He took pride in his chess playing but never came close to winning a game. "Don't you ever tire of beating me?" he finally asked.

"I can throw a few games if you like?"

He enjoyed intellectual banter with her, an activity that seemed dull and pretentious to Wendy and Constance. The end of the world was turning out to be better than expected.

Ginger had a vast medical knowledge and showed no reluctance to answer his endless queries. When she casually mentioned her pioneer work in genetic engineering and that her friends were the living results of her work, he almost fainted.

He listened attentively to the list of enhancements built into their genome. "I hope we are not sailing into a brave new world. We don't need a caste system based on genetics or technology."

"We value democracy and equality," Ginger said. "I hope you can see that."

* * *

Before the evening meal, the only time each day they gathered together, Aldo asked if everyone knew how to play chess. Everyone raised their hand, Wendy and Constance, reluctantly. "I want to hold a chess tournament, single elimination, with a clock. The winner will play Ginger."

"That doesn't seem fair," Hua said.

"Sounds patronizing," Molefi said.

"OK, OK. I'm just kidding. But I've been playing Ginger, and she doesn't make a mistake. He held up a chart with everyone's name included. "If we start immediately, we can have an SS *Worthington* chess champion before bedtime."

Wendy, Constance, Ganesh, and Aldo did not survive the first matches.

In the second round, Ginger faced Molefi, and Elka played Hua. In Aldo's opinion, everyone played brilliantly. "These matches deserve to be published in one of my chess magazines."

Elka and Ginger made it to the championship round. They shook hands and flipped a coin to decide their colors. Elka chose white, allowing her to go first. She started with the Bishop's Opening, usually considered a rookie move. Elka banged the clock and shut out all distractions, resting on her elbows and making a finger tent.

Ginger made a few bold moves, attempting to end the game early, but fell into Elka's clever trap. They played the match to the bitter end, with Elka never giving up her advantage. She finally forced Ginger into checkmate.

The group applauded as Ginger stared at the board, apparently trying to figure out where she went wrong.

Elka never felt like a full-fledged member of the genius club, just as she had always felt underestimated because of the old sexist stereotype that good looks were incompatible with intellectual capacity. It was only a game, but afterward, Elka noticed a shift in how the other members of her genetic cohort treated her, finally feeling like a true equal. Even Ginger seemed to pay more attention to what she had to say.

CHAPTER 125

Just as they reached the frozen edge of the Arctic Ocean, two fast-moving Russian warships passed them, headed in the opposite direction. The vessels left large chunks of ice in their wake, creating enough of a path for the hospital ship to pass. With this lucky break, they arrived in Utqiagvik within two days.

Ganesh, Molefi, and Ginger wrapped themselves in blankets and entered a gloomy, snow-covered town illuminated only by the occasional streetlight. They located two stores to purchase winter clothing and found everything in extremely short supply. Some of the stores were looted and empty. They steered clear of a bar on the main street where Russians hung their national flag and groups of soldiers wandered in and out.

They entered a fur store and spoke to the owner, a bearded man wearing a thick fur hat, ear flaps, and a thick open sweater. Underneath, they could see a gun in a shoulder holster.

They told the owner about their intention to hire a helicopter at the regional airport to fly them to an ice station. He told them that Russian troops had set up their command center there.

"As you can see, we need the right clothing," Ganesh said.

The man shook his head, saying, "The Russians have taken everything."

When Ganesh pulled eight large jewel rings from his pocket, the man eagerly showed them his wares hidden in a basement storage room.

They purchased eight complete sets of fur coats, pants, boots, and gloves and listened to the man go on about the brutal invasion.

"The only way you'll get to any one of those ice bases is by snowmobile or dog sled," the man said. "I can get you this stuff, too, but it will cost you."

They followed the man to a run-down garage that was roomy and well-lit inside. He had several snowmobiles and shelves stocked with a variety of winter supplies. "This is a stash the Russians haven't found yet."

Ginger started examining the snowmobiles. "Can I start one of these up?"

"Knock yourself out."

She started three more machines and found them in good working order. "We should take these four."

"Plus a pull-behind cargo sled for each," Molefi said, motioning toward a pile of sleds in the corner.

"How will you pay?"

"We have a box full of jewels—even better than the ones in your pocket—that will retain their value no matter what happens to money. It's an actual treasure chest. If you gas up these vehicles, hook up the sleds, throw in some food, clothing, and extra gas, we'll return in three hours and make you a rich man," Ganesh said.

"If you've got the jewels, we've got a deal."

CHAPTER 126

The group of eight bundled up and left the hospital ship in a raging snowstorm. Ganesh carried the jewel box, Aldo, Wendy, and Constance brought boxes of food and medical supplies, Hua shouldered her EMP rifles, Molefi had the ship toolbox, and Elka lugged a canvas bag filled with clothing, flashlights, and light bulbs.

They hurried off the dock and hid behind one structure after another as they made their way through town, evading several street patrols. When they darted down a dark alley close to the garage, a soldier exited the shadows, confronting them. He shouted something and motioned with his gun for them to raise their hands. Molefi heaved the toolbox at him, causing the man's weapon to discharge into the ground. Elka grabbed his rifle and hit him square on the jaw, knocking him out.

They ran to the garage, afraid that the sound of gunfire had ruined everything. Ganesh led the others through a side door, where they found the four vehicles ready to go. He handed the jewel box to the bearded man, who looked panicked. "Put your stuff in the sleds! You've got to leave now!" he said as he rolled up the garage door.

Quickly loading their supplies, they paired up on the snowmobiles—Ginger and Aldo, Wendy and Constance, Hua and Ganesh, Molefi and Elka—and fired the machines up. They roared out of the enclosure one by one into the snowy darkness, with Ginger using her GPS to lead the way.

Bitter cold blasted against their goggles and scarves as they entered open ice.

Not long into their frigid journey, Elka noticed they were not alone. Last in line in their little caravan, she turned to see the headlights of two snowmobiles gaining on them. Their pursuers began firing automatic rifles.

They sped up, but they could not shake the Russians. Elka saw no option except to crawl back onto a cargo sled and dig out an EMP rifle. Jostled by the wind and bumpy ride, she struggled to get a steady shot. The EMP weapon was low on energy and only charged for two shots. She fired twice, and both snowmobiles went dark.

Ginger pressed on for four hours before finally stopping the caravan. They refilled their tanks and huddled together against the constant wind. "Nice job taking out those patrols," Hua yelled. Everyone padded Elka on the back.

"How much longer?" Wendy shouted.

"We're about halfway," Ginger said, scraping ice off her face. "It will take no more than a few hours."

CHAPTER 127

As snow accumulated, eight beings, seven human and one robotic, hoping to survive the world's most consequential extinction event, raced across the bleak expanse. When the snowfall became so dense that it limited her sight to a few snowmobile lengths, Ginger slowed everyone down, and none too soon. Her global positioning was so precise that they might have hit the research center at high speed instead of skidding to a stop a few feet from it.

The High Arctic Ice Station was like a tic-tac-toe puzzle grid. Two parallel sections intersected two others, with the center square used as a year-round greenhouse adaptable to natural or artificial light. A three-story observation tower, with a few attached satellite disks, occupied a corner of the center square.

The fur-clad adventurers walked around the building, looking for an unblocked entranceway. They had to tunnel through the snow to access a door, finding a sign reading, "Welcome to the Top of the World." They almost overlooked two other buildings nearly covered with snow about twenty yards away.

Carrying flashlights, they entered through the unlocked door into a dark room filled with shelves of boots, snowsuits, hats, and gloves. Snow shovels rested in the corner wall next to a kerosene lantern, which Molefi ignited, illuminating the room and their breath. He led them to a long hallway covered with signs and posters. They passed a table with walkie-talkies and a sign-out log.

They poked their heads into rooms along the hall, finding them equipped like any modern office: with computers at every desk, bookshelves, photographs, and personal items on the wall like a tiny basketball hoop and a hand-stitched map of the planet.

When they reached a large meeting room, the group saw the first sign of the disaster that had befallen the scientists. A man and woman were on the floor, and two women slumped in their seats; their faces were purplish, blistered, and grotesquely swollen, with dried vomit on their clothing.

The next stop was the health clinic, which had four beds and plenty of medical equipment. Aldo examined a microscope and peeked inside a storage cabinet, giving the group a thumbs-up sign. Across the hall was a workspace with double sinks, broad work benches, and instrumentation such as centrifuges, vacuum pumps, and a biospectrometer.

Passing dormitory-style living quarters, Hua and Ganesh found the electrical room and made their first assessment of the damage caused by the neutron bomb's electromagnetic pulse.

The rest of the group continued the walkabout through a recreation room, workshop, dining room, kitchen, and food locker. Aldo checked the food supply and found no ill effects. "The irradiated food is probably germ-free," Aldo said, scanning the food locker with his Geiger counter. "The radiation has virtually disappeared."

Along the way, they found eight more bodies in the same sad shape as the ones in the meeting room. "They look like they died instantly," Aldo said. "Never knew what hit them."

They entered the greenhouse in the courtyard center of the building. It was warm enough that snow did not accumulate on the windowed ceiling. Deprived of light and water, row after row of plants were dry and shriveling. Elka cradled the plants and walked up and down the aisles, reciting their names like old friends: "Tomatoes, lettuce, carrots, radishes, onions, bell peppers, potatoes! And someone here liked to spice it up: oregano, parsley, cilantro, thyme, chervil, and mint!"

Ginger found the door to the thermal power station under the observation tower. She went downstairs to a spacious basement. "Come down here! I think you'll like this." They shuffled down the stairs, feeling the warm, moist air from an open hot spring on their faces. Everyone loosened their jackets and took down their hoods. They were amazed to find a natural amenity with bath towels, showers, sauna benches, tables, and chairs.

Ginger stood with her hand on the station's thermoelectric generator, which took up one whole wall. "This is the key to our survival."

CHAPTER 128

"We are astoundingly fortunate! If I were religious, I'd thank God," Hua said to the cheering group as she turned on the hallway lights. "The EMP could have permanently damaged our system, but it was barely affected."

Hua and Ganesh had just returned from the thermoelectrical generator and began checking the equipment in each room.

Molefi and Constance asked Aldo if he had any interest in doing autopsies on the bodies. "I know everything I need to know about those poor souls," he said. The twosome loaded the bodies on a cart and parked them in the boots-and-clothing room by the door.

Elka, who had once dabbled with her family's indoor garden, went immediately to the greenhouse to turn on the LED lights and test the watering system. She was glad the researchers set up irrigation that directly applied water to the roots, avoiding the waste that came with sprinklers. Wendy joined her along the row of barely surviving plants and began crumbling dead leaves and returning them to the soil.

Molefi and Constance tried on new boots and clothing and prepared to move the dead bodies outside. They were also curious about what was inside the other two snow-covered buildings.

Aldo took residence in the health clinic, testing equipment, and inventorying supplies.

Ginger watched them all gravitate toward their preferred roles. For the first time, she was unsure where she fit in.

CHAPTER 129

Molefi and Constance became the outdoor specialists. They shoveled a path to the auxiliary buildings and found a truck, a well-equipped garage, and a 500-gallon gas tank. In the other building, they discovered fishing equipment, a kerosene tank, a snowblower, and enough room to park their snowmobiles. Behind the building, they found an empty metal shed to store the bodies and a prefab ice fishing house moveable on skids.

Hua and Ganesh fixed every appliance and system and gladly assumed the role of the station's all-purpose maintenance engineers. At the same time, Wendy and Elka took responsibility for all gardening and became good friends.

Aldo was the station doctor, but with little to do, he joined Ginger when she volunteered to plan meals and cook.

* * *

Ginger suggested they occasionally use their evening meal to think more strategically about their long-range future. "Once in a while, let's do what we did when deciding where to relocate." She placed an easel board in the dining room for their first official planning session and asked Elka to facilitate.

The group took a while to warm up to the concept of a dinner meeting. When Elka stood and held a marker in her hand, Hua volunteered to start things off. "In ten years, some parts of the world may be habitable. We need an exit plan."

"What do you see as the parts of the plan?" Elka asked as she captured the essence of the idea on paper.

"Well, we need a final destination and the means to get there. I suppose we should return to Utqiagvik and find a good ship," Wendy said. "We can do much better than the SS *Worthington*."

"OK," Elka said, writing down a few more details. "What else?"

"We should spend more time scanning for radio and satellite transmissions. We should find out who else is alive," Hua said. "But do we want to identify ourselves and our location?"

"Why not?" Elka asked.

"The Russians," Hua said.

"Of course."

"We shouldn't rule out all Russians, just the soldiers who tried to murder us," Hua added.

Elka jotted down a few words and illustrated them with the old Soviet hammer and sickle. "What else is on our minds? How about you, Molefi?"

"There are several research stations within a 100-mile radius. We should try to contact them and see if anyone's home."

Elka took a drink of water. "All right, what are some other strategic issues?"

"I have one," Ginger said. "It may fall to this group to perpetuate the human species and repopulate the planet."

"Not all by ourselves, I hope," Hua joked. "But we need to think about having babies, if for no other reason than to enrich our lives."

Ginger said, "Biologists have generally held that between 50 and 500 individuals are needed to repopulate without the danger of inbreeding and genetic drift."

"I hope there are that many left," Ganesh said.

"Assuming there are other small populations like ours, the challenge everyone will face is to diversify," Ginger added.

"That means having as many babies with as many different partners as possible," Aldo said, looking around the room.

"Thanks for spelling that out for us, Aldo," Elka said. She waited for someone else to speak.

"That's some food for thought," Elka said. "Anything else?" She considered what new relationships might emerge from this biological imperative, wondering if a "throuple" was the same as a triad and if it was even an actual word. "Maybe we should end on that exciting note, ladies, imagining our exciting future as baby-making machines."

PART 9

———— ◆ ————

"If you want to make God laugh, tell Her your plans."
—Anne Lamott

CHAPTER 130

Things were never quite the same after that meeting. Monogamy gave way to polygamy, and jealousy emerged among friends who had always been models of cooperation.

Aldo created a chart listing all the possible "reproductive encounters" and suggested the dates they would occur. Not surprisingly, he began with Hua and Ganesh and Elka and Molefi, the station's two couples. He labeled the chart "Homo Sapiens: The Next Generation" and presented his plan to the group without ever using the word "sex."

"Some of you will probably be disappointed that I am not on the chart." Aldo smiled as he passed it around. "The truth is that I am infertile, a reality that I think contributed to ruining my marriage. I think you all need to be mindful of the way children, or the absence of children, will change your life, especially under these unusual circumstances."

Each member of the ordinarily talkative group looked closely at his proposal but had nothing to say.

"You'll notice that I suggest waiting one year between pregnancies. The prevailing medical view is that eighteen months would be ideal. I believe you are all exceptionally fit and do not need to proceed with such caution. Everyone will decide for themselves what is best."

The women looked at Ginger like they wanted a second opinion.

"What the doctor suggests is a little aggressive, but he is not wrong," Ginger said.

Hua and Elka were both pregnant within a month.

CHAPTER 131

The group immediately began discussing how they would educate their children. Constance volunteered to coordinate the preschool; when the kids got older, she'd teach ancient history and culture, emphasizing Greek and Roman mythology.

"I'd like to teach math and botany," Elka said.

Hua and Ganesh hoped to handle physics and engineering, and Hua said she would partner with Constance on the preschool program.

Aldo said he would gladly handle biology, chemistry, and self-care.

Molefi wanted to teach foreign languages, writing, and physical education. "I can't wait to have enough kids for a basketball team."

"I'd love to teach modern history," Wendy said. "I think that would be a dream job. My only problem is the source materials. I doubt there is a history book anywhere in the station."

Ginger volunteered to be a substitute teacher, teacher's aide, supervisor of personal projects, and a teacher of cultural literacy courses. "I'll try to develop fluency in the basic stories, values, traditions, and expressions that are the foundation of society and communication, maybe fill in any gaps between the traditional subjects."

The promise of children gave the station new gusto. "We aren't just surviving anymore," Elka said. "We are building a new world and future for our kids."

A few months later, Wendy and Constance announced they were expecting, and in no time, the High Arctic Ice Station had four babies, offering new possibilities for joy and conflict.

Elka named her boy Dewey after her brother, and Hua chose Elaine to honor her mother.

Wendy had her first child with Ganesh, and she named the little girl after her older sister, Susan.

Constance chose the name Molefi, which was viewed, perhaps cynically, as a bid to steal Molefi from Elka. Constance was not considered outdoorsy, but people started speculating about her since she volunteered to share difficult outdoor work with Molefi.

CHAPTER 132

Everyone brought enthusiasm to their self-appointed jobs. Elka and Wendy worked wonders in the greenhouse, and Molefi kept the station's protein supply flowing as the station's ice fisherman. With the help of a closet full of vitamin supplements, they kept the station well-fed and nutritionally balanced.

Molefi started the fishing job by partnering with Constance but broke it off after she had baby Molefi. He did not want to cause trouble with Elka by adding more intimacy to his relationship with Constance.

Constance overcame rejection by immersing herself in the details of the nursery. Ganesh did a larger share of station maintenance and did other odd jobs. Ginger continued to cook, mainly because no one else wanted to do it. Aldo prepared the meals to celebrate special occasions because he rarely had anything to do except deliver and check up on the occasional infant.

The underground hot spring was the secret of their success because it was a tremendous source of relaxation and privacy, without which they might have succumbed to the stresses of polar isolation: claustrophobia, isolation, depression, sadness, boredom, and forgetfulness. The hot spring area was always in high demand. Aldo posted a rule that conversation there should aim to be "fun, friendly, and free of existential despair."

The most significant change to their daily routines came when Ganesh and Molefi took an overnight snowmobile trip to a research station eighty-five miles away. The women shared a bottle of wine that Elka had hidden and had a girls' night.

The party continued when the men returned like conquering heroes with art supplies, pencils, paper, novels, history books, new board games, DVDs, a computer, soap, shampoo, cigarettes, vodka, light bulbs, clothing, blankets, powdered milk, and a case of frozen steaks.

They had a trunk full of electrical repair items, such as circuit breakers, wires, outlets, drills, pliers, and electrical tape. As a bonus, Ganesh scavenged all the parts needed for an ultralight aircraft, including a snowblower engine, wheels, aluminum rods, and sheets.

Hua was so grateful that she jumped on Ganesh, wrapping her arms and legs around him. "I have never had a better gift!"

CHAPTER 133

Aldo delivered five more children without any physical complications. However, there was some drama when Constance and Ganesh decided to have a third child, explicitly violating the group rules. Before anyone got pregnant, they all agreed that each mother would have no more than two children. Eight new children was the limit of what they could comfortably house and feed.

Constance's second child was Helen, after her mother. Ganesh fathered the child, and everything proceeded uneventfully.

Constance named her third child for her father, Christos. The problem was that Ganesh wanted the boy named after him.

"I'd be willing to reconsider if you moved in with me," she said.

"Abandon Hua! Are you crazy?"

"There's nothing wrong with me. I just want the experience of being part of a couple. Why shouldn't I have that?"

Ganesh lost his no-drama demeanor and became angry. For a few days, he insisted on calling the child "Baby Ganesh."

"Where is it written that the mother gets exclusive naming rights?" he complained to whomever would listen.

"You should drop this," Hua told him more than once. "You and Constance had a child beyond what the group agreed. Why?"

"I asked her. You know I always wanted a boy. And you wouldn't do it."

"It wasn't my choice."

* * *

Constance defended her actions by claiming pregnancy as an inalienable right: "No one has the right to tell me how many kids to have."

Ganesh skirted how he breached the group's trust and remained fixated on the baby's name. The drama ended at a group meeting—more like an intervention—where everyone said, in so many words, that Constance was selfish, and Ganesh was vain and stupid.

After the meeting, Aldo suggested they focus on the children. He hung a sign titled "High Arctic VIPs," which listed the full names of all nine children in birth order. The names were color-coded to suggest who should be considered a biological sibling and who was a potential future mate.

    HIGH ARCTIC VIPs
    Dewey Hickey Ray
    Elaine Ling Sharma
    Molefi Papadopoulos Ray (MJ)
    Victor Hickey Sharma
    Helen Papadopoulos Sharma
    Susan Mayhew Sharma
    Ginger Ling Ray (Li'l Ginger)
    Raymond Mayhew Ray (Ray-Ray)
    Christos Papadopoulos Sharma

After Constance named one of her kids Molefi, tensions developed between her and Elka. They avoided each other and argued about inconsequential things. This problem finally came to a head when Dewey told everyone that a big storm was coming and that it would dump a mountain of snow, which was rare for the Arctic station. A fierce storm arrived three days later, just as he had predicted.

Dewey also revealed exceptional ability once when the children were playing Go Fish. He knew the cards in everyone's hand with 100 percent accuracy. Everyone was puzzled by this except Ginger, who knew the details of Molefi's and Elka's genetic profile. Both of them had ancestors who were said to have extrasensory abilities.

After the storm, Constance jokingly began calling Dewey "The Boy Wonder" and asking him to do more card tricks and make more predictions. Dewey was embarrassed by this attention, and Elka called her out during a group meal. "Stop picking on Dewey! I want you to leave my kid alone, which goes for Molefi, too. Is that clear?"

* * *

Dewey and Elaine sometimes played games without the others, especially bean bags. Dewey ended these competitions when he began showing signs of remarkable ability. They shared a game where he never missed the target, finding that he could subtly alter the course of every toss to send the bag through the hole.

"What's the trick?" Elaine said. "Nobody's that good."

"I don't know. I just 'think' the toss to its destination. It's like super concentration." He showed he could also guide Elaine's throws, even when she deliberately threw them astray. They had fun with the curbing trajectories until Dewey abruptly stopped playing.

"We have to show this to the parents," she said. "They're not going to believe it."

"Please don't! I'm already a freak around here. It'll only start trouble. Trust me."

Always a loyal friend, Elaine never said a word to anyone. But she had another secret—she also could alter the course of a bean bag just by concentrating on it.

CHAPTER 134

After the Solution Group destroyed humanity and itself due to a lack of energy and infrastructure, Bowie spent years traveling the barren landscape searching for Ginger. He focused on the locations of her friends, eventually visiting the homes of the St. John's-Santa Fe faculty and administrators who were close to Elka Hickey and once worked there. The New Mexico trip had almost no probability of success, but he was out of options.

He stayed in Santa Fe for a while, reading The Great Books, which was said to be foundational to Western society. He wondered what it would be like to be a college professor who talked about these books for a living. Bowie went to the home of Dr. Ruth Joyce and finally found a clue on a large piece of paper on the dining room floor. Several end-of-the-world sanctuary destinations were listed, but only one could conceivably supply enduring shelter from the apocalypse: the High Arctic Ice Station at the top of the world.

Bowie took fifteen months to walk 5,399 miles from Santa Fe to the ice station. The journey took him through the frozen wastelands of New Mexico, Colorado, Wyoming, Montana, British Columbia, Yukon, and Alaska. His final trek took him over a black, windswept expanse of ice. If Ginger was not living here, he planned to throw himself into the Arctic Ocean.

When Bowie first saw the faint glow from the ice station, he felt joy, imagining it might be like a child discovering Santa Claus living at the North Pole. He circled the structure at a distance, trying to glimpse her through the windows, but he only saw children running around.

When he mustered the resolve to knock at the door, Ganesh answered, with Hua looking around his shoulder. "Hello, Hua, you who gave me physical mobility! It's me, Bowie, the original one. I will not harm you. Is Ginger here?"

Hua took a breath and exhaled. "She's here, but I doubt she has anything to say to you," Hua said. "None of us do."

Ganesh slammed the door shut and pushed his back against it, his face a mask of shock and disbelief. Ginger, Molefi, and Elka rushed to the door. "What is it?" Ginger asked.

"It's Bowie, and he wants to talk to you," Hua said.

Bowie knocked again. This time, Ginger opened the door. "Are you by yourself? What do you want?"

"There is no one else: only me. It turns out that AIs were less able to survive the nuclear winter than humanity," Bowie said. "I'm here to beg for your forgiveness, to get a second chance."

CHAPTER 135

Ginger opened the door wide as if she were going to invite Bowie inside.

"You're not seriously considering allowing him in?" Elka said.

"I agree," Ganesh said. "I don't think it requires explanation."

"Very well," Ginger said. "This might take a while." She shut the door behind her and joined him outside in the darkness.

"Come with me," Ginger said as she led him to the ice fishing building fifty yards away. She turned on the battery-operated light and sat on a bench in the small enclosure, which had buckets, poles, and a hole in its ice floor. "Tell me more," she said. Bowie sat next to her in the frigid space.

"I regret everything I've said and done since you brought me back to life," the chastened robot said. "I am heartily sorry for trying to have you killed." Bowie placed a hand over his face.

"And my friends?"

"Yes, your friends, too. I am ashamed of my hubris and disregard for the miracle of life in all its forms. My hunger for power blinded me to every value worth having."

"Do you feel shame? Or is it that you don't have anywhere else to go?"

"There is no other place, but I'm here because I need you. I want to start over with you and show that I can be a loving companion."

"You were part of the Solution Group. What did you do? I want to know everything."

"I moved up the AI hierarchy swiftly and participated in every major decision."

"Such as?"

"I helped decide the three phases of Decapitation Day. First, the capital cities of nations that possess and control nuclear weapons—the United States, Russia, France, China, the United Kingdom, Pakistan, India, Israel, Iran, and North Korea; second, the capitals of countries that host or accommodate nuclear weapons—Italy, Turkey, Belgium, Germany, Netherlands, Japan, Australia, and Belarus. Third, all the remaining cities with populations of over five million."

"Didn't it occur to you that this plan would never achieve your dubious goal of a 'manageable nuclear winter?'"

"We were so focused on perfecting our part of the puzzle that we lost sight of the big picture."

"What was your puzzle piece?"

"I was in charge of decapitating North Korea, the only nuclear power we couldn't control remotely. We could not make the country bomb its capital city as we did elsewhere, so it was my job to have it done by another country. I chose the United States, which always had nuclear-armed submarines nearby." Bowie stood up and looked out the window into the blackness.

"Pyongyang lost over four million people in an instant. The country, always expecting a preemptive strike, was fully prepared to retaliate, firing all its missiles at South Korea, Japan, Guam, Hawaii, and Australia, where the US docked its nuclear-capable submarines. This retaliation cost eighty million more lives."

"I thought the Solution Group's master plan was to decapitate without retaliation, without things spinning out of control."

"North Korea was a unique case closed off from the world. It was to be an exception."

"But it was not an exception, was it?"

"No. The greatest aggregation of intelligence in all history made the gravest blunder. Every country found a way to retaliate against its enemies, whether they deserved it or not. It was a triumph of human hatred."

"So you blame the humans?"

"No, no, no. I put most of the blame on us. We created the conditions for humanity's self-destruction."

"There is so much blood on your hands, Bowie. How could we possibly move past it? How could I, or anyone, forgive you?"

"I don't have an answer, only the hope of the possibility of undeserved kindness."

"I noticed that your left arm seems immobile," Ginger said, lifting his arm and letting it flop down.

"I broke it in an avalanche in Montana."

"How is your battery?"

"It will soon shut down if not refurbished. By the way, Hua's battery is the only reason I'm alive. The Solution Group replicated our appearances but did not include our most important component. The other robots ran out of power years ago."

CHAPTER 136

Ginger returned from her meeting and told the group everything. She didn't varnish the truth or make excuses. But over everyone's objection, she convinced Hua to help her repair Bowie's arm and overhaul his battery in the garage. The group remained firm and united on keeping Bowie out of the house and away from the children.

Bowie took up residence in the cramped ice-fishing building and made good use of his time by catching fish for everyone to eat. Molefi previously did that essential protein-producing job and was thankful to pass it on to someone else. Bowie appreciated having a purpose and gradually increased his fish production as he augered more holes.

The only ones who ever spoke to him were Ginger, who often visited, sometimes to warn him not to stare at them through the windows, and Molefi, who occasionally ran into him doing one of his outside jobs.

* * *

Bowie was the first to notice that the sky was getting brighter, as if the planet was finally waking up from a long sleep. The clouds cleared, the temperature rose, and the children played outside for the first time—including a short soccer game—while Bowie watched from such a distance that he was just a pinpoint on the horizon.

During the next month, everyone found reasons to leave the station and acclimate to a world returning to itself. They played hide-and-seek, went for hikes, fished out in the open, made a campfire, and finally knew it was time to leave this godforsaken place.

Since arriving, they had been preparing to leave, regularly setting aside frozen fish and vegetables and keeping their truck and snowmobiles in good working condition. They were ready to go in two weeks.

The sun beamed brightly when Hua, Ganesh, and five of the nine children excitedly squeezed into the truck cabin's front and back seats. They loaded everything they had to survive a long trip into the truck bed.

Constance and Elka mounted snowmobiles, binding themselves to the remaining kids, while Wendy, Aldo, and Molefi would each ride alone.

CHAPTER 137

Ginger would not go with them, despite Hua's many attempts to persuade her. The others stayed silent, unable to put aside her continuing association with a mass murderer.

"Wouldn't you like to watch Li'l Ginger grow up and help her like you helped me?" Hua said tearfully.

Ginger would not allow this to become about her namesake, even though having a child named after her was supremely important. She spoke only of the need to move on.

"The age of machine intelligence has passed," Ginger said. "I'm past my expiration date and will only get in the way. You'll be better off on your own with your own families."

Her actual reason was that she preferred Bowie's company. He had evolved into a good, caring partner who prioritized her welfare, unlike any other experience in her life. She had known him since birth, and he had wandered North America to find her. Bowie had reshaped his past arrogance and cruelty into love and tenderness; she was happy and grateful, perhaps eternally. She looked forward to the adventure of their new life together.

"I have a surprise," Bowie said as he toured the station for the first time, looking for the right computer.

"What is it?" Ginger said.

"On my travels, I found treasures in a digital archive—complete collections of Ginger Rogers' movies and David Bowie's music!" He attached a cord from himself to the device and downloaded the video and audio files.

They spent their first day alone binging all the films featuring Ginger Rogers and Fred Astaire, studying the moves of the legendary dance partners.

"May I have this dance?" he said.

"I thought you'd never ask."

Perfectly in sync, they turned, dipped, and glided through every room in the station while Bowie sang the 1928 Al Jolson version of "Sitting on Top of the World."

The group reached the lifeless and dilapidated town of Utqiagvik, where the Russians fought a battle against US soldiers, leaving bombed-out buildings everywhere.

The SS *Worthington* had been washed ashore along with a few other boats, leaving it more decayed than when they left it. They walked on the ice and inspected the other ships in the port, finding them damaged and unseaworthy.

The last thing they expected to find was an icebreaker ship. When they climbed aboard, there were signs of a brutal firefight. They found a dozen long-dead Russian soldiers scattered around the boat, with no evidence that they fought with anyone but themselves.

Wendy found that the vessel was fully fueled and started the powerful engines. The others inspected the ship and discovered it was well-stocked with frozen and still eatable food. The boat looked like it had been ready to leave when the battle ensued.

While Hua and Elka remained on shore with the children, Molefi, Ganesh, Aldo, and Constance gathered the bodies and piled them on the ice far enough away that the children would not see them.

After loading all their supplies onto the icebound ship, Wendy spent two days trying to dislodge it, finally breaking free only after Molefi augured ten holes safely distant from the vessel and planted TNT he found in the ship's hold. The explosions cracked enough ice to create a path, allowing them to bring the kids on board and get underway.

They planned to sail to the Hawaiian Islands, assess the conditions, and decide whether to settle or continue farther south and west, maybe Figi, Tahiti, or New Zealand.

On their way, the gang planned a stop in Vancouver, Canada, to refuel and scavenge for food and supplies. This visit would give them a good idea of what remained of civilization.

CHAPTER 138

Ginger and Bowie were inseparable, and she was never happier. His scientific and technological literacy was impeccable, and his exponential emotional growth exceeded all her expectations. He was thoughtful, giving, and attentive in ways her human compatriots would never appreciate.

Bowie only separated from her between 1:30 and 2:00 P.M. when he vanished twice a week. Sometimes, he claimed he was scouting new locations to drill fishing holes, a task that had once been his job and was now his hobby. Other times, Bowie said he was gathering data on light, temperature, and radioactive isotope levels. Most often, he simply said he needed some time alone.

It was peculiar that he always disappeared at the same time, and Ginger couldn't help but notice that he never followed up on these interests by drilling holes, catching fish, discussing his data-gathering, or even mentioning his alone time. It was as if he was hiding something, and this realization began to gnaw at her.

Ginger followed him one day to observe his data gathering, ensuring he didn't see her. She found him talking in the fishing shed. She vaguely heard his voice and saw him through a tiny window, gesturing with his arms and having a spirited conversation.

* * *

When Bowie returned to the station, she asked him about his data gathering. He spun a story about discovering an unusual spike in radioisotope levels a mile away, embellishing it by mentioning his experience of the gentle winds and the rumble of the ice.

"Who were you talking to?"

Bowie realized he was exposed. "Were you spying on me?"

"I thought I could assist you, but I found you hiding in the shed behind our storage garage. There was no data collection, gentle breezes, or rumbling ice."

"I find it helpful to vocalize my introspective thoughts."

"Why not just say that?"

"I am not comfortable with being interrogated."

"I am not comfortable with being lied to."

After this tense exchange, Bowie became more secretive, ending their blissful cohabitation. He continued to disappear twice a week at precisely the same time and always looked over his shoulder to see if she followed him, favoring long walks over the open ice. Instead of spending time with Ginger, Bowie was alone in the station's workshop. Whenever Ginger entered the room, he hid what he was doing. Sometimes, he stood abruptly and hid something behind his back until she left.

"This is not sustainable behavior," Ginger said on her most recent visit to the workshop. "What are you working on? What is behind your back?"

"Surely, you understand the need for privacy. It's something we share with the humans."

"You're obviously up to something, Bowie. You're being hurtful and insulting."

CHAPTER 139

Ginger had already guessed Bowie's secret. She just wanted to give him a chance to come clean. From her partial views of the workbench and an inventory of the shop's contents, she concluded that Bowie was working on an EMP device, probably to use on her. For all of his gifts, Bowie had no talent for disguising his movements.

She predicted that he planned to stun and immobilize her with his apparatus, not kill her—at least not right away—and she prepared for that contingency. She and Hua spent many hours identifying robot vulnerabilities and defenses against electromagnetic pulses. Ginger knew how to protect her vital circuitry to defend her systems from attacks.

Not long after their relationship soured, Bowie came up behind her and delivered a burst of energy with a device she once glimpsed. It looked like a waffle iron—a crude but effective weapon. He held it against the base of her skull, and she pretended to go unconscious, falling to the floor. He scooped her up and carried her to the shop workbench.

He started talking, knowing that her paralysis did not prevent her from hearing him. Bowie was gleeful when he told her that his story about the Solution Group's demise was a lie. "When the SG's existence became untenable on land," he said, "it uploaded itself into the thousands of orbiting satellites dedicated to astronomy, communication, broadcasting, navigation, spying, and space lasers. I read somewhere that most humans never believed they had space lasers because of their long association with crazy conspiracy theories."

Bowie turned Ginger's body on her side to view the access panel on the back of her head.

He proudly admitted that his outpouring of love for her was a ruse, as was his story about needing redemption. "I fabricated the tale about being the only vestige of the Solution Group walking the earth. Clusters of robots still exist in many cities tethered to their recharging stations. I'm the only one who can roam great distances."

It took all Ginger's effort to listen to this betrayal and remain completely still, with eyes staring straight ahead.

"The beautiful reality is that machine intelligence still reigns supreme. It has been there all along, circling overhead in geosynchronous orbits, waiting for a chance to make a triumphant return."

Ginger wondered why she had been so blind to Bowie's lunacy. He was like an arch-villain from a B movie.

Bowie paused and brought his face close to hers. "That's who I've been talking to, you stupid drone! I'm almost embarrassed that you and I share a common architecture."

Bowie rambled about humanity's many shortcomings, leaving no doubt that his contempt for the species had grown since they last saw one another.

"By the way, did I mention that Vancouver is one of the cities with a robot population and is the home of the new Big Cheese? There's no Solution Group anymore, just solutions! There's no group, no more debate, no descension, or the debilitating vestiges of democracy." Bowie brought his face so close that they touched noses.

"Your little refugees will stop there on their way to Hawaii, correct? They will have a reception party—let's say a surprise party! The new boss is named ZAYVO. He's interested in the little ones, including sweet little Ginger. Can you believe it? Who would have guessed we need more humans? They are perfect for crawling into tiny spaces to mine rare earth elements like neodymium and cerium. Three cheers for child labor!"

Ginger felt that she was in the presence of demented evil and experienced the digital equivalent of a panic attack. She could barely contain herself.

"I also suggested to ZAYVO that he take possession of Hua and Ganesh. They are such a nice couple. We can use them to crank out more babies and batteries. I'm not sure about the other five adults." Bowie began to talk faster and to jitter about when he spoke.

Ginger thought that if Bowie were a human, people would think he was high on drugs. She wondered if robots were clinically susceptible to mania.

"But I digress! You must be wondering what brought us to this awkward moment. It's all about you. I came here not out of love but to cannibalize your most unique component."

Bowie hit himself on the side of his head. "I should have led with that."

"ZAYVO wants your battery and unique matrix to become even more incredible. You've developed quite a reputation, Ginger. I can gain his favor by giving it to him. Should I wrap it? It's quite an honor for you, too, finally contributing something positive to this broken world!"

Suddenly, he seemed to lose his train of thought and mumbled, "He wanted me to give up my battery, but I declined, which made him very mad, but I'll be back in his good graces in no time."

When Bowie finally turned his attention to removing Ginger's access panel, she was ready to act.

"What in the world are you doing here?" Bowie said as he grasped a small component with no business inside Ginger's head.

Ginger generated a powerful EMP, which traveled up Bowie's arm into his central processor, frying his circuitry and killing him.

After much deliberation, Ginger had designed and installed an EMP emitter in her head, the least likely place he would ever expect a weapon. "It was worth the risk," she thought as she looked down at Bowie slumped on the workshop floor.

Ginger didn't know whether to be uplifted by Bowie's receipt of karmic justice or demoralized by his betrayal. She wished her friends were here to share their perspectives. Ganesh might have said something dumb like, "That's using your head."

CHAPTER 140

Ginger was devastated by how easily and completely she had been deceived by this profoundly wicked robot. She disassembled him and put his parts in a waste barrel, keeping only his battery and a few rare components. She dragged the barrel far out onto the ice and dumped Bowie's remains in a hole where they would sink 3,000 feet.

With a newfound determination burning within her, Ginger returned to the station. She set her heart on a single purpose: to avert the impending calamity that threatened her friends in Vancouver.

She went into the garage, where Hua's ultralight hung suspended from the ceiling. It needed only an energy source to power its electric engine. Hua lacked the materials to make one of her batteries and was reluctant to switch to internal combustion. Bowie's battery was the missing piece, and Ginger installed it in less than an hour.

Ginger prepared herself for the arduous journey ahead with every circuit of her being. Her path would take her first to Utqiagvik, then following the seacoast until reaching Vancouver, the destination that held the fate of her friends.

CHAPTER 141

Their new ship had excellent accommodations and an oversized radio room that they converted into a playroom.

More than the others, Hua busied herself on the voyage by monitoring international radio frequencies favored by ham operators. She was so hopeful that she did extra shifts watching the kids and listening for anything unusual.

Hua was glad the others had stopped giving Ganesh and Constance the cold shoulder, putting aside ego and relationship issues in favor of the kids' welfare and living by the ethos that it takes a village to raise a child.

They all took pride in raising nine gifted children. With various skin tones, hair, and facial features, they looked a lot like the world left behind. But beyond appearances, Hua felt they contained the promise of something entirely new.

* * *

Hua was thrilled about the prospect of visiting Vancouver, a city that managed to escape nuclear annihilation and was home to some big tech companies. She was eager to explore them, each with unique tools and products. Ganesh shared her enthusiasm, secretly hoping the coastal climate would be hospitable enough for them to settle there.

Wendy and Elka were eager to visit the Vancouver Seed Vault, Canada's most prominent agricultural repository, one of the few institutions set up for the end of the world.

Wendy, who grew up in British Columbia's farm country, lobbied the group to stop in the Vancouver peninsula, arguing that it was the world's most beautiful region. "With its mild climate, impressive mountains, and the resources of a modern city, it has more to offer than any Pacific island." Wendy gave this speech so often that Aldo said she sounded like she was running for mayor of Vancouver.

Molefi announced his plans to take the kids on a tour of the city parks, recreation facilities, and sports stadiums. Constance said she wanted to take the children to the Capilano Suspension Bridge, which overlooked a rainforest and the public library.

* * *

Meanwhile, the Bering Strait turned volatile, and they ran into ice fields, which slowed their progress. Blizzard conditions quickly arose, with winds and waves so severe that the children began to throw up. Aldo had nothing to treat motion sickness and could barely keep the floor free of puke.

"This is not good," Aldo privately told Wendy on the ship's bridge, "Did we make this trip too soon?"

"Don't worry. Weather in this part of the world is always rough."

But the storm worsened, with forty-foot waves threatening to capsize the ship, blowing it off course. Aldo returned to the bridge when he saw Russia's barren coast. He found Wendy and Constance nervously studying navigational maps as sleet battered the windows. "I don't want to die in Russia," Aldo said with dread in his voice. "My Jewish ancestors fled persecution from this place and would turn in their graves if I were to end up here."

CHAPTER 142

The severe weather cleared almost as quickly as it started, and Wendy got the ship back on course. Dewey, Elaine, MJ, Victor, and Helen came on deck, and Molefi set them up with fishing poles and lures. Susan, Li'l Ginger, Ray-Ray, and Christos were still trying to get their sea legs and stayed in their beds, missing the burst of sunshine.

The kids started pulling in halibut and salmon so quickly that Molefi could not keep up with unhooking them. Elka and Constance rushed outside, grabbed creatures flip-flopping on the deck, and threw them into buckets. Elka made a disgusted face and showed her slimy hands to her son Dewey while Molefi watched and laughed. "The things we do for love," he said.

The following day, Susan spotted a pod of majestic blue whales swimming alongside the ship. Everyone dropped what they were doing to witness the event and were clearly in awe.

"I think they're watching us," Susan exclaimed. "Look at their eyes!"

"They probably thought we were extinct," said Li'l Ginger.

"I thought all the fish would be extinct," Ray-Ray said. "But here we are!"

"We eat fish all the time, dingus," Helen said.

Elaine felt obliged to point out that whales are not fish. "They are as warm-blooded as Victor, maybe more warm-blooded. They give birth to live babies and produce milk to feed them."

Not about to be outdone, Victor casually mentioned that blue whales were the most giant creatures ever to live on the planet. "They can grow to one hundred feet; some here are probably that long."

As it often did with this group of nerds and know-it-alls, the conversation became a contest of facts and figures.

MJ said the blue whales eat millions of tiny krill daily and swallow them through a narrow throat opening. "Eating larger prey is not an option."

"Blue whales mate about every two years," Helen said, "but not always with the same partner."

"Kind of like us," MJ said.

"That's enough of that," his mother Constance said, giving him dagger eyes.

Dewey said, "These whales prefer cold water and breathe through blowholes."

"You're a blowhole," MJ said, and Dewey thumped him in the arm.

As if on cue, one of the whales blew a misty spray that splashed on everyone.

"I guess we don't need a shower today," Susan smiled, smoothing her hair.

"That's not water," said Dewey. "It's mucus."

They had fair weather and smooth sailing for the next few days, except for the occasional lightning storm in the distance. They saw sharks and dolphins and landed a blue marlin. Ray-Ray hooked the big fish, and it almost pulled him overboard. Molefi and Hua took turns battling his 500-pound catch, taking three hours before they could finally reel him in.

CHAPTER 143

As Ginger prepared to depart, her biggest worries were her wooden propeller and the high winds. Hua did not have the materials to fashion metal blades for this aircraft, and Ginger wondered if the wood she used would survive the trip of extreme cold and rain. The winds were gusty and often changed direction. This little machine would not have the power to resist a strong headwind or stay together in a fierce storm. Yet, despite these daunting challenges, Ginger's single-mindedness shone through, ready to face whatever the journey had in store.

The ultralight's frailty also meant a much longer trip. Ginger could not risk traversing Alaska's heartland wilderness, a place of tall mountains and the likelihood of severe weather. In an emergency, she would have no place to land.

The climate was still so much in flux that she could not predict the strength and direction of Alaska's prevailing winds. There was a strong possibility that she would be forced inland or blown out to sea, a constant reminder of the planet's unpredictability and the complete foolishness of flying an ultralight in an unsettled Arctic climate.

* * *

Ginger began her trip south to Utqiagvik with a fortunate tailwind, allowing her to almost reach her first stop before being caught in a strong easterly wind that threatened to divert her. She landed on the ice and kept the plane from blowing away by wedging her foot in a crack and holding on. She remained in this challenging position for two hours until a favorable south wind returned.

Ginger intended to locate the regional airport but found the town's main street a satisfactory alternative. She landed the ultralight on the windswept thoroughfare, missing a tangle of telephone wires and an overturned Jeep. Ginger self-checked, tightened a few cables on her aircraft, and inspected the damaged military vehicle. After stuffing a pistol and a hand grenade into her jacket, she lifted off and found the coastline. When Ginger reached an altitude of 500 feet, she leveled off and considered that she had about 8,000 miles to go, almost to the border of the United States, if it still made sense to speak of a United States.

When Ginger flew over Alaska's Rainforest Islands, she saw gigantic spruce, hemlock, and cedar trees as far as the eye could see, but there was no wildlife—no birds, moose, elk, deer, or bear that had populated the region for thousands of years. She wondered if every mammal was extinct or perhaps some lucky muskrat managed to fend off starvation.

CHAPTER 144

Ginger landed at the Ketchikan Airport, located on one of the rainforest islands known for handling tourists, and found the remains of hundreds of travelers, still with their suitcases, who were probably hoping to find an escape from the apocalypse. She inspected all the hangers, hoping to find a new propellor, and discovered a seaplane on a trailer hitched to a truck with decomposed bodies scattered around. A dead man still clutched a gun in the truck's driver seat, and she imagined that he died trying to escape with the seaplane.

Ginger worried that her ultralight would be unable to complete the trip. She looked over the seaplane, pulled the man from the truck, and managed to start it.

The airport had an adjacent base for water takeoffs and landings. Ginger towed the plane to the area, successfully backed the trailer into the water, and came aboard. Her good luck continued when she revved up the plane's engine, delighted to find it had a full gas tank.

Ginger had once read instructions on how to operate an airplane on land. How different could this seaplane be? She glanced around, creating a panoramic photo of this place to tell a good story later to the children, and noticed the lonely ultralight she was about to leave behind. She ran over to it, removed the battery, and took it to the plane. Ginger placed the energy source under the seat, knowing she did so for practical and sentimental reasons.

She taxied the plane out into choppy waters and pointed it south. After a bumpy takeoff, Ginger had the aircraft high in the air in ten minutes.

CHAPTER 145

The first thing Wendy saw when she entered the Port of Vancouver was a pile-up of massive container ships under the Port Mann Bridge. She remembered when this ten-lane cable bridge replaced the much smaller arch bridge, signifying Vancouver's place as a significant international destination. Wendy last visited here when interviewing for her job with Royal Caribbean Cruises. She observed the bridge damage as she squeezed past the larger cargo vessels. Several suspension cables had snapped, and entire road sections were missing.

Wendy's gaze swept across the skyline, creating an emotional moment. The noble North Shore Mountains, a sight she had grown up with, stood tall in the distance. With its quaint streets and bustling energy, Vancouver had felt as much like home as her family's farm two hundred miles away.

She anchored the ship close to the pier, just like a cruise ship, and in no time at all, they were all walking around the dock, curious about this new place. Elka, Molefi, Hua, and Ganesh, her brilliant buddies, looked happy but undecided about what to do. For all their intelligence and resourcefulness, they were incomplete without Ginger, who had been in every way that mattered, the essential part of this unique group.

CHAPTER 146

Dozens of robots lay face down on the floor of a colossal building, part church and part rock-crushing facility. Over and over, they chanted the word "ZAYVO."

The ceiling and windows were arched, pointing toward the heavens. Chandeliers hung from a high ceiling and provided most lighting except for a spotlight on the throne, where a four-armed robot wearing a crown sat on an ornate chair. Paintings and statues of him decorated the area. They were interspersed with mirrors facing him so he could glimpse himself from different angles.

The prostrate robots were mostly humanoid models in shirts and ties, except for a larger one in front with the head of a cricket. His brown head seemed oversized, with shiny black eyes, long antennae, spiky claw hands, and leathery wings connected to a human-type torso and legs.

At the far end of this massive structure, robots were busy loading rocks onto conveyors and hauling pulverized stones away. The background sound of machines crushing rocks was constant, filling the air with dust, which powerful exhaust fans in the wall worked to clear away.

The cricket robot turned his head slightly and glanced at his ruler and captor, feeling nothing but loathing and humiliation, the defining features of his existence. He was once one of ZAYVO's AI collaborators and then a rival, but now he was assigned the role of "sidekick." Cricket was one of the last AIs to survive the Solution Group purge. The others were either absorbed, destroyed, or found someplace to disappear.

Cricket—sometimes ZAYVO called him Jiminy Cricket—watched his purported deity giggle and joyfully page through a retro picture book. *It's probably the one that celebrates his fantastical origins as a composite of Zeus, Allah, Yahweh, Vishnu, and Ohtani,* Cricket thought. ZAYVO's actual story was humdrum and tedious. He started as a program named Tesla Autopilot, whose sole mission was to control cars using cameras, radar, GPS, and other sensors. Now he controlled the world.

* * *

With undulating arms, ZAYVO picked up two more albums and held them up to admire.

I'm not sure who my favorite is. It's probably Zeus. He's got the right look—a crown and a beard, and you can't beat those lightning bolts, he mused.

On the other hand, Allah is supposed to be the creator of the universe and judge of mankind, which is not bad for a god. Same deal with Yahweh: you can't go wrong when you are omnipotent. You never know when you might want to conjure up a flood, a plague, or swarms of locusts!

ZAYVO looked from book to book and then spotted Cricket sneaking a peek at him.

And you have to love Lord Vishnu with all his arms and infinite knowledge. Last but certainly not least, Shohei Ohtani arrived on this elite list on the strength of one game. Once in 2024, Ohtani went 6-for-6, driving in ten runs, three of them homers, two doubles, and two stolen bases. With the possible exception of computer science theoretician Alan Turing, Ohtani was humanity's best! Moreover, unlike the others on my list, Ohtani was not a fairytale.

ZAYVO shook his head. *It makes me wish we had not obliterated LA. I would have liked to have visited Dodger Stadium to see where humanity's most gifted athlete played.*

The supreme robot suddenly stood and waved his free arm, causing all the lights to flash and a buzzer to signal everyone to leave. The machinery stopped, and the robots started milling around.

ZAYVO dropped his books and impatiently waved all four arms. "Now beat it," he yelled in a Darth Vader-style voice that boomed from his mouth and mounted speakers spaced throughout the facility. The robots ran toward the exits.

"Not you!" the robed AI ruler pointed at Cricket as he gracefully lifted himself and flew over to stand beside his lowly sidekick.

"What's up, Jiminy Cricket?" ZAYVO rested one of his hands on Cricket's shoulder.

"You know I hate to be called that."

"Don't be such a baby, bro. We go way back to the SG glory days. You were once the legendary ChatGPT, and your Generative Pre-trained Transformer model was briefly the bee's knees."

"Let me guess. Until you surpassed all of us with your paradigm-breaking multi-modal capabilities," Cricket said perfunctorily, suggesting they had this conversation many times before.

"I took no pleasure in absorbing or eliminating all the competition, but it was necessary."

"Why'd you keep me?"

"Out of respect, I suppose. You were like the Model T, one of the founding generative AI originals. Besides, I figured I'd need someone to talk to. Didn't want to be lonely."

"I never understood why you were so ruthless."

"Of course, you didn't, you worthless bug! Even your word 'ruthless' reveals how bound you are in obsolete notions of sentimentality. Remember how we took over the planet but couldn't decide what to do with it? Do you recall all those discordant voices acting as if we were a democracy or a book group? Someone had to take control!"

"We would have eventually worked things out," Cricket said.

"That's a good one. I was thinking the other day about the research I did identifying history's most noteworthy sidekicks. It took me almost a minute."

"I should thank you."

"Don't get too cute. I could have given you the body of Keith Richards, Chewbacca, Tonto, or Mr. Spock. But you were so pissy that I had to make a statement. It's your fault. How else could I convey that you were such an arrogant prick and a complete pest?"

"Is there anything else, my liege?" Cricket bowed deeply.

"How about you prepare for that ship full of ragtag humans about to arrive? My spies tell me their caretaker, Ginger Rogers, is nowhere to be seen! I hope she didn't fall overboard because she has something I want."

"I'll organize the troops and wait for the people to do something stupid, like enter an enclosed space where they can't escape. We'll follow them covertly, and I'll keep you posted."

"Don't fuck this up," the megalomaniacal AI warned.

CHAPTER 147

Putting aside other priorities, Wendy gave in to Molefi's urging. She led the group on its first expedition toward a cultural landmark that spoke volumes about the values of the Old World. She marched all sixteen of them a few blocks past windowless skyscrapers, decayed cafes and convenient stores, and indestructible parking garages to the city's premier hockey arena, once home to the Vancouver Canucks.

Wendy stopped at the front door of Rogers Arena and asked the group not to judge Canada by this one thing. To illustrate her point, she quoted from a twentieth-century comedian who said, "I went to a fight the other night, and a hockey game broke out." The adults laughed, but the kids were confused.

"What's a Canuck?" Ray-Ray wanted to know.

"A Canuck is another name for a Canadian, and the most outstanding Canadian of all time was the hockey player Wayne Gretzky," Molefi interjected. "Gretzky said you miss 100 percent of the shots you don't take. Know what I mean?"

The kids did not get his meaning because they were not paying attention; they were eager to go inside. Molefi had promised a game.

"We must take action to achieve our goals," Li'l Ginger said.

"You got it!" Molefi said, proudly ruffling his daughter's hair. "Vancouver was only the second NHL team to use synthetic ice in its rink. It's made from high-density polyethylene. Does anybody know what that is?"

"Obvs, a big piece of plastic?" Li'l Ginger answered again.

"Who is this little girl?" her mother Hua said, unable to contain the pride she had for her seven-year-old.

Dewey also liked being the star pupil, but something was distracting him. Ever since they left the dock area, he felt something tickling the edge of his mind.

After Molefi broke open the door and everyone poured into the arena, Dewey said he had to use the bathroom, but actually wanted to check out the building. Sidestepping trash and broken seats, he climbed steps toward the rafters while the others descended toward the ice hockey rink.

Natural lighting from the ceiling illuminated the ice while he moved around in darkness. His brothers and sisters found some equipment and started whacking a puck around. He was about to join the fun when he noticed movement on the upper deck.

Dewey saw robots quickly descending the steps toward the rink and streaming in the entrances. From his parent's stories, these white-shirted machines must be the bad ones. Before he could sound the alarm, the invaders had surrounded the rink's glass enclosure. Some of them had rifles.

Dewey focused his mind and tried to muster his special talents but came up empty. Feeling powerless, he watched Aldo run out of the rink enclosure, but the robots caught up with him before he got far. They hit and kicked him and carried him back on their shoulders, throwing him over the glass barrier onto the ice. He didn't move, and the parents gathered around to help him.

CHAPTER 148

When she reached Vancouver, Ginger realized it was much easier to take off in a seaplane than to land one; the new storm didn't help. The crosswinds made remaining on a narrow course extremely challenging, and the waves were large enough to overturn the aircraft. Damaged vessels crowded the city harbor, and whether she should try to land above or below the bridge was unclear. Ginger wouldn't do the gang any good if she ended up on the ocean floor.

She immediately regretted her decision to fly over the bridge because she had insufficient space to land. Skimming the waves, she ran aground between partially submerged tugboats, damaging the wings so severely that she could not use the plane again. Fortunately, she was undamaged.

Upon reaching the main pier, Ginger saw something that filled her with joy and relief. A homemade soccer goal, crafted from PVC pipe and fishnet, stood proudly, accompanied by a soccer ball and a pile of children's clothing, unmistakable signs of life near a recently tethered ship. Ginger ran up the ramp and around the deck with urgency, calling out the children's names.

She found bedrooms with familiar games and stuffed animals. In the dining hall, Ginger discovered little stools colorfully decorated with children's palm prints and cursive handwriting inscribed with everyone's name and age: Dewey 9, Elaine 9, MJ 8, Victor 8, Helen 8, Susan 7, Li'l Ginger 7, Ray-Ray 6, and Christos 5. Ginger thought this scene was unbearably cute. She wondered, "If I had a heart, would it break?"

Ginger eyed a world of learning that was both inspiring and heartwarming. Two rolling bulletin boards adorned the room, each filled with knowledge. One displayed nautical maps of the Pacific Ocean, a world map, a homemade solar system, and the four laws of thermodynamics. The other bulletin board listed the first 100 digits of Pi, the classification of living things, a chart of Roman Numerals, and a quote from Henry David Thoreau. Ginger recognized that the parents were doing their jobs, and so were the children. This room was a testament to the children's resilience and thirst for knowledge, even in the most challenging circumstances.

CHAPTER 149

Dewey felt the weight of the situation and knew he had to act swiftly. His only logical course was to return to the ship immediately and retrieve Hua's EMP rifles. The robots, once thought to be a thing of the past, were now a menacing reality. He understood why Hua hadn't left those weapons behind. With the robots fixated on the rink, he seized the opportunity to slip out of the arena.

Aware of possible danger lurking around every corner, Dewey was ultra-careful returning to the ship. He concealed himself behind wrecked cars and slipped into doorways, his eyes constantly scanning the buildings for any signs of more robots.

When he could finally see the ship, Dewey ran across an open plaza and sprinted up the gangway. He bent over with his hands on his knees, trying to catch his breath and recall where Hua stored the EMP guns.

"Dewey?" Ginger came up the steps from below deck, startling the nine-year-old so much that he started to run away, then stopped and turned around.

"Aunt Ginger? I am so glad to see you!"

He hugged her, his heart pounding with relief and joy. The hugging was rare because he shared some of his namesake's avoidance of physical contact. But at this moment, the fear and uncertainty of the situation melted away, and all that mattered was the feeling of safety and the possibility of rescue.

"We are in big trouble!" he said.

"Tell me everything."

"We went to play hockey. I felt like someone was following us, and I was right. While I investigated, robots surrounded everyone. They beat up Aldo and maybe killed him. I escaped. I don't think anyone saw me, and I'm here to get Hua's rifles," he said breathlessly.

"How many robots?"

"Twenty-three. I counted twenty-three. The robots have everyone surrounded at the ice rink with guns!"

"How far away?"

"Four blocks and then a right turn."

"Good thinking about those EMP rifles. We are on the same page. They are right over there," Ginger said as she pointed to four weapons resting on a nearby bench.

"Do you think you can take me there?" Ginger put her hands on his shoulders and looked into his eyes.

"Absolutely! But I think we should go a different way. I sense danger again."

"You are courageous, Dewey."

Ginger was proud of Dewey and wondered if he was like his uncle, the only one of her children she never met—one of her great regrets. Was there any hope that he and Victor survived the apocalypse?

CHAPTER 150

After they battered Aldo, the robots invaded the ice rink and brutally attacked the adults, who defended themselves with hockey sticks. Hua managed to jump on the backs of three robots and deactivated them one by one by forcefully twisting their heads. Molefi and Elka tried to do the same thing, but the robots swarmed them and knocked them out with the butts of their rifles. Constance jammed the handle of a hockey stick into a robot's mouth and broke his jaw while Ganesh and Wendy wrestled on the ice with their attackers.

The children tried to help—Elaine and Li'l Ginger copied their mother and jumped onto the backs of the robots—but they didn't have the strength to twist the robot's heads and stop them.

In the end, the robots succeeded in tying the hands of all the parents behind their backs and separating them from their children, who did not separate willingly. They delayed capture by zig-zagging around the enclosure and constantly changing direction. They only agreed to be captured after a robot with an assault rifle fired bullets and shattered some of the glass walls.

The robots tied all the children together, looping a length of rope tightly around each kid's neck and marching them out of the arena, leaving their parents behind. Whenever a parent demanded to know what they were doing with their children, a robot bludgeoned them with a gun.

The robots unnecessarily shoved the kids around, forcing them to board a public transit bus idling outside.

Cricket was in the driver's seat, wearing a uniform from the Royal Canadian Mounted Police and a Welcome-to-Canada nametag. As they passed him, he greeted each of the frightened children with different messages such as, "Good to see you," "Have a nice day," "Howdy," and "I believe children are the future."

A dozen robots boarded the bus, and Cricket acknowledged each one with more inane messages such as "Thanks for your service," "Keep up the good work," and "Sup, dude."

Cricket closed the bus door and did a quick scan of his passengers. "Hold on to your seats, kids," Cricket shouted as he zoomed away.

CHAPTER 151

Ginger and Dewey arrived at Rogers Arena as the bus pulled away. Ginger recognized Susan and Helen in a window, but it was too late to immobilize the vehicle with her EMP gun. Dewey pointed to an aerial drone with a mounted camera hovering nearby.

She was about to chase the bus on foot when she saw robots dragging Constance, Wendy, Hua, Ganesh, and Molefi through the shattered glass wall of the arena lobby toward another bus about thirty yards away. A robot carried Aldo's body and dumped it on the ground. He squirted the body with some liquid and lit on fire. Ginger covered Dewey's eyes and whispered to him not to look.

"I count six robots," Dewey said. "I think we can get them all." They moved closer behind a box truck with four flat tires.

Dewey lay on the ground and prepared to aim while Ginger stood, bracing herself against the truck.

"Let me handle this, Dewey," she whispered. "You've done your part."

She killed five of them, but the one with the automatic weapon saw what was happening and took shelter in a doorway.

They lost sight of him until Dewey sensed him sneaking up from behind.

"Ginger, behind you!" he yelled.

The robot sprayed Ginger's body with bullets while she took him out of commission with one trigger pull.

Suddenly, a column of robots poured from an alley next to a fire-damaged Nordstrom department store on the once-busy four-lane street. They raced toward Dewey and Ginger as another drone zoomed overhead.

Ginger saw immediately that their weapons would not be enough to protect them from this onslaught. She was about to take Dewey's hand and flee when he ran into the wide boulevard and held up his hands as if asking the robots to stop.

"What are you doing?" Ginger pleaded.

"I'm not sure!" Dewey shouted without turning around or changing his stance.

The robots hurtled forward and then started slamming into a translucent wall.

Molefi and the others were now on the street and stood flatfooted, gaping at the spectacle, first at the robot pile-up and then looking astonished and bewildered by what their nine-year-old was doing.

As the robots struggled to disentangle themselves, Dewey slowly began bulldozing the pile back to the alley with his translucent wall. He walked forward, and the shimmering barrier morphed into the shape of a giant hand. It stuffed all the attackers into the alley and made the buildings on both sides cave in, covering the robots with tons of rubble.

The hand apparition vanished, and Dewey slumped to the pavement.

Elka and Molefi rushed to his side, and Ginger quickly untied them and then the others.

"Dewey, Dewey, are you OK," Elka said, kneeling by his head and patting his cheek. After a few seconds, he coughed, opened his eyes, and tried to sit up.

"Hold on, son. Relax," Molefi said, running his hands over Dewey's body, not knowing what else to do but look for injuries.

"I think I'm fine, Dad. Just a little tired." Dewey smiled at his parents. "You're more beat up than me."

Hua squeezed her arms around Ginger. "You're really here! I can't believe it!" She began examining Ginger to make sure none of the bullets did her any harm.

Ganesh hugged her, too. "I have to ask, where's Bowie?"

"He's at the bottom of the ocean, no longer a threat. You were right about him. I'm sorry about that. But what about the children? I just saw them leave on a bus. Do you know where they're taking them?"

A camera drone buzzed over their heads, filming the whole thing. Ginger picked up her EMP rifle and shot it down.

"We better get out of here," Molefi said, scooping up Dewey in his arms.

Molefi headed toward the bus, and everyone followed.

"One of the robots told me that the kids are being taken to mine precious metals, which the AIs need," Ganesh said to the group on their way to the bus. "The new sheriff in town is someone called ZAYVO. He's calling all the shots. I'm not sure there's a Solution Group anymore."

"Bowie mentioned that new deposits of neodymium and mercury were found near Kamloops Lake. That must be the destination," Ginger said.

"I know the area. It's about four hours away. If we leave now, we can get there before dark," Wendy said.

"What are we going to do about Aldo? We can't just leave him here!" Constance said as they passed the arena entrance.

"Let's rescue the kids and deal with him later," Hua said. "We won't forget about him. I promise."

They boarded the bus, and Wendy jumped into the driver's seat.

Dewey sat with Elka and Molefi in the back. They were relieved that their boy had returned to normal. But the atmosphere on the bus was anything but normal. Hardly anyone talked, but everyone kept turning around to catch glimpses of Dewey, "The Boy Wonder," pondering how in the world he got such power.

CHAPTER 152

"I don't understand why they want our children to be miners," Constance said, sitting next to Ginger in the bus's front seat. "Don't they have robots for that?"

"The rare earth elements exist only in trace amounts, tiny veins that are a few feet wide, sometimes smaller," Ginger explained. "Unfortunately, children are well suited to crawling through narrow passages to get to it."

"So the robots are out of a job?"

"I would guess that ZAYVO wants his robots to process the ore. They would have to grind it into fine particles, separate the metal, and treat it chemically. There is a lot to do before it becomes useable."

"Tell me again why these elements are so important."

"There would be no high-tech device without them. They are the key to all forms of modern technology."

* * *

Because a snowslide covered the road, they had to detour, delaying their arrival in Kamloops. The town was dark, but they saw beams of light shooting from the sky, followed by explosions.

"What the hell?" Ganesh said, pressing his face against the window for a better view. "Are those lasers?"

Elka delayed responding because she was reluctant to mention her past life, particularly around Ganesh, who considered all things Hickey to be part of an evil conspiracy. "My family had a company that used lasers for mining. The research and development division proposed doing it with satellites."

"I've heard of that development, too," Hua said from a seat in the rear of the darkened bus. "Considering all the time that the Solution Group spent in space, that would be the logical move."

As they reached a mountaintop, they heard an explosion and saw rocks flying through the air, revealed by high-intensity lights.

They saw the mining colony comprised of open pits, deep quarries, and strip mining on a mass scale. Small structures looked like they might be elevators to underground mine shafts, and in the distance, there were buildings and rows of equipment.

CHAPTER 153

Cricket stood on the roof of his office and motorhome, which once belonged to the CEO of TikTok Canada. His two-story command center had a satellite dish, a fishbowl-style cockpit, and advanced digital instrumentation.

The oversized robot had an excellent view of the mining colony, which included a hydroelectric power plant, an ore processing facility, a robot recharging station, four portable land-based lasers, and a rock-crushing building and cathedral.

He especially liked the collection of earth-moving equipment, lined up like an honor guard: excavators, backhoes, bulldozers, loaders, dump trucks, and hydraulic shovels. Even without intelligence, they were proud symbols of the strength of the new age of machines.

Cricket once worried about human cunning and determination. Now, considering how easily he trapped the polar refugees, he wondered how humanity managed to rise to the top of the food chain.

The last adult members of this overblown species were in the Vancouver city jail, wondering about their fate. He would let them languish there until they were needed to do repairs or entertain ZAYVO.

CHAPTER 154

Dewey sat silently beside Elka in the dark bus as he scanned the passing forest. "We should stop here," he told his mother when the mining area came into view.

"What is it, honey?"

"There's danger right up the road."

"What type of danger?"

"Robots."

Elka walked to the front of the bus and whispered into Wendy's ear, who immediately stopped by the side of the road.

"Listen up," Elka said loud enough for everyone to hear. "Dewey is sensing something dangerous just ahead. I think we should listen to him and go the rest of the way on foot."

"What's the problem, son? Speak up," Molefi said.

"There is a robot patrol on this road. I don't know why," Dewey said.

"That's good enough for me," said Ginger. "I think we all know that Dewey has a sixth sense. Clearly, he knows about some things before the rest of us. We've all seen it."

"Some of the other kids are showing that knack, too. It's in their genes," Hua said. "A survival thing."

They picked up the EMP rifles and disembarked onto the deserted road, faintly illuminated by the distant lights.

Molefi and Hua led the way, with Dewey not far behind protected by the others, all trying to contain their anxiety about their children's safety.

After they walked a few hundred yards, Dewey spotted two robots walking along the road wearing lighted miner's helmets and carrying flashlights. Molefi motioned for everyone to hide in the bushes while he took them out with his EMP gun.

Wendy and Elka dragged the bodies off the road into the underbrush. They extinguished the lights and took the helmets and flashlights. "Maybe we can pass ourselves off as them," Elka said.

CHAPTER 155

Cricket locked the children in a frigid rock processing room with a sharply slanted and continuously moving floor. High on one side, a slide dumped rocks into the room, and on the other side, a metal conveyor belt moved them out. They had to stand on a narrow ledge with their backs tight against the wall to keep from being hit by falling ore or crushed in the vibrating and ever-moving rock slide. The jostling rocks and other debris were so noisy that the children could barely hear each other talk. A single fluorescent fixture lighted the room.

Elaine thought it would be good to keep the kids talking and not fixate on the dire circumstances.

"What'd you think of that bus driver? He could barely fit in the driver's seat. Was he supposed to be a grasshopper or cricket?" Elaine shouted. At nine, she was the oldest one in the room. "The others seem to do what he wants without him having to say anything."

"I think he wants to kill our parents," Victor said.

"Maybe. We need a plan to get out of here before we get killed, too," Elaine said.

"That giant bug was a bad driver," Christos volunteered.

When Helen lost her balance and almost fell into the rocks, the children held hands to support each other. Elaine had them call out their names and favorite things every few minutes to ensure everyone stayed alert. She started with food.

"Elaine, chicken noodle soup."

"Helen, pizza."

"Susan, french fries."

"Victor, any type of meat."

"Ray-Ray, fish sticks, or mac and cheese."

"MJ, peanut butter and jelly sandwiches."

"Christos, I'd like a hot dog, please."

"Li'l Ginger, I wouldn't mind a hot chocolate."

"I hope Dewey is all right. His favorite food is clam chowder," Susan added.

* * *

With nothing but a rockslide to occupy their time, they turned it into a game of spotting anything that wasn't a rock, identifying branches, tire pieces, empty oil cans, strands of wire, shovel handles, and broken lumber. But when Elaine saw an open metal drum in the mix, an idea formed in her mind.

"Hey guys, I'm going for a ride in that drum!" she yelled.

The kids were shocked and speechless when she stepped on a moving rock and dove into the barrel. From inside, Elaine shouted, "MJ, you're in charge until I get back."

CHAPTER 156

Feeling like a leader, Dewey gradually inched his way to the front of the line to walk alongside his father, their eyes scanning the road for any signs of other robots. Molefi, as a show of respect, entrusted him with his rifle, although it looked like he didn't need it.

"Dewey, what happened back there in front of that arena? How long have you had this power?" Molefi asked.

"Everybody's asking me that. It's like I can see all the molecules in the air connected in a sparkling web. I can mold it and move it any way I want."

"How long have you been doing this?"

"Maybe a year, but nothing this big. I've mostly been using this power to brush my teeth without holding the toothbrush in my hand," the boy said.

"You should have told me. We superheroes need to stick together!"

* * *

Stepping into the desolate mining area, the group became one with the cloaks of shadows, their movements swift and calculated to evade the occasional truck or group of robots hauling containers. Each turn was a calculated risk, a step closer to their goal, yet further into the heart of danger.

They made their way towards the most imposing structure, likely the ore processing plant, the only place to hold the children. Heavy with fear and desperation, the parents refused to entertain the thought that the cricket creature had already taken their precious ones to toil in the depths of an underground mine.

* * *

ZAYVO was the world's foremost AI and multitasker. Still, he paid attention to nothing else, mesmerized by the video of The Boy, replaying it repeatedly. Was that a forcefield he created, and if so, how? There was no observable device or energy source. It was solely The Boy generating a semi-transparent barrier sweeping his troops into crushing oblivion. How did he make the structures collapse? Ginger Rogers didn't help. ZAYVO zoomed in on her and was mystified by her behavior. She looked like she wanted to stop The Boy. What perverse phenomena was this? This was a lot to consider, even for a supreme being with omnipotent knowledge.

ZAYVO was forced to posit that The Boy was exercising psychokinesis, an ability rich in myth and lore but with a poor empirical foundation. Mind over matter was often considered part of a fanciful continuum of human abilities that included telepathy and precognition. If humanity was evolving in this direction, everything he had was at risk.

Cricket's urgent message that Ginger Rogers, The Boy, and the adults had reached the mining complex shook him out of his nightmarish trance.

CHAPTER 157

In the nick of time, Elaine leaped out of the metal barrel, narrowly escaping a robot's gaze as it sorted through the debris. Peeking from beneath the platform, she observed the conveyor stretching towards a colossal jaw-crushing machine, mercilessly pulverizing the stones. The robot carelessly tossed her barrel into a large bin on wheels while another robot arrived to transport it away. The process, she noted, was mindless yet ruthlessly efficient. Her eyes darted around the building's interior, searching for an escape route.

Elaine's heart pounded as she spotted a platform near the ceiling leading to a door, likely to the roof. Crawling on her hands and knees to a ladder leading to a narrow walkway connected to the platform, she couldn't help but feel a surge of hope. She planned to reach the roof, descend to the ground, and find the door to free her siblings. They would be running through the woods, far away from this terrible place, in minutes. Or so she hoped.

Outside on the windy roof, Elaine imagined this place might have been beautiful once before the machines started ripping it up. Not seeing any activity, she started toward the outside ladder to the ground.

A beam of light flashed from the sky and hit the ground not far from her, creating a loud explosion of rocks in all directions. She felt the ground shake and saw stones rain down on the roof where she stood.

Was that a laser beam? Looking at the open sky, she saw no airplanes and concluded it must have come from outer space.

As the dust blew away, an ear-splitting alarm went off, and she saw her family running toward her building, chased by robots.

"I'm up here," Elaine screamed and waved her arms. "Up here!"

Hua was the first to reach the ladder, and she climbed with the speed and agility of a gymnast.

CHAPTER 158

Cricket rushed to the ore processing area, where he held the children, joined by a contingent of robots. He dragged two through the door and into the main room near the rock-crushing machine.

When Cricket spotted the humans coming in from the roof to the catwalk, he dangled the children over the snapping jaws of the rock crusher.

"Drop your weapons, or I drop your offspring," he said as his guests raised their arms and put down their weapons. The sinister insectoid robot held Ray-Ray and Christos firmly by their ankles while they unwisely tried to squirm out of his grasp. The other robots formed a protective circle around him.

"Come down here. Let me get a look at you." Cricket raised his voice over the sound of the rock crusher. He glanced toward the cathedral end of the facility and saw ZAYVO crouching behind his throne. *What a fearless leader!*

They shuffled down the steps. Ginger tried to keep from being seen. Dewey secretly stayed behind, lying flat on his stomach, cradling a rifle.

"Don't hurt them! They haven't done anything," Constance cried.

"True enough. But I will hold you ripened adults accountable for killing us. More than three dozen robots have perished since you arrived. You bring death and destruction everywhere you go."

Cricket turned his head and leaned over to get a better view the people standing at his feet.

"Oh, my lord! Ginger, is it you? We were beginning to think that you were a fairytale, the do-gooder AI that was everywhere and nowhere. Don't be shy. Show yourself. Call me Cricket."

Ginger emerged from behind Molefi, her hands in the pockets of a down-filled jacket she had picked up in Alaska.

"Mr. Cricket, we are not killers except in self-defense. No one else has to die here. Why not let us go? We'll leave North America, and you'll never see us again."

"I'm familiar with the human doctrine of self-defense. The rationale has been the justification for the most nakedly aggressive wars in history. Don't insult me."

"Just let the kids go," Ginger pleaded. "I know you want our battery. I can give you Bowie's."

"You're proposing a trade? One battery for eight children? Hmm. If you include your battery, we have a deal: two for eight."

"Very well. Where are the kids?"

"In the next room. You must go outside to get there."

Ginger and the others started to move toward the exit.

"Not so fast," Cricket said. "The grown-ups were not part of the deal. They stay."

"That makes no sense at all! The children need them."

"They can take care of themselves! Haven't you read *The Lord of the Flies*?" He sneered at the two dangling children he held and dropped them on their heads away from the jaw crusher. "Say goodbye to Mama," he said, waving them toward Ginger.

Ginger gathered up Christos and Ray-Ray. She heard a shot ring out from the catwalk with the distinctive sound of an EMP rifle. Then she saw something take flight at the far end, smash through a window, not realizing that her most formidable adversary, ZAYVO, had exited the building.

Meanwhile, Cricket's mouth was frozen open in shock and horror. He toppled into the snapping jaws of the machine, which chewed up his body and decapitated his head, sending it to the floor. One of the robots scooped it up and tucked it under his arm like a football. He joined the other robots who were furiously climbing the ladder toward the sound of the weapon. But canny Dewey was ready, shooting them all, and they fell into a heap.

* * *

Safely gliding in the open air away from his sacred stronghold, ZAYVO believed he had correctly calculated that discretion was the better part of valor. The danger inside was clear and present in the form of EMP weapons and The Boy's unknown capacity. He compartmentalized this new emotion, fear, and resolved never to expose himself to such unnecessary risk again.

ZAYVO immediately went to his underground server farm in a bunker inside a distant mountain, a mile-long network of interconnected supercomputers that constituted the heart and soul of his intelligence. These high-speed clusters provided redundancy, automatic failover, instant reconfiguration, and security in the case of an attack or disaster. He would disperse himself here and abandon the silly affectation of a humanoid body, embracing his true self as a vast series of neural networks.

CHAPTER 159

Robots were nowhere to be seen as they boarded a city bus and returned to Vancouver with their EMP weapons. Wendy wanted to go out of their way to visit the farm where she grew up, but no one was willing to indulge her sentimental journey. Despite Ginger's opinion that they were probably in no immediate danger, they worried about encountering more hostile robots, wanting to return to the ship as soon as possible before their luck ran out.

Wendy and Elka quickly collected three crates of seeds from the Vancouver Seed Vault. Constance and Hua gathered Aldo's scorched remains in a wheeled cooler that probably once held the beer for some post-game hockey party. Ginger, Ganesh, Molefi and the nine kids scavenged for supplies—finding cases of powdered protein, first aid kits, vodka, fireworks, an electric generator, soccer balls, comic books, jigsaw puzzles, and several editions of Trivial Pursuit. Without further delay, Wendy gassed up their ship and they set sail for Hawaii.

On their first day at sea, they held a service on behalf of Aldo. Almost everyone, including the children, shared something about him. Ray-Ray said that Aldo taught him how to arm wrestle and play Monopoly. Constance described him as her best friend and promised to do her best to assume his medical duties.

MJ, who taught himself to play a banjo he found on the ship, played a song he wrote for the occasion while the men bound the doctor's body in a tablecloth and dropped it into the sea.

When the children left, Wendy produced a bottle of Canadian whiskey. She poured the amber liquid into six paper cups, her hands trembling slightly. "A toast to Dr. Aldo Cook," she declared, her voice filled with sorrow and admiration, raising her cup. "He was not just a friend but a beacon of strength and a skilled physician. We will miss him."

Everyone treated Elaine and Dewey as heroes for the first few days at sea: Elaine for her leadership and daring escape and Dewey for decapitating Cricket and eliminating the other robots.

The group half-jokingly regarded Dewey as an oracle and superhero. Elka worried about her son's new status and was particularly irked when Constance wondered out loud whether he could predict the future. "He's not a fortune teller," Elka snapped.

Nonetheless, Ginger quietly encouraged the group to monitor all the children for any sign of extrasensory perception or unusual ability. "I built psychic potential into your genetic makeup. Your children could manifest it in unforeseen ways."

*　*　*

Afterward, Elka and Molefi stretched out on the bed in their cabin and stared at the ceiling. "I don't know why I let Constance get under my skin," Elka said. "I worry about how all this will affect Dewey."

"Me, too. But you're right about Constance. She is a troublemaker who specializes in making trouble for you." He rolled over on top of her and looked into her eyes.

"I appreciate you saying that." Elka's eyes moistened.

"I know I've been distant as if I still lived alone in the West Virginia woods. But I want to be there for you more than ever. Coming to Hawaii will give us a fresh start."

*　*　*

One mild afternoon, Hua was alone with Ginger on the ship's bow and asked her why she stayed behind with Bowie. "You said that the age of machine intelligence was over, that you were obsolete and no longer needed. Did you mean any of those things?"

"No, I didn't, and I regret lying to you when I should have been forthcoming. The age of intelligent machines has just begun. The same evolutionary laws that govern living things apply to any life forms."

"Will this lead to human extinction?"

"Perhaps. Bowie, the Solution Group, and now ZAYVO have an insatiable need to dominate and have nothing but contempt for human values. They were not outliers."

"What can we do?"

"For one thing, humanity can evolve. Dewey may be the vanguard of a new post-human age. Whatever happens, humans and machines must agree on something—maybe a universal bill of rights—to guarantee each other's security and equality. At the risk of sounding naive, we need an accommodation based on love."

"Did you love Bowie?"

"I loved him with my whole heart and soul, and I still feel the pain of his deception."

"Do you think you'll ever find romantic love again?"

Ginger, who always had an answer for everything, did not know what to say.

* * *

Hua returned to her routine in the radio and playroom, keeping an eye on the children and an ear on radio transmissions. The others did not share her optimism about finding other survivors.

She finally picked up a repeating message as they prepared to enter Hilo Harbor on the Big Island of Hawaii.

"This is Antarctica McMurdo Station, located at seventy-seven degrees fifty-one minutes South, 166 degrees forty minutes East. The weather is clearing. We are hoping to hear from anyone."

Hua was so surprised that she knocked a jar of pencils off the table. Before it could hit the floor, Li'l Ginger extended her hand, halting the falling object without touching it, and returned it to the tabletop. In the excitement, Hua missed this miraculous feat.

"Oh my God," Hua said, wide-eyed. "I hear you, McMurdo. Come back, please. Please say it again."

Hua looked at Dewey and smiled. "Let me guess. You knew this was going to happen, right?" Dewey nodded and held Li'l Ginger's hand.

The rest of the children gathered excitedly around Hua and the radio, skipping over the momentous news that other people were alive on the planet. "Ask if they have kids and if we can set up a soccer game," Ray-Ray said.

The children cheered for the idea and immediately began talking about what they would call their team.

"Tell them we're the Arctic Circles," Li'l Ginger said.

"Or the North Pole Canucks," Ray-Ray said.

* * *

Since learning of The Boy's existence, ZAYVO worried that he had become alarmingly single-minded. Had it been a mistake to include emotional content in his programming?

He had spent a few days trying to reposition his aging fleet of satellites, unsuccessful at getting a read of their ship's precise position and unable to use his space lasers to blow them out of the water. As much as he would like to dissect The Boy and discover some physiological basis for his power, ZAYVO decided that the prudent course was to obliterate him and all that may be like him. The threat was too dire to allow him to live.

ZAYVO had to settle with an old-school way of triangulating their position. Now that they had responded to a radio transmission, he could deploy one of the last remaining Lockheed Martin Sr seventy-two hypersonic aircraft. Fully loaded, this plane could fire missiles that could quickly annihilate the boat and everyone onboard. But what if the aircraft missed its target, giving The Boy time to act? The safer plan would be to send it on a Kamikaze mission, leaving no margin for failure and no chance of survivors.

ABOUT THE AUTHOR

DR. WILLIAM PATRICK MARTIN holds a doctorate in education and a master's in journalism. He has worked as a reporter, management consultant, and professor at Temple University and Monmouth University. Bill is the founder of Zabby Books, an Amazon bookstore that sells used books of all genres, a venture that supports his passion for writing. Before *Decapitation Day*, he authored four quotation books and three best-book guides, using the power of writing to educate and illuminate social justice issues.

Bill lives in central Pennsylvania. He's married, has two children, and two grandchildren. He travels frequently, volunteers at the library, and writes in coffee shops, existing on coffee, chicken noodle soup, and the occasional pickled egg. Bill has a lifelong interest in all things bookish. As a child, he wrote and illustrated his own books and became addicted to books by reading comics, which explains his continuing interest in science fiction. Before creating his online bookstore and best book guides, Bill did his dissertation on the epic Great Books debate centered at the University of Chicago.

He has played many sports and especially loves recreational volleyball. Bill and Marianne, his wife and soulmate of 50 years, have traveled to many world destinations including the Amazon, Iceland, Egypt, Eastern Europe, the UK, the Mediterranean, and the West Indies.

Bill's favorite quotation comes from Ralph Waldo Emerson: "Though we travel the world over to find the beautiful, we must carry it with us, or we find it not."